MEMENTO MORI

Rocky,
Thanks for
everything!
J. Morris

JANE MORRIS

Edited by Rocky Majors and Emma Poppe.
Cover art by Jafar Razgardani. Cover design by Lindy Martin, Hatch Endeavors.
Interior Formatting by Champagne Book Design

For

M.

Always for you

COMEDIC TEACHING MEMOIRS BY
JANE MORRIS

Teacher Misery: Helicopter Parents,
Special Snowflakes & Other Bullshit

More Teacher Misery: Nutjob Teachers, Torturous Training,
& Even More Bullshit

Crap My Students Make

What It's Really Like: Outrageous Stories from
Teachers Around the Country

NOTE TO READER

This story is very loosely based on the history of the Pre-Raphaelite Brotherhood and the women who inspired their greatest works of art and poetry. I have been fascinated with these peoples' lives since I first read about them as a teenager, which ultimately inspired my pen name. In 2020 when the coronavirus pandemic started, I desperately wanted to escape into a world like theirs—a world where the pursuit of art, beauty, and love was all that mattered. When I couldn't find a book like the one I wanted to read, I decided to write it myself. And as the saying goes, the story practically wrote itself. I used some of the things that occurred in the lives of Dante Gabriel Rossetti, William Morris, Jane Burden, and Lizzie Siddal as a road map to move the story along, but I infused it with my own themes and ideas. In this book, Gabriel's poems are based on ideas presented in Rossetti's poems that I rewrote for a contemporary audience. Lizzie's poetry is part of an original poem by Elizabeth Siddal called "Early Death." Jane's poems are my creations. If you're looking for an accurate account of the lives of the Pre-Raphaelites, this isn't it. But if you long to immerse yourself in a raw, all-consuming world of passionate obsession with love, art, and beauty, read on! And if you came here from my *Teacher Misery* books, thanks for giving this a chance.

Though you might be intrigued, don't look up the characters' real history until you finish the book. It might give things away!

Music was my greatest muse while writing this story. Each chapter has a corresponding song that helps capture the mood and atmosphere. To get the full experience, please listen to the music. You can listen to the entire playlist at bit.ly/Mementomoribook. If you'd like to see my visual inspiration for the characters and settings, check out my pinterest boards at https://bit.ly/3vnzLXA.

Do not be afraid; our fate cannot be taken from us; it is a gift.

Dante Alighieri

CHAPTER 1

Jane

"Love Interruption"—Jack White

I T WAS THE SECOND TIME I HAD MET HIM, THOUGH I COULDN'T remember the first. Lizzie had an interview for a job as an administrative assistant at the Museum of Modern Art. I tried to tell her that for someone so brilliant, who had a full scholarship to Yale, it was beneath her. But after years of her parents refusing to let her study art, she had to start somewhere. I hadn't seen her so excited in a long time. I wandered the first floor of the museum while she went in for her interview.

I wanted to understand what made these things special enough to be in a museum. I always thought that art involved some kind of skill, but the things I saw seemed ridiculous. In one corner, there were huge colored blocks stacked in a pile. People were looking at it from every angle and discussing the various meanings of the positions and colors. To me, it was something a toddler could have done.

I moved on to a room where a person's messy bedroom was on display. Next to an unmade bed was a pile of garbage, including used tissues, period-stained underwear, cigarette butts, empty vodka bottles, a pregnancy test, a half-used tube of lube, and used condoms.

Next to me, a woman taking notes said, "Striking in its vulnerability," to the man at her side.

"A brave self-portrait," he added. "Quite a contemplative atmosphere."

I couldn't help but laugh, and it came out a bit too loud. The couple turned to sneer at me, and I decided since I had already insulted them, I might as well have fun with it. "I never realized that the time I shit my pants in kindergarten made me an artist. I'll be exhibiting those underwear next month. I do hope you'll come!"

The woman looked me up and down and quickly spun on her fancy heels and stomped away. "Some people don't understand the power of symbolism!" the man hissed before joining his companion. I kept laughing and pulled out my phone to see if Lizzie had texted that she was done yet.

"It helps to know the background of the artist," a man's voice said. I put my phone away and looked up. He was so gorgeous that it disarmed me for a moment as he continued to explain the artist's background. "She grew up really poor, was raped at 13, and had to have an abortion. This is what her bedroom looked like when her boyfriend left her because he couldn't deal with her depression anymore." He held a sketchbook and pencil and kept glancing down to add detail to whatever he was working on.

"That's terrible," I stated. "And it does explain why her room would look like this. But I still wouldn't call it art."

The side of his mouth went up into a sexy smirk. "I agree completely."

I glanced at him with confusion before I moved on to the next room. There was something familiar about him, but I couldn't place it. The following installation was a gigantic tank with a dead shark suspended inside. The title had something to do with people's inability to fathom their own impending death. I stood there staring at it while people commented, "Oh, this is iconic!" and "Fascinating!"

"I don't understand," I said to them. "Did the artist *make* the shark, or is it real?" They stared at me like I was a pile of rotting trash.

"It's a real tiger shark suspended in formaldehyde," one replied.

"So, the artist didn't really *make* anything. He just put a dead shark in a tank and said it was his art?"

They turned away from me, and one mumbled, "You don't get it."

"So explain it to me. Isn't art supposed to involve some kind of skill? Couldn't I have taken a shark and put it in a tank and said it was my art?"

An amused voice from behind me answered, "But you didn't, did you?" I turned around and locked eyes with the beautiful guy from the last room.

"Excuse me?"

The warm expression on his face told me he wasn't trying to dismiss me the way the others did. "That's how the artist answered critics when they said exactly what you just said."

"Is that right?" I responded, trying to hide how attractive I found him. He had the kind of face you just can't stop looking at, and he seemed to know it.

"It originally sold for $12 million," he added. The people next to me smiled smugly.

"Well, *shit*. I need to start putting random dead things in tanks and calling them art!"

"The thing is, you have to be the first one to think of it."

"Come on! You don't really think this is art, do you?"

He bit his bottom lip and contemplated for a moment. "I don't know if I'm qualified to say whether it's art or not. But it's definitely bullshit."

The people around us gasped in shock as I answered, "*Exactly.*"

"Wait till you see the next one!" he exclaimed. We walked together into the next room, which had blank white walls and a white floor covered with brown mud or clay splotches.

"Oh, this must be the *shit* room!" I called out as heads twisted in my direction. He turned away to avoid laughing as I read a text from Lizzie asking where I was. "In the shit room," I wrote to her.

"Huh?" she wrote back.

"The room with the brown shit splashed everywhere—1st Floor next to the sculpture garden."

"Gotcha. Meet you in five."

As I put my phone back in my bag, I peered at the same guy who seemed to be following me. He was fucking stunning, with perfectly tousled golden brown hair and the most incredible smile. I'm a sucker for nice teeth, and his were pristine. His facial structure was angular and defined, and even though it was obnoxious that he was wearing a t-shirt with the sleeves cut off, his heavily-tattooed arms had just the right amount of muscle tone. When I saw that he was wearing a Jack White concert tee, my heart skipped a fucking beat.

He sensed that I was staring. His olive-green eyes darted from his sketchbook to my legs, then up to my hips, chest, and eyes. He squinted a bit like he was trying to see my face more clearly. "You seem familiar. I definitely know you from somewhere."

I shrugged, and he put his sketchbook in his bag and moved closer. "You hungry?" he asked. "They have a decent café."

"Unfortunately, I'm stuck in this shit room till my friend joins me." He nodded as Lizzie rushed in.

"They said they'd let me know by the end of the week," she announced.

"This is your friend?" he interrupted. She turned to face him, and I actually saw her eyes widen as she very obviously looked him up and down.

"Hi, I'm Lizzie!" She giggled nervously.

"Dante," he said as he held out his hand. She shook it awkwardly and glanced back at me with flushed cheeks.

"Your name is Dante?" I asked incredulously.

"Yes. And yours is?"

"Jane."

"Lizzie," he said as he moved closer to her, "I was just asking Jane if she would join me for lunch. I'd love it if you'd come too."

Lizzie immediately answered, "Of course!"

I cleared my throat audibly. "Lizzie, we can't. We have that thing we have to do, remember?"

She knew what I was doing and chose to ignore it. "What thing? I don't remember a *thing*. I'm free the whole afternoon!" He gave her that smirk, and she blushed.

I'll admit, he was one of the most stunning men I had ever seen in person, and I understood why she was so eager to spend more time with him. I tried to ignore his appearance, but it wasn't just how he looked. There was a confident, sexy aura about him, and it was magnetic. I started to get lost in a maze of conflicting thoughts and assumptions and concluded that he was probably used to getting any girl he wanted, and we weren't going to be his shiny new toys.

"I'm actually not feeling well, so we should go."

Lizzie's jaw tightened with irritation. "Come *on*, Jane. Just one coffee?"

He looked deeply into my eyes, and I had that intense déjà vu feeling I got from time to time. I felt like I knew him, and while it was a comfortable and intriguing familiarity, it was mixed with a panicky feeling as well. "Fine. Answer one question correctly, and we'll have lunch with you."

His eyebrows went up in surprise. "Okay. Shoot."

"Guess my favorite Jack White song." He studied my face for signs of trickery, and one eye squinted a bit. "Won't you just say I'm wrong, no matter what my answer is?"

"Gimme a piece of paper. I'll write it down."

He tore a page out of his sketchbook and gave it to me with a pencil. I scribbled a song title on it, folded it, and gave it back to him. He shoved it into his back pocket and started to ponder. Jokingly, he looked me up and down, and I rolled my eyes. His eyes closed for a moment then flew open. "Lazaretto!" he announced.

"Nope, sorry! Nice meeting you!" I took Lizzie's hand and yanked her away from him before she could say anything.

"Are you crazy?" she whisper-yelled at me.

As we walked away, he took the paper out of his pocket, read it, then chased after us. "Love Interruption! That was my second choice! I can play it for you!"

I turned my head and smiled inadvertently but kept my quick pace.

"Wait, please!" He moved faster and followed us out of the exit. Then he stood directly in front of us, blocking our path.

"Yes?" I said a bit bitchier than I meant it.

"I'm sorry. I know this must seem weird. There's just something about you. I can't let you go just yet."

"What the fuck is that supposed to mean? You can't let us go until *what*?"

"Until you let me paint you," he said as he stared intensely into my eyes. "Both of you."

"Oh my god! You're an artist?" Lizzie squealed with excitement. "So am I!"

"I'm sure there are a lot of girls who would die to be painted by you," I offered. I can't say I wasn't flattered, but it seemed like a cheap pick-up line.

"I don't *want* other girls. I've had *plenty* of other girls-"

"Oh, I'm sure you have!"

"I mean, I've *painted* lots of other girls!" His face was inches from mine. Then he turned to face Lizzie. "You have one of the most stunning faces I have ever seen. It's like you just stepped out of a Florentine fresco. Your hazel eyes that change in the light, that pouty bottom lip you see so often in paintings of saints, and your dazzling blonde hair that shows a touch of copper when you step into the light… You are just what I've been looking for, and I've been looking for a long time." She swooned while I laughed out loud. But then he turned to me and stepped up so close that our noses practically touched.

"We have definitely known each other before, but where or when, I can't quite say. Your long neck, blue-gray eyes, graceful hands… You're so profoundly beautiful; it's startling. I want to paint you as a goddess or an ancient queen. Please, let me preserve your beauty forever in my art." He turned a page in his sketchbook and held it up. There was a sketch of me in front of a mass of trees, and he captured my likeness really well but made me look much prettier than I actually was. Stunned by his words and the sketch, I was locked in silence, unable to speak. "I'll admit," he continued. "I was drawing you for a while today before we spoke. I couldn't help it. You captivated me." It seemed sincere, and I almost leaned in to kiss him but shook it off.

"Look, this is really weird. We don't *know* you at all." I couldn't come up with anything else to say, so I crossed my arms and waited for his response.

"Have dinner at my house tonight. And if you feel comfortable, maybe after that I can do some sketches of the two of you."

"This is crazy. I don't think this is a good idea." As cliché as it sounds, my mouth was saying *no*, but my body was screaming *yes*. I knew there was no way I *wasn't* going to his house, but the sixth sense I had developed for bullshit was begging me not to.

Lizzie, who had a newly found habit of living merely on impulse, stepped in front of me and exclaimed, "We'll be there!"

He flashed that coy smile as he took out the scrap of paper with "Love Interruption" written on it and scribbled his address on the back, then handed it to Lizzie. He turned to me and whispered, "Isn't there something so familiar about this, you and me?" He looked so intensely into me that I couldn't even formulate a response. There was definitely something familiar about him. But I wasn't about to let my guard down just yet.

"I don't know about that."

"I feel like we've been here before. You feel it too, don't you?" If he weren't so fucking stunning, I probably would have laughed in his face. But instead, I was wholly riveted.

"I'm not sure what you're talking about, but we have to go."

"7 P.M. tonight," he said more to Lizzie than to me.

"Yes, we'll be there!" she called back as I pulled her away from him.

"Don't count on it!" I added.

We exited the museum in silence until we were far enough away. Then we turned to each other and screamed, "Holy shit!"

I swiped the scrap of paper from Lizzie's hand and studied it. I felt like I had seen his handwriting before. Suddenly, there was a premonition I will never forget. A flash of white light erupted behind my eyes. The sensation seemed to last for years, but it was only a few seconds. In that flash, I glimpsed the rest of our lives. It was a whirlwind of exhilaration and joy, but there was overwhelming anguish and misery too. There was a tremendous feeling of push-ing and pulling between us, constant despair and uncertainty. But it was unbelievably thrilling, like living in a dark fairy tale. I turned my head, and the feeling was lost.

"Déjà vu again?" Lizzie asked.

"Yeah, a big one."

"Do you remember any of it?"

"Not really."

"Was it about that guy we just met?"

"I don't think so."

It was a lie. I couldn't recall the details, but I still had the knowl-edge that we had known each other before. It came with a vivid surge of warmth and need, but there was also the impression of im-pending doom. I shrugged my shoulders as she grabbed the paper from me. "I better put this somewhere safe," she said as she stuck it into her bra.

I let out a huge sigh. "I don't know if that's actually going to happen."

She looked at me like I was nuts. "*Like fucking hell.* Either we *both* go, or I go *alone!*"

CHAPTER 2

GABRIEL

"Fire"—Two Feet

I RECOGNIZED HER RIGHT AWAY. WE KISSED AT AN INCUBUS concert in Amsterdam a few years ago. She was definitely high on something, which is probably why she couldn't remember. But it left a permanent impression on me. Under the dark blue lights, we crashed into each other in an ocean of bodies, with a magnetic force neither of us could deny. From the moment our eyes locked, there was a knowing that flowed between us, that we had known each other before.

There's just something about her. Aside from her body, which is fucking perfect, and her long dark hair and big blue-gray eyes… There's a fire in her that gets me going like nothing I've experienced before. I think she's my muse. I was sure of it back then, when I thought I'd lost her forever.

It's hard to see through that concrete veil she puts between herself and the world. Some might say she's bitchy, or maybe even frigid, but I'm pretty sure I've got her figured out. She wants more than anything to give in to the fire that burns inside her. Her body screams for touch, and her soul begs to get drunk on passion, drunk on life. But she judges her feelings and desires too much. She punishes herself for her raw impulses. She is her soul's own jailer, and I'm going to break her out.

I want to pull her into the rain and fuck her senseless in the mud. I want to rip her veil away and hear her scream my name and beg for more. I want to reveal her naked soul to her. It won't be easy, but I love a challenge.

CHAPTER 3

Jane

"You're Mine"—Phantogram

WE ARGUED ABOUT WHETHER OR NOT TO GO TO HIS house the rest of the afternoon into the early evening. Of course, I wanted to go. But the more that time passed since seeing him in person, the more contrived the whole thing seemed. I didn't need to be wooed in his cheesy little bachelor pad, where he had easily seduced dozens of other girls under the guise of art. And Lizzie couldn't be trusted in that situation at all. She had a habit of falling into those kinds of traps and relying on me to pull her out. But she looked at it as an adventure, and she was right about that. We were about to enter into the most exciting and intoxicating time in our lives.

I only gave in when she grabbed her keys and said she would go alone.

"*Fine!* Let's go. But only for a few minutes."

"Suuuuuuuure, just for a *few* minutes," she mocked. "Did we meet the same scorching hot guy, or were you in some other reality this afternoon?"

I didn't answer.

We left way past seven, and we got lost a few times too. While arguing about how long we would stay, we didn't notice that we were entering a town we had heard about but never been to.

"This can't be right," I called out as we drove onto his block. "You've got to be *kidding* me." These were the most stunning old mansions I had ever seen. The word *mansion* doesn't even begin to describe these homes. They were estates, chateaus, *compounds*. We drove along a stretch of famous estates owned by some of the country's wealthiest people, and I felt like we didn't even belong on their roads.

We eased to a stop in front of an enormous iron gate with ornate scrollwork. There was a plaque attached to it that said "Red House" in fancy script. "This is it!" Lizzie announced. "This is the address."

"Well, how the fuck are we supposed to get in?" I pulled the car a few inches closer to the gate, and immediately it creaked open. "Woah," I whispered. "What the fuck? This is too creepy. We should go back."

"Maybe there's a motion sensor. Since when are you such a pussy?"

I gave her my middle finger as we slowly rode along the extensive driveway. Gigantic weeping willows lined the pavement, and old-fashioned lanterns hung from iron posts. It was something out of a fairytale.

A massive Gothic-style mansion came into view. With faint lights illuminating the facade, I could just make out the details of an old medieval-looking estate. It was bigger and more beautiful than any house I had ever seen. But there was something a bit sinister about it. The windows were sharply arched, many of them made of stained glass, and it had peaks, vaults, and several small towers. The strangest part was the red hue of the bricks. The effect was somber and weird but definitely romantic.

"Still want to forget it?" Lizzie teased.

"Well, I don't know. So who cares that he lives in a huge mansion? Besides, we're almost two hours late. He might not even be home."

"Jane, are you fucking crazy? Take a look around. It's worth knocking on the door!"

"Okay. I'll admit, this is pretty fucking amazing. It looks a lot like the haunted mansion at Disneyworld, don't you think?"

"It *totally* does! I hope we have the right address," she said. "What if he doesn't live here?"

"Well… What's the worst that could happen? Some weirdo

answers, and we apologize for having the wrong address and make a run for it?"

"Right!" she called out as we popped out of the car.

"What if he's a fucking vampire?"

"Or a creepy-ass murderer answers the door and forces us in at gunpoint?" she added.

"Or maybe it's a Satanic cult that will sacrifice our bodies to the devil?" I joked as we approached the intricately carved wooden doors and looked at each other with apprehension. "If I scream for you to run—*don't hesitate*!" I warned. She rolled her eyes and banged the colossal iron ring that hung from the door. "Do you still have that little bottle of mace in your bag?" I asked. She pulled the mace out of her bag and held it up as we waited for someone to open the door.

"Should I knock again?" she asked. I shrugged, and she banged the ring a few more times.

"There must be a doorbell," she said as she searched the doorframe.

"I think we should go. We tried, right?"

She pushed a button next to the doorway and a loud chime rang out, but after another minute, there was still no answer.

We had just turned around to leave when he appeared in the doorway, hair soaking wet, with a towel wrapped around his hips. *Holy fuck,* he was hot. He had the perfect amount of muscle, like his body was well-defined and golden from a life spent climbing mountains, swimming across lakes, and trekking rugged landscapes. I couldn't quite decipher the tattoos on his chest, but they looked like dripping black paint.

"I didn't think you were going to show up," he said with a very pleased look on his face before he raked his hand through his slick hair.

"Sorry. We'll go!"

I snatched Lizzie's hand and tried to pull her towards the car when he called out, "No, please! Come in!" She yanked back her arm and flashed me a pissed-off look before she followed him into the house. I entered the doorway, trying my best not to stare at him.

The size of the house was ridiculous. The floor was made of white marble and had a black marble mosaic of snakes entwined with wild birds. There was an enormous staircase with ornately carved flowers under each step. Hanging above was a massive crystal chandelier.

"You didn't mention that you live in a fucking castle," I joked. He grinned as he sauntered past the staircase and through a doorway. We passed through a room with dark wood walls and a white ceiling carved with intricate designs that looked like a wedding cake. The atmosphere was dark and ominous.

"I made pasta earlier. I can warm it up," he offered as we entered a huge solarium.

"We're not hungry," I answered. He ushered us through double doors at the back of the room, and Lizzie and I grabbed each other's hands. "Holy shit!" I blurted out.

We were gazing at an incredible expanse of land. The grass seemed to go on forever. There was a little table set up on the patio with a few lit candles and three empty wine glasses. "It's beautiful out tonight. Not too humid. I was hoping we could have dinner out here."

We sat down, and he excused himself and came back wearing jeans and a tight black t-shirt. He was holding a guitar and a bottle of wine. After filling our glasses, he pulled out a cigarette and lit it with a candle. "What's the guitar for?" I asked.

"I promised I'd play your favorite Jack White song," he said between drags of his cigarette. He finished it as we sipped the wine, and then he grabbed the guitar and began to play. I was hoping it would suck a little bit because why should someone get to be so good-looking *and* live in a castle *and* be unbelievably talented in art *and* music? But he played the guitar masterfully, and his voice was flawless. It sounded a lot like Chris Cornell, ranging multiple octaves.

He kept trying to connect with me while he sang, but I would glance down at his guitar or up at the house. Lizzie was dying for him to look at her as she leaned in closer and closer, but he kept his eyes on me. When he finished, we were silent for a moment, and I inadvertently murmured, "*Shit*."

"Not that good, huh? I haven't played that in a while."

I sighed deeply. "Actually, it was really, *really* good."

"Ya think?" he asked with that fucking smirk that equally frustrated and excited me.

"It was *amazing*!" Lizzie declared as she gulped down the rest of her wine.

He held up the bottle. "More?"

She held out her glass, and he filled it to the top, then turned to me. I showed him my glass, which was still mostly full. "I'm good."

"Any requests?"

"I'm more into classic rock," Lizzie stated. "You have another acoustic in the house?"

"Sure do! You play? What kind?"

"Gibson J-45."

"The old workhorse! You have the vintage sunburst?"

"Yep."

"Nice!"

"Any electric guitars?"

His face lit up. "I've got a 1963 Stratocaster owned by Jimi Hendrix."

"No shit! What does it sound like?"

"No idea. I've never taken it out of the glass case."

"I can't even imagine what that cost you."

"A lot. I've got a G-45 you can play. Not as nice as yours but-"

She finished a gulp of wine and exclaimed, "But still pretty nice! *Yours* is beautiful. I've never seen anything like it."

"It's custom," he said with a wink. "Lemme go get that acoustic. Jane, do you need anything?"

"Got a tambourine or a triangle, maybe?"

"I think I have some bongos!" he joked before he went inside. I immediately turned to Lizzie.

"So, five more minutes and we go?"

"*You* can go any time you want!"

"Lizzie, come *on*! You can't see what's going on here?"

"You mean how a gorgeous guy who lives in a medieval castle and plays guitar like a God wants to hang out with us?"

"Yeah. *That*. If by *hang out,* you mean *hit and run*!"

She guzzled the rest of her wine and answered, "Get in a car accident?"

"I mean smash and dash? Hump and dump? Hit it and quit it?"

"So what if we *are* just a booty call? Might be fun."

"Speak for yourself."

"I *am* speaking for myself, but I'm also speaking for your *fuck-strated* ass!"

"That's the wine talking, and just because it's been a while doesn't mean I'm desperate."

"*Uh-huh.*"

"I ain't no hollaback girl!"

She giggled and leaned in. "What about *rail and bail*? I just made that up!"

"That's a good one. How about *slam and scram*?"

"I like it. Wait, I got one. *One night delight!*" A snort slipped out of my nose before I cackled. "Wait, wait," I said through gasps. "It's on a *need-to-hoe* basis!" She spewed wine in my direction, and we were laughing so hard that we were practically crying as he joined us with a guitar for Lizzie.

"What's so funny?" he asked.

We struggled to pull ourselves together. "Nothing," I croaked, wiping tears from my face. He put his guitar back in his lap as Lizzie adjusted hers.

"So classic rock, right?" he asked, ignoring our residual giggles. "Umm, how about Guns N' Roses?"

"Guns N' Roses is *not* classic rock!" I insisted.

"Sure it is!" he responded. "It just needs to be 25 years old or older."

"No, that's what makes a *car* a classic. For rock, it's not just a

25-year time span because, by that logic, shitty rock songs from the late nineties could be considered classic rock."

"So what's your criteria for classifying something as *classic* rock then?"

"If it came out in the '60s, '70s, or '80s, *and* stands the test of time, meaning it's listened to by more than one generation."

Lizzie chimed in. "So what about rock songs from the early '90s that are still listened to, like Nirvana?"

"Just rock," I stated.

"Okay," he jumped in. "By your definition, Guns N' Roses would definitely be *classic* rock. 'Welcome to the Jungle' came out in '87. *And* it's still played on the radio all the time."

"Guns 'N Roses are early '90s," I maintained.

"*Appetite for Destruction* came out in '87. You're thinking of *Use Your Illusion*."

"I'll settle this," Lizzie stated as she searched her phone. "He's right. They formed in '85; their first album was in '87."

"I still don't think they qualify for the label *classic*."

"Why not?" he challenged as he put another cigarette between his lips and lit it.

"Would you classify Metallica, Motley Crue, or Bon Fucking Jovi as classic rock?"

He blew the smoke upwards, avoiding our faces. "Motley Crue—yes, Bon Jovi—maybe, Metallica—probably not. Well, maybe."

"Metallica as classic rock?" Lizzie asked. "That doesn't sound right."

He took another drag and put the lit cigarette on the table. "Well, I've got a mindfuck for both of you. Guns N' Roses covering 'Knockin' on Heaven's Door,' which was originally a Bob Dylan song. Doubly classic, in my opinion."

Before I could respond, he began to play. Lizzie, who also had an incredible singing voice, sang along with him. This time he didn't look at me once. The two of them played and sang together as they stared into each other's eyes, and both were glowing with joy. I swiped my wine off the table and drank half the glass. They finished the song, and I clapped and cheered to be a good sport and to hide my utter jealousy. I wasn't jealous of the attention he was giving her; I was envious of their talent. If I were as brilliant as Lizzie academically, and as gifted in music and art, I would have carried myself with a lot more confidence.

"You're really good," he told her. "How long have you been playing?" I could tell she had an intense buzz going on because her head was swaying a bit, and she couldn't stop smiling.

"Only three years. My parents forced me to learn the violin growing up. They wouldn't even allow a guitar in the house."

"They sound like scumbags."

"They're not *scumbags*. They're just very concerned with appearances."

"Lizzie." I leaned in closer before I continued. "Your parents are *major* scumbags."

"Yeah, I guess they are."

"You play really well if you've only been playing a few years!"

She grinned and played again. He listened for about ten seconds, then joined in. I wasn't sure what they were playing until they both started singing the first verse to The Doors' "Light My Fire."

They really seemed to be connecting, and I was jealous but also worried. Lizzie had developed a habit of leading men on and then freaking out when they actually tried to have sex with her because she was still a virgin. I saved her twice from practically being raped. The amount of wine she was drinking and the seductive little jam session they were having put me on edge. But I knew the more I tried to pull her out of the situation, the more she would want it. Her parents stunted her maturity so much that she seemed to be living through her rebellious teenager stage in her twenties.

They finished the song and complimented each other.

"How about 'House of the Rising Sun?'" she asked.

"I don't know that one."

She strummed the guitar and sang, and he listened for a bit, then joined in. I finished my wine and poured another glass. I began to feel stupid, like I didn't even exist in the same universe as them. Would they even notice if I left?

I brought my glass of wine with me as I descended a stone staircase that led to a walkway lined with lush pink peonies and bursts of white roses. I stepped out of my sandals and felt the damp grass between my toes. Turning back for a moment, I saw him pour more wine into Lizzie's glass before they played again. They didn't seem to notice my absence at all. I should have stayed with her, but I was sick of being the fucking babysitter.

I followed a faint glow of golden light peeking through the branches of a mass of pine trees. After a long trek on a worn dirt path, a lovely, still lake appeared. A small group of solar lanterns surrounded a stone bench. I sat down and swallowed a huge mouthful of wine while staring at the reflection of the lanterns on the water. A swarm of fireflies danced in circles near the surface, and I took in a deep, cleansing breath.

My thoughts swirled in every direction. It was so quiet, so still, and I had never seen so many stars in my life. All I could think about was why someone like him got to live somewhere like that, a place so beautiful and perfect. Why did some souls have to suffer so much while others seemed to be living in an idyllic dream? Perhaps I misjudged him, I thought. I didn't know his story. Maybe there was a layer of pain buried underneath the polished surface he presented? Had he suffered greatly, and was he still suffering? Did he bring us into his world to alleviate some great loneliness?

I felt a hand rest on my shoulder, and I jumped and flung it away.

"I didn't mean to scare you," he said softly as he sat next to me.

"Where's Lizzie?" I replied, looking back through the trees.

"She went inside to prepare."

"Prepare for *what*?"

"The sketches. I'd really like it if you would come too."

"Well, I kinda *have to* now. I'm not leaving my friend alone. She tends to get herself into these kinds of situations a lot."

"What kind of situations do you mean?" he said through that devious grin.

"Dangerous ones."

"And you don't like being in dangerous situations?" he asked as he moved a bit closer.

"No, not rapey situations. That's not the kind of thrill I'm into."

"So what kind of thrill are you into, Jane?" He took my glass of wine, sipped it slowly, and licked his lips.

"*Fuck,* he's hot," was all I could think. I took my glass back from his hand, drank the entire thing, and replied, "I think I'll keep that information to myself… for now."

My mood suddenly changed. I wanted to play his game, just a bit. I stood up, gave him the empty glass, and said, "It's warm out here tonight," before I slipped my sweater off to reveal a lacy little camisole. I wasn't wearing a bra, and I knew I looked good in that tank. Why was I toying with him when I was just chastising Lizzie for doing the exact same thing? There was no way in fucking hell I was going to hook up with him. But the wine was drawing out my flirty side. In truth, there was nothing I enjoyed more than teasing a fuck boy and leaving him high and dry.

I dropped my sweater onto his lap and asked, "So where are we doing this?" With a look of surprise, he took my hand and led me back up the pathway. His hand was cool, and his grip was just tight enough to send tingles up my arm. The wine was definitely kicking in, and I'm a notorious lightweight. When we entered the solarium, I glanced down at his hand and noticed a few tattoos. I stopped and pulled his hands closer to my face to examine them. One hand had an entire paragraph of Italian scrawled on it. The other had a black crow with the initials "M.M." under it.

"Who is M. M.?" I asked.

"It stands for *memento mori.*"

"What does that mean?"

"Remember, you must die."

"Huh?"

"It says *memento mori,* which means *remember, you must die* in Latin."

"That's kind of creepy."

"It's not creepy at all. It's truth. It's the *only* truth. The only certainty in life."

"Yeah, I guess. But why would you want to be reminded of that every time you look at your hand?" I swayed a bit as he stepped closer. I could feel his breath on my face, and it smelled like cigarettes and wine.

"You can't escape it. It doesn't matter who you are, how much you have, or what you do, you *will* die. For me, it's a constant reminder to make the most out of every moment. To not just exist, but to truly live."

He bent down a bit, leaned in close, and pressed his lips to my neck just under my ear. I closed my eyes for a moment and felt my legs turn to jelly. "You don't really think I'm dangerous, do you?" he whispered into my ear. I turned my head and said, "I wouldn't still be here if I did."

One of his eyes squinted just a bit and he started to bring one hand towards my hair. I backed away and cleared my throat.

"So what does this one say?" I gestured towards the paragraph on his other hand.

He spoke in perfect Italian, without looking down at his hand.

"In quel libro che è la mia memoria,

Nella prima pagina del primo capitolo,

Che è il giorno in cui ti ho incontrato per la prima volta,

Appaiono le parole, Qui inizia una nuova vita."

"Okay. The most I can translate is nuova vita. New life."

"That's right. It's the introduction to Dante's *La Vita Nuova.* It says, 'In the book of my memory, on the first page of the first chapter that is the day I met you, the words appear: here begins a new life.'"

"That's Dante talking about Beatrice, right?"

"Yes."

"So, who do you have that written on your hand for?"

"I don't know. I haven't met her yet."

There was a pause, and I thought he might try to kiss me. His eye contact was too intense, and I grasped for a way to continue the conversation. "Any other tattoos?"

He grinned and swiftly pulled his shirt off. The sight of his muscular, tattooed chest and arms and that warm familiarity between us made me lightheaded.

I'll be honest. If he had been just a bit more forceful at that moment, I would have given myself completely.

I tried to concentrate on the tattoos. There was a skull on his chest that looked like it was melting. On one shoulder leading down his arm were pieces of a broken clock, an angel, stormy clouds, a skull, roses, and a human heart. Scrawled across his hip was another line in Italian.

"la morte non è la fine dell'amore, la morte non è la fine"

I knew that morte meant death. "Wow. You're like, *obsessed* with death," I muttered.

"Quite the opposite really. I'm obsessed with *life*. I want to experience as much life as I can in every moment."

"Maybe your tattoo should say remember *life?*"

He stared at me and seemed to be searching my face for something. "You can put your shirt back on now," I commanded as I began to walk away.

"You haven't seen the tattoos on my back."

"I got the gist. Death and carpe diem stuff."

He put his shirt back on, retook my hand, and led me back into the house. Slowly, we went up the grand staircase and down a shadowy hallway. The walls were made of elaborately carved mahogany wood, and there were many painted portraits of women. The pictures were all different sizes, but each featured a gorgeous woman, and many were naked. I stopped to admire one. The woman had long auburn hair, juicy red lips, and was baring one breast with a delicate pink nipple. In one hand, she held an arrow. In the other was an apple. Pink and white flowers surrounded her.

"Venus, the Roman goddess of love," he offered. "See that arrow she's holding? Ready to pierce hearts. And the apple is, of course, for temptation." I tried not to look at him because every time our eyes met I felt like I would melt into a warm, gooey puddle. I kept my eyes on the painting. It had an inscription on the bottom of the frame with the name "Dante Gabriel Rossetti" inscribed in fancy script.

"*You painted this?*" I asked in shock as he nodded. "Did you paint *all* of these?"

"Only the good ones," he said playfully. "What do you think?"

"It's beautiful, but…"

"What? Tell me what you think. I really want to know!"

"She's a bit… manish."

"*Manish?*" he said with genuine confusion. "What does that mean?"

"I don't know. Like, her head, her chin, jawline… Seems a bit like a man to me."

"Shit," he pondered. "I've never noticed that before."

I wasn't even trying to be critical. I was just being honest. I don't think he had received any real criticism before. "Is her mandible that pronounced in person?" I asked. "Is she kind of like a dude?"

"*Alexa?* There is nothing manish about her. She is *all* woman!" His eyes glossed over like he was lost in a daydream. I'm sure he was thinking about Alexa, her pink nipples, and her man chin.

"Well, maybe you need to redo that part." He broke from his little reverie and stared at me with an expression I couldn't decipher. I studied the painting on the other side of me. It featured a pretty woman with a big feathery hat.

"Did you paint this too?"

"That boring piece of shit? No. That's John's painting. He's talented, but his choice of subject matter is definitely lacking. He's a bit of a prude." I wandered down the hall and stopped in front of another painting. It featured a man sitting at a piano with a pretty young woman sitting in his lap. She had a look of shock on her face. An inscription read, "An Awakening Conscience."

"This is interesting. Is it yours?"

"No, that's Will's painting. He's really into virtue and honor and all that shit. See, this is the man's mistress, but she suddenly has a moment of revelation that she's a whore and wants to seek redemption."

"It's not boring," I replied. "But if *he's* the married one, then *he* seems like more of a whore to me than her. Perhaps *he* should be the one seeking redemption?"

He looked amused. "Yes, I suppose you're right. But I don't believe in whores, or virtue, or judgment. There don't have to be so many rules."

"*Interesting*," I said as though I knew something he didn't.

"*What?*"

"It's just interesting that you seem to look down upon chivalry given your interest in Dante's *La Vita Nuova*. I only studied it a little in college, but from what I remember, the entire basis was courtly love and a man's lifelong admiration for his wife."

"Yes, courtly love is about devotion and admiration for one's love. But not necessarily for one's *wife*. Since most marriages throughout history were arranged, courtly love was considered an escape from a loveless marriage."

"Isn't love supposed to lift you up to the highest level of spirituality? That's what Dante thought, right? So how does one attain such high spirituality when potentially causing another such pain?"

"That's exactly why marriage is completely insane." I scrunched my eyebrows together to show my disagreement, but he added, "*Unless* you marry your greatest love."

"Your Beatrice."

"Exactly."

"But I remember one specific part about courtly love that was pretty important. And I have a feeling it would make things very difficult for you."

"What's that?"

"Courtly love was meant to be *unrequited*, and had to remain that way, otherwise, tragedy would occur."

"Unrequited, as in…"

"No fucking."

He paused for a few heavy moments, then said, "It's all just a bunch of fables anyway. Won't stop me from finding my muse."

"Well good luck finding her. And if you uncover a knight in shining armor or a guy in armor that isn't completely rusted to shit, send him my way!"

"You've been burned, have you?"

"Yeah, definitely *not* going into that with you. So who are these other painters? Friends of yours?"

"More than friends. We're partners. We're a brotherhood. They live here too."

"Wow! How many are there?" I was thrilled with the idea of a house full of artist guys. If they were half as attractive as him, I might never leave.

"There's five of us. They're in London at an exhibition, but I stayed behind. I don't need a bunch of asshole critics telling me what's wrong with my work." Okay, maybe he *had* gotten some criticism before.

"What do you mean by brotherhood? Is it like a cult?"

"No, I wouldn't say we're a cult. But we do have a set of shared beliefs that we live by. Come here."

He walked further down the hallway and pointed to a framed document. It read,

"In the modern age, beauty and spirituality have been lost. We seek a return to the freedom of simpler times in contrast to the slavery of the modern age. The fine arts have always relied upon truth, and truth must be unconfined, infinite, immaterial, and impossible of reduction into formulas or of conversion into machines. Society thinks itself more radically civilized due to its advanced technology, which it now uses to generate art. Digital art has a form and function unto itself and is still valid. But lost is the reverence for fine art that has forever defined all that is in man, the mysteries of the soul, thoughts and emotions, beautiful, vast, ponderous, gloomy, and awful. There is a power and a spirit that flows when man creates with his own hand. Poetry written

pencil to paper while sitting under a tree, hundreds of hours spent painting a woman's form with soft brush strokes mere inches from her naked body, a song conceived note by note running one's fingers upon strings-, these are the forms that capture our genius, our souls, and preserve them well beyond our inevitable death. We seek a return to the creation and reverence of fine art in its simplest form, as nature in its simplest form is most perfect. We shall dedicate our lives to this noble pursuit."

There were five signatures at the end of the scroll.

"Shit. That's deep. Who wrote it?"

"I did."

"So you hate technology?"

"Not at all. I'm grateful for it. I love flicking a switch and having instant light, but it can't compare to the warm glow of candlelight. I love my car, but it doesn't let me soak in the rain. I love my phone, but it cannot possibly capture the power of connecting with someone face to face."

"I feel the same way. I couldn't give up air conditioning, but a few months ago, my neighborhood lost electricity for three days. My phone was dead, and I was bored as fuck, so I started walking and I went further than I've ever gone in my town. I followed a stream to a little waterfall that I never even knew existed. I swam for hours and drank fresh water right from the falls. At night, I read a book by candlelight and fell asleep looking out my window at a sky full of stars that I was never able to see before because of all the light pollution. I was sweaty, but I slept better than I have in years."

"Have you ever had sex like that? Outside, covered in sweat, under a summer night's sky?"

"Umm, not that I can recall. I would worry about dirt and bugs crawling into... places."

"All you need is a thick blanket. I highly recommend it." He leaned in a bit closer, and I quickly backed away and cleared my throat.

"Where's Lizzie?"

He pointed down the hallway towards an open bedroom door.

As I entered, I saw Lizzie sprawled out on the bed asleep, wrapped in a large white drape. The bed was a tremendous, carved mahogany work of art with curled feet and an intricately engraved headboard. The room smelled distinctly masculine, like leather, musk, burnt matches, and freshly chopped wood.

I could see that she was drunk. Her teeth were stained purple. I tapped her on the shoulder, and she sprung awake and self-consciously repositioned herself. He held out what looked like a white curtain for me. "You can change in the bathroom if you'd like." I took the cloth, wrapped it around myself, and then undid my pants from underneath and dropped them. I pulled my camisole off from under the sheet, handed it to him, and said, "How should I pose?"

He cleared his throat nervously. "I'm working on some Biblical scenes. I'd like to do a painting of Lilith and Eve," he said as he set up his easel and tools. "Lizzie, you'll be Eve. You should be lying back on the bed with your arm above your head on the pillow. Jane, you'll be Lilith. Please pose next to Lizzie, but keep your arms by your side. I'm going to paint snakes around them." He continued to set up his tools as we tried to get the positioning right.

"So, this painting doesn't really make sense," I stated. "Lilith and Eve were never together in the Garden of Eden. Lilith left after refusing to be subservient to Adam, then God made Eve for him instead."

He looked confused until Lizzie chimed in. "Actually, Lilith left Eden but snuck back in later after Eve was created. Some interpretations claim that the snake that tempted Eve with the apple was actually Lilith in disguise." He grinned and excused himself for a second.

"Figures," I said to Lizzie. "Not only did Lilith become a demon because she wanted to be on top during sex, but apparently she's also responsible for the fall of man."

Lizzie turned her head to me and winked. "I'd still rather be an evil temptress than made out of a man's rib!"

"Being an evil temptress actually sounds like a lot of fun!" I joked.

He came back in and handed me a shiny red apple.

"What's this for?"

"Just hold it. Like this." He moved my hand to my hip and put the apple into it. Then he made little adjustments to our arms and legs and the angle of our faces. Every time he adjusted my face or arm, I burned inside.

His eyes moving from us to the canvas with such intensity drove me mad, especially because we couldn't move. The way a small piece of hair hung down over his eye as he looked at us with a furrowed brow was turning me on. I wondered how he could see us in the faint glow of the candlelight as he stopped for a moment and lit a joint.

He took a few hits and stepped back to look at his work. Then he sat down next to me on the bed and asked if I wanted a hit. I sat up and nodded slightly, and he told me to open my mouth. I raised my eyebrows, not realizing my mouth was half-open. He leaned in closely, blowing smoke directly into my mouth. It took me entirely by surprise, but it was also really sexy, having his lips so close to mine. I pulled away, coughing, a bit embarrassed that I wasn't smoother about the whole thing.

"More?" he asked.

I didn't really answer, so he leaned in and blew smoke into my mouth again. Then he smiled and went back to his canvas. The weed hit me immediately, and the first thing I felt was extreme hunger. I glanced down to the apple in my hand and sat up. I bit into it and chewed slowly, really savoring the sweet and sour flavor. I asked Lizzie if she wanted some and she sat up as I held it out to her mouth and she took a big bite. She looked into my eyes as she chewed, and I took another bite and held it out for her again.

When I looked up, he had stopped sketching and was staring at us intensely. "What?" I asked. He shook his head a bit. "That was really sexy," he stated. My face twisted in confusion. "What was?"

He looked amused. "The apple…"

I shrugged my shoulders and took another bite. As he started sketching again, he casually said, "You know, I'd love to do this painting nude," without looking away from his work.

"So take your clothes off then," I responded, trying to remember the position I was supposed to be in.

"Not me, Jane. *You*. Lilith and Eve lived in the Garden of Eden before the fall of man. They were nude, and there was no shame." I instantly sat up, and the spell was over. The wine, guitars, candlelight, weed, posing in his bed in a piece of cloth? "*How dumb were we?*" I thought. I wasn't willing to play his game anymore.

"We are *not* getting naked! Are you fucking crazy? We don't even know you!" I cried, walking away from the bed. As I neared the bedroom door, I looked back and saw Lizzie carefully unwrapping her drape while trying to maintain her position on the bed. "*What are you doing?*" I yelled as I ran back to her. I tried to push her hands from her underwear, but she flung me away.

"I can make my own decisions, Jane. I'm a grown woman," she said with irritation.

"Lizzie, I know you can make your own decisions. I'm just not sure you've really thought this one through. You don't know him *at all*. Why are you willing to get naked in front of him?"

"I'm not ashamed of my body. It's for art."

"I'm not ashamed of my body either. But this feels sleazy to me! Lizzie, *please*! I don't trust him!"

"Leave me the fuck alone, Jane! You're not my fucking mom!"

"*Fine*. Stay with the pervert then!" I got close to his face. "If you hurt her, *I'll rip your fucking eyeballs out*."

"Understood," he whispered with a smug grin that I wanted to slap off his face. "You can trust me, Jane."

"Uh-huh," I muttered as I leaned across him and snatched the joint and lighter from his table. Then I picked up my clothes and turned back to Lizzie. "If you need me, I'll be nearby. Just *scream*." If she wanted to be used by this sleazebag, what could I do? I decided to smoke some more and explore the house.

I lit the joint and stepped slowly through the dark hallway, admiring all of the paintings. Many of the girls probably weren't even that attractive in person. Still, the way they were depicted, amongst wild roses and burning candles, draped in luscious silks tied with golden ropes, made them look like absolute goddesses. Dante had done most of the nudes, which wasn't surprising. He seemed quite adept at charming the clothes off of girls. "Not me," I whispered to myself. "*Never* me."

I entered the first open door I saw. It was a huge bedroom, and it was breathtaking. The domed ceiling had elaborately carved beams leading into the middle, where an eight-pointed nautical star was painted. In between the beams were windows, and white light from the full moon poured into the room. Across from the bed was a white stone fireplace, engraved with intricate leaves and flower buds and a coat of arms in the middle. I ran my fingers over the leaves and took a deep breath, noticing the fresh scent that filled the room. It reminded me of the smell of salt water and warm sand that filled the little beach house my family used to own.

The crest had a ribbon below it that featured the words, "Virtute et valare luceo non uro." I assumed it was Latin, but the only words I recognized were virtue and valor. I approached the perfectly-made bed and lifted the pillow, inhaling the same enticing scent. It was strange, but I was getting turned on, dreaming of the man who inhabited that bedroom.

A framed picture on the bedside table featured a very tall, skinny blonde guy with a pretty little girl in a white dress in his arms. They were sitting on the stone bench near the lake. I felt like I was invading his privacy too much, and I left the room.

The next door was wide open and drew me in immediately. It was the loveliest bathroom. Everything was sparkling white, from the floor to the pedestal sink, to the gigantic claw foot tub. Above the tub hung a delicate crystal chandelier, and behind it was a floor-to-ceiling window. In the middle of the window stood a stained glass tree dripping with red flowers. Moonlight shone through the tree, casting a soft red glow across the room.

I unwrapped the fabric I was wearing, climbed into the tub, and re-lit the joint. I took a few hits, leaned my head back, and imagined

Red House was my home. I almost caught a glimpse of the many times we would bathe under that tree, where he would whisper, "You have been mine before, and you will always be mine." I needed to hear it. I needed to hear that I belonged and would always belong.

When I stood up, I was so fucked up from the joint that I didn't even put my clothes on. I continued exploring the house in my underwear. A catwalk overlooked a vast living room, with sumptuous fabric chairs and elaborate curtains on the floor-to-ceiling windows. It led directly to a fascinating wooden door that looked straight out of *The Lord of the Rings*. It was pointed at the top, and the hinges were made of intricate iron scrolls that stretched out to the middle. The door was slightly ajar, and I pushed it open a bit more to peek inside. There must have been motion-activated lights because as soon as I stepped into the room, it became illuminated. I called out, "Holy fucking shit!" when I saw what was inside. I was standing on the top floor of a massive library—row upon row upon row of books with ladders on wheels attached to the shelves. Several wrought iron chandeliers hung in the center of the room. The walls, shelves, and ladders were made of dark mahogany wood. The shelves were lit from inside and cast a warm yellow glow. I ran my fingers across row after row of books and looked over the balcony to the main floor. Amongst more bookshelves were cozy-looking armchairs and little mahogany tables with small candelabras on top.

The focal point of the room was a giant painted mural on four panels above a stone fireplace. The panels portrayed four versions of the same woman. Each seemed to represent a different season. The first was summer, and she was wrapped in a sheer cloth, revealing her curvy body underneath. Wild roses surrounded her, and purple wildflowers grew over her bare feet. Autumn wore cranberry-colored silks and looked quite tired. Not nearly as lovely as summer, which makes sense. Winter was covered in heavy blue fabric. Her hair and even her face had a blue hue. An ocean roared behind her, and she looked as though she was a moment away from a deep sleep. Spring held a branch of cherry blossoms and had pink flowers in her hair and on her shoulders. The scene was cheerful, though she did not look all that happy. I noticed each panel had an engraved plaque underneath, and I longed to see them up close. I spotted a small spiral staircase at the end of the row where I stood.

I stepped down and looked at the first plaque. It read, "Love is not love which alters when it alteration finds." The second plaque said, "Love's not Time's fool." The third read, "Love alters not with his brief hours and weeks." And the last read, "But bears it out even to the edge of doom." It was from a Shakespearean sonnet, one I always admired. "Who created this?" I wondered. "It couldn't possibly be that boy upstairs." He just did not seem that deep to me. But maybe there was more to him than I realized.

I felt cold, so I took a wool blanket from one of the armchairs and wrapped it around my body. Then I sprawled out on the ornate floral rug underneath the fireplace and stared up at the mural. I wondered about the woman in the paintings as I started to feel sleepy.

Being in that house was like stepping back in time several hundred years. I had never seen such beauty and attention to detail in my life. I imagined I was one of the women in the paintings that covered the walls—cared for, glorified, worshipped. While picturing myself clothed in those delicate fabrics and wildflowers, I fell asleep.

I awoke in the early morning, stunned that I had stayed overnight. There was a profound sense of peace as rays of early morning sun beat down on me through the massive windows. But I immediately stood up with a sharp pang of anxiety as I remembered I was in a stranger's house, in my underwear, and Lizzie had been alone with him the entire night.

I bolted up the spiral staircase, out the door, through the hallway, and back into the bathroom. I threw on my pants and camisole and dashed towards his bedroom. From the doorway I could see that Lizzie was asleep on his bed, tucked halfway under the puffy white blanket, and she was still naked. He appeared in front of me shirtless, his jeans hanging low on his lean hips. I could clearly make out a deep V leading from his hips downward. His hair was mussed just the right amount, and he held out a mug with a little grin. "Good morning, Jane. Coffee?"

"Did you sleep with her?" I growled while trying to avoid looking at his sculpted chest.

"Excuse me?" he responded softly, the same grin never leaving his face.

"You heard me! I asked if you fucked my friend!" I snarled, moving closer towards his face.

He cleared his throat twice and murmured, "I'd rather not talk about such private things. I consider them sacred."

I scoffed. "Yeah, I'll bet you do!" I gestured to the paintings hanging in the hallway. "I'm sure every one of these women you slept with is really *super* sacred to you!" His expression fell, and he stood motionless, waiting for my next move. I continued staring back with venom, and he gently put the mug to his mouth. That's when I asked, "Did you know that she's a virgin?" He choked on the coffee and began coughing like an idiot.

I shoved past him and tossed the blanket off of her. "Lizzie! Get up! Let's go!" She groaned and turned onto her stomach. I picked up her clothes and dumped them onto her back. "Get dressed! We're leaving!" She slowly sat up as he came into the room.

"Please don't leave yet! At least stay for breakfast," he pleaded.

"Fuck you!" I yelled as I shoved him over, so I could get to her shoes. All I could think about was him taking advantage of my best friend with his stupid, obvious tricks. As I gathered our things, I noticed that he had a very amused look on his face. "What are you so happy about?" I demanded as I dragged Lizzie out of bed.

"I've found you!" he announced. "I wasn't entirely sure last night, but there's no doubt. You are *her*!"

"What the fuck are you talking about?" I barked as I put on my shoes.

"You're my muse," he said, looking completely sincere.

"Yeah, I'm sure you have many, *many* muses. Lots of paintings of them in the hallway there!"

"No, no, no. You are Venus, Persephone, Astarte, Lilith,

Beatrice! You are not *a* muse. You are *the* muse. When that irrational anger lights that fire in you… *Fuck*! It's *breathtaking*!" Before I could answer, we heard a door slam, and the sound of lively male voices entered the room from below.

"The guys are back," he said with almost no emotion. Then a knowingness lit up his gaze. "I can't wait for them to meet you! *Both* of you!"

CHAPTER 4

GABRIEL

"Put Me to Work"—Big Data

No, Jane, I didn't fuck your friend. I had planned on seducing *you*, but you proved to be much icier than I had initially judged. After you fled my room, I realized I had fucked things up pretty badly, but I didn't want to look desperate chasing after you.

I figured I would get to know Lizzie a bit more. Maybe gain some valuable information. But she fell asleep, and I couldn't wake her. I tried to continue my sketch, but her snoring was constant and beyond irritating. I searched the house for you, but I couldn't figure out where you went. I slept in the guest room. The night was a total disappointment. This will be harder than I thought, but I'm not letting you go just yet.

CHAPTER 5

Jane

"Youngblood"—The Naked and Famous

I DRAGGED LIZZIE DOWN THE LONG STAIRCASE BY HER WRIST, and she protested by whispering, "Come on, Jane! Let go!" but I held on tighter.

"We need to get the fuck out of here before you get tangled up in more of this *bullshit*!" As we reached the bottom of the stairs, the group of guys let out all kinds of cheers and whistles.

"Oh *shit*! He had *two* here last night!" one called out.

Another added, "Only *two*, Gabriel? Are you having some kind of dry spell?"

They were all laughing except one, who had a serious, almost embarrassed look on his face. He was the tallest fucking person I'd ever seen. He had messy blonde hair and a plain, pale face. He stepped closer to us and said with a delicious English accent, "I apologize for my mates. They're not usually so rude. I'm Will." He held out his hand for a formal handshake.

"What are you, like eight feet tall?" I responded, not shaking his hand. One of them snickered, and Will replied, "6'7 actually. And you are?"

"I'm only about 5'4."

"She's fucking funny!" another cute blonde guy said as he moved closer to introduce himself. "Hey, my name's also Will, but everyone calls me by my last name, Hunt."

One of the other guys put his arm around Hunt. "And *we* call him *Madman*!"

"I'm sure there's a fascinating story behind that nickname," I responded.

"There definitely is!" one of them exclaimed.

But I cut him off. "But we were just leaving. Lizzie, let's go!"

I went for the door and heard Will say, "*Damn it*, Gabriel. What did you do to make her so angry?"

"I didn't do anything! I mean *seriously*!"

"Then *that's* why she's so mad!" Hunt joked.

"Dude, stop. It's not funny."

"Why did he call you Gabriel? I thought your name was Dante," I said.

He looked uncomfortable. "Gabriel is my first name. Dante is my middle name."

Hunt cut him off. "Yeah, like one of ten of them!"

"Shut up, dick!" Gabriel said as he shoved his friend playfully.

"So you lied about your name?" I said, squinting my eyes in anger.

"I didn't lie. Dante is my artist name. It's who I really am."

"Uh-huh."

I turned around to get Lizzie just as one of the guys stepped up to her. He was kind of short, with wild hair and dirty glasses. He had a nice face but looked like he needed a shower.

"Hey, I'm John. I've been working on a painting of Ophelia, and you would be absolutely perfect! Would you consider posing for it?"

"I love *Hamlet*. That would be fabulous!"

Then Hunt chimed in. "I've been working on a painting based on The Lady of Shalott, and you're just what I'm looking for! Your hair is *perfect*."

"Wow! You guys really like to paint suicidal women!" Lizzie exclaimed. Then Gabriel stepped in front of her and announced, "No one paints her but *me*! I'm the one who found her, and she belongs to *me*!" The guys were quiet, and Lizzie just grinned awkwardly.

I couldn't take it anymore. "She's not a fucking object! She's a person! She doesn't belong to *anyone*!" The guys all exchanged looks.

"You're right, Jane," Gabriel responded. "I didn't mean that she belongs to me in *that* way. I just meant that I didn't want anyone else to paint her."

"That's great, and I can assure you that no one will because we're leaving. Lizzie, come on!" She didn't move, and a guy with gorgeous brown skin and golden eyes stepped towards me.

"Hi, Jane. I'm Ed. It's great to meet you. I was just wondering… And don't take this the wrong way, but is Lizzie your girlfriend?"

I tried not to overreact and took a deep breath. "No, *Ed*. Lizzie is not my girlfriend. She's a very close friend of mine, and I care about her a lot. I don't like to see her taken advantage of."

Ed thought for a minute and said, "With all due respect…"

"Dude, *don't*!" Gabriel tried to cut him off.

"No, no, man. It's fine. So as I was saying, she does appear to be a grown woman and can probably answer for herself." Lizzie giggled and everyone was silent as a look of worry appeared on Gabriel's face.

"You know what, you're right. She *is* a grown woman, and so am I. I'm leaving. Lizzie, you want to stay here and be the center of this orgy or whatever the fuck this is, be my guest!"

"Jane, come on. Don't be like that."

I whipped around and flung the door open, and I didn't bother to close it as I marched to the car. We had been in so many situations like this where I had to bail her out later. I was over it.

As I reached out to open the car door, Will stood next to it and faced me.

"I'd just like to apologize again for my mates. They're idiots, but they mean well. They're good guys. And they genuinely want to paint your friend. It's not a trick or a ploy. We're artists."

"You know what, Will? I almost believed that last night when I agreed to pose for a painting, but then I was asked to remove all my clothes."

Will sighed. "Yeah, that's Gabriel. He's also not a bad guy. He does have a good heart somewhere inside. He's just really, you know…"

"Horny?" I offered.

He laughed. "Well, yes. But again, he would never do anything to hurt anyone or force a woman to do something she didn't want to do. I've known him for a long time. Please believe me."

He seemed very genuine and sweet, and I couldn't help but soften a bit. "Thank you for apologizing. I appreciate it."

"Can I convince you to come inside for coffee or tea? Please?"

My neck was hurting from looking up at him. "Make it breakfast, and I'll consider it."

"Absolutely. Painting is my first love, but cooking just happens to be my second. How about an omelet?"

"Eh, maybe. What else you got?"

"Hmm. French toast?"

"French toast? What kind of Englishman *are* you?"

"You're not saying you want an English breakfast, are you?" He seemed very amused.

"Never had one. Maybe I do."

"Eggs, sausage, back bacon, mushrooms-"

"What's *back* bacon?"

"It's from the pig's loin."

"Eww."

"Don't forget baked beans and blood pudding."

"Blood pudding? That's not literally what it sounds like, is it?"

"Pork blood, fat, and a bit of grain."

"I think I'll just go to IHOP," I joked as I reached for the door handle.

"Wait!" he called out as he put his hand on top of mine to stop me from opening the door. I looked down at his hand and then back up at him. I wasn't mad. It was just awkward. He quickly removed his hand and asked, "What's your favorite fruit?"

I put my finger to my mouth like I was thinking. "Strawberries."

"I've got it! Strawberry and cream crepes!" I lifted my eyebrows and nodded slightly. "And mimosas!" he added. "*Strawberry mimosas!*"

"I'm in. Can we go sit down now? My neck is killing me from looking up at you."

"Sure. I just have to pick up a few things at the market. Not much in the fridge."

"I'll go with you," I responded without thinking. "Get in!"

We were laughing and flirting as we entered the kitchen with bags of groceries. I liked being with Will. He was easy to talk to, easy to be with. I was attracted to him, but nowhere near the intense feelings I had for Gabriel. I could tell he was into me, but there wasn't any overwhelming energy about it. It was sweet.

Gabriel was sitting at the table with Lizzie. When he saw Will and I flirting with each other, the muscles in his face tensed, and he squinted his eyes in anger.

"We were wondering what happened to you guys!" Ed stated.

"Just got a few things to make breakfast," Will answered.

Ed came closer. "Jane, I'm so glad you decided to join us." I was starting to think I misjudged Ed. He seemed like a genuinely nice guy.

"I couldn't say no to strawberry mimosas!"

"Strawberry mimosas?" Ed asked with genuine confusion. "We have those?"

Will answered, "We will momentarily!"

"Interesting."

"Hope you like strawberries because we'll be having strawberry crepes too!" I announced.

"Crepes!" John called out. "Jane, you're making crepes?"

"I am," Will answered with a hint of irritation.

"Woah!" Ed blurted out as he approached Will, who was taking out pans and other utensils. "I didn't know you could make crepes, Will! I'm a little insulted that you never made them for *me*."

"Can you fuck off, please?" Will said playfully, shoving Ed away. Ed went over to John and leaned into his face.

"Did you hear that, John? Will is making crepes for us!"

John giggled. "I know, I heard. I'm pretty psyched! I haven't had those since Paris!" It was cute how they were teasing him. Gabriel whispered in Lizzie's ear until Hunt draped his arm around his shoulders.

"Gabriel, did you hear about the crepes Will is about to make?"

Gabriel had no response. I joined the fun and announced, "Don't forget about the mimosas! Will, where are the champagne glasses?"

Hunt spoke softly into Gabriel's ear. "Strawberry mimosas will be served as well, Gabe."

Gabriel immediately flung Hunt off of him and called out, "Will! Can I talk to you for a minute? In *private*?" Will didn't even look up from what he was doing. "Can it wait? I've got my hands full at the moment."

"No, it can't wait!"

I turned from the champagne glasses I was filling and brought one over to Gabriel. "Champagne, *Dante*?" I batted my eyelashes at him, and he gave me a death stare and turned away.

"Will! *Now*!"

Will sighed and called me over. "Would you mind whisking this? I'll be right back. I don't want it to get lumpy."

I happily took the whisk from him. "No problem at all!"

As I whisked, I looked up and noticed a punching bag hanging from the ceiling in the corner of the kitchen. I pointed to it and looked at Ed. "What's that doing in the kitchen?"

He grinned. "Just wait. You'll find out."

Will and Gabriel marched back in from the hallway, both looking pissed. Will took the whisk from me and thanked me for my help. He quietly continued whisking for a moment as I stood next to him, sipping my champagne. "If you want to blend up the fruit for those, the blender is in the cabinet above the fridge." I began to drag a chair over to reach the cabinet, but Gabriel stopped me.

"No need. I got it," he said.

I moved out of the way as he tried to reach the cabinet, but it was just a bit too high. He tried again and stood back in defeat. He went to grab the same chair I had just dragged over, but Will stepped in and quickly opened the cabinet and took the blender out.

He handed it to me and went right back to cooking. Gabriel wasn't exactly short, but Will was *ridiculously* tall. The other guys looked highly entertained, and one even said, "Oh shit," under his breath.

"Thanks so much, Will," I said while looking right at Gabriel. I picked up my glass and gulped the rest of the champagne down.

"Lizzie and I were thinking about going for a swim," Gabriel announced.

Hunt called out, "I'm in!"

"Let's do it!" Ed said with excitement.

"I can't. I've got a commission at noon," John told us.

"For who?" Ed asked.

"Ruskin."

"Oh shit! Will you be painting his hot naked wife?"

"No, his mother this time. Not naked though. I mean, I hope not!"

"Eww," Hunt responded.

"Look, money is money. And I'm getting 25 grand for this."

"Hot naked wife?" Lizzie inquired.

"Ruskin is our neighbor. Every morning at 6 o'clock, his hot young wife swims naked in their pool. If you go to the other side of the lake and hike up the hill a bit, you get an amazing view!" Hunt explained.

"What is a hot young thing with *that* body doing with that disgusting old man?" John wondered aloud.

"Money, John. *Money*," Ed insisted.

"I don't know. There's something about her that doesn't strike me as shallow. She just doesn't seem like the type."

Ed and Hunt started singing Kanye West's "Gold Digger" very passionately to each other.

"Alright! Alright! You made your point!" John called out.

"Just lemme know if you get to see her naked golddiggin' ass close up!" Ed remarked.

"*Anyway*," John continued. "I'm sorry I won't be able to spend the afternoon with you ladies. It's been lovely."

"Thanks, John. Good luck with your portrait. And let me know when I can pose for Ophelia!" Lizzie emphasized.

"I certainly will!"

Gabriel walked over to Lizzie and held out his hand. "Let's go."

"Not yet. I'm looking forward to this breakfast Will is making!" Gabriel took off his shirt and dropped it into her lap.

"Meet me there. I'm not hungry," he spat and strode out of the kitchen. Seeing him with no shirt on again sent a flash of energy between my legs. *Fuck.*

We sat around the island eating, drinking champagne, and laughing. The alcohol, combined with Gabriel's exit, helped me let my guard down and relax. At some point, Ed turned to me and said, "Jane, I know I might risk getting kicked in the balls, but I have to tell you that you are magnificent."

I rolled my eyes. "*Magnificent*? Come *on*."

"No bullshit. You're stunning. I can see why Gabriel is all fucked up over you!"

"He *is*?" I said innocently.

"Umm, yes. I haven't seen him wound this tight in a long time."

"I don't think I've *ever* seen him like this!" John added. "Must be love."

"*Please!* I just met him *yesterday*!"

"Then it's love at first sight!" Hunt announced.

"He seems pretty enamored with Lizzie as well," I offered. "Is it possible to be in love at first sight with two women, who, I might add, are complete opposites in every way?"

"*Totally* possible," Ed said matter-of-factly. "Though highly unusual."

"I always thought the idea of love at first sight was utter bull-shit," I said. "*Lust* at first sight? Fine. But *love*? Without knowing the person? Come on! Didn't you guys read *Romeo and Juliet* in high school? That kind of shit can only lead to destruction."

"Or amazing art," Will offered.

"Or both," John added. "I'm pretty sure Madman over here could tell you a few things about love at first sight!"

"Fuck! Don't start, John!" Hunt spat.

"Come on, man! Tell them about Annie. You could use a woman's perspective!"

"I am *really* not in the mood to talk about this!" Hunt said through gritted teeth.

I couldn't help myself. "Come on, Hunt! I'd love to hear about Annie. Maybe Lizzie and I can give you some advice!"

Hunt stood up and yelled, "Thanks, guys! I hadn't even thought about her yet today!" Then he stalked over to the punching bag and started beating the shit out of it. I turned to Ed and nodded my head. Now I knew why that bag was there. Hunt started to sweat. He pulled his shirt off and beat the bag even harder. He was ridiculously ripped. It looked like he could compete in a bodybuilding contest. After he was sufficiently sweaty and flushed, he marched to the back door and announced, "I'm going swimming!" before he kicked it open.

Ed turned to me, "And *that* is why we call him Madman."

"Got it. Seems a little over the top. What did this girl do to him?"

"She just wants to fuck him really bad and is kind of unrelenting about it."

"And he likes her?" Lizzie asked.

"Likes her?" John said. "He's fucking *obsessed* with her!"

"I don't see the problem," I responded.

The guys looked at each other, and John jumped in. "He's saving himself for marriage."

"Oh," I said.

"Yeah."

"It's so stupid," Ed said. "A total waste of energy. He could just pop his fucking cherry already, calm the fuck down, and refocus his energy back on his art. All he does is get angry and punch that fucking bag. He's created nothing good in months!"

"I don't think guys have cherries to pop," John pointed out.

"I don't think it's stupid that he wants to wait," Will said. "It's important to him, and she plays with him too much. If she loved him, she'd respect his decision and back the fuck off."

"Yeah, she's kind of a *slag*," John said.

"Brilliant word choice!" Will noted.

John grinned. "Okay, I have to get going. Lizzie, I'll be in touch!"

"I think we'd better head out," I said. "We don't even have bathing suits."

"Jane," Ed said. "Are you wearing underwear?"

"Come on," Will said. "Don't be a fucking wanker."

"*Yes*, I'm wearing underwear, Ed."

"Then you have a bathing suit! Let's go!"

"I'm gonna stay behind," Will said. "I'm exhausted." He got up and collected the dirty plates.

"Lizzie," I said. "I think we should probably go."

"Oh, come on. Don't be such an old lady!" Lizzie teased.

"I'm not being an old lady! I need a shower and clean clothes. And I don't feel like swimming in my underwear."

"Jane," Lizzie said, "It's almost noon. Gimme till 1 o'clock, and I promise we'll go!"

"Ugh, *fine*. Do you have chairs by the pool?"

"We don't have a pool. We have a lake. And no chairs. Let's go!" Ed flung the back door open and turned to Lizzie. "Last one there has to pose for my next painting!"

Lizzie answered, "It's gonna be a self-portrait then, bitch!" and they giggled and ran out. I sighed and turned to Will, who was doing dishes. "Don't feel like swimming?"

"The lake isn't my favorite place," he answered without turning to look at me.

"Oh," I said, unsure how to respond. There was an uncomfortable silence until I added, "Well, thanks for breakfast. It was fun!"

He nodded and continued washing. I slowly stepped towards the door, and he called out softly, "Jane." I turned back, and he was facing me. "I would be honored if you would consider allowing me to paint you. Fully clothed, that is."

I smiled warmly. "I'll consider it."

He smiled back and said, "Cheers."

I took my time walking to the lake. In the sunlight, the landscape was incredible. Everything was so lush and green. The flowers and vines were slightly overgrown but clearly cared for. I strolled down the path, stopping to take a closer look at the unusual flowers I had never seen before.

As I got closer, I heard lots of laughing and splashing. The water came into view, and I saw a little sandy beach in front of it. Hunt was furiously doing laps, and Ed was standing on the end of a small rounded cliff that stuck out over the lake. Gabriel came up from under the water and slicked his hair back. Droplets of water glistened on his muscular chest, and he looked sexier than ever. He swam over to the rocks where Ed stood and yelled, "Come on, man! I wanna see some of that gymnastics shit!"

"Yeah, yeah. I got you!" Ed braced himself for some kind of dive, but he suddenly spun around as though he sensed my presence. "Jane!" he called out. "Get up here!"

"I'm good. I'm just gonna sit over here and enjoy the view!"

"Come on, girl! I won't bite. Come sit with me up here!"

"No *way*! You're gonna push me in! I'm not *that* stupid!"

"I swear on my grandmama that I will *not* push you in!"

Hunt called out, "That's serious! He fucking *loves* his grandma."

I rolled my eyes. "Okay! But if you push me in, I can't guarantee Grandmama's safety!"

"Yeah, yeah! Come on! This is the best seat in the house!"

I flung off my shoes and went up the beach to the cliff. I could feel Gabriel's eyes on me the whole time, but I refused to give him any attention. I sat down next to Ed at the edge. "Look out at that water. Tell me that's not the most wonderful thing you've ever seen," he said into my ear. You could see how huge the lake was from up there, and the sun was glittering on the surface. The sky was full of huge, cottony clouds.

"Now watch *this*!" Ed exclaimed as he stood up and put his arms in the air. He looked down at me and winked and then did what looked like at least five flips in the air before slicing down into the water. He quickly swam back to the surface, put his hands up in the air, and turned in a circle saying, "Eh? Eh? *Okay*?"

Gabriel answered, "Meh. I'm not impressed. I wanna see that backward!"

"I was pretty impressed!" I called out. Suddenly I felt hands shove me and a cold shock went through my body. I swam to the surface and coughed water out of my throat. "What the fuck!"

Lizzie was leaning over the edge of the cliff staring down at me. She was soaking wet, and in her underwear, with a proud grin on her face. "Love you!" she said before jumping in next to me. The scar on her chest, which she was usually really self-conscious about, was in full view. I was proud of her for not being afraid to let it show.

I swam back to the sand, and slowly pulled off my drenched pants and shirt. Thankfully, I was in plain black underwear that matched my tank top. I tied my hair into a bun on top of my head and looked out at the water. Gabriel and Hunt were standing in the water, staring at me. I pretended not to notice, but it was fun having them admire my body.

I swam over to Lizzie and splashed at her a bunch. She sprayed me back, and Gabriel swam to the beach, picked his jeans up off the sand, and took something out of the pocket. Then he went down the beach towards the cliff. He was wearing boxer briefs that clung to him, and I realized I was staring too long. I dropped underneath the water and tried to shake his image out of my head as I swam closer to Ed. "So where'd you learn to flip like that?"

"I used to do gymnastics competitively. My bros here like to tease me about it. I don't think they understand how strong you have to be to do some of the stuff I used to do."

"I'm sure they're just jealous. Those gymnast guys are hot! And those pants they wear… *Lord*! They show *everything*."

"Yup. You gotta be packing something decent, or it's just all balls!"

"Yuck! Nobody likes balls!"

"Speak for yourself!" He winked at me and swam away.

Gabriel called out from the edge of the cliff, "Anyone want a hit?" He was taking long drags off a blunt.

I knew I shouldn't. I had smoked too much the night before and needed to get my head straight, but I wanted to sit near him and share something intimate. He had a magnetic pull, and I couldn't help myself. I yearned to be close to him.

I climbed up the rocks from the water and approached him. He had a huge tattoo in the middle of his back of two snakes entwined into an infinity shape and a bunch of strange symbols across his shoulder blades.

I bent down next to him, and he held out the blunt without looking at me. I took a puff and started coughing immediately. "Shit. What kind of weed is this?" I said through coughs.

"The really good kind."

I took another hit, held it in as long as I could, and gave it back. I already felt lightheaded.

There was a weird silence until he stated, "I didn't sleep with her," while gazing out at the water. He pulled deeply on the blunt and kept staring ahead. I didn't answer, and he continued. "I didn't touch her. I sketched her until she fell asleep."

"I'm sorry I overreacted. I know I'm too protective of her, but there's a reason." He held the blunt out for me. I paused and added, "She's fragile." I took a small hit and gave it back.

"What makes her more fragile than anyone else?" he asked before hitting the blunt again.

"She had cancer."

He turned and locked eyes with me but didn't say anything, so I continued. "A few years ago she had a cough that lasted for months, but she didn't think anything of it. She was in her first semester at Yale on a full scholarship, and she was completely consumed with studying. Then she started getting weird pains in her ribs, but she didn't tell anyone. She passed out in the middle of a huge lecture hall. They did a CT scan at the hospital and found cancer in her lungs."

"Fuck," Gabriel muttered as he held the blunt out for me again.

"I'm good, thanks."

"So it was lung cancer? I've never heard of a young person getting it."

"It's super rare. But the mass took up most of her lung, and it had to be removed."

"Wow," he said under his breath as he looked out at Lizzie, who was having a splash fight with Hunt. "Is she okay now?"

"Yeah, she's fine. It's just that after the surgery, she changed *drastically*. She didn't go back to school. She didn't want to do anything anymore unless it was for fun. She became kind of reckless."

"Well, I can imagine that looking death in the face like that would really make you prioritize. And she chose to really live her life. It's like memento mori is written on her chest with that scar."

"Is that what really living is? Throwing away major opportunities and just getting drunk all the time and letting guys take advantage of you?"

"Maybe to her it is. Who am I to say?"

We were silent for a while. I kept peeking at him from the corner of my eye as the weed began to distort my thoughts. All I could focus on was how beautiful he was. He was looking at me too but trying not to be obvious about it. Our faces moved closer, and he closed his eyes. I had that warm, familiar sensation, and I almost let him kiss me.

"Jane!" Lizzie interrupted. "We have to stay for the party tonight!"

"What party?" I called out, feeling disappointed yet relieved that the kiss didn't happen.

Gabriel answered. "It's Hunt's birthday tomorrow. We're having a party tonight."

"We should go soon. I don't have any clean clothes and-"

He interrupted me, "I have some clothes that are about your size."

"Mmmhhhmmm," I said with an attitude. "I'm sure you have plenty of women's clothes left behind."

"It's not like that. They're my sister's."

"I've got to get up early for work tomorrow anyway. We should go."

I stood up and felt dizzy. I tried to get my bearings as I called out to Lizzie. "Come on! You said we'd leave after a swim!" I stepped slowly off the cliff as the world spun around me. I sat down on the beach and watched Lizzie continue to play with Hunt, climbing onto his back and covering his eyes till he threw her over his shoulder. Gabriel dove back into the water, and I felt sleepy. I rested my head on his balled-up jeans and closed my eyes for a minute.

I woke up in a soft, cozy bed. The pillow under my head had that comforting beachy scent. I slowly opened my eyes and looked around. The setting sun created a bright orange glow in the room. I brought my eyes up to the dome above the bed and marveled at the pink and orange twilight sky. I turned over and faced the framed picture of Will and the little girl on the nightstand I had seen the night before. I couldn't remember how I had gotten to his room.

My camisole and underwear were still a bit damp, and I felt desperate for a shower. I sat up and noticed a pile of neatly folded women's clothes and two cream-colored towels at the end of the bed. I took the clothes and towels and entered the bathroom that was connected to the bedroom.

The design of the bathroom was very minimal and more masculine than the rest of the house. None of the bedroom's adornments were there, but it was still the most gigantic bathroom I had ever been in. Everything was gray, from the stone floor to the rectangular marble sink to the stone tiles on the walls. It took me a minute to figure out where the shower was because it had no doors or curtain. There was a large platform at the far end of the room with a rectangular showerhead that hung down from the ceiling. I took off my underwear and stepped onto the platform. There were several potted and hanging plants on one side, and on the other side were tons of shampoos and body washes. I turned the water on, and it sprayed down on me like a warm waterfall. All of the soap smelled like eucalyptus and herbs. I was still a little stoned, and it was one of the best showers of my life.

A white peasant blouse and jeans were laid out for me but no underwear or bra. The jeans fit pretty well, but the top was quite snug, and with no bra, it revealed more than I would usually be comfortable showing. I shrugged my shoulders, twisted my wet hair into a bun, and went back into the bedroom to find my shoes. We had been there long enough, and it was time to leave.

As I searched Will's room for my shoes, I heard laughing outside the window. I peeked through the curtains, and the patio was filled with people who were drinking, dancing, and laughing. The sun was almost gone, and there were lanterns with lit candles everywhere. I spotted Hunt with a girl on his lap. She was kissing his neck and sucking on his ear, and he looked like he was in pain. "That must be Annie," I whispered to myself. Then I noticed Gabriel sitting on a ledge playing guitar. He had an audience of almost a dozen females surrounding him, and one of them was Lizzie. She threw her arms around him as he finished the song. He put the guitar down and embraced her with a grin; then she pulled him into a chair and sat on his lap like they had known each other for years.

I bolted out of the room, into the hallway, down the stairs, through the kitchen, and onto the patio. I slid into the crowd and quietly made my way over to Gabriel and Lizzie, but Will stood in front of me before I got to them.

"You're up! How are you feeling?"

Gabriel's eyes were on me, and I could tell he didn't like that I was talking to Will. "It's too crowded. Let's go for a walk," I suggested. I held out my hand and continued to stare at Gabriel as I let Will lead me away from the party, down the stairs, and into the garden. There were tons of fireflies, and the cool grass felt soothing under my toes.

"How did I end up in your bed?"

"I carried you."

"Why?"

"You were lying on the beach by yourself, and it was getting dark. It didn't seem right."

"That's very sweet of you. That weed Gabriel smokes is really strong."

"I trust you found the shower?"

"I did. It was wonderful."

"I'm glad."

There was an uneasy silence between us, and I glanced behind me to see what Gabriel was doing. He was standing at the top of the steps watching us with his arms crossed. Will looked up and saw that we were staring at each other.

"You must be starved. You haven't eaten since breakfast."

"I'm fine," I answered, turning back to him.

"Would you like me to make you something?" he asked. "Or we can go out."

"Leave the party?" Gabriel and I continued to stare at each other as I added, "Yes, I think that might be nice."

"Great! This time *I'll* drive!"

We went back up the garden steps, and I practically hit Gabriel's shoulder as we brushed past him and navigated the crowd together. He ushered me to the front of the house and told me to wait for him there. A few minutes later, he pulled up in a white Tesla. He got out, walked around, and opened the passenger door for me. As I got in, Gabriel came out of the front door of the house and jogged towards the car.

"Where are you taking her?" he spat at Will, as though I wasn't even there.

"We're just going to get something to eat," I said with a grin.

"We have food *here*." Will didn't say anything, and he went around and got in the car. Before I could shut the door, Gabriel got right in my face and looked intensely into me. "Please stay, Jane."

I giggled, leaned in closer, and whispered, "We're just getting something to eat. We're not eloping." He frowned as I closed the door in his face. He put a cigarette between his lips, and we glared at each other as the car pulled away. I bit my lip to stifle a laugh. This was fun.

"What kind of food should we get?" Will asked.

"Well, I'm barefoot and not wearing a bra, so most restaurants are probably out." His eyes went to my feet and up to my chest. His eyes darted away nervously when he realized he was staring at my breasts.

"Cheeseburgers?" he asked.

"Yes, please!"

"Have you ever been to All-American?"

"No, what's that?"

"You are about to have the best cheeseburgers and fries of your life!"

"Wow! That's a pretty big claim!"

"*Just you wait!*"

There was another bit of uncomfortable stillness between us before we both talked at the same time. He insisted that I continue.

"How did all of you guys meet?"

"At art school. We were all in the same painting classes, and we just sort of formed a bond. We agreed that the teachings were shit and that good art was lost in the past. We decided to form a brotherhood based on our ideals and dedication to painting."

"How did you end up living here, in that *amazing* house, together?"

"It's my family's house. We needed a place to stay, and no one was using it."

"*No one was using it?* Wow! How do you have a house like that that no one uses?"

"My family mostly lives in London. We have properties all over the world."

"Shit. Are you royalty or something?"

"Of course not. Just lucky to be born into old money. My great-grandfather owned a very successful shipping company."

"So you're rich, and the guys just mooch off you? Pretty nice of you!"

"They do quite well for themselves. They do a lot of commissions for wealthy people in the area. People pay them tens of thousands for one painting."

We pulled into the parking lot of a pretty rundown, old burger joint. You had to walk up to the front window to order. "Be right back!" Will announced as he jumped out of the car. Minutes later, he came back with a bunch of greasy paper bags and three big shakes.

"Three?" I asked about the number of drinks.

"I didn't know if you wanted chocolate or vanilla, so I got you both. Now get ready to have the absolute *best* cheeseburger of your entire existence!" He handed me a bag.

As I unwrapped the burger, I said, "Kind of ironic, isn't it?"

"What?"

"If this is the best burger I've ever had and it's from a place called All American…"

"Then you will have received this glorious burger from an Englishman?"

"Exactly!"

"Go on…" he said as he took a huge bite. I bit down and chewed thoughtfully. He stared at me for a few moments. *"Well?"*

"Well…" I hesitated. "That is absolutely the best fucking cheeseburger I've ever had!"

"And the chips are amazing as well!"

"Chips? Oh, you mean the fries."

"Yes, I mean the *fries.*"

I wolfed down the rest of the burger and ate a bunch of fries. They were greasy but yummy. "I'm eating like an animal," I said with a full mouth.

"I've just had three cheeseburgers while you've only had *one.* And you haven't tried the shakes yet!"

I sipped the vanilla, and it was unbelievably good. Then I tried the chocolate, and it was the best chocolate shake I've ever had by far.

"Holy fuck!" I called out.

"I know," Will said as he shoved almost an entire burger into his mouth.

"How do you eat like that and stay so thin?"

"A lot of surface area, I suppose."

"Must all go to your legs," I joked, and we both laughed.

"Did you want another burger?" he asked.

"No, I'm getting really full. If I eat any more, I might vomit all over this lovely car."

"We could go outside and sit at that picnic table. That way, you could vomit and then eat some more!" he said as he pounded more fries.

"No, seriously, I'm good."

"Is there anything else I can get for you?"

"No. For real. I'm *super* full!"

"Anything you need, Jane. Please let me know," he said with a serious tone.

"I think we'd better get back. I have work tomorrow."

"Of course," he said as he collected my trash. He pulled out of the parking lot and up to a garbage can and tossed everything. We drove in silence for a bit.

"Where do you work?" he asked.

"At a bookstore."

"Corporate or independent?"

"Independent. It's a really cool place. Mostly titles you wouldn't find in a mainstream bookstore. A lot of self-published authors too."

"Sounds wonderful!"

"It's alright. Not a bad place to work. It's just until I figure out my shit."

"We've all got shit to figure out."

"What shit do *you* have to figure out? Your life seems pretty well figured out!"

"What makes you say that?"

"You live in a castle that's paid for already. You're an incredibly talented artist, and you live with your best friends and make crepes, and go swimming, and have parties. What more is there to figure out?"

"Money and friendship. In your estimation, that's all a man needs?"

"For the most part. You don't have to worry, and you don't have to be lonely."

"And what of love, Jane? And what of loss?"

"They're about one and the same, I think. The more you love, the more potential for loss. So just hold onto your friendships and keep chasing your passions."

"What if love is what drives my passion, my art?"

"Then you're fucked."

We both laughed as we entered the long driveway to his house, and I noticed he was staring at me.

"Watch the road, Will."

"Sorry. You make it hard to concentrate."

I felt myself blush, and he grinned. When he parked near the front door, I turned to him before I got out. "Thank you for dinner. It was really nice."

"Maybe next time we can go inside of an actual restaurant," he said a bit awkwardly.

"I'll be sure to wear shoes *and* a bra!"

He instinctively looked at my chest, so I looked down too. He had the A/C up pretty high, and my nipples were popping out. He coughed nervously, and I giggled. He shut off the engine, and I reached out for the door handle.

"Wait," he said. "Let me open your door." Before I could say it wasn't necessary, he was outside opening the door. He held his hand out to help me up. There was a little tingle on my skin when I put my hand into his. We looked into each other's eyes, and I felt my face light up.

As he walked me to the front door he said, "How can I convince you to sit for me?"

"Sit for you?"

"I would love to paint you."

"I don't know, Will. I think my modeling days are over."

"Please. Don't make up your mind so quickly. Just think on it."

"I *shall*!" I said, mocking him a bit. Then I did a little curtsey, and he bowed in response. I chuckled and started to open the door. "Are you coming in?" I asked.

"I think I'll go for a walk. Would you like to come?"

"Thank you, but I need to get going. I'm worried about what Lizzie's up to in there."

"Raincheck?"

"For sure," I said, and he started to walk away.

"Will!" I called out, and he turned back to me. "What are you doing on Thursday?"

"Not much. Why?"

"I'd like to sit for you."

"Brilliant!" he exclaimed with a huge grin.

I entered the house. It was dark and mostly quiet, but I could hear the noise outside. I moved towards the kitchen, but someone grabbed my wrist and shoved me up against a wall. I screamed, but Gabriel looked into my eyes and put his finger to my lips to silence me.

"Jesus *Christ*! You scared the shit out of me!"

"Why are you playing games with me?" he said through gritted teeth. His face was so close I could smell the beer on his breath.

"What the fuck are you talking about? Let go of me!" He was still holding my wrist.

"Are you actually *into* him?" I kept squirming, and he grabbed my other wrist to get a better hold on me.

"Into *who*? Let me go!" He leaned closer until his lips were an inch from mine.

"I'm talking about Will! Are you actually interested in him?"

"Maybe! What the fuck do you care?"

"He's a pussy."

"He's not a *pussy*. He's a *gentleman*. You could learn a thing or two from him about how to treat women!"

"What I *meant* is that he's not right for you."

"Oh, *and you are*?" I tried to headbutt him, but he saw it coming and moved his head back without letting go of my wrists.

"Yes," he declared, then he put his face against my neck and inhaled deeply. The feeling of his breath on me sent waves of energy throughout my body. Then he whispered into my ear, "Maybe he's a gentleman. But there's one thing I know for sure. He can't make you come like I can."

I shivered, which was very irritating because I didn't want him to know he was getting to me. He held my face. "Let me kiss you." It was a command. He held his grip on my face as he leaned in and slowly ran his tongue between my lips. I instinctively opened my mouth, and we kissed fiercely. Our kissing styles were different, and we both struggled for control. I could feel that he wanted to dominate me, and maybe if I trusted him more, I would have given in. But instead, we battled each other with our tongues. Despite the combative feeling of it, it was the most electrifying kiss of my life. But a sense of dread crept into my chest, and I pulled back and shoved him away. He was breathing heavily and came back in for more. He almost touched his lips to mine, but I pushed him again.

"Come *on*," he said, half-amused, half-annoyed. "I know you feel that connection between us. Stop fighting it." He leaned in again, and I slapped him as hard as I could across the face. My ring caught his bottom lip, and I ripped it away. He slowly brought his hand up to his lip and swiped at it. He looked down at the blood on his hand with amusement and then bent towards me again.

"*Why?* Why won't you kiss me?" he demanded. I paused for a moment.

"Because…"

I slowly moved towards his face and looked directly into his eyes. "This is more fun." Then I grinned and sauntered away.

CHAPTER 6

Jane

"Fire for You"—Cannons

THE NEXT NIGHT, I WAS CLOSING THE BOOKSTORE BY myself. The girl who always closed with me on Sunday nights faked sick again, so she could leave early. I preferred to be alone anyway. As I returned stray books to the shelves, my head was in a dreamlike state. I slowly stepped through each room in Red House, going over every beautiful detail, trying to etch them into my brain.

I sauntered barefoot down the hallways in a white linen dress, the kind I used to wear all summer at our beach house. My hair was loose and flowing freely as I descended the grand staircase and dashed out the back door. I ran through the garden to the lake, where I saw him waiting for me on the sand, in the blinding sunlight. When I reached the shore, Will turned around and took my hand. We gathered objects in the sand together. A tiny cracked hourglass, shards of a porcelain teacup, and a sea glass heart wrapped in weeds. I scraped my foot on a jagged piece of driftwood and bled warm water, as Gabriel pressed his salty lips to my wound. He carried me inside and laid me on his crisp linen sheets. I inhaled his salty, woodland scent and reached out to run my fingers through Will's hair.

The chime on the front door of the bookstore ripped me from my dream and back into reality. "Shit," I whispered. I forgot to lock the door.

"We're closed!" I called out, not bothering to turn around.

"I just need five minutes of your time," he replied. I knew the voice right away. "Five minutes and thirty-eight seconds, to be exact."

I spun around and saw Gabriel's face on the other side of the register. He looked fucking gorgeous in a white linen button-down shirt, tight jeans, and thick-rimmed black glasses.

"I'm sorry, sir, but we're closed."

"*Sir*? Ouch."

"How did you find out where I work?" I asked, trying to hide how pleased I felt.

"I have my ways." I stared at him blankly until he added, "Lizzie told me."

"Great. What can I do for you?"

"I have something I need to show you."

"Okay, what is it?"

"Not here. You have to come *with* me." He grinned so warmly that I felt his energy spread throughout my body.

"I'm not going anywhere with you. I'm at work."

"But you just said you're closed."

"I still have work to do. I have to clean and reshelve all those books," I said, pointing to a few stacks of books in the corner.

"I'll help you. Happy to."

He grabbed a stack of books and looked for where they belonged. I took the pile from his hands. "*I'll* reshelve the books. You can clean." I held out the vacuum, and he nodded.

We worked quietly, but the tension was there. We kept catching each other's eyes and smiling. Finally, everything was done, and I ran to the bathroom to pull myself together. I fixed my makeup as best I could and brushed my hair out but then put it back into a messy bun. I didn't want him to realize I was putting any effort into my appearance. When I came back out, he was leaning against the wall with that smirk. "Ready?"

"Five minutes, right?"

"Five minutes and thirty-eight seconds. Not including the walk to my car."

"Your car? You said five minutes. I'm not going anywhere with you."

"We're just going to my car. Give me five minutes and

thirty-eight seconds once we get there. Do you trust me?" He held out his hand for me to take.

"No, I don't," I replied, but took his hand anyway. We went out to the parking lot holding hands, and there was only one other car besides mine. "*That's your car?* Of course it is!" It was a black two-door Maserati.

"It was a trade for a painting."

"*One* painting?"

"Yup. I painted this lady, and she didn't have any cash on her. So she said I could wait or take one of her cars. She had like 20 luxury cars in her garage."

"*Jesus.* All you did was *paint* her?"

"Yup."

"Uh-huh. I'll bet she was a very satisfied customer."

"It's not like that. She had recently gotten divorced, and she got all of her husband's cars. She didn't even know what was in there, and she didn't care. I think she just wanted to get rid of all of it."

"So, you didn't fuck her?"

"Jesus Christ, Jane! *No*, I didn't *fuck* her. She was old and gross, and her kids were there the whole time. It was their idea. They wanted her to have a portrait to replace the picture from her wedding that hung over the fireplace."

"Were the kids young and female?" I asked as he opened the passenger-side door for me.

I got in as he replied, "Why do you think I'm such a man-whore? You don't even know me." Then he slammed the door and got in the driver's side. The first thing I noticed was that the car was manual. Fuck. I was a total sucker for a guy who drives stick. My senses were then overtaken by how good the car smelled, like a musky cologne, but subtle.

He got into the car and slammed his door. He didn't say anything as he touched a bunch of buttons on the illuminated dash. Then he turned to me and said, "Close your eyes."

I turned back to him with one eyebrow cocked.

He looked irritated and replied, "*Just close your eyes.* I'm not going to do anything. I'm going to play a song for you." I huffed and closed my eyes.

As soon as I heard the Chinese lute, I was transported to another time and place. In the summer after we graduated high school, my friends and I traveled through Europe for six weeks. We were in Amsterdam and had several hours to waste before going to an Incubus concert for my friend's birthday. Of course, we had to check out the local weed shops. I knew I shouldn't smoke anything because it would be much stronger than anything I could handle. I wanted to have my wits about me in a foreign country at night. I explained this to the guy behind the counter, and he pulled out a small cookie. "This is the tamest thing we have. It barely has anything in it." I happily ate it, and about an hour later, I heard my friends screaming my name from the corner of the café. "What!" I responded. "You don't have to yell!"

"We've been calling your name for the last five minutes! *Are you okay?*"

"What are you talking about? I'm fine."

When I tried to get up, the room spun so fast that I had to sit down again. Every person in that café seemed to be staring at me. "Jane, get up! We're going to miss the concert!" My friend grabbed my hand and yanked me out of my seat. I was pulled onto a tram, and as it quickly moved forward, I went flying into a glass partition. I felt like everyone was laughing at me. We kept calling out our station's name because we didn't know where we were. We also didn't know how to get the tram to stop when we needed it to. I pictured us having to get out at the last stop, not knowing where we were, and wandering the streets alone. We were the cliché of the young American tourists, making fools of ourselves in front of the locals.

Finally, the tram jerked to a stop, the doors opened, and a man got on the loudspeaker and called out, "Your stop, ladies!" The whole train erupted in laughter, and while we felt pretty dumb, we were relieved to have arrived in front of the concert venue. After that point, things got blurry, but the song Gabriel played brought me back to a specific moment.

It was standing room only and packed with people. The lights went completely dark for a moment, and I felt like my heart stopped. Terrible thoughts ran through my head about losing my friends and being stranded by myself. Then bright blue lights beamed down from the stage into the crowd, and they began to play "Aqueous Transmission." I never heard the song before, and it was so different from all the other songs they played. I closed my eyes and swayed back and forth. I pictured myself lying in a boat and being carried off into the dark blue night. I opened my eyes, and a boy was standing there staring at me.

Something came over me at that moment, and I grabbed his face and kissed him. Then I leaned back, closed my eyes, and continued swaying to the music. He paused and then took my face and kissed me back. I gave in to what was happening, and we continued kissing throughout the entire song. It was gentle but intense, and it felt like a dream or a hallucination. When the song ended, I opened my eyes again, and he was gone. I never told anyone about it, and I wasn't even sure that it had really happened.

The song stopped, and I crashed back into the present. My eyes flew open, and the blue lights from the dashboard were illuminating Gabriel's face.

"That was you," I whispered. He continued to study my face until we both leaned in at the same time and kissed. The kiss became deeper and more frenzied, and he pulled me on top of him. As he kissed my neck he tried to take off my shirt.

"Wait," I said softly, not really stopping anything. He took off his glasses and tossed them onto the dash. Then, with one yank over my head, he removed my shirt and attempted to undo my bra. "Wait!" I yelled this time.

"Why?" he murmured as he continued unhooking my bra.

"Because!" I shrieked as I caught my bra with my arm just before it fell down completely. He leaned back and searched my eyes for a clue as to what was wrong.

"What is it?" he asked gently, trying not to piss me off.

"I just…" I wasn't quite sure what was wrong. I wanted him,

and the connection felt real. But something also felt profoundly *wrong* though I couldn't verbalize it.

I grabbed my shirt from the passenger seat and slipped it back on. I leaned back against the wheel while still in his lap. "I'm stunned that was you at the concert. I'm shocked that it was real, and I'm even more shocked that you remember."

He came in closer to my face. "Don't be so shocked. That was the most memorable kiss of my life, and I've been looking for you ever since. I knew you seemed familiar when I saw you at the museum. I was lying in my bed last night thinking of you because you're all I've been able to think about, and the vision of us at that concert just appeared in my head. But I don't think that's the first time we met. I think we've been together before."

"Before the concert?"

"Before this lifetime."

I wanted to laugh, but I couldn't because I felt like what he was saying was true. He held my face firmly with both hands and looked intensely into my eyes. "You have been mine before, and you will always be mine. You're my muse." He drew my face into his and gently moved his tongue into my mouth. Every time I pulled away, he brought me back in, and I wasn't fighting very hard because it felt so good.

I unbuttoned his shirt and felt his smooth chest while he kissed my neck. I whispered "fuck" without even meaning to. Then he lifted my shirt and held my breasts with both hands. He gently pinched my nipples as he sucked on my earlobe. He was driving me insane. My body was on fire, but I couldn't let it go any further. I murmured, "Wait," but he ignored me and dove his mouth onto one of my breasts and gently bit my nipple. I moaned loudly but shoved his chest back as hard as I could and yelled, "Stop!"

He dropped my nipple from his mouth and looked up at me, panting.

"Just because we had that kiss years ago doesn't mean I'm going to let you fuck me in your car in a parking lot!"

His breathing was labored, but he wasn't mad. "Jane, I'm not trying to fuck you in my car. I'm… I'm…"

"Yes?" I quickly put my bra back on and jumped into the passenger seat.

"I don't know!" he yelled, exasperated. "I was just feeling connected to you. I wasn't planning anything. I'm just in the moment! And I *know* you felt it too!" We both sat quietly, staring out the windshield, not knowing what to say or do. Then he turned to me and said, "Won't you ever just give in to how you feel?"

"No," I responded coldly. "Not with you."

"*Why?*" he demanded.

"I might have been yours before, but I will *never* be yours again."

"I don't understand. Tell me *why!*"

"Because," I said as I opened the door and got out. Then I leaned back into the car and declared, "I want to be the one you can't have."

I slammed the door, got in my car, and sped away. The drive home was more exhilarating than anything I had ever experienced, even more than that first kiss with Gabriel years before. If he really wanted a muse, I would give him one that would inspire his greatest works. *One he couldn't have.*

CHAPTER 7

GABRIEL

"Your Love"—Glass Animals

THIS FUCKING GIRL. I WASN'T KIDDING WHEN I SAID I FEEL like I've known her for a long time. There is something so familiar about her, so comfortable. It's hard to describe the feeling exactly. It's like she was my girlfriend for years, and I lost my memory, but there's still an inner knowingness that she's mine. It's frustrating that she won't give into me, because I'm certain she feels the same way.

I don't think she's a tease. I've dealt with those before, and it doesn't take much to break that shit down. She *wants* to surrender to me. The fucking fire is there. We both feel it. It burns hotter than any girl I've been with. Maybe I'm just hung up on her because she keeps rejecting me. I'll admit, I've never had a girl say no to me for very long.

That's not it. It's something else. She's inside me, swimming through my veins. I *need* her. I can't believe I'm saying this. I've never *needed* anyone, especially a girl. If she's going to be mine, I need to get creative. I must be patient. She *will* be mine.

CHAPTER 8

Jane

"It Could Be Sweet"—Portishead

WILL OPENED THE FRONT DOOR WITH A WARM GRIN. "I'm so glad you're here." He led me past the staircase and down a hallway I hadn't been in before. The walls were dark mahogany like the walls upstairs, and there were luxurious brocade couches and chairs in various locations.

"Where are we going?"

"The library. The light in there is perfect this time of day."

"I love it there."

"You've been?"

"Saturday night, when I came here with Lizzie, I kind of wandered in there. I think it might be the most beautiful room I've ever seen."

We passed through two large wooden doors and into the library. The curtains were tied back, and daylight was streaming directly through the windows in long beams. "Yup," I said. "This is definitely the most beautiful room I have ever seen."

He nodded in agreement and gestured to an armchair made of golden silk. "Please sit."

I sat down and noticed he already had an easel and various tools set up. I began to feel nervous. "Are we the only ones here?" I asked, looking around.

"Nope. Ed is upstairs, and John's outside sketching Lizzie."

"Lizzie's here?"

"She hasn't left since the weekend."

"Oh my god, are you serious?" I was glad he was busy setting things up because the whole thing felt too awkward, and I wished

I hadn't agreed to pose for him. I hoped that continuing a casual conversation would ease some of the tension. "I'm sorry. I hope she hasn't been a burden."

He kept lining up his pencils and trying to decide on the placement of the canvas. "Not at all. I've barely noticed her. She's been working with John quite a bit."

I chewed on my bottom lip. "I see. Only John?" I asked, hoping he didn't realize I was looking for information pertaining to Gabriel.

"I haven't been taking notes, but I'm quite sure I've only seen her with John." I stood up and paced nervously.

"I'm sorry. I just worry about her."

"Don't apologize. I understand. But as I told you, there's nothing to worry about." He stopped what he was doing and stepped towards me. "Ready?"

"I was just admiring this mural. It's incredible. Which one of you made it?"

He blushed just a bit. "It's mine."

"The way you capture the feeling of the seasons in their expressions... It's breathtaking."

He seemed uncomfortable.

"I'm glad you think so."

"Did you add the Shakespeare lines too?"

"Yes. It's all related."

"I love that sonnet. I never understood much Shakespeare in high school, but I definitely knew what he was saying with that one. What made you add those lines?" He shifted a bit on his feet and looked down. "I'm sorry. Maybe I shouldn't have asked."

"No, it's alright. I painted this for my girlfriend. *Ex*-girlfriend, I mean. She kept saying her feelings were changing, and she was always so hot and cold with me. One day, I was the greatest love of her life, and the next she would say we should just be friends. But I always felt the same. So I painted this for her... to show her how I felt about love. How I felt about *her*. That my feelings wouldn't change."

I gazed up at the mural and felt resentful of the girl who was featured in the four panels. How could your feelings run hot and cold for someone like Will, someone so wonderful?

"So that's her? In each season?"

"Yes," he said softly. "Can we..." he didn't finish the question but pointed towards the chair.

"Oh, I'm sorry! Of course." I plopped back down and crossed and uncrossed my legs and put my hands in a few different positions.

"How do you want me?"

"I think for right now I'm just going to practice drawing your hands, so don't worry about the rest of you. Just get as comfortable as you can. You're going to be sitting there for quite a while."

"Like how long?"

"How long can you stay?"

"Umm..." I moved my eyes side to side and pursed my lips, and he laughed.

"Just let me know when you're tired and need a break."

He arranged my hands in my lap. There was a definite tension between us, and when our eyes met, he quickly glanced back down at my hands.

"There," he said. "Please don't move." He went back to his easel and started sketching. I stayed silent for a while, amused by his furrowed brow and how he would get frustrated and start erasing. "Can I talk?" I mumbled through closed lips.

"Yes, just don't move your hands."

"What will this painting be about?"

"Tristan and Isolde," he replied from behind the canvas. "Well, just Isolde really."

"I've heard of it, but I don't know the story."

"It's a very old fable," he answered without breaking his concentration, "that's about a love triangle of sorts."

"Oh, it sounds scandalous! Do go on!"

He chuckled and continued. "Tristan was a knight who was sent to retrieve Isolde from Ireland to marry his uncle, the king of England. But on the way back they fell madly in love. When they got to England, she married the King, but she and Tristan found a way to be together each night after the king went to sleep. His advisors found out and told the king to kill them."

"Shit! What did that douchebag king do to them?"

"That's what makes the story so interesting. The king wasn't a bad guy at all. He truly loved his nephew and his new bride. He didn't want to believe it. Tristan felt terrible because his uncle was a loving father figure to him, and Isolde felt bad because her new husband treated her so well."

"That *is* interesting!"

"Jane, you moved your hands."

"I'm so sorry! Were they like this?" He came over and gently repositioned my hands. Then he looked down at me.

"If you can't stay still, I won't tell you any more fairy tales."

"I'm sorry, sir," I whispered. "I won't move. I promise."

He whispered back, "Thank you," and returned to his easel.

"So where were we?" he asked as he began sketching again.

"The king didn't know how to handle the news that his nephew was fucking his wife."

"*Right*. So eventually, the king saw them together and knew for certain the rumors were true. He sent his nephew to the gallows, and his new wife to burn at the stake."

"That fucker! See? I knew it would end like that! How come he couldn't just accept defeat and let them be together?"

"I suppose he felt some kind of ownership over his bride. That's how things were in the 13th century."

"Fuck *that* shit! I don't care what piece of shit century it is. No one has the right to treat anyone else as property."

"Agreed. But there's more. Tristan escaped on his way to be hanged and rescued Isolde, and they lived happily in the woods together."

"A happy ending? I was totally not expecting that."

"That is until the king found them."

"Oh shit!"

"The three made peace, and Isolde agreed to be with the king, and Tristan left the country and married a different woman named Isolde."

"What! That's bullshit! Tristan just gave her up like that?"

He stopped working and looked down at me. "She was never his to begin with."

"She was never anyone's but who she *chose* to be with! She didn't *want* the king. She *wanted* Tristan. And the king should have been a man and honored their feelings."

"I suppose you're right. It's only a story, though." He continued working.

"It's a terrible story," I announced. "Why would you want to paint that?"

"I don't want to paint the story of Tristan and Isolde, Jane. I want to paint you, as Isolde. Only you."

"Why?"

"Because you have the face and spirit of a woman that many great men would fight for."

I didn't say anything. I didn't move or react. I just sat there and tried to embody the essence of the woman he had just described.

"Jane, wake up." I opened my eyes, and Will was kneeling in front of me.

"I fell asleep?"

"Yes."

"Oh god. You must think I have narcolepsy or something. "

"No, I just think it's quite boring to sit still for four hours."

"I was asleep for four hours?"

"Almost three."

"I'm so sorry!"

"It worked out really well, actually. You didn't move at all, and I did exactly what I had hoped to do." There were over a dozen sketches of my hands scattered on the floor.

"I also came to the conclusion that I am shit at drawing hands."

I picked up one of the sketches. "This is good. The proportions are a bit off, but I think they really look like my hands!"

"I know I can do better. I've always struggled with hands."

"Well, I can't draw anything at all so…"

"You must be hungry."

"Stop trying to feed me!"

"You're not hungry?"

"No, I'm good."

"Alright, well, I'd love to move on to a silhouette."

"Wait, I'm not done yet?"

"Unfortunately not. This is a bit of a commitment, I'm afraid."

I stood up and stretched. "Maybe we can go for a walk first? While it's still light out?"

"Of course. Where to?"

"I'd love to walk in your garden again."

"Have you seen the maze?"

"There's a maze? Let's go!" I took his hand and pulled him out of the library as though I knew where I was going. He seemed happy to let me lead him around.

"Where does it start?" I asked, taking him through the kitchen to the backdoor.

"You're going in the right direction."

I let go of his hand and quickly went down the stone staircase. "This way?" He nodded yes, and I kept moving down the path until he yelled, "To your right!"

I stopped and looked right, but all I saw were a bunch of over-grown rose bushes. "What's here?"

"This is going to be tricky. Lots of thorns." He spotted a fallen tree branch and hit the thorny rose branches with it. "It's been a while since anyone has been in here," he said as he chopped away at the branches.

"We don't have to-" I offered, but then I saw a door emerge underneath the vines. "No *way*!"

A weathered wooden door with an iron ring for a handle came into view. "Is this like a secret fucking garden?"

"Sort of," Will answered as he cleared the rest of the branches off the door. "It's a maze that my grandfather made. It wasn't really meant to be a secret, but my sister loved the book, so my grandfather attached this door for her."

"Wow! Do you also have a hunchbacked boy hiding in your attic?"

"Hmm? Oh, Colin? We keep him in the basement."

He pulled on the handle, but it didn't budge. "Is there a key?" I asked.

"They did give her a big fancy key, but it was for show. I think the door just hasn't been used in a while." He slammed his shoulder into the door, and it flew open. Then it flung back and hit him in the head.

"Oh, God! Are you okay?"

"I'm fine," he said as he rubbed the side of his head. "A bit of wounded pride is all." I couldn't help but laugh at him.

"I'm so sorry! I don't mean to laugh! I just have a thing about people falling or getting hit in the head…"

"I see," he said with a sly smile. "You enjoy having a laugh at other people's pain, do you?" I kept giggling.

"Kind of."

"Then let me ask you… How do you feel about being tickled?"

"Huh?" I blurted out. "What do you mean?"

"Do you enjoy being tickled?"

"No, I fucking hate it!"

"Good!" he called out as he stepped closer to me. I shrieked in his face.

"Come on. You wouldn't! That's creepy as fuck!"

"Maybe *I'm* creepy as fuck," he replied before he lunged forward. I quickly began running. I ran as far into the mess of leaves and branches as I could and stopped to catch my breath. Then I heard him yell, "Jane! I was just kidding!" and I took off again. I almost went right into a moss-covered wall and skidded over just in time.

I just kept running. I don't know what came over me, but the whole thing felt so exciting. I wasn't paying enough attention to where I was going as I kept making random turns. Will called out my name a few times, but then I couldn't hear him anymore. I stopped and put my hands on my knees, letting the burning sensation in my chest subside.

I heard a crunch of leaves behind me and bolted again. Just as I got to what looked like an opening back into the garden, I slipped and landed in a huge mud puddle. The entire right side of my face and body was submerged in mud. I lifted my head and saw Will step into the opening from the other side. His eyes grew wide when he saw I was lying in the mud.

"Oh, fuck! Jane, are you alright?" he called out, trying to contain his laughter.

"My shoulder!" I screamed. "I think it popped out of the socket! Help me!" I moaned in pain.

"Don't move!" he yelled as he got on his knees next to me. "It's really important that you don't move at all, or we might make this much worse! Which arm is it?"

"This one!" I announced as I took a huge handful of mud and smashed it across his face. We were both frozen for a moment, waiting for the other's reaction.

A chunk of mud fell from his face onto the ground, and he called out, "You're fucking dead!" Then he took a handful of mud and mashed it onto the top of my head. I screamed and pelted him with huge handfuls. He flung some back at me, and then he picked me up by my hips and sat me down directly in the puddle. We were both laughing so hard as we continued to wrestle in the mud. I stopped to catch my breath and put my hand out to call a truce. "Okay, okay," he panted, and we stared at each other through laughter and heavy breathing. Then he leaned in and pressed his lips onto mine.

His eyes were closed, but mine stayed open. I didn't push him off, but I didn't kiss him back because I wasn't entirely sure how I felt about him yet. He waited a few seconds for my response, but then opened his eyes and saw that mine were wide open and backed away.

"I'm so sorry. I thought-"

"No, no. I'm sorry! I just…"

"I shouldn't have."

"No, it's okay! I'm just… so dirty…" I looked down and laughed.

"Right," he said matter-of-factly. "Should we get cleaned up?"

"I can't believe I have to shower and borrow clothes from you again."

"I don't mind at all. I rather like having you in my shower." I smiled awkwardly. "I mean…" His face turned crimson. "I didn't mean…"

"It's okay. Let's go! I'm feeling the mud drying in my scalp!"

He stood up and held out his hand for me. I let him lead me out of the maze and back into the house. We tiptoed up the staircase, trying not to drip too much mud everywhere.

"Has anyone ever had a wedding here?" I asked. "It would be a shame not to have a bride descend this staircase with a huge train trailing behind her."

"No, there haven't been any weddings as far as I know. But I agree. I'd love to have my bride descend these stairs before taking my hand."

"Well, how about a ball? I think these stairs would be great for a ball too!"

"We do have a ballroom that hasn't been used in about 80 years," he said as he held his bedroom door open for me.

"*You have a ballroom?*" I asked in amazement. "You *must* have a ball! A *masked* ball!"

He was quiet but gave me this look like I was the most adorable thing he had ever seen. "There are fresh towels in the cabinet next to the sink, and a clean robe on the back of the door as well. Will that be alright, or should I look for some clothes for you?"

"A robe is great, thank you!"

"I'll wash your clothes when you're finished."

He turned to leave. "Aren't you coming in?" I asked. His

eyebrows shot up. "I mean into your room. To shower. When I'm finished," I quickly clarified.

"No, no. I'll use another bathroom. Please let me know if you need anything." He gently shut the door.

I took my time showering off all the mud. Then I wrapped myself in the plush navy bathrobe that was hanging behind the door and slowly combed out my hair. When I went back into the bedroom, I noticed a bookcase in the far corner with an old armchair next to it. I sat in the chair and searched through the titles.

You can tell a lot from the books people keep. I'd like to think I can tell whether the books have actually been read or if they are only there for show. Will's books definitely seemed well-read and well-loved. Most of them had tons of bookmarks, post-its, and notes scribbled inside. There were quite a few art history books, which I expected. There were also several shelves of philosophy texts. What moved me the most were all the classic love stories. *Pride and Prejudice, Wuthering Heights, The Great Gatsby, The Princess Bride, Great Expectations, Gone with the Wind, Anna Karenina, Jane Eyre, Romeo and Juliet,* and on and on. There was also a ton of classical love poetry. I held up a very old and weathered book. The cover was probably red when it was first published, but it had faded into an ugly orange color. It simply said, "*Love Poems*" on the front and nothing on the back. On the inside cover, it had an inscription that read,

For my William,
'God is love
and those who dwell in love
dwell in God
and God dwells in them.'
1 John 4.16
All of me,
Christina

A loud knock at the door startled me, and I inadvertently flung the book across the room and yelped. "Jane, are you alright?" Will called out. I quickly grabbed the book, shoved it back into the bookcase, and opened the door.

"Sorry, you just startled me."

"My apologies. Do you need anything?" His hair was wet and slicked back, and I could smell his crisp cologne. Part of me longed to lean in and continue the kiss he had started in the mud.

I held up the pile of muddy clothes. "Can you show me to your washing machine?"

He held his hands out, and I placed the clothes in them. "I've got it." He grinned and added, "You look good in my robe."

We went downstairs side by side, as I inquired about his book selection. "So, which of those love stories is your favorite?"

"Come again?"

"You have a lot of classic love stories on your bookshelves."

"Well, when you study literature, you're bound to come across those titles."

"I thought you studied art."

"I double-majored in art and literature before I dropped out."

"I was an English major before I dropped out," I admitted.

"Do you mind if I ask why you left?" he asked gently.

"I just couldn't pay the bills anymore, and I didn't want to take out any more loans. Halfway in I already owed $80K, and I didn't know why I was there or what I wanted to do. Really, I just wanted to write and to read books. So I left, got a job at a bookstore, and kept devouring literature, for free."

"That makes quite a lot of sense. That's why we created the brotherhood. We didn't feel we were learning anything useful at the academy. In fact, we felt the teachings were taking away from our natural abilities."

He led me into a room near the kitchen. There were leaves of ivy painted all over the walls and a huge stained glass window with leaves and flowers growing all over it. There was a concrete floor, and it didn't quite match the rest of the room. He lifted the washer's lid, threw my clothes in, then added detergent and turned it on. I noticed a large wooden table next to the washer and dryer with beautiful carvings all over the legs. The table was covered in wrinkled clothes. "*This* is your laundry room?" I asked in amazement.

"It's got to go somewhere."

I stepped over to the window and ran my fingers across the beveled flowers and leaves. "Isn't there somewhere less… lovely?"

"Not really. This does have an awful floor. Haven't quite gotten around to that yet."

"Who made this stained glass?"

"I did. All the stained glass in the house is mine. I'm much better at painting glass than canvas."

"I think you're quite good at both," I said as I walked over to him. "I have to admit I'm a bit hungry now."

"Of course. Should we have something here or go out?"

"Let's just find something here since I'm in a bathrobe."

"Right."

We entered the kitchen, and I sat at the island as he looked through the fridge. "How hungry are you?" he asked.

"A snack will do," I answered as I squinted to see the stained glass windows above the sink. There was a man with wings standing next to a beautiful woman in a garden. "Who is that supposed to be?"

He popped his head out of the fridge and looked towards me. I pointed to the window.

"That's the Archangel Gabriel and Mary." I got up and looked closer. The face of the angel looked a lot like Gabriel.

"Wait. Is this…?"

"Yes, Gabriel sat for it. It's the only thing I've ever gotten him to sit for. He's quite impatient."

The woman's face looked like the paintings of the woman in the library. "Will, is this the same girl-"

"Yes, that's Christina. My ex."

"Wow. She's beautiful."

"Is she?" he mumbled from behind the fridge door.

I could see that this wasn't his favorite topic, so I walked over to the pantry door and grabbed a cereal box. "Do you have milk?"

"I do!"

I held the cereal up. "Shall we?"

He lifted the milk carton into the air. "We shall!"

We sat on stools at the island, eating cereal and learning more about each other.

"So, Will. Tell me your favorite classic romance story."

"Let me think for a moment." He paused and then added, "Probably Gatsby."

"Really? *Ugh*, that's probably my *least* favorite. The characters are the most hateful people ever!"

"Why do you say that?"

"They have everything in the world, and they're miserable!"

"You really are convinced that money is the only thing one needs to be happy, aren't you?"

"It's not just that they have money. They're selfish and abusive. How could that possibly be your favorite love story?"

"I suppose I relate to the lengths that Gatsby goes to in order to win back the love of his life."

"Yeah, and after all of that, she takes his heart, plays with it, stomps on it, and literally leaves him for dead."

"None of that, in my opinion, takes away from the beauty of his love for her. But it is quite sad, now that I think about it. How about *Princess Bride*?" I sucked back a giggle before it came flying out.

"What!"

"Nothing. That's just very cute."

"And?" he said with his eyebrows up, waiting for my response.

"And cheesy as fuck!" I added.

"How is it cheesy?"

"Oh, I don't know. The whole *death cannot stop true love* thing. Pretty fucking cheesy!"

"Some of us believe that, I'll have you know!"

"It always bothered me how Buttercup couldn't tell it was him just because he had a mask on! Like, lady, this is your one true love!

You couldn't tell it was him? He didn't even disguise his voice! It's like when Superman puts a pair of glasses on, and suddenly Lois doesn't know who the fuck he is! These women are idiots. I'm pretty sure if I had *one true love*, I'd recognize him in a pair of glasses or a mask."

"I don't have a good excuse for Lois Lane, but as far as Buttercup, she had believed for years that her love was dead, and it utterly devastated her. So it wouldn't enter into her mind as a possibility. It couldn't. She had closed herself off to love and the world at that point. But he promised her he would always come for her. And even though she was engaged to another man, he still came back for her."

"You really believe in all that chivalry shit, don't you?"

"I suppose I do. Do you pity me?"

"Not at all. I envy you."

"Envy? *How?*"

"You believe in true love. I don't know if I do."

"Well, even if you don't, your mind can be changed, can't it?"

"Perhaps," I answered with a sly grin.

"Is there anything else that might come after that 'perhaps'?"

"*Perhaps* my mind could be changed if I saw a certain ballroom?" I tapped my finger slowly on my bottom lip until he responded.

"I'll make you a deal. I'll show you the ballroom if you promise to let me continue my sketches of you when we get there."

"Ugh, *boring*."

"That's just fine. I didn't quite feel like visiting the ballroom anyway."

"Fine! Deal."

He took me through the same hallway that led to the library, but we turned and went in a new direction. As we proceeded through the dark hallways, he asked, "So what's *your* favorite love story?"

"Probably *Pride and Prejudice*."

"You're more like Elizabeth Bennet than any woman I've ever met, so that makes a lot of sense."

"I take that as a great compliment! She's quite a heroine, in my opinion. When all anyone cared about was money and status, she wanted to marry for love. And she *demanded* respect."

"*You.*"

"I love the banter between Lizzy and Darcy too. They're just fun."

"I was glad she didn't fall for Wickham. She seemed more intrigued by him at first. I'm always happy when the good guy wins. That's how it should be, always."

"Agree. I don't think she ever really bought into Wickham's bullshit. She was too smart for that."

He opened a door at the end of the hallway and flicked on a light switch. We entered a massive dining room. The walls were a cream color and had what looked like hand-painted gold wreaths on the walls. In the middle of the wreaths were golden candelabras. The dark wooden table in the middle of the room seemed to go on forever. There were at least 50 chairs. On both sides of the table were stone fireplaces. They each had a similar coat of arms carved into them. I stopped to take a closer look, as Will stood by the double doors at the end of the room.

"Come on!" he called. I quickly joined him, and he turned to me with both hands on the golden door handles. "Are you ready for this?"

"Honestly, I don't know. This dining room is kind of blowing my mind right now!"

"You haven't seen *anything* yet, madam!" He flung the doors open, and my jaw completely dropped. It was the largest room I had ever seen in my life. It felt like the size of several football fields. The floor was made of dark wood with an intricate pattern of leaves made of lighter wood lining the entire room. In the middle of the floor was a giant "M" that looked like it was painted in liquid gold. Three of the four walls were lined with floor-to-ceiling windows that curved at the top, and in between each window was a giant mirror with lacy gold frames. Ornate golden scrollwork crept all over the ceiling and around the windows. But the most astounding part of the room was the massive stained-glass dome. I couldn't make out the design completely because it was so high up, but it featured angels and a starry night sky. The sun shone through the glass panes, creating an ethereal blue light across the dance floor. There were about a dozen crystal chandeliers, and the one that hung from the center of the dome was dripping with delicate crystal teardrops that cascaded halfway to the floor.

We were still standing in the entryway when he asked, "So? What do you think?"

"I think that somewhere in this house is an enchanted rose, and when the last petal falls, you'll be transformed into a beast forever!"

"Huh?"

I rushed into the middle of the room, stood upon the giant golden "M," turned to him, and yelled, "This is the ballroom from Beauty and the fucking Beast!"

He looked amused and called out, "Oh! Got it."

When he reached me, he remarked, "It was actually modeled after the Hall of Mirrors." I assessed my surroundings and realized it was absolutely a mini version of the "Galerie des Glaces" at Versailles in France. I had visited there when I traveled through Europe before college.

"Oh my god! This is insane. I *went* there!"

"My great-grandmother was a bit of a Francophile."

"But the rest of the house is so medieval. It doesn't fit!"

"The house was built in the Gothic style in the 1830s by my great-great-grandfather. His daughter married a French nobleman and lived in France for decades before she inherited this place. This room was originally a chapel but she turned it into a ballroom and tried to add some French touches."

"This dome! There are no words, Will. "

"35,000 individual panes of glass."

"How could you *not* use this room? What a waste!"

"Seems a bit decadent to me. But I guess my great-grandmother was trying to show off her wealth just like Marie Antoinette."

"Woah, woah, woah. Wait just a minute. Don't go hating on my girl Marie Antoinette!"

He scoffed. "How exactly would you like to defend her? Wasn't she responsible for the economic downfall of an entire nation?"

"You're about to get schooled. You might want to take a seat."

He turned and pointed to a large platform that stuck out from a sidewall. The platform had a shiny white piano on it. He sat down on the top step of the platform and said, "Proceed."

"I'll make this quick. She was only 14 when she was forced to leave her family to marry a man in a foreign country. She was constantly blamed for not immediately producing an heir even though her husband basically didn't understand how sex worked and didn't touch her for eight years."

"How is that even possible?"

"Think about it. No internet. No encyclopedias. No manuals. And it was considered improper to talk about it at all. They were all clueless!"

"Right."

"Finally, someone explains how a key goes into a lock, and he gets her pregnant."

"Seriously?"

"*Seriously.*"

"That's bloody hilarious!"

"Yeah. Anyway, everything she did and said was scrutinized by the entire country from the moment she got there. They made fun of her tomboyish clothes, so she wore fancier shit, but then they said she was too extravagant. She hated how everyone attended to her every move. Even when she went to the bathroom, a group of people had to watch. Can you imagine? They judged her for wanting privacy. She was only 21 when she became queen, and she was told to spend money like crazy because that's what royalty has always done! So to please everyone and get them to shut up, she bought even more fancy clothes and jewelry and redecorated the palace. But of course, everyone blamed her for bankrupting the country, even though they were out of money long before she even got there!"

"Well, what about that whole 'let them eat cake' thing?" he challenged.

"*Never happened!* That quote came from a man like a hundred years before she was born! She was actually quite caring and generous with the poor."

"So why would they want to portray their own queen as a callous piece of shit?"

"Simple. She was an easy scapegoat, as women always are! And they did the classic thing people do when they hate a woman. They spread gossip about her being a whore. They said Catherine the Great fucked horses, and Anne Boleyn fucked her own brother, so it could be worse. They only accused Marie of regular affairs. But there was no evidence of that at all!"

"Didn't she have an affair with a Count?"

"Ferson? They were friends. But I guess men and women can't be friends without it somehow turning sexual, right?" I rolled my eyes deeply to show my sarcasm.

"I do think there's some truth to that."

"Come *on*. Look at us! I'm a woman, and you're a man, and there's nothing sexual between us. Right?"

There was a very awkward silence where I felt him say so much without saying anything. Then he stood up suddenly, sat down at the piano, and said, "So... Any requests?"

I went up the steps of the platform. "You play piano too? Of course you do. Are you any good?"

"Fifteen years of lessons. Ms. Doreen always said I was a natural."

"Ms. Doreen?"

"My piano teacher."

"Got it. So, how about a Beatles song?" I sat down on the top step of the platform.

"Come on," he answered. "Too easy."

"*Really?* Can you play *all* of them?" I demanded.

"Pretty much!" He started to play, "Can't Buy Me Love," and I called out, "Eleanor Rigby," and he quickly transitioned into it. I stood up and yelled, "Hard Day's Night," and he smoothly changed the tune. "Umm…" I thought aloud, "I Wanna Hold Your Hand!" He instantly banged out the notes, tapping his foot, and bopping his head. "You're amazing!" I called out. I started to dance around the piano. "How about 'Let it Be?'" He played it without hesitation, but I changed my mind. "Rocky Raccoon!" The music abruptly stopped.

"Shit. I don't know that one."

"Golden Slumbers!"

He paused for a minute, then tapped his head again, and played. "I love this song!" I announced. His face was beaming and I loved how he moved his head with the notes. "Can you sing too?" I called out.

He sang, "Sleep pretty darling, do not cry, and I will sing a lullaby." He had a pretty good voice. Not the best I'd ever heard, but pretty damn good. I sat down next to him on the bench and sang with him, and his face lit up. We continued singing together, and he kept gazing up from the piano and into my eyes. I got a little choked up at the end.

"Jane, are you crying?"

I sucked my emotion in and yelled, "No!" He tilted his head towards me, and I added, "*Maybe.* I love that song so much. I want to hear it when I walk down the aisle one day."

One of his eyebrows went up. "*That* song? A bit unusual for a love song, no?"

"It's better than any love song. It's a lullaby. What says love more than rocking someone to sleep? But it *has to be* the Ben Folds version."

"Didn't know he covered it."

"It's amazing. You sound a lot like him actually."

There was a silent pause between us before he said, "Didn't he cover this one too?" and he began playing "Bitches Ain't Shit" and sang it so sweetly too.

"Oh my god!" I shouted, and we sang the unbelievably

disgusting lyrics together through laughs as the ballroom doors busted open. Lizzie, John, and Gabriel wandered in carrying art supplies.

Lizzie called out, "Hey! Why'd you stop?"

John yelled, "I want to hear 'Yellow Submarine' next!"

Gabriel had a murderous expression and growled, "What the fuck are you doing in here?" Neither of us answered, and he added, "*Why is she wearing your robe?*" He didn't wait for an answer before he threw his things on the floor and stormed out of the room.

Lizzie yelled, "Gabriel, wait!" and ran after him.

John came closer to us. "Uh, did I miss something?"

Will and I both shrugged our shoulders, and I turned to Will. "I think it's time to put my clothes in the dryer."

He gestured towards the door and said, "As you wish."

CHAPTER 9

GABRIEL

"Tearing Me Up"—Bob Moses

I S SHE SERIOUSLY FALLING FOR WILL? THIS IS THE BIGGEST bunch of bullshit.

Don't get me wrong. He's a good guy, and I consider him my brother, but he's not right for her. He needs a nice, quiet, boring girl with a plain face and average body to pour his chivalry bullshit onto. And Jane needs a man who has the same craving for life that she has. The same hunger for experiences, adventure, and fucking fire. A man who doesn't merely exist, waiting for life to happen *to* him. Someone who fucking lives life like the world around him is on fire, and he has only moments to take in the pleasures of everyone and everything around him. She needs *me*.

How can I make her see?

Sure, he can give her love. Tedious, uninspiring, mind-numbing, but reliable love. She'll be ripping her hair out from boredom in six months. I can challenge her, give her the excitement she requires to live. We can make this world our fucking playground, and these people our pawns. What can I do to show her? *What can I do?*

She has me writing poetry again.

Her Love

She loves him, for her infinite soul is love
and he may be her guiding star.
Passion in her is a glass facing
outwards, where her bright light is mirrored,

And the heat returned;
yet move that glass, and it shall turn,
in an instant, as ice to the moon;
while her pure fire for whom it burns,
clings close in this man's heart.

CHAPTER 10

Jane

"Tongue Tied"—Grouplove

I HADN'T HEARD FROM LIZZIE FOR SEVERAL WEEKS AFTER I saw her in the ballroom, so I asked her to meet me for lunch. She came into the café with such a light breeze about her, I thought she must be high on something.

"Hey, ladybug!" she called out as she flung her arms around my neck. We sat down, and she fumbled around in her bag. Then she started touching everything on the table.

"I'm worried about you," I said.

"Ugh, you're *always* worried about me!" she responded without making eye contact.

"I only worry when you give me reason to. Where've you been?"

"Doing my thing. Enjoying life. How about you?"

"Working a lot. Reading a lot. What kind of enjoyable life experiences have you been having?" She sighed and a huge, sly smile grew across her face, but she didn't say anything. "Lizzie. It's me. I know you better than anyone. What's been going on?"

"Don't judge me."

"I'm not going to judge you! When I worry about you, it's not because I'm judging your decisions. I'm scared that you are being reckless and putting yourself in danger."

"Yeah, yeah. I'm not in danger. In fact, this is the happiest and safest I've felt in years!"

"Wow!" I said, pretending to be happy for her. "What's been going on?"

"I kind of, like, moved into the house."

"The house?"

"Red House."

"*That* house."

"Mhhm," she practically sang.

"How did that happen?" I asked, trying to sound non-judgmental.

"I've been working a lot with John. He's painting me as Ophelia. Really long hours. It takes him like 20 hours to paint a few inches. I ended up just sleeping over for a few nights, and a few nights turned into a few weeks. It's not a big deal. They have like five extra bedrooms."

"So, are you and John a thing?" I asked, hopeful that she would say yes. John was sweet and trustworthy, and he'd make a great boyfriend for Lizzie.

"John!? Uh, no. We're not a thing."

"Oh. Okay. Well, I'm glad you've been having a good time with John. He's a good guy."

"And Gabriel's been teaching me to paint," she quickly added.

"Is he?"

"You know I've always wanted to study art, but my parents wouldn't let me. Why not learn from a master?"

"A master, huh? I mean, sure. That's cool, I guess." I looked down into my lap.

"*What*, Jane? Just say what you're thinking. "

"I don't trust him."

"Who? Gabriel? Why don't you trust him?"

"Because he's a fuck boy of the highest magnitude!"

"Why? Because he's hot?"

"No, because I can see his intentions from 50 miles away. Once he gets into your pants, he'll dump you like yesterday's trash."

"Come *on*. You don't know that!"

"Have I ever been wrong about a guy? *Have I*? You know I have a sixth sense for assholes."

"Whatever. I don't care if he's a fuck boy. I'm having fun."

"And that's all that matters, right?" I said sarcastically. "Are you gonna lose your virginity to him?"

"Maybe. Don't you think it's time?"

A text from an unknown number pinged on my phone. It read, "Jane, it's Will. I'm so sorry to bother you, but I really need your help."

"What's up?" I responded. I hadn't heard from him since I gave him my number weeks before.

"I can't tell you much right now," he texted. "Can you meet me at my house at eight? I'd really appreciate it."

"Okay, sure. Dress code?"

"Formal."

"Formal???"

"If you don't mind."

"I'll try my best!"

"Jane! You okay?" Lizzie asked.

"Yeah, fine. Will you be at Will's tonight?"

"No. Will texted all of us that we should find another place to stay tonight. I think there's something going on with his family. He's been in London the past few weeks."

"Hmm."

I had no idea what I was walking into that night, but I felt sort of honored that Will wanted me to be a part of it and no one else. I wore my favorite black cocktail dress. It was the right amount of classy and sexy. I hated wearing heels, but since he said it was formal, I sucked it up and wedged my feet into my black satin peep-toe heels.

There was a piece of paper taped to the front door that said, "Jane, please meet me in the dining room," and the door was unlocked. I was startled by how dark it was inside. All the lights were off, and there were a few lit candles in lanterns on the floor near the staircase.

I went down the hallway where Will had taken me weeks

before. It was so dark that I walked directly into a chair and fell over into it. I stood up and took a deep breath. I tried to find a light switch somewhere in the blackened hallway, but I was unsuccessful. Finally, I stood before the doors of the dining room. I paused and pressed my ear to the door, but I heard absolutely nothing. Not knowing what the fuck was going on, and resisting the urge to make a run for it, I opened the doors and stepped in.

The dining table was covered in lit candles and flower petals. I walked slowly to the end of the table and saw an elaborate place setting for two. Someone moved in the shadows on the other side of the room.

"If you wanted to have dinner with me, you just could have asked," I stated. Gabriel emerged from the darkness dressed in a black suit.

"Would you have come?"

I started to move back towards the door. "Where's Will?"

"In London," he said casually as he made his way towards me and blocked the door.

"Where are you going?" he said with his stupid, sexy smirk. I was angry that I had been lied to. I don't like being in a situation where I don't have control, and he made me feel completely out of control whenever he was near me.

"Please move."

His hair was combed back, and the suit was exceptionally tailored, showing his toned chest and arms. The sight of him up close made my legs shake. He looked down into my eyes and softly said, "Come on. *Please* have dinner with me?"

"You tricked me."

He stroked my cheek and said, "Just a little white lie. Won't you give me a chance?"

I flung his hand away. "You just can't accept that I *don't* want you!"

"I won't accept it because *I don't believe it.*"

He took a slip of paper out of his pocket, slipped it into my purse, and calmly said, "I wrote this for you." Then he leaned in and lightly placed his lips on mine. I let him kiss me for an instant, and then I leaned back.

"I have to go. Please move." He stepped to the side like he was letting me go, but as I moved forward, he grabbed my wrist and flung me up against the door. He had his knee pinned between my legs, his hands tightly gripped my wrists, and his face was inches from mine.

"You look incredible," he whispered into my mouth. "I can't let you go." He slowly swirled his tongue on my lips and into my mouth. He was the most sensational kisser. I came away panting, and he ran his tongue up my neck and nestled his face into my hair near my ear. "Fuck, Jane," he whispered. "What you do to me…"

"You only want me because you can't have me." That was exactly how I felt. He wasn't used to being rejected, I thought, and as soon as he had me, he'd move on to the next girl.

Ignoring my comment, he kissed my neck and cupped my breasts. He yanked the top of my dress down and very slowly ran his tongue over my nipples while staring up at me. Then he moved his tongue back into my mouth while he crept his fingers up my thigh and underneath my dress.

I wasn't wearing underwear because I didn't want any panty lines to show in my dress. He grinned when he found me bare, and I gasped as he dragged two fingers between my legs and gently moved them in circles. Then he slid them inside me as he whispered in my ear, "Fuck, you're wet." It felt so good that I had to close my eyes and brace myself against the door, so I wouldn't collapse. Slowly, his fingers went in and out as he rubbed me on the outside with his thumb. Then he suddenly drew his fingers out and brought them up to his face, which was so close to mine. He showed me how his fingers glistened in the candlelight. Then he put them in his mouth and sucked on them. "So sweet," he murmured.

My legs were shaking so intensely that I could barely stand as I responded, "You're the fucking devil."

He looked pleased with that comment and answered, "Yeah? Then so are you. We're the same, baby."

"Take me upstairs."

He searched my eyes for a moment, then gripped my hand and yanked me away from the door. He forcefully led me through the dark hallway and towards the stairs. When he got to the bottom step, he turned, and his mouth came down onto mine. I let him completely consume me for a moment before I begged, "Please! I can't wait any longer!" That devious grin spread across his face, and he continued guiding me up the steps. When we got into his bedroom, I spun around, so my back was towards the door.

"You wanna know what I wanna do with you?" I said.

"You can do whatever you want, baby. I'm yours."

"Get on the bed," I commanded. As he backed up, I yelled, "Wait!" His eyebrows went up, and I added, "Take off your jacket." He did as I asked, and I told him to remove his shirt. He slowly undid the buttons with a look of amusement and dropped the shirt to the floor. "Pants," I said, and he swiftly pulled them off. The moonlight shone down through the windows onto his flaw-less body, and it took everything I had not to take a running start and jump on top of him. He was wearing black boxer briefs, and I paused, admiring him for a moment. "Now get on the bed."

He complied and sprawled out in the middle of the bed. "I'll be right back," I declared.

I went into his closet and turned on the light. The harsh fluores-cent light brought me back to reality. I giggled to myself and felt a rush of excitement. This was going to be fun. I searched through his closet until I saw a bunch of ties hanging from a hanger. I grabbed them and went back into the bedroom. He was still spread out in the middle of the bed, looking very pleased with himself.

"What are those for?" he asked.

"This is my fantasy, Gabriel."

"Get over here."

I climbed on top of him with a fistful of his ties. He tried to kiss me, but I yanked my head back. "Uh-uh. Not yet. Be patient." Before he had time to answer, I secured a tie around his eyes as a blindfold.

"Shit," he called out. "Kinky." I put my finger to his lips and shushed him. Then I took one wrist and tied it to the bedpost as firmly as I could. When I moved on to secure his other wrist, he made a noise to show his discomfort. "It's a bit tight."

"Are you a pussy?" I teased.

He paused and responded, "Do the other one tighter." I did as he asked and sat back to admire my handiwork. Then I mounted him again and took off his boxers. He moaned, "Yeah." He was huge and ready. I got off the bed, leaned over his face, and whispered his name. His face turned towards me, and I kissed him gently on the cheek. Then I whispered into his ear, "Goodnight," and softly padded out of the room. He was quiet for a moment or two, but as soon as I descended the stairs, I heard him calling my name. His calls got more and more frantic, and just as I opened the front door, I heard, "Are you fucking kidding me, Jane!?"

I practically skipped to my car, and I thought I heard him screaming in the distance. I turned the radio on, and "Tongue Tied" by Grouplove was on. It was sublime. I spun the volume all the way up, rolled down all the windows, and sped home so fast that I almost lost control of the car. When I got to my apartment, I laid down on the floor in the dark and laughed until tears poured from the corners of my eyes. Then I ripped off my dress and rubbed myself while imagining getting on top of Gabriel and riding him like I wanted to. I came harder than I ever have when I thought about him tied to his bed all night, alone.

CHAPTER 11

Jane

"Dissolve"—Absofacto

I WASN'T ENTIRELY SURE WHAT TO EXPECT AFTER I LEFT HIM tied to his bed all night. I thought there would be some kind of backlash. Some display of anger or resentment. I watched the door at work for the first few days, waiting for him to burst in and verbally attack me. A week went by, and there was no word from anyone, not even Lizzie. I can't pretend I wasn't disappointed. What I did was over the top, and I wanted something to happen in response. I needed that excitement in my life. Then came a second week of silence. I started to think they had all turned on me—that he told them what I did, and they all agreed that I had gone too far.

Just as I contemplated dropping by their house, I got a phone call from a number I didn't recognize.

"Jane, it's Will. How are you?"

"Is this *really* Will?"

"Do I not sound like myself?"

"You do. I just thought perhaps it was someone faking an English accent."

"How can I prove to you that it's really me?"

"Umm, text me a picture of you picking your nose."

A moment later my phone dinged, and a picture of Will with a half-smile and his pointer finger up his nostril appeared. I laughed out loud.

"Okay, it's you."

"Right. Would it make you angry if I admitted that I've missed you?"

"Why would it make me angry?"

"I'm not sure."

"Would it make you angry if I said I kinda miss you too?" It was the truth. I wasn't sure what my feelings for Will were, but I really enjoyed being around him.

"Certainly not," he responded. "That's something I'd love to hear right now."

"Okay. I kinda miss you. Where have you been?"

"Why don't you come over, and I'll tell you all about it."

"Ehh, how about we get dinner instead?"

"I'd really like that. When is a good time?"

"Now."

"Now? I wasn't expecting that! How about in an hour? I'd be happy to pick you up."

"Have you ever been to The Witches' Cauldron?"

"No, I don't believe I have."

"It's not that far from you. I'll text you the address. Meet me in an hour."

"I will!"

I'm not sure why I chose that obnoxious café. Lizzie and I used to go there all the time as teenagers, trying to embody what we thought cool people were like. We'd stand outside smoking clove cigarettes while trying to pick up cute goth dudes. The people who went there took themselves too seriously. I think I just wanted to take Will somewhere he would feel utterly out of place. He was so calm and cool all the time, so I wanted to see how he'd be out of his element.

I made myself cozy on an old couch in a back corner. The place was very dark, lit with strings of orange and purple lights and some red light bulbs in old lamps. I saw Will wandering around, looking a bit confused. He was wearing khaki pants and a light blue polo. His blonde hair was combed more neatly than usual. I held my arm up and waved until he spotted me. He looked around for a place to sit and I gestured to the empty spot next to me on the couch. "Right," he stated as he sat down. "This is an interesting place."

"Is it too much?"

"Too much of what? I think it's fun. I'm really liking the flexible seating!"

"Yeah?"

"Quite a dodgy neighborhood, I think."

"I think that's the most British thing I've heard you say!"

"Oh, right. Sorry."

"Don't be sorry! I love it!"

The waitress came over with the frozen chai I ordered. Then she asked Will what he wanted to drink.

"A cuppa tea please."

"What kind of tea would you like?"

"Just black tea. With lemon."

She looked a bit confused. "As far as black tea, we have good tidings, caramel vanilla, moulin rouge, sleepy hollow, dragon moon, black velvet, angel's dream, cinnamon plum, Marrakesh, ginger peach, blackberry sage, raspberry quince, mango, earl grey-"

"Earl grey would be perfect, thanks!"

"Anything to eat?"

He turned to me and said, "I'll leave that to you!"

"You sure?"

"I trust you," he said with a wink.

"We'll have the goat cheese crostini and vegetable spring roll appetizers. For a meal, we'll share the butternut squash gnocchi and the Middle Eastern platter."

"Perfect," she responded as she took the menus off the table.

"Sounds delicious," Will declared.

"The food here is really good. So tell me where you've been!"

"My grandfather has been quite ill, so I flew to London to visit with him."

"I'm so sorry to hear that. May I ask what's wrong with him?"

"Pancreatic cancer."

"Shit," I replied.

"He was diagnosed just a few months ago, and he's been in rapid decline ever since. He doesn't have much time left."

"That's awful. I'm so sorry. Are you close?"

"Very. My grandparents raised my sister and me for the most part. My mum and dad weren't that enthusiastic about being parents."

"Got it. How is your grandmother handling his illness?"

"She passed away just days before he was diagnosed. They had a very strong marriage and were quite attached. She wouldn't have been able to handle seeing him like this."

I took a few sips of my drink and thought of what to say next. The appetizers and his tea came, and we began eating. "This is really, really good!" he told me.

"Are you surprised?"

"A bit. I wasn't entirely sure what to expect."

"This place is a bit over the top with the decor, I'll admit. But the food is awesome!"

"The tea isn't bad either!"

I considered whether or not to bring up the subject of his family again. I genuinely wanted to know more about him, so I did.

"How long were your grandparents married?" He took a minute to finish his last bite of food before he answered. "Almost 70 years."

"Wow! That's quite an accomplishment!"

"Yes, and an even bigger accomplishment was that they were still truly in love."

"That is so sweet! You don't hear that very often."

"No, you don't. The success of their marriage was all about the effort my grandfather put into it. He vowed to always treat her like a queen, from the day they got married, and he followed through with that each and every day."

"Oh god. I'm going to cry!"

I shoved more food into my face. Normally when I was on a date with a guy, I would have been very self-conscious about eating. I'd be preoccupied with making sure there was no food on my lips or in my teeth and that I didn't order anything that would leave a lingering odor on my breath. But it was different with Will. He made me feel so comfortable; I didn't even worry about things like that.

"They were my role models," he continued. "I learned about honor, manners, and how to treat women from them."

"Oh, I see. That's where all of this chivalry stuff comes from!"

"Absolutely. Even when my grandfather could barely walk, he brought my grandmother breakfast in bed every day. It just took him much, much longer!"

"That is so cute!"

"I hope to have a marriage like they had one day," he said as he went for the last spring roll with his fork. "Hold on. Did you want this last one?"

"No, no. Please. It's yours."

"Are you sure?"

"One thousand percent sure."

He chewed for a while and said, "So Jane. I heard your birthday is only a few weeks away."

"Oh, you heard that? From who?"

"Lizzie, of course."

"Yup. October 31st. Halloween."

"What a wonderful day for a birthday! Must have been fun growing up!"

"Not really. It's like having your birthday on Christmas. You feel kinda jipped."

"Jipped?" he asked.

"Robbed, in a way. You don't get the full celebration. Your birthday is just kinda tacked on to the celebrations that are already happening."

"Oh, I see."

"You don't celebrate Halloween though, right? You have Guy Fawkes day."

"We never really celebrated Halloween, right. But it's kind of becoming a thing now in some parts of England. Lots of costume parties at the local pubs."

The waitress brought our entrees, and we continued our conversation as we ate. "The reason I'm bringing this up is that my mates and I are planning something special for your birthday," he said with a mouth full of gnocchi.

"Your mates?" I asked.

"The brotherhood."

"*The brotherhood* is planning something special for me?" I asked in disbelief.

"Well, yes. And Lizzie too."

"How about Gabriel?" I blurted out. He dropped his eyes and kept them on his plate as he spoke.

"Well, he wasn't too keen on the idea."

"That's what I figured."

"After that stunt you pulled, I'm not sure he'll be very enthusiastic about you visiting."

"You know about that?" I didn't regret what I had done, but I felt a bit stupid about it in front of Will. He was so mature and proper; he probably thought what I did was ridiculous and childish.

"We all know. Not because Gabriel told us. I'm quite sure he had intended to take that information with him to the grave. Ed is the one who told us about it."

"How does Ed know? Gabriel told him?"

Will giggled a bit. "No. Ed had the pleasure of finding Gabriel and untying him." I made an "oops" kind of face, and Will added, "I must admit, it's one of the funniest things I'd ever heard."

"You don't think it's stupid of me?"

"Stupid? *No.* I think it's brilliant. And I hope that he used the time to really contemplate some of his choices while he was tied to his bed all night."

"I only did it because he tricked me. I thought it was you who had invited me over."

Will's eyebrows went up with surprise. "Now that detail I was unaware of," he said.

"I don't like being lied to. He tricked me, so I tricked him."

"You don't need to justify anything to me. I quite enjoyed hearing about it. Especially the irony of Ed being the one who found him."

"What do you mean?"

"Ed's a bit in love with Gabriel."

"Really? Oh shit! That must have been… awkward."

"Awkward and hilarious."

"So tell me about my birthday surprise!"

"No, no," he answered. "The plans will be revealed in due time."

"Oh, come on! I don't like surprises. Just ask Gabriel."

"You will like this one, I think." We finished our meal and the waitress asked if we wanted dessert. Will looked at me and said, "Do we?"

I turned to the waitress. "We'll take a brownie sundae to go!"

"We will? To go?" Will asked me.

"Trust me," I said as I pointed behind him where they were setting up for open mic night on a small stage. He turned around as a teenaged boy with a purple mohawk sat down on a stool and began screaming the lyrics to "Disarm" by Smashing Pumpkins into the mic. He turned back to me and said, "Right. So where will we eat our dessert?"

"There's a park a few blocks from here. They have plenty of picnic tables."

"Sounds nice. Shall I drive?"

"We can walk!"

I stood up as the waitress brought our dessert box, and I took it from her. "Come on!" He dropped two $100 bills onto the table and quickly followed me to the door.

"So how many blocks is it exactly?" he said as he looked around nervously.

"I don't remember, but I know it's pretty close."

"Right."

We walked side by side, and he seemed uneasy. "Are you alright?" I asked.

"Yeah, I'm alright. I just can't believe how dark the streets are. Don't any of the street lights work?"

I shrugged. "Are you afraid of the dark? I'll protect you."

"Oh, good. I feel a lot better now," he said sarcastically. "Are you cold?" he asked. "Please take my jacket." He started to take off his jacket, but I stopped him.

"It's fine! I'm fine."

We moved in silence for a bit, so I tried to cut down the awkwardness with small talk.

"I love looking into people's windows at night," I declared.

"Well, that's a bit creepy," he replied.

"I don't mean I go right up to them and look in like a psycho. I mean from far away. I was on the track team in high school, and I had to run around my neighborhood for hours and hours. To make the time go faster, I tried to see into people's windows. You can really see a lot at night!"

"I would imagine listening to music would help with that too. But I admire your creativity."

"Yeah, yeah. Look at that house over there. The bedroom lights are so bright, and the curtains are open. It's better if we're further away. Come here."

We crossed to the other side of the street and stopped to gaze up at the window. All we saw was a fan whirling around on the ceiling. "Wow, Jane. I'm riveted." I smacked him gently on the arm.

"Okay, that one wasn't so great. Let's keep going."

We passed a few more houses, and there was a bright light shining down from a living room window. Will pointed to it. We stopped and waited, but all we saw was some very old furniture. We moved past a few more houses, and Will noticed colorful lights coming from a bedroom. We crossed the street again to get a better view, and there was a lit Christmas tree in the person's bedroom. "Now that's weird!" I declared.

"A bit early for Christmas, I agree. But not *that* unusual."

I huffed with frustration. "I know we'll see something strange eventually!"

We walked further and reached the entrance to a trail at

the end of the road. I pointed to it, and Will said, "What is *that*? Where people go to get themselves murdered?"

I laughed. "That's the trail that leads to the park."

He rolled his eyes and answered, "Right…" Then he whispered, "Look!" into my ear and pointed across the street where there was a very clear view of someone watching porn in their living room on a gigantic T.V. screen.

"Holy shit!" I called out. The scene featured a woman with platinum blonde hair and gigantic fake boobs riding some hairy dude. "Pretty fucking gross," I added.

Will turned to me with a look of disgust and said, "Definitely not my thing either." I kept walking forward down the trail and turned to him.

"So what *is* your thing exactly?"

"What do you mean?"

"You said that nasty porn wasn't your thing. But everyone likes *something* right?"

"What are you asking me? What kind of porn I watch?"

"Yeah, I guess that's what I'm asking," I said.

He was quiet for a moment and then said, "Horses."

"Whores?" I responded.

"No, horses," he said.

"So you watch horse porn?"

"Yes," he said with a serious tone.

"What exactly do you watch these horses doing?"

"Oh, just your standard kind of equine intercourse. Nothing too out of the ordinary."

I smacked his arm again and said, "Come on! Answer the question!"

He laughed and replied, "I'd rather not talk about that stuff. I find that people who talk about it aren't doing it enough."

"Oh, I see. So you must be getting a lot more action than me!"

"Ah, you just proved my theory to be inaccurate!"

At this point, he noticed we were deep in the woods. Some

kind of bird squawked, and he turned to me and said, "Did you bring me here to murder me?"

I leaned in and whispered, "No. I just want to drink your blood." I grabbed his hand and pulled him further down the trail as he got visibly uncomfortable.

"Jane, I really think we should turn back. It's really isolated here."

"What's wrong with a little isolation?" I countered. "Besides, you haven't seen the best part yet!" At that moment, we could see the most phenomenal view of the lake. The waxing moon was the brightest I had seen in years, and it created a long silver bar across the water.

"That is bloody brilliant!" Will exclaimed.

"I know!" I answered. "Let's go!" I took his hand and began to drag him closer to the edge of the water.

"Jane, wait," he said calmly.

I ignored him and kept pulling. "It's almost as pretty as your lake, huh?"

"Yes, definitely. Can we just sit right here?" he pleaded as he tried to pry his arm from my hand.

I let him go and declared, "I want to put my feet in!" He planted his feet and kept asking me to come back. "What's wrong? Can't swim?" I teased.

"I can swim. I would just rather you didn't." I ignored him and ripped off my socks and shoes and went running into the water. "Fuck!" I called out. "It's fucking freezing!"

"You'll come back now, then?"

I ran out of the water and scurried back to the grassy area where he was sitting. "Shit. I'm an idiot. Is that why you didn't think I should go in?"

"Something like that." I started to rub my feet to warm them up. "Here, let me," he said as he held out his hands.

"You really want to rub my feet?"

"I would be honored."

"*Okay*," I said as I dropped my feet into his hands.

"*Shit!* That water *is* freezing! Your feet are like ice!"

He rubbed my feet very quickly like he was rubbing sticks together to start a fire. It wasn't sexual, just a bit embarrassing. I giggled, and he asked, "Is this helping at all?" I lifted my feet out of his hands and put my socks back on.

"Thanks. I do think that helped!" He must have seen me shiver because he insisted I take his jacket. He draped it over my shoulders and that clean, fresh beach scent drifted into my nose. "You smell really good, Will." The words fell out of my mouth inadvertently.

"I'm so glad you think so. I would imagine you smell quite nice, but I haven't gotten close enough to be able to judge." I rolled my eyes and scooted closer. "No pressure. I don't want to smell you if you aren't ready," he joked. I dropped my head into my hands and snickered. "Sorry. That sounded really strange."

He moved closer and put his face close to my neck. I had the chills, just a bit. I turned my face towards him, lifted my eyebrows, and softly asked, "Well?" His eyes were closed, and he took his time before answering.

"*Absolutely* the loveliest scent on the planet."

"Oh, stop!"

"I mean it. When I paint a goddess... *that* is what I imagine she would smell like. Flowers, and fresh rain, and some kind of dessert."

"We forgot to eat dessert!" I remembered.

"I don't want dessert, Jane," he said as he looked intensely into me.

"What do you want?" I knew what I was asking, and I knew what I would get. I wanted it to happen. He closed his eyes and leaned in. Just as our lips touched, we saw a light flashing behind us, and a man's voice called out, "Hey! Who's out there?" Will turned back to look, then looked down at the ground with defeat.

"What should we do?" I whispered.

"Did we do something wrong?" he whispered back.

"I don't think so."

He stood up and shouted, "Hello?" The man shined the flashlight right into Will's face and yelled, "Police! Put your hands up and slowly walk towards me!"

He immediately put his hands up and yelled, "My girlfriend is here too!"

I stood up, put my hands up, and called out, "Hi!"

The cop flashed the light into my face and said, "Alright, you two. Party's over. Let's go." We slowly marched over to where he stood. "Do you both have your licenses? I need to run them before I can let you go."

"Of course, officer," Will replied.

"Either of you have any drugs on ya?"

We both laughed, and Will said, "Not that I'm aware of."

The cop looked a bit confused. "Not that you're aware of?" he repeated.

"We do not have any drugs. Only dessert."

He looked Will up and down with squinted eyes and said, "Follow me."

The cop led us down the trail and back onto the street where his patrol car was waiting. "Lemme get your IDs." We both pulled out our wallets and took out our IDs.

Just before he turned to go back to his car, Will asked, "Officer, were we breaking any laws?"

"The park closes at dusk," he answered before he got into his car.

I shrugged my shoulders and muttered to Will, "Oh, big deal! So we were at a park after hours. It doesn't *belong* to anyone. It's public property. We weren't trespassing!"

Will looked a bit worried. "I knew you were trouble. Now I'm going to have a criminal record!"

I shoved him teasingly. "Good thing you have enough money to pay everyone off and have it expunged!"

He cocked his head and said, "Good point."

The cop returned with our IDs. "Are we in trouble?" I asked.

"I won't give you a ticket this time, but listen carefully, alright? It's not safe in that park at night. You understand?"

I scoffed and said, "You sound a lot like my boyfriend here."

The cop had a severe look on his face. "These rules exist for a reason. It's not a joke."

"I think we both understand the gravity of the situation," Will responded, "and we can assure you that it will not happen again." He held his hand out, and the officer shook it.

"So you two need to find somewhere safe to do your sexy time, alright? Take it indoors!" I covered my mouth so I wouldn't react as Will gave me a gentle nudge with his elbow.

"Absolutely, officer. I can guarantee that our sexy time will only happen indoors." I busted out laughing, and the cop lifted an eyebrow.

"Lemme drive you two home."

"Our cars are just a few blocks up the road," I said.

"But we would love a ride!" Will added. "Just to be safe."

He opened the backdoor to his car and said, "Get in."

We jumped into the backseat, and I shouted, "Can you put the siren on too?"

The cop looked over at Will. "Does she always think everything is a joke?" he asked.

Will turned to me and grinned. "Yes, she does."

When we got to our cars, Will asked if I wanted to come back to his house. He was hoping to work on the sketch from weeks before. I said I was tired and kissed him lightly on the cheek. I wasn't tired in the least, but I just couldn't handle the thought of seeing Lizzie or confronting Gabriel that night. I promised I'd let him continue his sketches soon.

When I got home, as I was getting undressed, I noticed a piece of paper on the floor of my closet.

Sudden Light
For Jane

We have been here before,
But when or how I cannot tell:
I know that voice beyond the door,
Your sweet familiar smell,
That sigh you make as you lie upon the shore.

You have been mine before,—
How long ago I may not know:
But that pang I felt from deep within my core
With your neck turned just so,
When your veil did fall,—I knew it for sure.

Have we been like this before?
And shall time's swirling flight
In this life our love restore
In death's despite,
So we can be together once more?

I folded the paper back up, sat down on the edge of my bed, and held it to my chest as I let out a long sigh. I knew what he was feeling, what he meant. I knew the veil he described, the one I put between myself and the world. I felt guilty for not thinking about Will. We had a great time, and I had affectionate feelings towards him. But I felt Gabriel's words in the depths of my being.

That night I dreamt of him over and over. In each sequence, we looked completely different and wore strange clothes, but I knew for sure that it was Gabriel and me. There was always turmoil, always disquiet between us. But there was the most incredible infatuation as well. I woke up exhausted and confused. I tried to expunge him from my mind, at least for the day, but it was hopeless. He had buried himself in me.

CHAPTER 12

Jane

"Live in the Moment"—Portugal. The Man

WHEN I GOT HOME FROM WORK A FEW DAYS LATER, there was a big package waiting for me. An enormous white box with a smaller box on top in the most beautiful champagne color sat in front of my apartment door. Both were tied with a bow made of white tulle, and there was a rhinestone fleur-de-lis in the middle. I brought them inside and carefully placed them on my bed. I started to think that there was a mistake, and the boxes were not actually for me.

I untied the bow and opened the smaller box. Inside was a delicate mask made of champagne lace. It had the tiniest sparkles, and the scrollwork of the lace crept up higher on one side. Underneath the mask was a message etched in gold on a satin background.

THE PLEASURE OF YOUR COMPANY
IS REQUESTED AT A
MASQUERADE BALL
IN HONOR OF

Lady Jane

ON THE ANNIVERSARY OF HER BIRTH
TO BE HELD AT "MAISON ROUGE"
ON THE 31ST OF OCTOBER
AT 10 PM
NO MASK, NO ENTRY!

Okay, so the boxes were for me. I cannot even describe the excitement and honor I felt at that moment. The box, mask, and invitation were absolutely breathtaking, and I didn't quite feel worthy. I immediately called Will.

"Lady Jane!" he exclaimed before I could say anything. "I trust you've received the invite?"

"Will. This is too much. I can't..."

"You can't what? Come to your own birthday party? It's going to be-"

I cut him off before he could finish. "I can't accept this. You can't throw a party like this for me. It will be too expensive, and you barely even know me!"

"If it makes you feel any better, we've had a big Halloween party here for the past three years. We just haven't had it in the ballroom or required masks."

"But in my honor? And with these fancy invitations?"

"You're the only one who received an invite like that. Everyone else got a text. Feel better?"

"I guess."

"How about the gown? Does it fit?" I glanced down at the other box that I hadn't opened yet. "I didn't even open it!"

"Then you haven't seen anything yet."

I opened the bigger box and separated the gossamer tissue. I gasped and dropped my head down to the bed. Inside was the bodice of the most incredible ball gown. I took it out and held it up in front of the full-length mirror. It was really thick and heavy. The entire gown had a pale golden hue, with flowers and vines stitched all over the front and shiny silver and gold beading. The sleeves went to the elbow and bursts of gold and white tulle hung down the rest of the way. The skirt was perfectly draped like a golden waterfall, and the back had a huge train of golden satin that started at the top of the dress and cascaded down to the floor. I couldn't stop admiring the details until I heard Will call out, "Jane, hello? Are you there?" from the phone I had dropped onto the bed.

"Will. This is the most beautiful thing I have ever seen and absolutely the most incredible gift I have ever received. But I can't accept it."

"Well, that's a shame because it was custom-made and non-refundable. And I'm quite sure that it wouldn't fit me, so I suppose it's going into the trash."

"No! No! Of course it's not going in the trash. What do you mean it was custom made?"

"Lizzie provided the design and measurements. It was *made* for you, Jane. Only you can wear it."

I glanced back at the box it came in and saw a few white feathers and a folded-up fan. "Wait a minute!" I exclaimed. "Am I? Is this… Marie Antoinette?"

"Oui, bien sûr!"

"Will. I… I don't know what to say."

"Say you'll be there!"

"Okay. I'll be there!"

"Brilliant."

"Hey, Will? I have a wedding to go to the weekend after Halloween. It's my old roommate from college. Would you like to be my date?"

"I would be honored."

I called Lizzie next, and she obviously knew why I was calling because she answered the phone with a fancy, "Is this the Dauphine of France?"

"Lizzie! Oh my god. I don't even know what to say."

"A simple thank you will do, Madame."

"Is this for real? Like…"

"I know. This all seems too good to be real life."

"Exactly."

"It's real. Trust me. It's really real."

"Lizzie, I miss you so much. I miss *us*."

"I know. We'll be us again soon. But a better version. A *fancier* version."

"Well, that's for fucking sure."

"You have to get here early, so I can help you do your hair." I held the phone to my ear with my shoulder, put the dress up to my chest, and spun around and around.

"Did you try it on yet?" she asked.

"No, I called you before I had the chance."

"Hang up right now, put it on, and call me back!"

"I don't even think I can get this thing on by myself."

"I know for a fact that you can."

"Oh?"

"I tried it on to get the measurements right. Don't worry, I had them leave a lot more room for your enormous cans!"

"Shut up. Okay, I'll call you back." I hung up and tossed the phone onto the bed. Then I ripped off my clothes, unzipped the dress from behind the train, and stepped into it. It took a lot of stretching, but I was able to zip it all the way. It was a bit tight in the chest, but it was obviously supposed to be. It smashed my boobs together just the right amount. It was classy cleavage. I piled my hair on top of my head and clipped it in place, and then I stuck the feathers in. I took a few selfies and sent them to Lizzie. She sent back about 50 heart emojis and thumbs up. I wrote back, "I love you."

"Love you too," she texted back. "See you Saturday the 31st at 7 PM for hair and makeup!" I threw the phone back on the bed and practiced greeting Will and Gabriel from the top of the sprawling staircase at Red House.

CHAPTER 13

Jane

Fête de la Maison Rouge Playlist
bit.ly/PartyAtRedHouse

THE DAYS AND WEEKS LEADING UP TO THE PARTY WENT faster than I thought they would. I tried my dress on every night, twirled around in front of the mirror, and practiced dancing with the weight of the fabric on my body. I spoke on the phone with Will almost every night for hours. He kept trying to get me to come over to pose for a painting, but I resisted. I didn't want to go to his house until my special day.

I worked the day of the party, so I would be busy and not obsessing over every detail of what I should say and how I should act. I left work at 6 and texted Lizzie, "On my way!"

"Text me when you're here!" she answered immediately. I spread the dress across the backseat of my car and kept moving my rearview mirror, so I could study it. It was the most lovely thing in the world, and I kept trying to convince myself I was worthy of it.

I rolled down my windows and blasted "Bulletproof" by La Roux. I pictured myself slowly stepping down the grand staircase in my gown and seeing Gabriel's harsh stare from the corner of my eye but purposefully ignoring him as I opened my fan and gently moved it about. I imagined him wearing a regal military uniform, just like Count Ferson would have worn to a ball with Marie Antoinette. In the scenario that I kept replaying in my mind, he wore black leather boots that went up to his knees, a bright red cape, and a shiny golden sword hung at his side. I held out my hand and let him kiss it, and then I moved past him like he was nothing. But when I walked down the hallway holding Will's hand, I turned to

see him again and our eyes locked. He gestured towards the staircase with his head, and I excused myself from Will and my guests
for a moment. Then I joined him behind the staircase where we
fucked like it was our last day on earth.

Before long I pulled up to the driveway of Will's home. I figured being three hours early, I would be the only one there, but the
place was buzzing with commotion. There were about 15 trucks
lined up by the front door and tons of people bringing in huge arrangements of red, orange, and black flowers, gigantic platters of
food, box after box of candles, giant swaths of black, white and gold
fabric, and huge speakers. Two men rolled in the biggest and most
well-stocked bar imaginable. The front doors were wide open, and
a group of women were frantically decorating the doors, threshold,
walkway, and bushes with sparkly spiders, wicker pumpkins, black
crows, fall foliage, lanterns, and little twinkling lights. I followed one
of the workers in and saw dozens of people decorating the staircase,
entryway, and hallways. I moved towards the hallway that led to
the ballroom, but Lizzie spotted me from the top of the staircase
and called out, "No way! You get your ass up here right this second,
birthday girl! You're going to spoil the surprises!"

"Wait!" I called out. "I need to get my dress from the car!"

She stomped her foot and yelled, "I don't trust you. I'll have
someone bring it up! Now get up here!"

I made a face that said, "Well, excuse me!" and began running up the stairs. She met me in the middle, and we embraced
and jumped up and down together. "This is fucking crazy, Lizzie!"
I said into her ear.

"I know! Come on!" She grabbed my hand and led me the
rest of the way, past Gabriel's and Will's bedrooms. I was partly
disappointed and partly relieved that their doors were closed. We
went past the bathroom with the gorgeous red tree, and she flung
open a door to a room I hadn't seen yet. She pulled me inside and
slammed the door behind me. It was a lovely, very girly bedroom.
Everything was a soft shade of pink and white. The wallpaper had
thin white and pink stripes with bursts of roses throughout. A big

picture window was framed with sheer white curtains tied back with bunches of pink silk roses. In the middle of the room was a huge white sleigh bed with elaborately carved roses all over the headboard. There was a ridiculous pile of pink and white pillows on the bed, and a crystal chandelier hung from a white medallion that had similar carvings to the bed.

"So this is where you're staying?" I asked.

"Yup!" she replied as she opened the double doors to the massive closet that had crazy piles of all her crap strewn about.

"It's adorable!" I exclaimed as I pointed to the overstuffed armchair covered in teddy bears and bunnies.

"A bit girly for my taste, but I can't complain. It's clean, beautiful, and the rent is free."

"Is this a guest room?"

"No, Will's sister's," she said as she set up a ton of makeup on a little table in front of a mirror.

"Guess she doesn't visit much," I offered as I sat down at the little desk and looked at the pencil sketches that were scattered about.

"She died," Lizzie said and paused for my reaction.

"Oh god!" My hand went to my chest. "That's horrible!"

"I know," Lizzie whispered. She opened the drawer of the makeup table, took out a picture and brought it over to me. It was a picture of an angelic little girl with shiny blonde hair blowing in the wind behind her. She was wearing a yellow sundress and laughing. I turned the photo over and "Emma Rose, summer at Red House" was scrawled on the back.

"She was beautiful. Do you know what happened?"

"She drowned," she replied as she took the picture back from me.

"That's fucking horrible. Do you know the story?"

"The only thing John told me was that it was a few years ago, she was nine years old, and she drowned. He seemed pretty uncomfortable, so I didn't press him for more details."

"Fuck. That's so sad."

"I know."

"Lizzie. How can you stay in this room? Isn't it…?"

"Creepy?" she offered.

"Well, yeah. And like... I don't know. Shouldn't this be a place that's left alone?"

"Will offered me the room. He said there are other rooms I could stay in, but he thinks this one suits me best. I told him that I know about his sister, and all he said was that he'd rather someone use the room then have it sit here collecting dust like a mausoleum."

"Wow."

"I know."

I wanted to change the subject immediately. Since Lizzie had been diagnosed with cancer, we never talked about death. It wasn't like we avoided the subject on purpose. I just sensed that she was preoccupied with it, and I understood why.

"Who did these sketches?" I asked, holding one up for her to see.

"Me!" she answered proudly.

"*Really?* Lizzie! These are *really* good!"

She smiled uncomfortably and said, "Ya think?" I shuffled through the rest of the pile.

"Umm, yes! I didn't know you could draw like this!"

"I didn't know either. I never really tried. My parents always made me feel like it was a waste of time. But I love it! When I'm drawing, hours go by like seconds. The other day I sat on the terrace and sketched for *six hours.* I had no idea how long I was out there until my stomach growled, and I realized I hadn't eaten anything since the day before!"

"You're a natural. If this is what you love, then keep doing it!"

"Gabriel and John have been teaching me. It's been... *amazing.*"

I have to admit, I felt a little jealous. I didn't know what Gabriel's feelings were for Lizzie, and I started to wonder if they had something going on.

"So, are you, like, romantically involved with any of the guys?"

She rolled her eyes at me and said, "Romantically involved? *Really?*"

"You know what I mean!"

"No, I'm not *romantically involved* with anyone... yet."

"Yet? Oh shit. Come on! Who is it?"

She walked over and sat on the bed facing me. "Don't act like you don't know," she said, looking down at her nails and avoiding eye contact.

"Gabriel?" I asked. She grinned and pursed her lips a bit. "Has anything happened between you?" I asked, afraid of the answer.

She began chewing her cuticles. "Not really."

"Not really?" I said sharply. "What does *that* mean?"

She kept looking down at her lap. "Nothing's happened. There's just been a few... moments."

"Moments?" She didn't answer, and I yelled, "Lizzie! Look at me!" Her head snapped up.

"Don't get all bent out of shape. I just mean... like... there's times when he's showing me how to draw, and he'll be holding my hand a certain way and the way he looks at me... I don't know. Maybe it's nothing. I mean why would a guy like *him* be into someone like *me*, right?" I sat down on the bed next to her.

"Lizzie, are you kidding me? You're brilliant and fun and funny, not to mention the fact that you're absolutely beautiful. A guy like him, or any other guy, would have to be brain damaged not to be interested in you." Her eyes looked red and a small tear fell.

"Then how come I've never had a boyfriend?" she said softly.

"Because you have standards, and no one has been good enough!" She gave me a slight smile, and I added, "Plus, I don't really let them get anywhere near you. So that's sort of a problem."

She laughed and replied, "That's true."

I wanted to tell her how he had come on to me several times, but I didn't want to crush her feelings. I was pretty sure she was aware of it anyway and choosing to ignore it.

"I'm sorry that I'm so overprotective. I just love you so much, and I don't want to see you get hurt."

"I know, and I love you for that. But isn't getting hurt part of being in love? If I never get hurt, that means I've never loved!"

I sighed. "Yeah, getting hurt is part of it. For sure. But I've been hurt, badly, and used and treated like trash. And you deserve so much more. If you get hurt, hopefully it's because it just didn't work out with a wonderful guy who truly cared for you. Not because you got used by some piece of shit who gets off on sleazy conquests."

"Gabriel's not a piece of shit, Jane."

There was a sharp knock on the door. I jumped up and grabbed my chest. I was on edge for some reason. Lizzie opened the door, and someone I didn't recognize was holding my gown. "Please hang it on the closet door," Lizzie ordered, and the woman quickly complied. Then Lizzie asked her to get us two glasses of champagne, and the woman responded, "Right away!" and scurried out.

"Getting rather adjusted to your new lifestyle I see!"

"Will hired her to help us get ready. I don't want to waste his money."

"Wow. Our very own lady-in-waiting! What else can I ask her to do? Brush my hair? Feed me? *Wipe my ass?*"

"Come on, Jane. Just chill the fuck out for once and enjoy it!" The woman knocked again and entered with two crystal champagne glasses and a bottle of Cristal.

"Shall I open it for you?" she asked.

"Yes, please do," Lizzie responded. "It's my dearest friend's birthday today." She leaned down and kissed me on the cheek with a smile. I mouthed "love you" as the woman popped the cork and poured our glasses.

"Happy birthday madam. Is there anything else I can get for you?"

My stomach growled so loud that we could all hear it. "I guess something to eat might be nice."

"Of course. What kind of food would you like?"

"Something sweet?"

"Right away!" The woman left, and we took our glasses and held them up.

"To you, Lizzie. And your enduring good health and happiness!" I exclaimed.

"Fuck *that*! To *you*, ladybug. And your endless love and friendship. *And* the wildest, outrageous, fucking *epic* birthday you will ever have!" I clinked her glass with mine and gulped the whole thing down. She refilled my glass and put her hands on my shoulders. "Makeup and hair time!" she announced.

"How exactly am I going to make my hair look like Marie Antoinette? Do you have any birds' nests and baby powder lying around?"

"I've got that all figured out." She opened the door and ushered in three very fabulous-looking men. "Jane, meet your glam squad! Dom, Drew, and Ash." They all had a ton of boxes, shopping bags, and luggage, and they were spreading the contents out on the bed.

"Wow! Will hired us a glam squad too? This is too much!"

"Actually, they're *my* birthday gift for you."

One of them whipped around and said, "Heyyyy! Happy birthday! I'm about to take you back a few centuries and up a few classes!" And with that he opened a box and pulled out a gigantic white-blonde wig. It was a fucking masterpiece. It had curls and braids all over, with golden pearls, sparkly butterflies, and bunches of pale pink roses. There was even a tiny white bird in a little nest peeking out from the side.

"Holy fuck! That's for me? Lizzie, how much did this cost? I can't accept all of this!"

"That shit was custom made, and I can't return it. So if you don't wear it, I *will!* And it doesn't go with my costume at all." My eyes lit up as I considered all of the literary characters she might have chosen for her costume. She was a huge Shakespeare nerd, so I expected Lady Macbeth or Juliet.

"How could I not have asked! What's your costume?"

She winked and said, "Be right back," before she disappeared into the closet. A few minutes later she came out wearing a flesh-colored body stocking. There was a beige thong underneath but no bra, and I could see her nipples quite clearly.

"Okay. There's your goodies. But where's the costume?"

She giggled and said, "This is it!"

I scrunched my eyebrows together. "I don't get it. You're a naked person?"

"Not *really* naked!" She turned to one of the makeup guys and asked for her wig. One of them handed her a ridiculously long auburn wig and she put it on her head and adjusted the strands to cover her chest. "See? It covers my boobs."

The guys slathered my face with foundation as I admitted, "I'm still confused. What are you supposed to be?"

"Come *on*, Jane! Use your head." She stood there with her hands on her hips, waiting for me to guess. Then she exclaimed, "Wait!" and ran into the closet. She came back with a fake horse head on a stick. "How about *now*?"

"Crazy naked lady on a horse?" I guessed.

The guys giggled, and Lizzie called out, "What the fuck are you even talking about? I'm Lady Godiva!"

"Ohhhhh! *Okay!* But how many people will get that?"

"I don't care. I think it's *badass*!"

"Totally!"

One of the makeup artists whispered, "Who is Lady Godiva? A drag queen?" I busted out laughing, and one of the other guys said, "Y'all don't know the story of Lady Godiva?"

"Does it have to do with chocolate?" he asked, and we all laughed.

"I don't think so. It was something about her defying her controlling husband, I think."

Lizzie jumped in. "Exactly. Her husband was a king who was unfairly taxing his people into terrible poverty. Godiva kept asking him to lower their taxes, and he said he would do it if she rode her horse naked through town. I'm sure he was joking, but she did it!"

"That's *definitely* badass!" I remarked. "Weird costume though."

She slapped me on the back and yelled, "Shut up! Do you think Gabriel will like it?"

"Unless he's gone blind in the last few hours, I'm sure he'll enjoy getting a glimpse of those tatas!"

She looked down and shrugged. "Not like there's much to see, unlike *some* people!"

"Oh, you got big ones?" the guy who was pinning my hair up asked. I was wearing a big t-shirt that hid my chest for the most part.

"I don't know. I guess," I said uncomfortably.

"They're perfect," Lizzie explained. "I've always been jealous of them." There was a soft knock on the door, and the assistant entered with a plate full of the most delicious-looking brownies.

"Will this do?" she asked.

"Perfect! Please put them right here," I said, pointing in front of me. I grabbed one of the brownies that were covered in caramel, marshmallows, and chocolate chips and shoved it into my mouth. "Lizzie, you gotta try one of these."

"I'm good."

I ate another brownie as the guys finished my makeup.

"So where's your mask?" I asked Lizzie.

"Shit."

"No mask, no entry!"

"I fucking live here. I don't give a shit!" There was another knock on the door. "Who is it?" Lizzie called out.

We heard, "It's Ed," on the other side of the door. She undid the latch and let him in. "You locked it?" he asked.

"I'm not letting anyone see us before the illusion is complete!"

As Ed came closer, I was awed by his costume. He was clearly dressed as the Phantom of the Opera, but there were feminine elements to his costume, like the bottom half of a ball gown and a rose in his hair on the opposite side of the mask. "The phantom is here!" I called out.

He smirked and responded, "*And* Christine!" He was letting me know that he was dressed as both characters.

"Very cool!" I responded.

"I can't wait to see you all done up, miss!"

"Well, you better go. This is the part you are definitely *not* supposed to see."

"Will wanted me to ask if you have any musical requests."

"Oh! Umm, that's a big question." I looked at Lizzie and said, "There's one song we both absolutely must hear." She came closer and at the same time we both called out, "Tainted Love!"

"You got it, ladies! If you think of anything else, let me know." Then he leaned close to my face and said, "You better save me a dance."

"Of course. You don't even have to ask."

"I don't want to have to compete with the hundreds of men who will be lined up to dance with you."

"Don't be ridiculous."

He pointed a finger directly at my face and said, "I mean it. Save me a dance!"

"You got it!" I called out, and I blew him a little kiss. He acted shocked and caught it in the air and gently pressed it to his lips.

"Magnifique!" he called out and promptly left the room.

I thought we'd be waiting around for hours after our hair and makeup were done, but mine took so long that it was almost 10 o'clock when the guys finally announced that I was finished. They made me promise not to look in the mirror until I had my dress on. I closed my eyes as they helped me step into my gown and zipped it up. At last, they allowed me to look.

I couldn't even believe the woman I saw reflected in the mirror was me. The hairdo was really heavy but so incredible, and I had about five pounds of makeup on. I looked positively regal. "Jane, you look fucking amazing!" Lizzie exclaimed.

"You do too!" I told her. "I'm worried the wig might fall off."

"As long as you don't turn upside down you should be fine. They put about 5,000 bobby pins in there. Ready?" she asked with a nervous energy.

"Hold on," I said as I leaned over and repositioned my boobs, so they were spilling over the top of the dress a bit more. "Shit. I just realized I don't have any shoes to wear. I can't wear my sneakers!"

"Lemme see what I have," she offered as she walked towards her closet.

"You're like two sizes smaller than me. I'll never be able to wear your shoes."

"Just wear your sneakers."

"You know what? I'll go barefoot."

"You sure?"

"Yes. I like the idea of feeling the dance floor under my feet."

She held her hand out and said, "Shall we?"

I gently placed my hand into hers and said, "We shall!" But as she put her hand on the doorknob, she hesitated and asked me what time it was.

"I'm not sure. Close to ten, I think." She went over to her bedside table and picked up her alarm clock.

"9:50," she stated. "We can't go yet."

"Why is that?"

"We can't be early. That is *so* not cool."

"Do we really care, Lizzie? How late do we have to be to maintain our coolness?" I was already feeling the weight of the hair and how hot it was going to get under the gown, and I was starting to feel irritable.

"I don't know, but we definitely cannot go down yet," she insisted.

"How about we watch from the window, and when enough people have arrived, we can make our big entrance."

"You can't see the front from my window, only the back."

My eyebrows went up. "We'll have to sneak into Gabriel's room then."

She smiled and opened the door just a bit and stuck her head out. "Let's go!" she whisper-yelled to me.

We tiptoed as quickly as we could down the hallway and into Gabriel's room and slammed the door and locked it. I looked around to make sure he wasn't there, but it was just the two of us. I had to stop myself from looking through his drawers and jumping onto his bed to smell his pillow. His room smelled so good that I didn't want to leave. I was immediately drawn to his desk where there was an open sketchbook amongst scraps of paper with bits of writing. The sketches in the book that were visible looked a lot like Lizzie.

I grabbed the first scrap of paper I saw and started reading.

Warmed by her hand and shadowed by her hair
As she leaned close and poured her heart through me,
eloquent throbs flow with the smooth dark stream of hair that
makes her face so fair,—
Sweet fluttering sheet, even of her breath aware,

Before I could finish reading, Lizzie ripped the paper out of my hand and placed it back on his desk. Then she rolled her eyes at me and dragged me over to the window. We stood behind the closed curtains and moved them over slightly to peek out of the window.

"What the fuck!" I called out, and Lizzie slapped me for being too loud. The huge U-shaped driveway was packed with cars going as far back as we could see. There were hundreds of them, bumper to bumper, and hordes of people were streaming through the front doors. They were all dressed in elaborate costumes with masks. "Who the fuck *are* these people?"

Lizzie looked as shocked as I was at the number of guests pouring into the house. "I don't think it matters when we go down, Lizzie." She nodded, and we walked back to the door. But before Lizzie could see, I grabbed the scrap of paper I was reading from his desk and stuck it into my cleavage. I was intrigued and wanted to read more. What I really wanted was that sketchbook, but it would have to wait.

We stood at the top of the staircase in awe of how the house had been transformed into a haunted mansion. The entire entrance was covered with what seemed like thousands of pillar candles, and it was otherwise dark. The constant flow of people continued as we heard the first few notes of The Black Keys' "Howlin' for You" come blasting into the room. We jumped into each other's arms with excitement. People danced and moved down the dark hallway towards the ballroom, and we quickly descended the stairs and followed them.

The hallway was lined with trees that had bare jagged branches covered in little twinkling lights. It was completely dark except for the lit candles that bordered the walls and the lights on the trees.

There were strands of crystals hanging down from the ceiling that shimmered in the candlelight.

At the end of the hallway was the bar I saw being rolled in earlier. There were two women dressed as evil, broken dolls who were serving drinks. We waited in line until we were handed a menu.

Before she even read the menu, Lizzie pointed to someone who was drinking purple liquid from a martini glass with smoke pouring out of it and exclaimed, "I'll have one of those!"

"One Witch's Brew!" the bartender said.

I turned to Lizzie and pointed to the last drink name. "Do you think?" I asked.

"I don't think. I *know* it's for you!"

I whipped around and said to the bartender, "I'll have a Lady Jane!"

She smiled and said, "You got it!" Then she handed Lizzie her smoking martini glass and put a large glass down onto the bar. She quickly poured different liquids in, and it took on an orangey-red hue. Then she dropped a lit match into the glass, and it went up in flames. "There you go!" she said as she slid the flaming glass towards me.

"I don't know whether or not to be insulted!" I yelled to Lizzie, so she could hear me over the music that was getting exponentially louder.

She yelled back, "Try it first!"

I blew out the flames and took a sip. "Sour… bitter… but somehow sweet!" I announced.

"Sounds like you!" Lizzie called back as she took a sip from her smoke-filled glass. "Mine is delicious!"

Someone called out, "There they are!" and we spun around to see a man dressed as a knight, helmet and all.

"Hi?" I said, not sure who I was looking at.

He took the helmet off, and it was Hunt. He held his elbows out and said, "Ladies! Allow me to be your escort?" We both curtsied and hooked arms with him. "You both look absolutely lovely!" he called out as he led us further down the hallway, and we pounded our drinks.

"Thanks, you make an excellent knight!"

"I'm not just *any* knight! I'm Saint George. He's like *the* knight. Slayed a dragon and everything!"

"That's awesome. Where's Annie?"

"Probably at the other bar. She was supposed to be dressed as Princess Sabra, the woman Saint George saved, but she came as Catwoman."

"There's another bar?" I asked as he led us into the dining room.

"The good stuff is at the bar in the ballroom," he informed us.

"Good stuff?" Lizzie asked.

"The *real* stuff! Not these girly drinks."

"I'm enjoying my girly drink very much, thank you!" I countered.

The massive dining table was covered in candelabras, huge floral arrangements, fake skulls, and platters of food. Lined up against the walls were tremendous coffins filled with ice and different kinds of beer. I pointed to them and asked, "Are those coffins real?"

Hunt shrugged and said, "Probably!" Then he turned back to the food. "Hungry?"

"This looks amazing!" I exclaimed, but I was too nervous and excited to eat. The closer I looked at the food, the more familiar it seemed. They had goat cheese crostini, vegetable spring rolls, butternut squash gnocchi, hummus, tabouli salad, falafel balls, and olives with pita bread. It looked delicious but a weird swirl of nausea rose up from my belly and I turned away.

Lizzie pulled me into the corner where a huge table of desserts was set up. There were apples dipped in white chocolate with sticky red blood dripping down, little cups of chocolate mousse with candy gravestones, and red velvet cupcakes with white frosting and shards of candy glass tinged with blood sticking out. "These are incredible!" I grabbed a shard of glass from one of the cupcakes and looked closely at it. Lizzie grabbed it from my hand and shoved it into her mouth.

"I hope that's not real glass," I warned.

"It's candy."

"Wait till you see the cake!" Hunt called out.

"Don't tell me! I want it to be a surprise. Where's Will?"

"This way."

We followed Hunt through the open doors to the ballroom, and he pointed towards the platform. The ballroom was quite dim, with the lights from the chandeliers turned down low. There were dark blue lights shining from various locations, which gave the room the most dreamy, surreal feeling. It was beautiful, but it made me feel a bit disoriented.

On the platform a band was playing a cool, modern version of "Paint it Black." I didn't recognize the drummer or one of the guitar players, but I could tell who the other guys were despite their costumes. The guy on keyboard was dressed like a pirate in all black, but based on his ridiculous height, I knew it was Will. The bass player was wearing a dragon costume, and I knew that John was the only one weird enough to wear that. Front and center on electric guitar was Gabriel, dressed in a tight black leather jacket and leather pants. His hood was pulled up, and he had black makeup smudged around his eyes. Under the jacket was a white t-shirt soaked in blood. It looked like he had a massive wound in his chest.

His voice was really powerful and soulful. He was also brilliant on guitar, and in that moment, I was probably more turned on than I had ever been in my life. They started playing Jack White's "Would You Fight for My Love," and he was singing into the same mic as a gorgeous girl. She was wearing a long, flowing white dress with a crown of wildflowers in her hair and a sheer piece of black fabric over her eyes. In the middle of her chest was a huge wound dripping with blood, just like Gabriel's. I suspected she was the one he had written about in the poem that was wedged into my cleavage.

"Who's the skank he's singing with?" I blurted out.

"Jane!" Lizzie scolded, but Hunt laughed.

"That's his sister, Christina."

My jealousy melted away for a moment, and I couldn't believe how good they sounded and how fucking gorgeous he looked. I imagined myself ripping off his jacket and pressing my chest into his. Then I realized something. "Wait. Is that the same Christina who Will dated?"

"Yup," Hunt answered. "Sore subject for him. Don't bring it up."

I watched as her perfect face emitted a totally angelic voice, and her sleek little body swayed back and forth. I came to the conclusion that I hated her guts, and I was going to make her jealous as fuck. The song ended, and I ran over to the platform and waved to Will. He immediately joined me on the dance floor. I jumped into his arms, and he spun me around. "You look absolutely bloody perfect Jane!"

"And you make a very handsome pirate!"

"I'm not just any pirate. Don't you recognize me?"

I made a face that showed my confusion. "Shit. I have no idea!"

The band continued without him, and he said into my ear, "Let me give you a hint! 'Life is pain, highness. Anyone who tells you otherwise is trying to sell you something!'"

I jumped up and yelled, "Westley!"

And he bowed and replied, "As you wish." I tried to hug him, but he was so fucking tall that I hugged his lower chest and stomach. He leaned his head down, so I could hear him. "I considered dressing as Count Fersen, but I didn't want to put myself in the friendzone!" I wasn't sure how to respond, so I didn't. I peeked around him to see if I was making Christina jealous, but she wasn't looking at us at all. Gabriel, however, was staring directly at us and looking rather angry while he sang "Fresh Blood" into the mic. I winked at him and turned back to Will. I could feel Gabriel's eyes on me, and the song was so hypnotic that I struggled to focus as I gripped Will's arm to steady myself.

"So, I noticed that the food seems rather familiar!" I called out, hoping he could hear me over the music, which seemed much louder than it had been just moments before. He pointed to his ear to show me that he couldn't hear, and then he gestured to a far corner where there were fewer people. I nodded and followed him there, and I briefly noticed that Lizzie was gone. Then I turned to face the stage, so I could get another glimpse of Gabriel singing.

"What was that?" Will called out while bending down to my level. I was jarred out of my reverie and had to think about what I was saying. However, I couldn't remember, so I changed the subject.

"Umm, who are all these people?"

"It's pretty much an open house."

"So a real ax murderer could be amongst us right now?" I joked as I turned away from the stage, so I could focus.

"Yes, I suppose. Are you worried you might lose your head?" He gave me a sly smile.

"I'll just make sure not to tell the people to eat cake!" I answered.

Christina began singing K. Flay's "Blood in the Cut," and her voice was flawless. I tried to swallow down a bitter pang of jealousy.

I was surrounded by the most talented people, and I couldn't help but think about my own lack of talent and purpose. How did I belong with them?

Will was looking at me so lovingly, desperately waiting for my next words. I tried to keep the conversation going. "I noticed that the food seemed familiar."

He grinned. "That's because I had The Witches' Cauldron cater the event. It seemed appropriate."

"That is fucking awesome, Will!"

"I'm glad you're enjoying your party, Jane."

"Is this really for *me*?"

"Technically it's my house, and technically I paid for everything, so if I say it's your party, *it's your fucking party*!" Since he was already bent down towards me, I leaned in and kissed him on the cheek.

"You are wonderful!" He turned his face towards mine and came in closer just as the music stopped.

I almost kissed him, but Gabriel announced into the mic, "This goes out to Jane," and they started playing a hard rock version of "Tainted Love."

Lizzie grabbed my hands and screamed, "It's our song!" as she forced me away from Will and onto the middle of the dance floor.

We were in heaven, dancing to a much cooler version of the song we sang all the time growing up. Gabriel sang with such emotion, it was moving. I wondered where his passion was coming from as Lizzie and I spun around and around. Towards the end of the song, Will approached me and held out his hand.

"Dance with us!" I yelled, ignoring his hand.

"I can't!" he yelled back.

"Sure you can! Get over here!"

He frowned, and when the song ended, he looked relieved. "I have something I'd like to show you."

Ed suddenly stuck his face between us. "So sorry to interrupt but Jane promised me a dance!" I smiled awkwardly, and Will looked pissed and threw his hands up.

"I'm yours after this. I promise!"

I took Ed's hands as "Possum Kingdom" filled the room. Will went to the bar and made himself a drink as Ed sang to me, and I rolled my eyes. "What!" he exclaimed.

"This song is so cheesy!" I yelled.

"Cheesy but so good!"

We sang and danced, and I kept trying not to look at Gabriel because I didn't want him to know I was thinking about him. But every time I caught a glimpse, he was already looking at me while he sang. I loved knowing he was watching me dance. I felt sexy as hell. As the song ended, Ed took my face and kissed me on the mouth. It felt like more than a friendly kiss.

"What was *that* for?"

"I've just wanted to do that for a long time." I felt myself blush, and he added, "You do know how fucking beautiful you are, don't you?" I pushed him playfully and told him to stop.

"If you ever get bored playing with these boys, let me know."

"Wait a second. I thought you had a thing for Gabriel!"

"I do." I didn't reply, and he added, "Not everything is so black and white, Lady Jane," then he sauntered away.

A burst of dizziness rattled me. I spun around and moved right into Gabriel. I shot backward, and he smiled.

"Jane, this is my sister Christina." I gave her daggers with my eyes, and she put her hand out for me to shake.

"Hey, it's so nice to meet you! I've heard a lot of great things about you," she exclaimed.

I ignored her hand. "Really? I've never heard of *you*." She awkwardly retracted her hand and mouthed "okay" to herself.

"So what are you guys supposed to be?" I asked.

"Francesca and Paolo Remini," Gabriel said, as though I would know who they were.

"And they are…?"

"Characters from Dante's *Inferno*."

"Have you read it?" Christina asked.

"No, but I think I know the gist. Hellfire, suffering, burning. Stuff like that."

"No, no! There is so much more to it than that! Take Paolo and Francesca for example. They're based on real people."

"And what happened to them? Something violent I'm guessing."

Gabriel chimed in. "He was her brother-in-law. They had a secret affair for ten years. When her husband caught them in the act, he put a sword right through both of their hearts at the same time."

"That's pretty fucked up. Gabriel, why are you so obsessed with death?"

"It's his namesake," Christina announced.

"Huh?"

"The archangel Gabriel was the angel of death."

I paused before answering. "It's kind of weird that you guys are related and pretending to be lovers. Is there any truth behind that?"

Christina turned to Gabriel with wide eyes. "Yeah, I think I'm gonna go get another drink. It was nice meeting you, Jane."

"Uh-huh," I muttered as I walked away. I felt nauseous again as "Dead Souls" by Nine Inch Nails began to play, and I wondered if maybe I had gotten food poisoning. Gabriel took my hand and spun me towards him.

"I have to go!" I yelled. He yanked me harder until we were nose to nose.

"Dance with me."

I leaned closer to his ear. "Will's waiting for me. I have to go." I tried to escape his grip again, but he held me tightly.

"Will can wait."

I looked back to the corner, and Will was talking to Lizzie but was watching me over her shoulder. I didn't want to make him jealous, but I figured this was a good opportunity to question Gabriel about Lizzie.

I put my hands on his shoulders and made space between us as we both started swaying.

"So what are your intentions with Lizzie?"

A look of confusion came over his face. "I don't have any." I rolled my eyes as he moved me closer.

"You aren't interested in her at *all*?" He spun me out at arm's length and then quickly spun me directly back into his body.

"No. I'm not interested in her at all." He gave me a burning look like he was about to devour me.

"Well, I don't think she knows that," I said as I pushed him away from me again.

"Why are we talking about Lizzie?" he asked as his face got closer to mine.

"Because she's in love with you."

He looked genuinely surprised. "Well, I'm not in love with her. I'm in love with someone else." He pressed his lips against mine, and I instantly became inflamed with need. My body wanted nothing more than to completely succumb to him and let him do anything and everything he wanted. My mind, however, was completely focused on not hurting the feelings of Lizzie and Will, who were watching us intently. I hated having to push him away, but I did.

I shoved him and said, "Don't."

"You get off on rejecting me, don't you?"

"Umm, no. I wouldn't go that far."

He bent down, put his nose to mine, and said, "*I* would."

The music cut off, and Will spoke into the mic. "Alright, mates. The haunted maze is now open!" I whipped around, and he was staring right at us, looking amused that he interrupted our little exchange.

"A haunted maze?" I called out as I ran to Lizzie and took her hand. We followed the crowd down the hallway, into the solarium, and onto the patio. There were what must have been thousands of white pillar candles melting into the concrete all along the edges of the patio, on top of the stone fence, and down the staircase that led to the garden trail. As we moved through the cool grass to the opening of the maze, Lizzie called out, "It's fucking freezing out here!"

"Well, you're literally wearing nothing. Go inside and get a sweatshirt!"

"Okay, I'll see you in there!" She pushed against the crowd to get back in the house. My shoulders were a bit cold but otherwise,

I was very warm under my giant wig and the several pounds of fabric of my gown.

On either side of the maze door were huge fire pits with a big pile of skulls in them. The flames were shooting up to the top of the maze walls. A rush of uncomfortable feelings ran through me as I entered the doorway. It was a hellish mixture of nausea, vertigo, and terror. I stopped moving, which caused everyone behind me to crash into each other.

"Move!" the guy behind me yelled.

"Get the fuck out of the way!" someone else shouted, and then I heard, "What's the hold-up?"

I turned around to try to escape, but with so many people pushing against each other, I was swept into the maze amongst a group of wild drunks.

It was utterly black inside, and the ground felt like it was rising up to my face. I stopped moving again, and bodies kept speeding by, forcing me further and further into the complicated depths of the maze.

I turned a corner to get away from the surge of people, and I found myself alone in the blackness. The vertigo became too much to bear. I slid down the wall and pressed my cheek into the damp, cold grass. With my eyes closed, I saw an image of Lizzie covered in strips of hardening plaster. She looked like an old, weathered statue.

A thick crimson drop of paint fell from the corner of her eye, leaving a red streak down her face as she opened her mouth and let out a high pitched wail. Bits of plaster crumbled from the corners of her mouth, and I could see a tiny spider sitting in the middle of her chalky tongue. It crept from her mouth to her neck, and then into a large gash in her hard chest cavity. Red and black paint gushed from the wound, and she shrieked so sharply, I had to cover my ears.

"Lizzie, *please*!" I called out into the inky night, my eyes still clamped shut. Her powdery fingers slid between her legs as watery red liquid gushed down her thighs. Then her lips parted, and hordes of tiny black spiders scurried out of her face. My eyes opened abruptly as a massive wave of sickness crashed over me. Gradually sitting up, I tried to concentrate on my breathing. A girl dressed as Little Red Riding Hood sat down next to me in the grass.

"Hey, come this way!" she beckoned as she snatched my arm and tried to launch me off the ground.

"I can't," I argued. She released my arm, and I slammed back down on the grass. Then she leaned over me, and a monstrous, gaping wound that spanned the entirety of her face and neck was right in my line of view. She looked like she had been attacked by a wolf.

"Cool costume," I mumbled.

"*What* costume?" she asked as the whites of her eyes filled with a swirl of dark matter. I gasped, and she cackled loudly and vanished into the dark. An intense chill crept across my shoulders, and I regretted not going back into the house for a jacket.

"Are you cold?" a delicate female voice asked. I cloaked my shoulders with my arms and hands as the shivering became more extreme. Looking left and right, I couldn't figure out where the voice was coming from, but there was a faint orange light a few feet away. "It's warmer over here," the friendly voice stated, and a girl in a shimmery royal blue gown stepped in front of the orange glow. I edged closer to her to feel the warmth of the fire, and she turned to me with a wicked grin. One shoulder and arm were engulfed in flames, but she didn't seem to mind at all. She popped a cigarette between her lips and leaned down to the flame on her body to light it. She inhaled deeply and asked, "Cigarette?"

I whipped around and launched myself forward as my face smashed into someone's forehead. His hand flew up to his head as black ooze seeped from a jagged crack in his forehead. Removing his hand, he looked down at the blackness on his palm as a beam of white light burst through his skull. The light swirled into a spiral galaxy above him as he wrapped one hand around my neck.

"Watch where you're *fucking* going!" he blared into me. I screeched, and he unclasped my neck and left me there. My belly churned again, and I tried to ignore it as a mass of people rushed by. I kept hearing ticking noises, like a clock was strapped to my ear, and the words of the Nine Inch Nails song I had danced to with Gabriel kept reverberating in my brain.

"They keep calling me. They keep calling me. They keep calling me. Tick. Tick. Tick."

I felt bile rise in my throat and slouched forward to heave, but nothing came out. "Are you alright?" a familiar voice asked. I jerked my head back, and Gabriel was standing in front of me, a look of concern on his face.

"I don't know," I whispered, but he didn't seem to hear me. He kept asking me over and over if I was alright. "Stop asking me that!" I yelled.

He replied, "Asking *what*?" Then he held my face in his warm hands and stared aggressively into my eyes.

"In the end, it's only us, floating through dimensions," he said softly. "With us go translucent bits of memory, glowing projections of people and places we've loved, who carved themselves into our core." Then he kissed me so fiercely, I stumbled backward. Catching me with his open hand on the back of my head, he propelled me back into his lips. His tongue pushed into my mouth, and I felt nausea rise up again. I shoved him off as aggressively as I could.

"Stop! I feel sick. I need to sit down!"

"There's no time. You'll be in the ether in just a moment, where you can sit for all eternity!"

He had a crazed, wild look in his eyes as he rammed his hips into mine, and his hands tried to squeeze down into my corset. I howled as I dug my nails into his face. He muttered "fucking bitch" as he looked me up and down with rage and disgust. When my eyes met his, I realized that it wasn't Gabriel at all, but a man I didn't know. His face was painted like the grim reaper, with slim black lines on his lips that made it look like his mouth was sewn shut, and a cavernous black hole where his nose should be.

I swiped at my mouth and saw black and white makeup on my hand. Leaning over, vomit poured from my mouth onto his shiny black boots, and he ran off into the night.

Swaying back and forth with my head down, I moaned as I felt a presence behind me. A girl dressed as a nun crouched down. She had a pretty face and kind eyes. "You should sit," she said gently, and she took my hand and helped me to the floor. She sat down next to me and pulled a small floral teacup from her robe. "Something to drink?" she asked. I nodded my head, desperate for water. She handed me the empty teacup and held a knife up to her arm. "Sometimes the light leaks through me," she whispered as she dragged the blade across her outstretched arm. Thick, black blood seeped down, and she held the wound over the cup, filling it to the top.

"I can't drink this," I told her.

She shushed me and said, "Look closer." I peered into the cup and tiny glowing stars were floating in her blood. When they collided, I heard a faint sound of chimes.

"So beautiful," I murmured.

She whispered into my ear, "You don't walk into heaven, you swim."

Then she took her blade and sliced through the grass, leaving a trail of light behind. The ground started to shake, and the earth opened up around the crack of light. I should have been terrified, as an intense gravitational force pulled my body towards the center of the crack, but I felt strangely calm like I was going home. Thick, warm liquid engulfed me as the same glowing stars I saw in the teacup floated by. I looked up, and the nun was lying on the ground looking down at me. "You're swimming in the soul of the earth," she said with a warm smile.

"Why is this happening?" I asked.

"You're dying!"

Panic set in, and I kept trying to grasp the edge and pull myself out. Each time I tried to launch myself from the hole, the ground would move, and I would lose my grip. I closed my eyes and called out, "This isn't real!" and when I opened them again, I was back in the cool grass by myself.

I slowly stood up and inched along the wall, dragging my hands across the rough bricks to center myself. I could hear my heart beating so loudly that it was almost deafening. As I tried to escape the maze, an onslaught of terrifying images moved past me.

A woman with no eyes or nose and a dead baby in her arms reached out and cried for my help. A man had a distorted, rotten pumpkin for a head with huge black fangs. A skeleton climbed out of a hole in the ground and crept towards me while cackling. I kept moving around corners, trying to exit what seemed like a never-ending nightmare. At one point, I stopped to vomit again, and when I picked my head up, a man completely covered in blood revved up a chainsaw near my face. Shoving past him, I ran faster than I ever have. My chest was on fire, and my feet were throbbing with pain.

Finally, I saw a light in the distance and felt immense relief when I realized I was close to the entrance of the maze. As I got closer, I felt a sharp pain in my foot. I tried to walk on it but that made the pain much worse, and I collapsed onto the ground. The night sky went in and out of focus, and my foot hurt so badly that I squeezed my eyes shut and prayed I would wake up in my bed.

I heard Gabriel's voice, and I saw him dive onto the ground next to me.

"Jane! What's wrong?"

"My foot," I murmured, lethargically moving my head in his direction.

He moved the fabric of my dress aside and held my foot up to examine it. Then he gently put it back down and took my hand.

"You have a huge piece of glass in your foot. Someone must have dropped a beer bottle. I'm going to carry you inside." He swept me off the ground and carried me out of the maze and through the garden path towards the patio. I hung my head back and closed my eyes.

"Jane, are you feeling okay? Talk to me!"

"I don't want to be carried," I mumbled, my head swaying back and forth. "I want to lie down."

"We need to get you inside and clean up your foot. You can lie down then. Try to stay awake, okay?" My body felt like a massive stone slab was pressing me down.

"I'm too heavy. It's because I'm dying," I told him.

"Jane, you're not dying. Look at me." I had to try a few times to pick up my head. Finally, I held my head straight and opened my eyes. We were nose to nose. Even though I felt nauseous, dizzy, disoriented, and was in immense pain, I felt completely safe and at ease, which caused me to smile brightly.

"Hi," he said very sweetly in response to my smile. "We're going up the stairs now. We're almost inside."

I pulled his hood off, and his hair was all disheveled in that way that made him look that much sexier. I leaned in and gently kissed his ear. His face lit up but he tried to keep a serious expression. I kissed his neck and inhaled his delicious scent. "You smell so good."

He tried not to react as I kissed the side of his mouth. "You're killing me, babe," he confided as he flung the kitchen door open and brought me inside. Will was standing by the island talking to Christina, and he seemed irritated. When he saw me in Gabriel's arms, he immediately tried to take me from him.

"What happened to her? What's going on?"

"She stepped on a piece of glass. It's fine. I've got it."

"Put her on the counter!" Will ordered.

"Why? I was just going to put her on the couch."

"The lighting here is best!"

Gabriel looked annoyed but didn't respond. He turned around and gently placed me onto the island in the middle of the kitchen. He got on his knees as Will scrambled around the kitchen gathering supplies. Gabriel held up my foot and examined it as his sister knelt down beside him.

"You should go away," I told her, my head bobbing around as I gazed down at them.

"Why?" she asked.

"Because I don't like you." I was so amused with my own comment that I cackled in her face. She and Gabriel exchanged a look, and she quickly left the room.

"It should come out easily," Gabriel said as he grasped the huge shard of glass and yanked it out. I cried out in pain and heard him mutter "shit" to himself.

"What?" I yelled as I tried to move all the fabric of my dress over, so I could see. I caught a glimpse of the blood that was all over the floor, and a huge surge of dizziness came over me. "I'm definitely dying!" I announced.

Will put all kinds of instruments on the counter next to me and put gloves on when he saw the blood.

"Gabriel! Did you pull it out?"

"Yes. Give me the alcohol."

"Are you fucking daft? She needs stitches! Did you even wash your hands?" Will kneeled down in front of me and held up my foot.

"Her foot is filthy. This is going to get infected!"

"She doesn't need stitches. I have surgical glue!"

"Well, get it!"

Gabriel ran out of the kitchen, and I murmured, "They keep calling me," over and over.

Will looked up at me with concern. "Who is calling you?"

"The demon lady with the dead baby, and the nun who made me swim in the soul of the earth, and the Grim Reaper who was Gabriel. He kissed me, but then he wasn't Gabriel. I think they're calling me to the other side."

He looked worried. "Jane, you look very pale. I think you need to lie down." I sighed and slowly fell back onto the counter. Gabriel came in with the glue and knelt down beside Will.

"I think we need to get her to the emergency room," Will stated. "I'm going to wrap her foot as tightly as I can. Then I'll pull the car around the back."

Gabriel sighed. "She doesn't need stitches, Will. I've had much deeper cuts than this and-"

"You're not a bloody doctor!"

"Neither are you. Use the fucking glue."

Lizzie entered the kitchen and screamed out, "What the fuck happened? What's all this blood from?" She stood beside me and stroked my hair. I dropped my head to the side, and she asked if I was okay.

"I'm going to throw up again."

"*Again?* You threw up?"

"Help me up, Lizzie. I think I'm dying." She pulled me up and brought a small trash can over. I heaved a few times, but nothing came out. She rubbed my back lovingly, and I turned to her with my eyes closed.

"Is this what it's like when you're dead? Because I think I died, but this isn't at all what I thought it would be like."

"Umm, guys? She's acting really weird."

"I'm so fucking thirsty!" I announced.

"Get her some water!"

Gabriel went to the fridge and came back with a bottle of water. He opened it and handed it to me. I tried to drink it, but I just poured it down my face. "My mouth doesn't work anymore," I said matter-of-factly. He looked confused, and Lizzie quickly found a straw. I sucked down the entire bottle like I hadn't had water in days.

"More," I panted. I felt Will doing all kinds of things to my foot as Gabriel retrieved another bottle of water from the fridge and brought it to me.

"Wait a second," Gabriel thought out loud. "Umm, Jane. Did you eat anything today?"

Lizzie answered for me. "She only had a few brownies."

"Oh, fuck," Gabriel blurted out.

"What!" Will demanded as he wrapped my foot with gauze.

"I think she ate my hash brownies."

"Are you fucking kidding me, Gabriel?"

"Lizzie, how many did she have?" Gabriel asked.

"Two, I think."

"Two whole brownies? Fuck. That's a lot. I usually only eat a fourth."

"That's just fucking great!" Will announced. "How could you let this happen?"

"She'll be fine. It's not like she's going to die!"

"Gabriel, just go. Go back to the party."

"Will, it's not his fault," Lizzie tried to intervene.

"Of course it's his fault! How could he just leave those out without a label? He does shit like this all the time because he's fucking irresponsible!"

"I didn't mean to-"

"Just go!" I called out, and everyone got quiet. Gabriel froze, and I pointed directly at him. "This is *your* fault. I want Will to take care of me. *Go.*"

He instantly left the room. I leaned over the counter and vomited out most of the water. Then I slammed my head back onto the counter and closed my eyes again.

CHAPTER 14

GABRIEL

"War Paint"—Boy Destroy

S HE CHOSE WILL. SHE LITERALLY TOLD ME SHE WANTED WILL and not me. I lost my chance. I wasn't really angry at him, more at myself. I needed to forget about her for the night. I stomped back down the hall where I saw a bunch of guys doing bumps of coke, and I shoved my way in and did two. Then I went back into the ballroom and grabbed Will's five thousand dollar bottle of Japanese whiskey off the top shelf of the bar. If he got to have my girl, I got to have his fucking whiskey.

It took me the entire walk from the bar to the fucking doors to get the bottle open. Finally, I took a huge swig. Annie was standing by the doors dressed as Catwoman, and she grabbed my hand and pulled me towards her. She whispered into my ear that I looked hot, and she wanted to take me upstairs.

"Hunt is my best friend, you fucking whore!" I yelled as I shoved her away. Then I kicked the doors open and took another huge gulp of the disgusting liquid as I remembered how much I hated whiskey.

Standing by the staircase was Alexa, with her long, red hair hanging over her bulging cleavage. She was dressed as a sexy nurse, and she looked like a fucking hooker. It wasn't even sexy. Jane was sexy. Alexa was cheap. She gave me a smirk and sauntered over in her shiny spiked heels. "What's that?" I asked, pointing to the mask in her hand. She proudly held out a gigantic gas mask.

"Why the fuck would a nurse wear a gas mask?" I spat at her and gulped down a huge swig of whiskey.

"Maybe I work at a dentist's office."

"That's a WWI gas mask, not a dental mask, you fucking moron!" I barked as I chugged more of Will's disgusting drink.

"What's your fucking problem, Gabriel?"

I turned away and went right into the bathroom and locked the door. Staring at myself in the yellow glow of the candlelight, I couldn't figure out what the fuck my problem was. Since when did I let a fucking girl get in my head like that? I watched myself chug more whiskey in the mirror, and I spit it at my reflection and yelled, "Get your shit together!"

I needed to calm the fuck down. I considered taking Alexa upstairs, but I'd need a lot more whiskey for that. There was a gentle knock on the door, and a meek voice said, "Is anyone in there?" I opened the door, and Lizzie was standing there holding a red cup and swaying back and forth a bit. I grabbed her wrist, yanked her into the bathroom, and locked the door again. I immediately started kissing her and stuck my tongue into her mouth. She dropped her cup and tried to pull away to look for it, but I wouldn't let her. I kept kissing her, but she wasn't very receptive. She'd been on my dick since the day I met her, and now she had me and wasn't even into it.

I stepped back, took her face into my hands, and looked deeply into her eyes.

"Tell me what you want."

She hesitated and then said, "You."

There was almost a question mark at the end of the word, but I took it as a green light. She'd asked me more than once to take her virginity, but I refused because I didn't want to ruin my chance with Jane. It didn't fucking matter anymore, and I was gonna give her what she wanted.

I couldn't figure out what she was wearing and how to get it off. I tried picking it up over her head, but it was nylon and slid through my hands. I tried pulling it down, but that didn't work either. Finally, I grabbed the fabric with both fists and ripped it all the way down until she was standing there naked except for her underwear. She immediately tried to cover her scar with her hands, but I gently moved them away.

"You're fucking beautiful," I stated, and I wasn't lying. She was like a porcelain doll with a delicate crack in the middle. She looked extremely uncomfortable standing there, so I grabbed her by the ass and pulled her towards me. "Come here."

I kissed her mouth and neck and sucked on her earlobe. That usually drives girls crazy, but she had no reaction. I gently licked one of her nipples, and when I looked up at her face, she looked terrified. I stood back up and asked, "Do you still want to?"

"Yes. Don't stop."

I was pretty fucking drunk by that point, so I did as she asked. I took her down onto the floor, ripped her panties off, and kissed her all over her body. She didn't move or react at all. I pulled my shirt off and unzipped my pants. "Ready?"

She nodded and without thinking too much about it, I entered her, and she gasped. "Should I stop?" I asked, as any guy who's not a total piece of shit is supposed to do.

"Don't stop," she said, though she sounded unsure. I pulled out halfway and went back in, trying not to hurt her too much. There was no reaction. It was like fucking a doll. I grabbed her breast, and she looked bewildered and between her lack of reciprocation and the whiskey, I started to go limp and froze inside her. She picked her head up off the floor and said, "Why'd you stop?"

"Sorry. I didn't think you were into it," I admitted.

"I am!" she cried with her first show of emotion.

I tried to keep going, but it wasn't happening. I closed my eyes and pictured Jane in that dress with her tits pushed together, and I immediately got hard. I forgot where I was and what was happening and just thought about Jane. I thought about her pulling her wet clothes off by the lake, straddling me in my car, and tying me to my fucking bed. I pictured her climbing on top of me and riding me with all that passion and fire that flares behind her eyes. I grabbed her ass and began fucking her like I knew she wanted to be fucked. I pushed her knees up to her shoulders and went as deep as I could. She cried out. "Is that how you want it?" I asked.

I rubbed her clit while I fucked her with everything I had. I whispered into her ear, "Fuck, Jane!" as my cum shot far inside her. I pulled out and opened my eyes, and Lizzie was lying on the floor with a look of horror on her face. Tears streamed from the corners of her eyes, and I knew I had just made a huge mistake.

"Fuck! I'm so sorry! Are you okay?" She turned her head to the side to avoid looking at me. "Fuck, Lizzie. Are you alright? I'm sorry. I got a little carried away. Look at me, please." She curled up into a fetal position and shook her head. "Please put this towel on and come upstairs with me, so I can find you some clothes."

She kept shaking her head and crying. I draped the towel over her, scooped her up, and brought her upstairs. She kept crying, and I didn't know how to calm her down. I gently placed her on the bed and pulled the blanket up to her chin. Then I laid down next to her and put my arms around her. "I'm so sorry," I whispered. She was so pale and delicate, and I felt horrible. "It shouldn't have been like that." She was quiet for a while, and the crying subsided.

Then she whispered, "You called me Jane." I didn't know how to respond, so I gently shushed her and rubbed her back over the blanket until we both fell asleep.

I woke up about an hour later, and the bed was empty. I changed into jeans and a t-shirt, grabbed my cigarettes, half a joint, and a lighter off my desk, and went into the hallway. I noticed a faint light coming from Lizzie's bedroom. I walked over and saw her sitting on the terrace outside her window. She was hugging her knees to her chest and staring out at the night sky.

"Hey," I said lightly. She looked up at me but didn't react or say anything. "Anyone sitting here?" I gestured to the empty seat next to her, and she shook her head. "May I?" She nodded yes without looking at me.

I sat down, lit the joint, and took a long, deep drag. Then I held it out to her. She turned to me and pulled her shirt down to reveal her scar. "Oh, fuck," I responded. "Sorry." I took another hit and blew it towards the stars.

"You know what?" she said. "Fuck it." And she held her hand out for me to give her the joint.

"You sure?" I asked. She nodded yes, and I passed it to her. She took three deep hits and held it in, and then she blew it out and started coughing like a maniac and turned a bit purple. I leaned over and took the joint from her hand. "That's probably enough." I put it in my mouth and went inside to get a glass of water from the bathroom.

I held out the glass for her. She smiled, so I sat back down beside her. We were both silent for a while as I finished the joint, and she drank the water. It wasn't awkward. It was actually kind of peaceful. I began to feel more relaxed. "So, do you want to talk about it?"

She shrugged her shoulders. "What is there to talk about?"

"That probably wasn't how you pictured it would be, huh?"

Without looking at me, she said, "Is it ever?"

I laughed and replied, "No. *Never*."

She finally turned to me. "What was your first time like?"

I hesitated. "Eh, not the best story. I was 14 and obsessed with getting it over with, so I found a girl online who was willing and had my brother drop me off at her house. It lasted about two minutes, and then I left. Never saw her again. I'm sure she was pretty disappointed."

She looked disgusted and asked, "Do you wish it would have been with someone you loved?"

"No. But I wish it was with someone I knew or cared about in the least." She turned from me and continued staring out at the sky. "Do you regret it?" I asked.

She paused and answered, "No. I just-"

"Hoped it would be different."

"Yeah."

"I'm sorry. I really am. I was drunk and angry, and it had nothing to do with you."

She was silent again. Then she said, "She's getting to you, huh?"

I went through five different possible replies in my head and went with, "Who?"

She looked intensely into my eyes. "*Really?* You kinda called her name out while you were fucking me, remember?"

"Right." I shoved a cigarette into my mouth and lit it. I blew the smoke out of my nostrils as I admitted, "She's driving me fucking insane, and I don't even understand how or why."

She smiled warmly. "She has a way of doing that."

"Does she just like to play games?"

"Yes and no. She definitely likes to lead guys on, but it's usually the ones she thinks are shitheads. She doesn't intentionally try to hurt anyone… I don't think."

"She definitely thinks I'm a shithead," I admitted.

"Yup. But I think you've gotten to her too."

"What makes you say that?" I asked, eager for information that might help my cause.

"I just know her. She can try to pretend she doesn't give a shit about you all she wants. But I can tell she's intrigued by you. You boil her blood, and that wouldn't happen if she didn't think there was more to you than just a cute guy who's trying to get in her pants."

"So what is it about me that gets her so worked up?" I lit another cigarette and hoped the smoke wasn't reaching her.

"I think she sees that there's a lot more to you, but she's terrified of being hurt or taken advantage of, so she keeps her defenses turned way up."

"*Way* the fuck up."

"Don't tell me you aren't having fun though!"

"Fun. Frustrating, humiliating, *infuriating fun.*"

"*Sexy* fun."

She was right. The games Jane played *were* fun. I liked the torture she was putting me through. But it had to lead somewhere. I couldn't live like this forever. I had to win her over somehow, and Lizzie was helping me figure out how.

"So, maybe I shouldn't be asking this after what happened between us but-"

"You want my advice?"

"*Please.*"

"Be honest. Be real. Be yourself. And don't stop fighting to break down her walls. Pursue her heart relentlessly. You'll break through somehow. The two of you are so much alike."

"I hope that's a good thing."

She shrugged and added, "One more thing. And this part is essential. Leave sex out of it as long as you can. That's how you'll gain her trust." I was quiet, and she asked, "Is that even possible for you?"

I scoffed. "Of course. I'm not an animal." She gave me a knowing look and I added, "It'll be hard. But I can do it."

"And Gabriel. If you hurt her, I'll rip your fucking heart out and eat it."

I stood up, kissed her gently on the cheek, and whispered, "Thank you." She gave me a half-smile and looked down at her feet.

"You're an angel, Lizzie. Truly."

"Not anymore, thanks to you. You defiled me, remember?"

"Shit. I really am sorry about that."

"I know, Gabriel. I know."

CHAPTER 15

Jane

"Heartlines"—Florence and the Machine

I OPENED MY EYES, AND I WAS IN A ROOM I DIDN'T RECOGNIZE. The walls were a light yellow color with hand-painted ivy leaves bordering the ceiling. I was sprawled out on a satiny chaise lounge. I tried to lift my head, and I heard, "How do you feel?" Rolling my head to the side, I saw Will sitting in an armchair across from me. There was a small table between us that was filled with food and several bottles of water.

"Where are we?" I mumbled.

"A sitting room. How are you?"

"Dizzy. Nauseous."

"I know you're nauseous, but you really need to eat something." I slowly sat up, and he said, "Easy. Go slow."

My head swayed a bit from the weight of the wig. "I really want to get this thing off my head."

"Sure." He sat down next to me and gently tugged on my wig. "How exactly does this come off?" I closed my eyes and dropped my head back.

"There's like a million pins. You have to pull them out."

"Right. Tell me if I hurt you." He started to locate the bobby pins and remove them. "I can't believe how many bloody pins are in your hair."

I smiled but didn't open my eyes. Finally, the wig felt loose, and I pulled it off. "Oh god, that feels so much better."

"I'll bet. This thing is a true work of art, but I'm not sure it belongs on a human head." I combed my hair with my fingers and asked for water. He handed me an open bottle and urged me to eat again.

"I'm just so nauseous."

"We'll start slowly. How about a strawberry?"

"Okay." He handed me a strawberry, and I bit into it with my eyes closed.

"How's that?"

"It's nice."

"Would you like another?"

"What else is there?" I opened my eyes and looked over the food selection. "No cake?"

"If you're in the mood for cake, you are going to be very happy." He left the room and stuck his head in a few minutes later.

"Close your eyes."

"They're already closed."

"Okay, don't open them."

A few seconds later, he told me to open my eyes. The lights were off, but the room was dimly lit by the dozen or so sparklers that protruded from a ridiculously enormous cake. It was light pink, trimmed with golden bows and drapes, and was probably about as tall as I am. My mouth hung open.

"It's beautiful!"

"Happy birthday, Jane."

"Help me up, so I can blow out my candles!"

He came over and helped me onto my feet. I started to walk towards the cake, but I almost collapsed when I stepped on my injured foot. "Don't walk! Stay right there!" He wheeled the cake directly in front of me and held my hand as I blew out the candles. Suddenly, we were in the dark, and I leaned in and kissed him on the cheek.

"Thank you for this. For everything." He turned his head and kissed me gently on the mouth, and I kissed him back.

I expected the kiss to deepen, but he pulled away and said, "Let me get the lights."

He returned and cut a huge piece of cake, placed it on a plate, and handed it to me. "It's such a shame to see you cut into something so beautiful! Forks?"

"Shit. Be right back."

"No, it's fine. Look!" I lifted the giant piece of cake and took a huge bite. "Strawberry shortcake! My favorite! Aren't you going to have some?"

"Sure." He cut himself a slice and sat next to me.

"Here. Let me," I said as I took his cake off the plate and mashed it onto his closed mouth. He just sat there covered in whipped cream with no expression. "Sorry! I'm still pretty out of it."

"That's quite alright. Allow me to feed you as well." Before I could register what was happening, he took my slice of cake, slammed it onto my cheek, and smiled. My mouth hung open in shock.

"Will!" I yelled. "Come on!"

"Total accident. I think I may have had too much whiskey," he said with a giggle.

"Uh-huh!" I pretended like I was going to eat my piece in a normal fashion, but then I lunged at the giant cake in front of me, grabbed two handfuls, and mashed them onto both sides of his face.

He swiped a bit of cream off his face with his tongue. "Mmm. Buttercream." Next, he took his plate of cake and pressed it into the side of my face. "I hear buttercream is quite moisturizing," he told me.

I wiped the cream out of my eye and whispered, "You. Are. Dead." Then I jumped onto the cake and grabbed as much of it as I could with my open arms and launched myself at him. He fell back and caught me as I landed on top of him, and we were both covered in cake and laughing so hard. There was a pause, and then we kissed.

I unbuttoned the top button of his shirt before he stopped me. "What's wrong?" I asked, and he hesitated.

"We should get cleaned up." He gently lifted me off of him and handed me a stack of napkins from the table. As we wiped our faces clean, he asked, "How are you feeling? Are you still hungry?"

"I'm just really tired. I want to go to sleep."

"Of course. Let me bring you upstairs."

He picked me up, and I closed my eyes and fell asleep as he carried me upstairs to his room. When he put me onto his bed, I felt the tightness of the dress pressing into my chest. "I need to get this dress off. It's so uncomfortable."

"Right."

He helped me stand up and walked towards the door to leave. "Wait! I need you to unzip me!" I turned around and pointed to the zipper at the back of the dress. He slowly unzipped the dress, and I let it fall to the floor. Then I turned and smiled at him as I stood topless before him. He stood in place, not knowing where to look until his eyes stopped between my breasts, and he looked perplexed. I glanced down and saw the scrap of paper I had stolen from Gabriel was stuck to my skin. I quickly removed it and threw it on the floor. "It's nothing," I told him. Then I moved forward and kissed him, and as he kissed me back, I took his hands and put them on my breasts. He gently felt me, but then he moved back.

I was dizzy, so I sat down on the bed and closed my eyes. "You don't want me?"

He came closer. "Are you kidding me? I've never wanted something so badly in my entire life!"

"I don't understand."

He kneeled down in front of me and took my hands into his. "Jane. Look at me." I looked down at him with drowsy eyes, and he squeezed my hands a bit. "I want you more than anything, I promise you. But not like this."

"Not like this?"

"You're not in your right mind. I want you to be fully you, and completely sober, when you choose me."

"But-"

"If you feel the same way that I do, then we have all the time in the world to get to know each other… in that way."

"I need to lie down."

"One second." He opened a drawer, took out a sweatshirt, and put it over my head. Then he gently moved me down onto the pillow, pulled the blankets up, and kissed my forehead as I fell asleep.

❧

"Jane. Wake up."

I heard Will's voice, but I was too tired to respond. "Jane. I need to speak with you. Open your eyes." It took all my strength to open my eyes and keep them open. The sun was barely up.

"What time is it?" I asked, struggling to stay conscious.

"About 6 AM. Jane, my grandfather died last night."

"Oh god, Will. I'm so sorry! That's terrible."

"I need to go to London this morning."

"How can I help?" I forced myself to sit up and face him. He sat down next to me and took my hand. "I'd really like it if you would come with me."

"To the airport? I don't think I can drive."

"No, I'd like to take you to London. Introduce you to my family. Show you where I grew up."

"Oh Will! That is so… nice. But I can't just drop everything and leave right now."

"If you feel funny meeting my family, you don't have to. I'll probably have to be there quite a while to help with his estate, and I would love to have you by my side."

"Will. That is so sweet… and cool of you. And I wish I could. But I can't just leave. I have work."

"You don't have to worry about money, Jane."

"Umm, yes. I do. I'm so sorry about your grandpa, Will. But I can't leave."

"I understand." He stood up and zipped his suitcase then leaned over me. "I'll call you. And please feel free to stay here while I'm away."

"Oh no, I can't do that."

"Please, Jane. It would make me happy knowing you're here in my bed. I mean… my home."

"Okay."

I took his hand and kissed it. Then I plopped back down onto the pillow and started to fall back asleep.

"Jane?"

I kept my head on the pillow but called out, "Yeah?"

"Just… I want you to be careful."

"Okay. Careful of what?"

"Gabriel."

I immediately sat up. "What do you mean?"

He hesitated. "Just… be careful."

I nodded my head and slowly fell back down and into a deep sleep.

I woke up several times that day but didn't manage to drag myself out of bed until the late afternoon. I had completely forgotten about my foot, and when I walked on it, the pain was awful. I hopped the rest of the way to the bathroom, took a look at myself in the mirror, and almost fell over. Makeup was smeared all over my face, there were dark circles under my eyes, and lots of dried-up cake encrusted in my hair.

I took a long, hot shower and thoroughly scrubbed every inch of my body. Then I hobbled into Lizzie's room and borrowed a t-shirt and jeans and started to put on makeup. I stopped and asked myself why I needed to wear makeup and dropped the lipstick back into the drawer. I was still a bit fucked up from the brownies. I heard incessant ringing in my ears, and I had the worst headache of my life.

I slowly made my way down to the kitchen and saw Hunt hunched over a bowl of soggy cereal. He was wearing a tank top, and his muscular arms and shoulders were flexed. It suddenly hit me how attractive he was. I shook my head to remove the thought from my brain. There was already enough confusion for me as far as men were concerned.

"May I join you?" I asked.

His head popped up, and it seemed as though I had ripped him out of a daydream. "Yeah, yeah. Sure." I made myself a bowl of cereal and sat beside him. "You okay?" he asked me.

"Yeah. My head is pounding, my foot is throbbing, and I barely know what the fuck is going on, but I'm okay. Are *you* okay?"

"Yeah, I'm just confused. And kind of sad."

"Do you want to talk about it?"

"I guess. It's about Annie."

"I figured."

"We slept together last night."

"Like, had sex?"

"Yeah." He hung his head in what seemed like shame.

"So... help me understand. Why are you upset?"

"I didn't really want to."

"So, did she force you?"

"No. She didn't. But in a way, she did. I don't know how to explain it."

"Can I try to figure this out?" He nodded. "Your mind didn't want to, but your body did, so you gave in?"

"Yes. That's pretty much what happened. I had a few drinks, which I don't normally do, and it made it harder to think. To fight."

"Yeah, that's how it tends to unfold. But let me ask you this. What's wrong with giving in to what your body wants every once in a while? If you're not hurting anyone..."

"Because I had an ideal that I was dedicated to. I made a promise to myself, and I broke it."

"People change, and ideals change. That's not a bad thing. It could mean maturity and growth. It also doesn't mean you have to give up completely. You gave in once. You can start over."

"That's the thing. I don't think I can go back."

"Why?"

"Because it was fucking mind-blowing."

I laughed and said, "It was, was it?"

"I had no idea! I mean, I knew it would feel good, but I didn't know it would be *like that*. Now I know why men are completely ruled by it! And I don't want to be like that!"

"You don't have to be anything you don't want to be. You're in control, okay? You! Not your feelings or your dick!"

"You're right." I kept eating my cereal, and he added, "It's just so fucking good!"

I rolled my eyes. "So I've heard."

"Wait, you're not a virgin, are you, Jane?"

"Not that it's really your business, but since you opened up to me, I'll share, I suppose. No, I'm not a virgin. I've just never found it to be a particularly enjoyable experience."

"Does it hurt?"

"No, not after the first few times. And it's not terrible. It just isn't as fucking *mind-blowing* as it seems to be for the guy."

"Well, shit. That fucking sucks. Annie really seemed to enjoy herself!"

"Well I'm happy for her, Madman. Perhaps you were just *that* good at it!"

"You think?"

"Your first time? There's no fucking way. But I'm glad she gave you a good show."

"Thanks, Jane. Somehow I feel better."

"Just stop judging yourself for feeling what you feel. You're human, and it's fucking confusing sometimes."

"I think you might need to take your own advice, Lady Jane." He winked at me and took his bowl to the sink.

"Have you seen Lizzie today?"

"She's been in the bathroom with John for hours."

"In the bathroom?"

"They're working on that Ophelia painting. I think he has her in the tub."

"Wow. That's dedication."

"On both their parts!"

"I'm gonna go say hello. I'll see you later, Madman."

"Thanks for the talk, Jane. You're a real cool chick."

"You're pretty cool yourself."

CHAPTER 16

GABRIEL

"Bullets in the Dark"—No Love for the Middle Child

I T WAS LATE AFTERNOON THE DAY AFTER THE PARTY. I WAS doing work in my room when I heard Jane scream for help. I rushed into the hallway and followed the sound of her voice into the bathroom. She was on the ground holding a soaking wet and shivering Lizzie in her lap.

"What's going on?"

Jane looked up at me with the most desperate eyes. "Something's wrong! Her head is burning up, but her lips are blue and her hands feel ice cold! She's not responding!"

I dove onto the ground and took Lizzie's head into my hands. "Lizzie! Wake up! It's Gabriel. Please open your eyes!" Lizzie's eyes opened for a moment and then rolled all the way back into her head, and her shivering got worse. John was standing in the corner in shock.

"We need to get her to the hospital!" Jane called out. I scooped up Lizzie's limp, wet body and carried her out of the bathroom and down the stairs. I quickly slid into my shoes and grabbed my keys. Jane was limping behind us.

"Jane, be careful! Your foot!"

"Fuck my foot! *Go!*"

She followed us barefoot to the car. I opened the passenger side door and gently placed Lizzie onto the seat. "Fucking two-seater!" Jane yelled out. "I'm coming with you! Put her on my lap!"

"Jane, I don't think-"

"*I'm coming with you!*"

I carefully lifted Lizzie back up, so Jane could get in. Then I gently placed Lizzie onto Jane's lap. She cradled her like a baby and tried to get her to open her eyes. Then Jane's eyes snapped to me. "What the fuck are you waiting for?"

I jumped into the car and sped towards the hospital. "Fuck! My fucking phone!" she called out. I unlocked my phone and handed it to her. She frantically dialed.

"Mrs. Siddal? It's Jane. Lizzie's sick, and we're on our way to the hospital… I know you haven't heard from her in weeks… I'm not sure what's wrong with her! Good Samaritan, we'll meet you there. Because that's the closest hospital to us!"

She threw the phone into the console. "Bitch hung up on me! Can't you drive any faster, Gabriel! I'm really worried!" I revved the engine and almost lost control around a sharp curve. "Are you trying to kill us?" she barked at me.

"Jane, I know you're scared, but you have to calm down."

"I can't calm down! *You* calm the fuck down!"

I sighed and drove as fast yet as safely as I could until we reached the entrance to the ER. I got out and picked Lizzie up over my shoulder and carried her towards an EMT who was heading in our direction with a wheelchair. "She's very sick!" I called out as I placed her in the chair.

"This chair is for someone else," the man calmly replied.

"I don't give a fuck!" I yelled. "Get her to a doctor right now!" The guy nodded and turned around with Lizzie, who was limp and had a bluish color to her face. Jane hobbled after them. "Where are you going?" I called out.

"I'm going *with* her!"

The EMT told her she couldn't go back with them and to stay in the waiting room. Jane argued and followed them until a security guard stepped forward, and she backed off. She paced the waiting room like a maniac.

"Jane, I really think you should sit down. We could be here a while."

"I don't want to sit down!" She continued limping around the room until a nurse came out to collect information about Lizzie.

"You brought in the young lady with the red hair?"

"Yes, Lizzie. Elizabeth."

"Last name?"

"Siddal."

"Can you tell me what happened?"

"She was in the bath for a long time; the water got cold, and she lost consciousness. That's how I found her."

"You found her passed out in the bath?"

"Sort of. She was posing for a painting. She had clothes on. The painter didn't realize she was passed out."

"Uh-huh. And how long was she in the bath for?"

"He said since 10 in the morning, so like almost five hours, I guess."

"She was in the bath for *five hours*?" the nurse asked in disbelief.

I chimed in. "As she said, she was posing for a painting. It can take many hours to get the details right."

The nurse looked at me with a hint of disgust. "I see. Tell me what symptoms she had when you found her. Was she responsive at all?"

"The water was ice cold, and her skin was like ice too, except for her forehead, which felt really hot. She was very pale, and her lips were blue. She didn't respond at all, but her eyes rolled around a bit."

"Any coughing?"

"No."

"Does she have any issues with drug or alcohol abuse?"

"No. Not at all!"

"Do you know if she consumed any drugs or alcohol today?"

"I doubt it!"

"But you don't know for sure?"

"I know for sure! She's very smart and responsible, and she doesn't do stuff like that."

"Any medical conditions we should know about?"

"Yes. She only has one lung."

The nurse's eyes opened wide, and her eyebrows went up. "Can you tell me more about that?"

"She had lung cancer two years ago and had to have her lung removed."

"Is she currently undergoing treatment for that or any other medical condition?"

"No. She's been cancer-free for over a year."

"Any allergies?"

"Not that I know of."

"Insurance?"

"I'm sure she has some, but you'll have to ask her parents. They should be here soon."

"Okay, thank you for the information. You can go. We'll be in touch."

"I'm not going anywhere! You didn't even take my phone number!"

"You can stay if you like, but you won't be able to see your friend. We probably won't have a clear picture of what's going on for several hours. It would make more sense to wait at home."

"I don't care what makes sense! Thanks."

Just as the nurse left the waiting room, Lizzie's parents rushed in and approached Jane. "What happened!" they screamed at her with an accusatory tone.

These people looked like they had just stepped out of a Polo ad. The mom was dressed in white from head to toe, and her hair was pulled back tight. Her face looked like she dabbled with plastic surgery a bit too much. The dad was wearing khakis and a fucking V-neck sweater vest. They had a pretty douchey vibe. Rich, narcissistic douchebags.

Jane tried to explain the details of what was happening, but they kept interrupting her with various absurd claims. They accused her of being a bad influence, and they even had the balls to say that her lack of ambition had rubbed off on their daughter. Jane held it together pretty well. I would have knocked them the fuck out. Finally, they left us to go harass some nurses, who let them back to see Lizzie. Jane tried to follow them, but the nurse who was escorting them back said, "Family members only."

Jane called out, "I *am* family!"

And Lizzie's mom replied, "No, she isn't!" and let the door slam right in Jane's face.

She limped back over to where I was sitting and screamed, "Do you fucking believe those assholes?"

I was happy that her anger wasn't directed at me for once. "They're a fucking nightmare," I responded. "It's no wonder Lizzie is so repressed."

"Repressed?" One of Jane's eyebrows went up. "What do you mean *repressed*?"

"I don't know. She just seems... bottled up somehow, you know?"

"If you think that about her now, you should have seen her a few years ago. Her entire life consisted of pleasing those two assholes in there. Tennis lessons, crew, ballet, piano, SAT prep, straight A's, Ivy League, pre-med. They left very little room for her own interests."

"Or fun!"

"I tried so hard to get her to loosen up and break a rule every now and again, but she just couldn't. Until she got cancer... then it was a 180 in the other direction. She didn't give a fuck about anything anymore."

"Makes a lot of sense. Maybe, in a way, the cancer was a blessing?"

She gave me a look like I was absolutely awful for saying it, but then she responded, "I guess. As long as she doesn't get it again, maybe it *is* a blessing. I don't know."

"Would you sit down? I'm worried about your foot."

"Would you let that go already?"

"You know, since we're already in the hospital, you might as well have it looked at."

"I don't want to."

"Jane. Come on. Be reasonable. We should make sure it isn't getting infected."

"No. I don't give a shit." I left her and walked up to the desk. I explained what happened to her foot and that we'd appreciate it if someone could take a quick look. They said they'd take her back soon.

"What did you tell them?"

"Nothing. You hungry? There's some vending machines over there."

"I'm not hungry."

I got some M & M's, a Snickers, and a coke and held them out for her. "Are you trying to give me diabetes?" she said as she grabbed the soda and gulped it down. A male nurse came out and called her name. "What did you do?" she said with irritation.

"Just let them look at your foot for fuck's sake." She crossed her arms on her chest and looked away. I went over to the nurse and quietly explained that my girlfriend was worried about her friend and didn't want to leave the waiting room but needed a cut on her foot looked at.

"Sounds like my girlfriend," he commented. "Stubborn as shit, but cute as hell."

"Yup."

I saw part of an Air Force tattoo on the guy's bicep and got an idea. "Air Force too, eh? What unit?" I asked.

His face lit up, and he said, "Medic, aeromedical evacuation, five years. You?"

"58th pararescue. I'm Sam Wilson." I was directly quoting a Captain America movie.

He immediately shook my hand. "Mike Carruthers. Good to meet you, brother."

"You too, man. Listen, is there any way you can help me out here?" I gestured to Jane, who was still limping around the waiting room like a psycho, and he laughed.

"I can take a quick look in the waiting room."

"Thanks, man. I really appreciate it."

We went over to her, and she said, "Do you have any information about Lizzie?"

"No, but I'll make you a deal. If you let me take a look at your foot, I'll find out what's going on with your friend."

"Ugh, fine."

He kneeled in front of her and started unwrapping the bandages.

"So what happened here?"

"I stepped on a piece of glass."

"Ouch. How'd that happen?"

"Some idiot broke a beer bottle, and I stepped on it."

"I'll bet you wish you were wearing shoes, huh? Let's take a look." He held her foot up and examined it. "Looks like it's healing well. Is this glue?"

"Yeah."

"No swelling or discharge. I think it'll be fine. Just keep it nice and dry. I'll go and get some fresh gauze for you and see what I can find out about your friend. What's her name?"

"Elizabeth Siddal."

"Got it."

He strolled past me, and I whispered, "Thanks, man," and he gave me a fist bump. I sat next to her again. "Aren't you glad you had that looked at?" She shrugged and stared at the floor.

"You okay?"

"Not really."

She was completely preoccupied with worry for Lizzie, and I wanted to get her mind off it. But I knew if I tried to talk about anything else, she'd ignore me.

"How long have you and Lizzie known each other?"

"As long as I can remember. We grew up next door to each other."

"Really? Her parents look like they're wealthy. Are yours too?"

"No, not anymore. But they were." I paused and waited for her to continue. "I grew up in a wealthy neighborhood. I mean, my house wasn't on the level of Red House, but it was probably worth a few million. As I got older, my dad's spending became more and more over the top. We started traveling first class to exotic places, and we got a super fancy pool with a waterfall. Then he bought my mom a shitload of diamonds and a bunch of luxury cars. I was like

10 or 11, so I just thought it was awesome. Then one day the FBI knocked on our door and took my dad away in handcuffs."

"Shit. Drug dealer?"

"No, he was a financial planner, but he was stealing from his clients. The thing is, he'd been doing it for years and would've gotten away with it until he started stealing bigger and bigger amounts. Then it was obvious."

"So what happened to you and your mom?"

"We lost everything. We had to move to a one-bedroom apartment in a shitty town, and we struggled to pay the bills because my mom had never worked and didn't have any skills."

"But you stayed friends with Lizzie?"

"Yup. She was the only friend that kept in contact with me. She never treated me any differently, but her parents treated me like I was the criminal."

"They're pieces of shit."

"Yup. Just because you have money, doesn't mean you have class."

"So is your dad still in jail?"

"No. He got out a few years ago and moved to Mexico. Supposedly he became a priest." She rolled her eyes.

"Do you talk to him at all?"

"Nope. I haven't heard from him since the day he was shoved into that cop car."

"That makes so much sense."

"What makes sense?"

"I just feel like I understand you better now. Your relationship with your dad is the reason you hate men."

"I don't hate *men*! I hate *assholes*!"

"I'm sorry. That came out wrong. I meant you don't *trust* men because of your dad."

"Let me clarify this for you. I don't trust *fuck boys.* Grown men who act with honor and dignity, I trust!"

"I didn't mean to piss you off."

"You know what, why don't you just go? There's no reason for you to be here right now!"

"I'm here because I want to be here for you and for Lizzie."

"We don't need you!"

The nurse who had looked at Jane's foot came out and crouched down in front of her. He wrapped her foot in fresh gauze as he spoke. "They're still waiting for more test results, but it looks like your friend has a pretty serious case of pneumonia."

"Fuck. Are they giving her antibiotics?"

"Well, this is serious because she's immunocompromised due to the chemo she had. And the fact that she only has one lung. They're doing everything they can, but she'll need to be here for several weeks."

"*Several weeks*? Can I see her?"

"I'm afraid not. She's conscious and comfortable, but no one besides immediate family will be able to see her until she's stable. They can't risk reinfection."

"Okay. Thanks for letting me know. Can you please tell her to call me as soon as she's up to it?"

"Of course."

He came back to me and said, "Sorry I can't take her back there."

"No worries, brother. I appreciate your help." He gave me another fist bump and I added, "Hey, Mike. You wanna grab a beer sometime? It'd be good to know someone who gets it."

"Yeah man, definitely." He pounded the rest of his coffee, quickly wrote his number on the side of the cup, and threw it at me. Then he disappeared behind security doors that closed quickly behind him.

I entered his number into my phone, happy to have a contact in the hospital for Jane. I turned back to her and she was sitting there staring out at nothing.

"Come on. Let's go home," I said softly with my hand outstretched. She stood up and walked in front of me and out the door. I followed her out, and she got into my car like I wasn't even there.

As we drove away from the hospital, the sky turned dark gray and a downpour began. She was pressed against the door, as far away from me as she could possibly be. I asked if she was okay, and she didn't answer.

A little while later I asked if there was anything I could do to help, and again she ignored me. As I turned onto our block, I noticed she had moved her hand onto the center console, and I tried to hold it. She immediately ripped her hand away and yelled, "Don't fucking touch me!" As the doors of the gate creaked open, I drove off the pathway, put the car in park, and shut off the engine. Rain was pounding onto the car.

"What the fuck are you doing? The house is half a mile *that* way!" she yelled.

"I want to talk."

"Well, I want to go home, and my car is *down there*!"

"Jane. Look at me for a second. I'm worried about you. "

"I don't need you to be worried about me! I need you to keep driving!"

I stared at her and waited for her next move.

"Fine, dickhead! I'll walk!"

She flung the door open and hurried out into the torrential rain and started limping down the driveway. I got out and ran after her.

"Come on, Jane! You're fucking barefoot!" I tried to grab her hand, but she yanked it back.

"Leave me the fuck alone!" she yelled as she continued to stumble down the road.

"Why are you such a bitch to me? *What did I ever do to you?*" I shouted.

She stopped and turned to face me. "*Why am I such a bitch?*"

I just stood there, letting the rain beat down onto my face.

"I'm a bitch to you because I know your type *very* well!"

I flung my arms out in anger. "Yeah? Okay! Since you know me so well, *what's my type exactly?*"

"The type that's full of shit!"

"How am I full of shit? You don't even know me because you

won't give me a chance to show you who I am!" The enormous amount of rain made her white t-shirt completely transparent, and I tried to keep my eyes off her hard nipples that poked through the thin, little bra she had on.

"Are you in love with Lizzie?" she challenged.

"I already told you that I'm *not*!"

"Then why are you leading her on? You're going to crush her heart, and she's been through enough pain!"

"You know what, Jane? You are just as full of shit as I am!"

"*Me? How?*"

"Are you in love with Will?" She hesitated, and I repeated the question. *"Are you in love with Will?"*

"No! I'm not!"

"Then why are you leading him on? You're going to crush his heart! And he's been through enough pain!"

"Fuck *you*! It's not the same!" she spat out and began to turn away. I seized her hand, and she turned back to me.

"I know you feel the same way that I do! Why won't you give me a chance?" I shouted so she could hear me over the rain that beat down onto us.

"Because I don't trust you!"

"Let me change your mind. *Please*." I grabbed her face and kissed her, and it was fucking electric. I felt her protest for a second, and then she melted into me. It felt like we were stuck in time, standing there connecting in a freezing rainstorm, and I didn't want it to end. Somehow I knew that those brief moments when she let her veil down for me would always be fleeting. I felt her shudder from the cold, and I begged her to get back into the car.

"No. I want to walk."

She smiled warmly and took my hand, and we walked, very slowly, the rest of the way to the house.

"So much for keeping your foot dry."

CHAPTER 17

Jane

"Tempt My Trouble"—Bishop Briggs

WE OPENED THE FRONT DOOR, AND JOHN WAS SITTING at the bottom of the stairs with his head in his hands. He didn't lift his head when the door slammed shut. "Are you okay, man?" Gabriel asked. He slowly lifted his head, and his face looked drawn and tired.

"How is she?"

"She's okay. She's awake and comfortable," Gabriel replied.

"What did I *do* to her?"

"You didn't do *anything*. She got pneumonia. It's not your fault."

"I had her in the tub for five hours. I didn't think to check the temperature of the water. I didn't ask if she was thirsty. I didn't take care of her at all. It's *my* fault."

Gabriel sat down next to him. "John. Look at me. It's not your fault. She should have said something. It was an accident. She'll be fine."

"She's shivering," John stated. Gabriel looked up and saw that I had my arms wrapped around my wet body, and I was trembling.

"Shit, let's get you upstairs!" He led me towards the bathroom with the giant stained glass tree.

"Why are we in here?" I asked through chattering teeth.

"You need a hot bath. You need to warm up."

I looked into the tub and saw it was still full with water from when I had dragged Lizzie out. "I'm not using this tub."

He pulled the drain. "Jane. She didn't die. There's nothing wrong with the tub."

I started to shake more intensely and struggled to say, "I don't care. I'm not using that tub!"

"Okay. There are other tubs." He took my hand again and brought me down the hall in the opposite direction of the library. I had never been down that way. "This is John's bathroom." He opened the door and peeked inside and said, "Yeah, it's filthy in there." So we continued down the hallway.

"I don't need a fucking bath, Gabriel. I need dry clothes."

"I really think a hot bath would help you warm up."

"I'm not taking a bath with you."

"I know that."

"Don't you have a bathroom attached to your room?"

"Yeah, but I only have a shower."

"So I'll take a hot shower! I'm fucking freezing."

"We need to keep your foot dry."

I growled at him as he took me into another bathroom and turned on the light.

"Holy shit. This is enormous."

I stepped into an unbelievably large bathroom. One whole wall was made of glass and overlooked a little Zen garden covered in white pebbles and bamboo trees. The tub looked like the world's biggest soup bowl. "This is fucking beautiful. You've never been in here?"

"No. There's a lot of rooms I haven't seen."

"We should explore."

He winked at me as he opened a cabinet and started taking out towels and stacking them on a little wooden table next to the tub. Then he turned the faucet on and checked the temperature. "Do you need anything?" I was shivering so hard that I could barely walk to the tub.

"Aren't you cold?" I asked with rattling teeth.

"Nah. I'm super warm-blooded. Feel." He undid his top button and pressed my hand onto his chest.

"Oh god, you're so warm."

I put my other hand onto his chest, and he softly said, "Come here," and brought me into an embrace. He held me for a long time until I finally stopped shivering. Then he drew back and started to take off my shirt. I grasped his hands to stop him.

"I'm just trying to help you."

"Help me get naked?"

"Help you take off your soaking wet clothes and get into a warm bath."

I was absolutely depleted. I was physically and emotionally exhausted, and the throbbing pain in my foot was starting to peak. I couldn't fight anymore, so I sighed and gave in. I gave in to Gabriel, and I gave in to what I truly wanted.

He tugged my shirt over my head and gently unhooked my bra. As it fell to the ground, I saw him look down at my chest, and then his eyes flashed back up to my face. I almost laughed, but I was too tired. He undid my pants and pulled them down along with my underwear. I held onto his back as he took them off completely. He slowly rose back to his feet, took my hand into his, and guided me to the tub. He was obviously trying to avoid looking at my body, which I appreciated. But I also longed to have his gaze all over me.

He helped me step into the tub and reminded me to keep my foot out of the water. When I propped my foot up on the edge of the tub, he unraveled the muddy gauze and used a washcloth to clean the wound. He kept his eyes on my foot the entire time though I desperately wanted him to look up at me. Then he stepped backward slowly and said, "Better?"

I closed my eyes and murmured, "So much better." A few moments later I still felt him in the room, and I opened my eyes to find him staring at me. "What?"

"Sorry."

"What is it?"

"Nothing."

I rolled my eyes and closed them again as I heard him gently close the door.

⚜

He entered a while later with clean clothes, gauze, aspirin, and a tray of food. He put the tray down and kneeled next to the tub.

"How are you feeling?"

"Relaxed. Thanks."

"I brought you something to eat."

"What is it?"

"Grilled cheese and tomato soup. I hope that's okay. My cooking skills are pretty pathetic."

"Wait. When we first came here for dinner, you said you could make us anything we wanted."

"Yeah. That was bullshit."

"Well, they say acknowledgement is the first step to recovery."

"I am willing to acknowledge that I can't cook for shit."

"And that you're *full* of shit."

"Sometimes, yes. Aren't we all full of shit sometimes?"

I shrugged and reached for the sandwich. "This is one of my favorite meals," I admitted.

"I'm glad."

"Can you bring me my phone? I want to call the hospital and check on Lizzie."

"Where is it?"

"Will's room."

He gave me a half smile and replied, "Got it."

While he was gone, I inhaled the food, took the aspirin, and got out of the tub. I changed into the Incubus t-shirt and baggy sweatpants he brought me, which were clearly his. But no bra and no underwear. His delicious scent drifted up from the shirt, and I picked up the collar and pulled it to my nose to inhale him more deeply as he came back with my phone.

"Do you like the shirt?"

"It's cozy."

"It's from the concert when we first met."

"Really?" I turned around to look at the back of the shirt in the mirror. Amongst the dates and locations was Amsterdam. "Cool."

I took the phone and called the hospital's information line.

They put me through to Lizzie's room, but there was no answer. I tried her mom too, but she didn't pick up either.

"No answer?"

"No." I sighed and leaned into the vanity. "Wanna watch a movie?" he asked like we were kids having a fun little sleepover.

I almost gave a snotty response, but I caught myself. "Sure. I could really use a comedy."

"You got it." We walked side by side to his bedroom, and I examined his bookshelf while he set up his laptop.

"Why do you have so many copies of Dante's *Divine Comedy*?"

"They're different translations."

"Have you read all of these?"

"Most of them."

"Are they really that different?"

"Very. Some translators do a word-for-word translation. Some try to keep the rhyme scheme, which messes up the meaning. Others interpret things in their own way and just fuck the whole thing up completely."

"So which is your favorite?"

"I don't have a favorite; that's why I'm working on my own."

"*Your own translation*?"

"Yes. Not of *Divine Comedy*. That would take several lifetimes. I'm translating *La Vita Nuova,* a collection of poems."

"How do you know Italian so well?"

"My dad's from Italy, and he was a professor of Italian. I grew up reading Dante in Italian."

"That's pretty fancy. I grew up reading *The Babysitter's Club*."

"It's cool, I guess. I'm not a huge fan of my dad, but I'm grateful for what he taught me."

"I'm willing to admit, I don't know anything about Dante other than the whole hell thing."

"Okay, lemme give you a quick overview. Dante grew up obsessed with a girl he barely knew named Beatrice. She died young, and it motivated him to write his greatest works. He's the main character and has to go through the various levels of hell to reach paradise, where Beatrice waits for him."

"That sounds so much like one of my favorite movies, *What Dreams May Come*. A man travels through hell to save his wife who killed herself."

"Never heard of it. The title sounds familiar though."

I sat next to him on the bed and said, "'For in that sleep of death, what dreams may come…'"

He immediately responded with, "'When we have shuffled off this mortal coil…'"

And we both said, "'Must give us pause!'" at the same time.

"You know *Hamlet*?" I exclaimed.

"Of course. I'm obsessed with death, remember?" He yanked up his sleeve and pointed to a tattoo of a stretched-out arm with a skull in its hand. "'Alas, poor Yorick!'" I shouted.

"'I knew him well,'" he added and winked at me.

"I never thought I'd be turned on by a skull tattoo," I accidentally admitted.

He smirked. "You're turned on?"

I quickly got off the bed and started looking at the papers scattered across his desk. There was an open notebook full of notes in Italian. "So what do you think happens after death? Do you think Dante had it right?" I asked.

"No, I don't think it's that cut and dry."

"All those levels of hell? Doesn't sound cut and dry to me."

"I don't think it's as simple as heaven and hell. Good and bad. Punishment and reward."

"Do you believe in life after death?"

"Did you read the poem I wrote for you?"

I had read it every night since he gave it to me and kept it underneath my pillow, but I didn't want him to know it. "Yeah, I read it."

"So you know that we've been here before."

"I know that you believe that."

"It's more than a belief. I'm sure of it."

"How can you be so sure?"

"I can't prove it, yet. It's just *in* me. It's an ongoing feeling like déjà vu that I've had my entire life. But it gets much more intense and undeniable at certain times and with certain people. Like with you."

"Me?"

"Absolutely. Not all the time. When you have that veil up, I barely recognize you, but when you let me in and show me who you really are, I know without a doubt that you have been mine many times before."

"Okay, since you seem to know so much about life, why are we here? Why would we all choose to enter into this existence and to suffer so much only to lose it all in the end? To learn some kind of lesson?"

"Not necessarily. I think some people come here to learn lessons. But that's not why *I* keep coming back. And I don't think that's why you're here either."

"So enlighten me, please! *Why are we here?*"

"Because it's fucking fun."

"*Fun?* I'm not having *that* much fun! So much worrying and suffering and pain. Who in their right mind would choose this?"

"Do not the spirits who dwell in the ether envy man for his pain?" He stood in front of me, so close to my face.

"Huh?"

"We suffer, yes. But when we aren't in our bodies, I think there is a longing of sorts. A longing for the heaviness, the drama, the pain. It's exhilarating! Yes, life is impossible sometimes. But as fucking painful as it is, it's also an unbelievable thrill."

"My life isn't that thrilling, Gabriel."

He took my hand into his and whispered, "Stick around a while. We're just getting started."

I cleared my throat and walked towards the bed. "We have to watch *What Dreams May Come!* It's really sad though."

"Does it have a happy ending?"

"Yeah, it does."

"Let's do it."

CHAPTER 18

GABRIEL

"Inertia Creeps"—Massive Attack

I DIDN'T PAY MUCH ATTENTION TO THE MOVIE. I WAS TOO consumed with the fact that I finally had Jane in my bed. I kept thinking of all the things I had been wanting to do to her and strategizing how exactly I was going to control myself.

It wasn't bullshit. I wanted to relish every moment with her, not just rush through for a quick release. I wanted to earn her, be worthy of her. I wanted to worship her like a goddess.

She cried for the first half-hour of the movie, and she let me hold her in my arms. Reluctant at first, she finally folded into me after a few minutes. I closed my eyes and inhaled the sweet scent of her hair and that delicious caramel smell she always has. Soon after, she fell asleep on me.

Having her in my bed and wearing my clothes, with her long wisps of hair spread across my pillows, was paradise. I slipped her out of my arms, lit a bunch of candles, and grabbed my sketchbook. I couldn't waste the opportunity to capture her like that. I wanted to freeze the moment and live inside it for eternity. I sketched for about an hour and a half when she awoke and looked directly at me. But she didn't say a word. She just stared at me with a curious expression I couldn't discern, and when I picked the pencil up to continue, she lifted off her shirt and gazed at me with a bright, sexy smile.

Holy fuck, she had the most perfect tits. I threw my sketchbook and pencil to the floor, slid across the bed, clutched her face, and kissed her softly but eagerly. She kissed me back with an equal amount of desire, and there was no doubt in my mind that she was mine.

She took off my shirt and grasped for the button on my jeans. I seized her hands and held them at her sides while I kissed her neck and ran my tongue down to her nipples. I released her hands as I lightly swirled my tongue around her creamy skin. We both moaned at the same time, and she tried to open my pants again. It was so hard to refuse her, but I knew it would be worth it. This night was about her.

"Tell me what you like," I told her.

"Hmm?"

"What gets you off?"

"Umm, my right hand?"

She reached for my pants, but I drew back. "No, I mean what do you like having done to you? How can I make you come?"

"I'm hoping you can help me figure that out, Gabriel!"

"Wait. You're not a virgin, are you?" Suddenly I was terrified. I didn't want to fuck a virgin ever again.

"Jesus! No! I'm not a fucking virgin."

"You've never had an orgasm then?" The idea of making her come for the first time was exhilarating.

"*What are you fucking kidding me?* I think I gave myself my first orgasm in 6th grade!"

"Oh. No one *else* has ever gotten you off."

She sighed. "And I doubt anyone ever will. It's too complicated."

"Lemme give it a try."

I climbed on top of her and gently kissed her neck while I pulled her pants off. We were kissing so intensely, and she bit my bottom lip and smiled with her eyes closed. I almost lost my nerve, so I broke away and started gently sucking one of her nipples and lightly bit down. She whimpered, and I trailed kisses down her body and very slowly opened her legs up wide.

"*Fuck,*" I muttered as I stared down at her.

"What!" she demanded.

"You're fucking perfect."

She rolled her eyes and yelled, "Okay! How often have you used *that* line?"

"Umm, not once. I don't usually look very much. Jane, your body is a fucking work of art. Your pussy is so beautiful. It's so pink and-"

"Alright, I get it!"

"Show me what you do to yourself."

I thought she would protest, but her hand went right to her clit and made light circles, and I memorized the exact spot she rubbed. I kissed her hand as she rubbed herself and I took her fingers into my mouth and sucked on them while staring into her eyes. She stared back with equal intensity, and I kissed the spot she showed me very lightly, over and over. I was barely making contact with my lips, and it was definitely driving her mad. Then I leaned back and just looked her up and down and smiled.

"Thank you."

She looked at me with drowsy eyes. "For what?"

"Letting me do this to you."

I dragged my lips up and down her thigh and then started blowing on her clit, and she giggled.

"Do you like that?"

She let out a sexy little "mmhmm," and I kissed up and down her slit.

When I felt like I had sufficiently tortured her, I looked up and said, "Tell me what you want."

"Please, Gabriel."

"Tell me what you want."

"More."

"Tell me. I want to hear you say it."

"I want you to make me come."

I got my tongue really wet and touched the tip to her spot so delicately and then pulled it back and did it again. I kept teasing her, and I could tell it was working because she looked very serious and had that misty look in her eyes like she was losing herself. "*Please*, Gabriel."

I ran my finger up and down her pussy. "Fuck, you're so wet."
She moaned and murmured, "More. *Please*."

I kissed her entrance over and over and slid my tongue inside.
She arched her back and groaned. I gently moved my tongue as far
inside her as I could go, and I felt her get wetter. I pulled away and
whispered, "You taste so fucking good. You don't know how long
I've been waiting to taste you."

She opened her eyes and looked at me with intense desire.
"*Please*."

I knew she was close. I kissed her spot again and again then
made little circles with the tip of my tongue. Her moaning got
louder and more intense, and I ran my finger downwards and entered her. She grabbed my hand and yelled, "Fuck, Gabriel!"

I moved my finger upwards and slowly went in, up, and out as
I made tiny little circles on her clit with my tongue. I fingered her
harder and faster, and her breathing got more intense. I knew she
was about to come.

"Jane, I want you to come for me." She didn't answer. "Open
your eyes, Jane!" Her eyelids flew open, and she stared down at me.
"I want you to come for me, baby."

"Don't stop!" she called out. I dove back in and continued my
licking and fingering and increased the pace. She grabbed my hand
again. "Fuck, I'm coming!" I moaned into her as she writhed beneath me. I started to pull away, and she screamed, "Don't stop!" as
she came again. Then she put her hand on top of mine and guided
me to finger her really hard, which I happily did as she rubbed herself. She came really hard this time while staring into my eyes, and
it was the hottest thing ever. Then she yanked me up to her mouth
and passionately kissed me and started to unbutton my pants. I
grabbed her wrists and shook my head.

"*Really*?" she asked as she rubbed my rock-hard dick over my
pants. I pulled myself away from her hands.

"I'm good. That was fucking hot." She gave me a look of disbelief and then shrugged and flung herself down on the pillow and
closed her eyes.

"No one's ever done that for you?"

"Oh, I've had that done many times," she said with her eyes closed.

"But no one has ever made you come?"

"No one ever really took the time to try. It was always so rushed, a means to an end." I put my head down next to hers and savored the immense satisfaction. Then she opened her eyes and added, "Plus, it's *you*."

"Hmm?"

She was already asleep, so I ran into the bathroom and finished myself off.

CHAPTER 19

Jane

"Two Weeks"—FKA Twigs

I slept better that night next to Gabriel than I had in months. I woke up early and watched him sleep. The steady rise and fall of his bare chest was so peaceful. I put his t-shirt and sweatpants back on, opened the door, and walked directly into Ed.

"Jane, you stayed over?" He paused for a second and added, "In Gabriel's room!"

He gave me a sly smile, and I rolled my eyes. "Don't give me a hard time, Ed! It's been a rough few days!"

"Oh, no judgment on this end! I've been trying to get into Gabriel's bed for almost a decade! *How was it?*"

"How was *what*?" I said as I pushed past him and went towards Lizzie's room.

"Okay, play dumb. That's fine!"

I found a clean shirt and pants that might fit me in Lizzie's closet, and I fished my bra out from under her desk.

Ed stuck his head in the doorway and shouted, "I'll get the juicy details out of you eventually!"

I quickly got dressed and brushed my hair. I had to use Lizzie's toothbrush, but I knew she wouldn't mind. I went downstairs and made myself a cup of coffee. I wanted to get to the hospital as soon as visiting hours started.

I went back into Gabriel's room, and he was still sleeping. A fun little idea popped into my head. I put my coffee down and got two ties from his closet. I gently lifted his wrists and tied them to the headboard. It was a fucking miracle that he didn't wake up. Then I pulled the blanket off of him and he was only wearing a tight pair of boxer briefs. I dashed back into the closet and left the door open a crack so I could watch the show, but he didn't stir at all. He was a deep fucking sleeper. I tiptoed out of the room and went to the thermostat in the hallway. I switched it to cool and put the temp as low as it would go. Then I crept back into his room and into the closet. It took about a minute for him to feel the chilly air pouring out of the vent above him onto his almost naked body. He jerked awake, and his head instantly swung back and forth to his wrists. He started yanking on the ties, and when he couldn't break free, he started screaming my name.

I had to hold my mouth to keep from laughing too loudly. "Jane! It's not fucking funny! Get the fuck in here!" I let him scream and squirm another minute. Then I burst out of the closet while laughing my ass off.

"Haha! So funny! Untie me right now!"

I grabbed the elastic band of his underwear and said, "I don't know. I think maybe you need more air," and he started to shiver.

"Don't you dare!"

"Just for a few hours?" I climbed down and went for the bedroom door. "I'll be back later!"

"Jane! Fucking untie me! I'm not kidding!"

I turned around and went to the bed and untied his wrists. "I was just having a little fun."

"Why is it so goddamn freezing in here?"

He pulled on a pair of jeans and a sweatshirt. "Oh, lemme fix that." I went into the hallway and turned the thermostat back to heat.

"Well, that's an interesting way to wake up," he said as he shivered a bit more. I grabbed my coffee cup and handed it to him. "Hot coffee?"

"*Please!*"

"I was just trying to fully enjoy my life, Gabriel."

"Memento mori, eh? Your carpe diem includes torturing me?"

"Most definitely."

"Noted. I'll sleep with one eye open."

"Maybe both."

"So what do you want to do today?"

"Visit Lizzie in the hospital and then go to work."

"I said what do you *want* to do."

"I *want* to visit my friend."

"Yeah, we'll do that. But *fuck* work."

"Easy for you to say. Not all of us have people handing us luxury cars and a mansion to live in."

"I can arrange that. Move in here."

"Umm, no. And this isn't even your house, so you can't ask me to live here."

"Something tells me that Will wouldn't have a problem with it."

"Please don't talk about him."

"Why?"

"Just *don't*."

"Right. So fuck work. We'll visit Lizzie and go to the beach?"

"First of all, I'm going to work. Second, it's November."

"If you insist on going to work, I'll drive you."

"I don't need you to drive me."

"I know you don't need me to. I want to."

"Fine." I tried to shake off my attitude, but it was a habit I had gotten used to with him. "It sucks that you guys don't have a pool here," I offered. "Swimming does sound nice."

"Yeah, we'll have to get he-who-shall-not-be-named to put one in."

"Indoors, preferably."

Suddenly his face lit up. "I have an idea!"

"Oh no. What is it?"

"You'll see. After I pick you up from work later."

"Oh lord. So what will you do today while I'm at work?"

"I've been working on a project with Christina, so I'll probably drop by her place for a while."

I wrinkled my nose and made a yuck face.

"What do you have against my sister? You don't even know her."

"I know she broke Will's heart."

"There's two sides to every story, you know. What was *his* side?"

"He only told me that she jerked him around and couldn't figure out if she loved him or not. Then she just dropped out of his life. What's *her* side?"

"The truth? She *did* love him. *Like a brother.* There was some attraction there in the beginning; they're both artists, so they had a lot to talk about. But eventually, she realized that she loved him like a brother. Not a lover."

"Sounds like an excuse to me."

"Christina is a very passionate woman. She needs to be with someone who can match that. Will just doesn't have that fire in him."

"*Maybe* she isn't used to being treated respectfully. A lot of girls are turned off by that because they aren't used to it, and they've been taught that it isn't attractive."

"So why aren't *you* his girlfriend then, Jane?"

"I don't know. Maybe I *will* be."

"I think if you wanted to, you would be *already*. He's made his feelings pretty clear, hasn't he?"

"Sort of."

"So what's the problem?"

I got up and went for the door. "I have to call the hospital."

I called the information desk at the hospital, and they connected me to Lizzie's room. Again, no one answered. I tried her mom over and over until she finally picked up and yelled at me to stop calling. She said Lizzie went into respiratory failure the night before and was on a ventilator. Apparently, she wouldn't be able to have visitors until her condition improved a lot more. I slammed the phone down and told Gabriel what her mom had said. He tried to hold my hand, but I yanked it away. "It's fine. I have to get ready for work."

I wasn't used to having someone waiting for me after work. It was only 7 PM, but the sky was completely dark, and the air was frigid. I threw on my sweater, which was not warm enough at all, and saw

Gabriel leaning against his car smoking a cigarette. He was wearing a long black peacoat with the collar up, a black t-shirt, tight jeans, and beat-up leather boots. All I could think was, "How does he always look so fucking hot?" I bit the inside of my cheek to keep from smiling. I didn't want to feed into his colossal fucking ego. But after what he had done to me the night before, he must have known he had me.

He went around the car and opened the passenger door. I gave him a slight smile and got in. He didn't say anything as we quickly sped off.

"Where are we going?"

"You'll see."

"Can you just tell me?"

"Nope. Music?" He held out his phone for me, and I started to search for a song.

"Have you ever heard of FKA Twigs?" I asked.

"The name sounds familiar, but I don't think I've heard it before."

"I heard this song for the first time today, and I was stunned. It's a work of art."

"I'd love to hear a work of art right now."

I clicked "Two Weeks" and put his phone back in the console. The dark, sexy tones silenced us for the entire length of the song. I started to regret playing it. That song, the black night, and the silence between us that we both knew was filled with so much angst and longing and passion... *What was I doing?*

Watching his hand shift gears as he sped along the curves of some desolate road was too much. I kept thinking about what those fingers had done to me, and I wanted to grab them and put them in my mouth.

When the song ended, he murmured an emphatic "fuck," and all I said was "I know."

Neither of us spoke for what felt like an endless amount of time until he said, "That song."

"I know."

"There's so much there, beyond the lyrics. Something is captured there. A feeling that's impossible to express with words."

"Exactly."

He pulled to the side of the road in a heavily wooded area and shut off the engine. "Where are we?" He got out of the car, opened my door, and held out his hand. I put my hand into his, and he swiftly pulled me up and into him. His mouth crashed down onto mine, and his tongue dove into my mouth. I fell back onto the car but responded with an equal amount of passion. I fucking wanted him, and he knew it. He held my face as we continued to kiss. Then his hands dove underneath my sweater and bra. He gently felt me as his hands glided down to my sides. He grabbed my hips and pulled me into him so I could feel how turned on he was. We started rubbing ourselves together, and I wrapped one leg around his body. His hands went down my pants, and he used my ass to pull me in harder. The air was so chilled, but we were so hot together, and it made the whole thing so much more intense.

He yanked my pants and underwear down and started rubbing me as we continued to kiss. I wanted to protest. I didn't want to be on the side of the road, naked from the waist down, with a hand inside me. I didn't want to *want* it as much as I did. But I gave in. "*Memento mori,*" I thought and then my thoughts ceased.

He knelt down and started licking me. I grabbed the back of his head and ran my fingers through his hair. He licked me so much more intensely than the night before. "Gabriel, *Jesus Christ!*" Suddenly, he stood up and rested his forehead on mine, and looked down into my eyes as he slowly rubbed my spot.

"You have no idea how much I want you," he said through gritted teeth. It seemed like he was in pain. I plunged my hand into his pants and started rubbing quickly but gently. "*No!*" he yelled then, "Fuck! Don't stop!"

"Get in the car. I wanna get on top of you," I breathed out into his mouth.

His only response was a stern, "No."

I murmured, "Come on," but he got just the right rhythm going with two fingers inside and his thumb on the outside, and I was silenced by my impending orgasm. I grabbed the back of his neck as I shuddered and called out his name.

I bent down to pull my pants back up, and my legs were so unstable that I almost fell over. I looked at him with drowsy eyes, and he took my hand and yanked me towards the woods.

"Wait! Where the fuck are we going?"

He continued to guide me over fallen trees and piles of leaves until we came to a fence. He got down on one knee and held out his hands.

"Come on, Gabriel. I'm not in high school anymore. I'm not climbing a fence!"

"Yes, you are."

"No way! I'm fucking freezing!"

"I promise when we get over the fence, you will get super warm." I just stared at him, and he drew an X over his chest. "Cross my heart."

"A promise from you is like a promise from the fucking antichrist."

"Please?"

I sighed and stepped up onto his knee. He hoisted me over, and I found myself in a gigantic backyard. He jumped down next to me and started walking across the lawn. I quickly caught up.

"Whose backyard is this?"

"Don't worry about it."

"What are we doing here?"

"You said you wanted to go swimming."

He stopped in front of a huge covered pool that was long and narrow and spanned about 30 feet. He took off his jacket and shirt and kicked off his shoes.

"I'm not swimming! It's like 30 degrees out!" I protested.

He took a key out of his pocket and inserted it into a post near the side of the pool. As he turned the key, the cover slowly unfolded and blue lights and jets came on. He turned a dial and looked back at me. "Will 100 degrees be warm enough, or should I go higher?"

"100 sounds pretty toasty."

I quickly got undressed but left my bra and underwear on in case anyone saw us. I started to step in, but Gabriel unhooked my bra from behind. I caught it before it fell. "Are you sure we're alone?"

"Does it look like anyone's home?"

He gestured to the giant mansion in the distance, and all of the windows were completely dark.

"You sure?" I asked.

"Positive. They're only here in the summer."

"How'd you get the key?"

"I borrowed it when I was doing some work here last year."

"And by borrow you mean steal, right?"

"They didn't seem to need it."

He stood behind me and slowly pulled my underwear down and kissed my neck. I turned around and put my fingers under the elastic band of his boxer briefs. "You too."

He put his arms out to show he was open, and I yanked his underwear down. He took my hand, and we stepped into the warm water together.

"So who lives here?"

"Some old douchebag and his young, sad wife."

"Oh, is this the couple John was talking about? With the wife who swims naked every morning?"

"Yup."

"Interesting. What kind of work did you do for them? Something involving the young, naked wife?"

He sighed and moved closer to me. "What is it with you and your insistence that I'm a manwhore?"

"I like how irritated you get. Plus, I *know* there's some truth to it."

"Yeah, how do you know?"

"I have a sixth sense for that kind of thing. Why do you think I've been fighting you off for months?"

"I thought you just weren't into me." I didn't respond, and he added, "Then I thought you might be a lesbian."

"*Why*? Because I wasn't into you?"

He shrugged and then laughed. "Anyway. No, the work I did for them had nothing to do with the wife. He had me paint a mural on the ceiling above their bed."

"Sounds tacky."

"It *was* tacky. It was a Nativity scene with angels flying around and beams of light shining down."

"Eww. Above the bed? Isn't the Nativity scene a Christmas thing?"

"Not for him. He's an Evangelical Christian. He lives, eats, and breathes the bible. He has most of it memorized, and while I was working, he would recite passages to me. He said it was meant to inspire me, but all it did was make me want to throw a bucket of paint at his head."

"Don't you hate painting stuff that you don't care about?"

"Yes, very much. I don't even think I did a good job at all. I wouldn't want to claim it as mine."

"So why didn't you just say no?"

"Because he paid me fifty grand."

"Are you fucking kidding me?"

"I should have charged him more. I had to spend over a month with that motherfucker. He's annoying as fuck. I can see why his wife is miserable."

"Well, she married him. She must have known what he was like."

"Yeah, but I think you don't really know someone until you spend tons of concentrated time with them."

"If she didn't do that before they got married, she's a moron."

"Agreed."

He left the pool to get something from his pocket. As he swam away, I focused on the tattoos on his back. A series of weird symbols ran across his shoulder blades with two snakes entwined together underneath. I tried to figure out what they meant as I dove underwater and swam the length of the pool. The steaming hot water felt strange as it glided across my face, and the shock of the cold air when I surfaced was disconcerting but refreshing. There was a strong current at the end of the pool, and I swam against it for a while. Then I struggled to walk through it and sat down on a seat in the corner. The forceful current felt wonderful as it crashed into my body. Gabriel came from the side of the pool and jumped in next to me. He had a lit joint hanging from the corner of his mouth. He took a deep drag and held it out for me. I sighed and grabbed it.

"What? You don't have to."

"I know I don't have to. And I shouldn't." I took two hits and held it in as long as I could and gave it back. He flashed me a sexy grin and took another drag. Then he leaned into my face and put his lips right up to mine. I opened my mouth, and he blew the smoke in with his eyes closed. I held onto it then tilted my head back and blew it up towards the sky.

"What do those symbols mean?"

"Symbols?"

"On your back."

He flashed a coy smile. "I can't explain it. I'd have to show you."

"Okay, show me."

"When the time is right, I will."

"*Okay…* Well, since I told you about mine," I began, "Tell me about *your* childhood."

Smoke came out of his nostrils as he answered, "What do you want to know?"

"Brief overview, I guess."

"I'm the second of four kids. Two boys, two girls. We're all artists except for Maria who became a nun a few years ago."

"*Really?* That's surprising because you seem so anti-religion."

"My mother's very religious and kind of pushed it on us as kids. We all rebelled except for Maria. She really got brainwashed."

"Is she happy as a nun?"

"I have no fucking idea. She doesn't talk to any of us."

"That's sad."

"We were never close. I was always doing my own thing,

questioning the rules, making my own path, and she just watched in judgment from under my mom's skirt."

"That's a weird image."

"You know what I mean." He held the joint out for me, but I shook my head. "What else do you want to know?"

"Where did you grow up?"

"I was born here and homeschooled till I was nine. Then my dad became a professor at King's College in London, and I went to their lower school. When I was fourteen, I came back here to attend a fine arts school. I spent most of my summers in Italy though."

"Pretty fancy upbringing. So you're one of those weird homeschool kids?"

The weed was hitting me hard, and I tried to focus on what he was saying but paranoia was setting in. I kept thinking I was hearing footsteps.

"Homeschool was pretty great besides the religious part. We spent a lot of time exploring the woods near our home. I learned more there than any school ever taught me."

I had a very strong feeling that we were not alone. I kept whipping my head around to see if anyone was there.

"Jane, are you alright?"

"Yeah, yeah. Just thought I heard something. So when did you meet Will and the other guys?"

"We met at the Academy. We were all freshmen in this super exclusive art program and lived in the same dorm. One night we were all drinking in John's room, and we started talking about how the program was total bullshit. A waste of time, money, and youth. We agreed that their teachings were taking away from our natural talent. Will proposed we form a group and dedicate ourselves to making art the way we think is best, and here we are."

"Did you hear that?"

"Hear what?"

"I thought I heard footsteps again."

"You're paranoid. It's just us. I swear."

"I'm freaked out. There's a weird energy out here."

"Weird energy?"

A branch snapped, and I grabbed my chest and screamed. Gabriel laughed at me, then a window in the mansion flew open and a man's head appeared.

"Who's out there!" the voice demanded. I held my breath and grabbed Gabriel's hand. He put his finger to his lips to shush me.

I whispered, "We should go." He shushed me again, and I said too loudly, "I will not shush! *You shush*!"

His head dropped down in defeat, and we heard the man say, "Turn the light on!"

Light flooded down from the window, and we could see a shadowy male figure with no shirt and a woman hiding behind him.

"If you come out now and show yourselves, we won't call the cops!"

Gabriel got out of the pool and put his boxers on. Then he walked towards the house. I whisper-yelled, "Gabriel! What are you doing?" Suddenly he paused and strained to look in the window.

"John?" he called out.

"Who's there!" the voice answered.

"It's Gabriel."

I slapped my forehead. "Great, now he knows who the trespassers are," I thought.

The man in the window leaned his head out, squinted, and yelled, "Gabriel? What are you doing here?"

"I could ask you the same thing!"

The man turned to the woman and started arguing with her. Gabriel called out, "Hey, man! You think we could get some towels? It's fucking freezing out here!"

"You got it! I'll be right down."

Gabriel came back to the pool and grabbed his clothes. Then he knelt down to help me out. "It's cool. It's just John."

"John? As in John Ruskin?"

"As in John who's part of the brotherhood."

"No way!" I yelled as he hoisted me out and wrapped his arms around me, so I wouldn't be too cold.

"Let's go. He's bringing us some towels."

"This should be an interesting story."

"Definitely."

"Umm, Gabriel? I'm butt naked."

"Shit!" He ran back and got my clothes and slipped my shirt over my head and helped me into my pants.

John came to the back door and said, "Come in! Come in! You'll freeze out there!" We hurried into the house, and I saw them do some kind of handshake fist bump combo. I could tell it was about John being with Ruskin's wife. I rolled my eyes at him while John turned on the lights.

We were in a living room or den. It was enormous and tacky as fuck. Everything was either bright gold or zebra/cheetah print. There were four or five humongous gold chandeliers, three couches, and five armchairs made with shiny gold fabric, and the biggest zebra print rug I've ever seen. The floor was a shiny white and gold marble, and there was a huge painted gold fireplace. John was wearing some ridiculous, brightly-colored harem pants and no shirt. His chest hair was wild, and the hair on his head was sticking out in every direction. "Sit down! Please! Warm up!" he called out as he flicked a switch that ignited the fireplace. We sat down on one of the couches, and Gabriel took a cheetah-printed blanket and wrapped it around me.

"What can I get you two? Hot cocoa? Effie will be down in a minute," John said with excitement.

"Effie?" Gabriel asked. "You don't just call her Ruskin's wife?" We both giggled, and John started to turn red as Effie entered the room wearing nothing but a silk robe. She was probably in her early twenties and had long, flowing brown hair and bright blue eyes. She was beautiful and looked really nervous.

"Hi, I'm Effie. You must be Gabriel!" She went over to shake his hand, but Gabriel stood up and hugged her. "Oh!" she called out, and Gabriel looked down at her ass and gave John a thumb's up behind her back. I stood up and kicked the back of Gabriel's knee really hard. He fell down onto the couch, and I stood up and held out my hand.

"I'm Jane. It's so nice to meet you!" She vigorously shook my hand and sat on an armchair next to us while John stood beside her.

"I'm so sorry to intrude on you," I started. "I don't normally do things like this."

"I'm a terrible influence on her," Gabriel added.

"Oh, don't worry about it! I get it. I'm just glad my husband isn't home. He has guns in the house." John scoffed and took her hand.

"Where is the old guy?" Gabriel asked.

"Who cares," she responded and looked up at John lovingly. They continued talking, and I thought I saw something behind them move. I tried to focus on the conversation, but a huge wave of fear and paranoia washed over me.

"Jane? Are you okay?" Gabriel looked at me with concern.

"I'm fine. Why?"

"John asked you a question." I saw the same thing move again behind John, but it was hard to make out what it was.

"Jane?" Gabriel asked. "Hello?"

"I'm sorry. What was the question?"

"Are you warm enough?" John asked.

"Oh, yes. Very toasty. Thank you."

"Can I get you anything to eat or drink?" Effie asked.

"Do you have a cat?"

"Nope. No pets," she answered. "Why?"

"No reason. I think I just smoked too much weed. I'm a little paranoid."

"If you smoked too much weed, then you definitely need refreshments! I'll be right back!"

"Wait up, John!" Gabriel called out as he jogged after John. Just as they left, I saw the same image pass through the room, but it was even clearer this time, and I gasped.

"Is it a little girl?" Effie asked me.

"Huh?"

"Is that what you see? What you thought might be a cat?"

"Yes!"

"I see her too. All the time."

"Oh my god!"

"Was she wearing a white dress?"

"Yes!" I whisper-yelled. "And her hair kinda looks…"

"Wet?"

"Yes!"

"It's weird because I kind of see her in my periphery, but when I try to look straight at her she disappears."

"That's how it is for me too." She got up and sat down next to me. "Her name is Sarah. She's about five years old."

"How do you know that?"

"When we first moved in here about two years ago, weird things kept happening, like keys would disappear or objects would move by themselves. But the worst was someone always knocking on the front door. Whenever I would answer it, there was never anyone there. But these things only happened around me; it never happened when anyone else was around. Then I started seeing someone move in my peripheral vision when I was home alone. One night while my husband was out of the country, I heard footsteps in the hallway upstairs. So I went into the hallway, and I saw a little girl in a white dress run across the hall and into one of the guest rooms."

"That's so freaky!"

"I know. I don't know why, but I followed her into that room."

"You have balls of steel! I would have shit my pants and left the house and never come back!"

"I know. I wouldn't normally do something like that, but there was something that was almost compelling me to follow her. I didn't feel scared at all. Just curious. So I followed her into the room, and it was a room we hadn't redecorated yet. It definitely used to be a little girl's room. It had pink flowery wallpaper and light pink carpet."

"Oh shit."

"That's not even the freaky part. I saw the closet door close on its own, so I went over and opened it."

"Oh fuck! Was there a dead body in there or something?"

"No. There was a little white dress hanging inside the closet. The same white dress I saw the girl in. And it was damp."

"Eww! Are you kidding me?"

"The craziest part is that I had put some of my winter clothes in there when we moved in, and that dress was definitely not there!"

"That's so fucked up!"

"I was so freaked that I grabbed my keys and got in my car and drove for like a half-hour. Then I just pulled over somewhere and slept in my car."

"You poor thing!"

"I have a hard time being alone in the house, especially at night."

"Did you tell your husband about it?"

"Yeah. He said that either I'm losing my mind from a lack of moral purpose, or a demon is possessing me and making me see these things. I stopped talking about it when he brought up having an exorcism."

"Geez. He sounds like a real fun guy."

She made a face like she was going to throw up.

"Can I ask you a very intrusive question, Effie?" I didn't want to make her uncomfortable but I couldn't help myself. She giggled and responded, "Sure, why not?"

"Your husband sounds awful. Why did you marry him?"

She took a deep breath and let it out with a sigh before answering. "My parents. They forced me to marry him."

"Oh no. That sucks. You poor thing! Don't they know how terrible he is?"

"They don't think he's terrible at all. They're very religious, like him, and they think he's good for me. And they like his money a lot too."

Before I could respond, the guys came back with armloads of snacks. Effie looked very uncomfortable, so I changed the subject.

"Have you ever researched the history of the house? Maybe something bad happened here and that's why you have ghosts."

"*This* sounds like an interesting conversation!" Gabriel called out as he shoved a handful of popcorn into his mouth.

"You told Jane about her?" John asked.

"I didn't have to. She saw her!"

"I have a theory," John said to me. "I think she only appears to women for a reason."

"Or only women can see her," I added.

"Okay, would someone please tell me what the fuck you're talking about?" Gabriel exclaimed as he opened a beer.

"Her house is haunted by the ghost of a little girl," I told him.

"Cool!"

"It's not cool," Effie responded. "It's sad. She's stuck here. I didn't do research, Jane. But the answers came to me, literally, a few weeks ago."

I moved closer to Gabriel and grabbed his hand as I braced myself for more freaky details. I was still pretty fucked up from the weed, and the whole ghost thing was fifty times creepier.

"I was home alone again at night, and I heard the same knock on the door I kept hearing. But this time, there was a little old lady standing there. She said that she grew up in this house and wanted to take a look around."

"And you were alone?" I asked. "I would have punched that creepy old lady and slammed the door in her face! Fuck that shit!"

"Yeah, fuck that old demon lady!" Gabriel concurred.

"Well, she seemed trustworthy, so I let her in, and she looked all over the house and told me memories she had in each room. Then we went into the little girl's room, and she went into the closet."

"And she went in there and disappeared because she's a fucking demon?" Gabriel asked. I started to wonder if he was drunk, but I only saw him have one beer.

"No, she didn't disappear," Effie responded.

"Was the white dress in there?" I asked.

"Was Satan in there fucking your old husband in the ass?" Gabriel called out. We all turned and looked at him at the same time.

"Too much?" he asked.

"Just a bit," John said.

"*Anyway*," Effie continued, "the dress wasn't there, but the lady knew that there was a loose floorboard in the closet. She lifted it and took out a picture. In the picture was the little girl in the white dress. She handed it to me and said, "'This is my sister Sarah. This was her room.'"

"No way!" I exclaimed as I bit down on my fingers.

"Then she said, 'She died near here.'"

"No shit, lady!" Gabriel said, and I smacked him.

"I asked what happened to her, and she said her mother never let her father watch the kids because he was a drunk and irresponsible. But one day she had an emergency, and the kids had to stay with the dad. There was a knock at the door, and the dad answered it."

"Ax murderer?" Gabriel asked. I smacked him again.

"No, it was just a delivery. But the dad left the door wide open and went into another room. The little girl ran out of the house and they never saw her again."

"Fuck," Gabriel and I commented at the same time.

"Until a few years later when they found her at the bottom of the lake."

We all gasped at the same time.

"How can you still sleep here at night?" I asked.

She took John's hand. "It helps if I'm not alone. And if I'm with someone who makes me feel safe." They both stared dreamily into each other's eyes.

"Well, that's fucking adorable," Gabriel said as he opened another beer.

"Are you okay?" I asked him.

"Fan-fucking-tastic! Why do you ask?" He chugged the whole beer in one go and said, "Kind of reminds me of this really freaky abandoned villa in Northern Italy. We used to rent a house near there in the summer, and one night Christina and I snuck into the place. Scariest fucking night of my life."

"Yeah, I'm gonna need more details than that, bro," John said as he slid next to Effie and grabbed a beer.

"It's called Villa de Vecchi. People also call it Red House because it's made of red sandstone."

"*Really*? Like Will's Red House?"

"I guess. It's considered the most haunted place in Italy. It was built in the 1800s by a count. He came home one day and found his wife brutally murdered, and his daughter was missing. He searched for her for a year and then killed himself."

"That's awful."

"Yup. The place was left to his brother. When he started renovating it, he kept hearing and seeing weird shit, so he just left the place behind. It's been abandoned for like 80 years."

"Sounds creepy as fuck," I said.

"To add to the creepiness, a famous Satanist visited and supposedly had animal sacrifices and ritualistic orgies there. That drew weirdos from all over the globe who vandalized the place. They fucking ruined it."

"So what was it like when you went?"

"I was about 14 or 15. I was a cocky little shit who didn't believe in ghosts or any of that. A local kid I used to hang out with dared me to get something from the cellar to prove I was there. I made my sister come with me. I said I wanted to show her that ghosts aren't real, but really I was too scared to go in alone. It was dusk and really foggy out, which made the whole thing creepier."

"What did it look like?" I asked.

"Most of the red on the outside faded, and it's like an old Gothic castle covered in ivy and weeds. The front door is gone, so you can just walk right in. You can tell the house was really beautiful, with so much attention to detail and lots of hand-painted frescos. But it was covered in graffiti. Not even *good* graffiti. Just stupid tags and curse words in Italian. At the time I thought it was cool, but it's really just annoying that people go into beautiful old places like that and fuck it up for fun."

"Okay, old man," John interrupted. "Besides the annoying graffiti, what happened?"

"The first thing we saw in the main room was a decrepit piano.

The legs and top were missing. I don't think it had keys either. Moss and branches were growing all over everything. I remember being struck by the frescos on the walls and ceiling. Tons of Christian themes. Your husband would have fucking creamed his pants."

John and I laughed, but Effie just looked down at her feet.

"We went upstairs and into a bedroom that had a purple ceiling. For some reason, the purple hadn't faded as much as the rest of the paint in the house. I wasn't paying attention and almost fell right down a huge hole in the center of the room. Christina grabbed my hand just in time."

"Yikes."

"So what was so freaky about it? The holes in the floor?" John asked.

"I'm getting to that part. As we were leaving that room and coming back into the hallway, we heard a child laughing. We both turned to each other and said at the same time, 'Did you hear that?' Then Christina started running back down the stairs to leave. I ran after her and grabbed her hand and said I wasn't ready to go yet. She begged me to leave, but I made her come into the cellar with me. It was a fucking wreck, covered in debris and huge rocks and branches. It was already dark, so I turned on a flashlight and swung it around, and told her there was nothing to be afraid of. Then we heard a song playing on the piano upstairs. We turned to each other and froze. She looked fucking terrified."

"Maybe someone was playing a radio?" John asked.

"No. This was *live music* being played right above us. We heard a woman's voice singing in Italian. I grabbed Christina and shoved her through a hole in the wall that led outside, and we ran as fast as we could until she couldn't run anymore. I took a notebook out of my backpack and wrote down what I heard the woman singing. I crumbled it up and told her to put it in her back pocket. Then I had her tell me exactly what she heard the woman sing. She said, 'la morte non è la fine dell'amore, la morte non è la fine.' I told her to take out the paper and read it to me. She read the same words she had just spoken."

"And for those of us who don't know Italian? Can we get a little help?" John said.

"Death is not the end of love, death is not the end," Gabriel said as his eyes bore into mine.

"I have chills!" John called out.

"Me too!" Effie said as she wrapped John's arms around her.

"The creepiest part is when we got home, my sister hummed the tune we heard for my dad and told him the lyrics, and he turned white as a ghost but said it was nothing. Later that night I heard him talking to my mother, and he said it was an old Italian folk song from the early 1800s."

"*Fuck.*"

"Yeah."

I turned to Gabriel and lifted his shirt a bit to reveal a tattoo I remembered seeing weeks before. There scrawled across his hip were those same lyrics. I ran my fingers over the words and looked at him and nodded. He slowly closed his eyes.

"I think I might have been to a freakier place than that if you can believe it!" John said.

"What could possibly be freakier than *that* story?" Effie asked.

"Have you ever heard of Heart Island?"

"I have!" I answered. "It's part of the Thousand Islands, right?"

"The salad dressing?" John responded.

"No, there's a chain of islands between New York and Canada, over a thousand of them. Heart Island is a tiny, heart-shaped island where a rich guy started building a castle for his wife in the 1920s."

"That's so sweet!" Effie exclaimed.

"Very. Except she died suddenly in the middle of construction, and the husband completely shut down the project. The castle structure has been abandoned there for a hundred years. My ex took me there. It was supposed to be romantic, but it was just creepy and sad."

"Did you see any ghosts?" John asked.

"No. But there was definitely an eerie energy. I couldn't wait to get the fuck out of there. Plus, he was a total douche. He kept trying to make out with me and get me in the mood, and I was just like *hello*, I'm not fucking you in some dead lady's castle!"

"Nothing like being trapped on an island in a creepy, abandoned castle with a horny douche!" Effie responded.

"I know, right? The things we women endure!"

"Tell me about it!"

"Sorry to interrupt this little feminist fest, but that's not the Heart Island I'm talking about," John interrupted. "*This* Heart Island is in the Bronx. It has a really fucked up history. It was originally a Civil War prison where they tortured and buried hundreds of prisoners. Then it had a hospital for Yellow Fever patients, which they turned into an insane asylum, a tuberculosis hospital, a jail, a boy's reform school, a homeless shelter, and a rehab facility."

"Sounds like the worst fucking place on earth!" I said.

"That's not even the worst part," John continued. "It's become a burial site for unidentified bodies. Over a million people have been buried there."

"Please don't tell me you went there. There isn't enough money in the fucking world to get me to a nightmare place like that!"

"I *did* go there. I was a senior in high school, and a bunch of my friends and I thought it would be a fun idea to drop acid there at night."

"There is nothing more deranged than the teenage male brain! Am I right?" Effie said to me.

"You ain't lying!" I called out. I was really starting to like Effie, and I couldn't understand why she was married to that old piece of shit.

"It was definitely one of the worst decisions I've ever made. We had to steal my friend's dad's boat to get there."

"So you operated a boat while high on acid?" Effie asked.

"I already said it was one of the dumbest things I've ever done!" John answered. "We made it there okay because the acid didn't really kick in until we were already on the island."

"What was it like there?" I asked.

John blew a huge breath of air through his mostly closed mouth and said, "Really fucked up. The worst part was the fact that there was nothing there. *Nothing.* No headstones or markers of any kind. Just a huge open area and some piles of dirt and rocks. My friend thought it was a fun idea to jump into an open grave that was waiting for someone. We were all pretty fucked up at that point and couldn't figure out how to help him out, so he was stuck there till the next day."

"*Till the next day*? You just left him there alone?"

"No. We *all* got stuck on the island. We weren't there very long before we realized we'd made a huge mistake, and we completely freaked out. We ran to the boat and looked for hours for the key, but we couldn't find it. We felt bad for Sam, our friend in the grave, so we slept on the ground above him. The weirdest part was that he was a pretty hardcore atheist before that night, and when we woke up in the morning and the cops pulled him out, he'd decided to become a Born Again Christian. He'd never thought about it before, but he said Jesus sat with him in the grave the whole night."

"And that's why you won't catch me dropping acid!" I exclaimed.

"Or hanging out at a mass burial site!" Effie added.

"Amen!" I yelled with my hands in the air.

I realized that Gabriel hadn't said anything in a while. I looked over, and he was staring hard at something behind John and Effie. His eyes were really glassy, and he wasn't blinking at all. "Gabriel? Are you okay?"

He didn't give any indication that he heard me. I took his hand into mine.

"Gabriel? Hello? Are you okay?"

No response. I moved my face in front of his and yelled, "Gabriel! I want to fuck you right now on this couch!"

He shook his head a few times and let out a weird little "huh?"

"Gabriel, what's going on? I'm worried about you."

He responded to me a bit robotically as he continued to stare at the same spot. "I'm fine. We should go."

John softly said, "I think maybe he had a bit too much tea."

"What!" I called out. "What *kind* of tea?"

"The psychedelic kind."

"When did *that* happen?" I asked.

"When we went to get snacks."

"Is he okay? Is this normal?"

"He's fine. We usually trip together once or twice a month. I think he just had too much on an empty stomach. You should see the paintings we've made while high. Pretty wild stuff!"

"Well, he can't drive like this! How far is the walk back to Red House?"

"It's not just a walk. It's literally a hike through the woods and around the lake. It's too cold and too dark."

"Fuck. I can't drive stick!"

"You can stay here!" Effie announced.

"Oh no! We can't. I mean, that's really nice of you but-"

"Why can't you stay?" she asked. "I'd really love it if you did. My husband is gone for weeks, and I don't have many friends my age around here."

"Aww, you're so sweet!" I said. "Gabriel, do you want to stay over here tonight?"

He answered me while continuing to stare behind John. "*No way*, this place is haunted as shit."

I squeezed his hand as hard as I could and dug my nails in. He yelped and looked at me with concern. "We'd love to stay!" I said to Effie. Gabriel was silent but looked totally freaked out.

"Awesome! I'll show you to your room."

"Not that girl's room!" Gabriel yelled.

Effie giggled. "I won't even put you on the same floor. We have a beautiful guest room down here."

"Thank you so much," I said as I pulled Gabriel off the couch. We followed her down the hall and into a huge bedroom. Everything was white and baby blue. There was a very ornate bed covered in light blue satin bedding with about 50 frilly throw pillows. In the corner were three big steps leading up to a light blue Jacuzzi tub.

"Please make yourselves at home. If you need anything at all, please let me know."

"Thank you so much, Effie. You're a wonderful host."

She smiled warmly and closed the door behind her. "She is such a sweetie, but she has the worst fucking taste I've ever seen!" Gabriel stood next to me motionless as his eyes darted around the room. Suddenly, he grabbed my arm really tightly and said, "We have to get the fuck out of here. The energy here is so dark. I don't feel safe. We're not safe!"

"Gabriel, you need to calm down. You're just having a bad trip. Maybe you should let me know the next time you plan on taking psychedelics?"

"Jane, I'm not fucking kidding. I need to be back at Red House. We're not safe here!" He flung the bedroom doors open and started running for the back door.

"Where the fuck are you going?"

"Home! We're going home!"

"You can't drive! Just wait a minute!"

"I can't stay here!"

I called out for John, and he and Effie came running down the stairs.

"I'm so sorry, but Gabriel's freaking out. We really need to get back to the house."

"I'll drive you. It's no problem!" Effie said. "Just lemme throw some clothes on."

Gabriel had already gone out the back door. I ran out and started looking for him. I was getting really nervous thinking of all the bad things that could happen to him in the mental state he was in. I pictured him drowning in the pool, and I started screaming his name.

Then I heard, "Shh!" from the side of the house. He was standing next to a row of bushes with his face about an inch away from a bunch of leaves he was staring at.

"You scared the shit out of me!"

"Shh! They can hear you!"

"Who?"

"Them!" He pointed to the leaves in front of his face.

"The leaves can hear me?"

"Of course. Come closer. But don't startle them."

"Okay…" I joined his side, and he gently held a leaf in his hand.

"These are the most beautiful leaves in the entire world, aren't they?"

"Yes, they're quite beautiful. Listen, Effie agreed to drive us back so-"

"The fear in your voice is upsetting them."

"Fear? I'm not afraid, Gabriel."

"Of course you are. We all are. That's the problem."

"Right."

"Can you see the glow they're giving off? I feel like I can see the world through their eyes. And there is such compassion… and love. They love us so much, Jane."

"Are we still talking about the leaves?"

"Not just the leaves. It's everything! The grass, the soil, the air… it's all alive with the same spirit. And we're connected to it. It's us!"

"Okay. Sure. Let's go around to the front, so we can get home, okay?" He stared up at the sky and didn't move at all. "Gabriel! There are some amazing rose bushes in the front of the house that have a message for you!"

His head snapped to me. "This isn't a joke. Don't mock me."

I took his hand. "I'm sorry. I'm just worried about you. I want to get you home where you feel safe."

He held my hand up to his mouth and gently kissed it. Then we walked around to the front of the house together, and John and Effie were waiting in the car.

The short drive back to Red House was quite awkward. It was quiet as Gabriel stared out the window with a strange look on his face. I thought he might be feeling paranoid, so I put my hand on top of his to comfort him. His eyes closed immediately, and after a moment or two, he said, "Do you feel that?"

"What?"

"There's so much karma between us. It's so heavy." I didn't answer, and he continued. "You've been my teacher, my enemy, my mother, my daughter, my sister, and my lover, countless times. I know you'd feel it too if you would let yourself open up to me."

"You can really feel all of that?"

"You really *can't*?"

John cleared his throat and said, "We're here."

"Thank you guys so much for taking us back. We really appreciate it."

"Of course," Effie answered.

"Love you, brother!" John said to Gabriel. Gabriel put his hand on John's shoulder.

"Same to you, old friend."

We got out of the car, and I looked back at John with trepidation. "Take care of him!" he called out.

"Who will take care of *me*?" I answered with a smile and waved goodbye.

Gabriel stood near the front door gazing up at the night sky again.

"It's freezing out here. Let's go inside."

"Do you feel that?" he asked, not moving his head at all.

"Feel what?"

"Everything. It's all alive. And it's speaking to us. We just refuse to listen."

"What's it saying?"

"Love. A constant message of love. And connectedness. We're all one. There's no separation between matter and spirit." He swiftly turned his head towards me. "We're all *one*."

I whispered, "I agree. But *this* one is getting frostbite. Can we…?"

He held his hands out in front of him as though he was feeling something in the air and closed his eyes. A few seconds later, he opened them with a smirk and said, "After you."

As we entered the house and approached the staircase he said, "You don't think it's real."

"I don't think *what's* real?"

"The things I'm sensing. The ability I have."

"I don't really know what I believe right now."

"I'm going to prove it to you."

We went up to his bedroom, and he sat down on the bed. "I'm going to turn my back to you, and I want you to pick any book from my bookshelf that you've never read before. Don't tell me what it is."

He turned to face the opposite wall, and I looked at his bookcase. "Any book?"

"Yes. Just don't tell me what it is."

I scanned the shelves and tried to pick something that he couldn't possibly have memorized. The words "Plato's Symposium" shined in deep gold lettering, and I grabbed it. "Okay, I've got a book."

"Open it to any page and start reading, but *do not* say anything out loud."

"So just read it in my head? Why?"

"You'll see."

"Okay…"

I opened to a random page and started reading in my head. "According to Greek mythology, humans were originally created with four arms, four legs, and a head with two faces." He didn't say anything, so I turned towards him and said, "So what's supposed to happen?"

He was still facing the other way. "Start over, and read slower this time."

I sighed and started over. "According to Greek mythology," I heard in my head, "humans were originally created with four arms, four legs, and a head with two faces."

I kept reading, and suddenly he was saying exactly what I was reading. "'Fearing their power,'" he said as I read along in amazement, "'Zeus split them into two separate parts, condemning them to spend their lives in search of their other halves.'"

My jaw dropped. "Holy shit! How are you doing that Gabriel?" I whipped around to see if he was behind me, but he hadn't moved at all and was still facing the other direction.

"Keep going!" he called out. "This is the best part."

"'When one of them meets the other half,'" I read internally as he said the words at the exact speed I was reading them, "'the actual half of himself, the pair are lost in an amazement of love and friendship and intimacy, and one will not be out of the other's sight, as I may say, even for a moment.'" I went to the other side of the bed and stood in front of him. "You're freaking me the fuck out! How are you doing that?"

His eyes flew open and he smiled. "I'm reading it through your eyes."

"That can't be! You have this memorized!"

He put his hand on top of my hand that was holding the book and said, "How would I know what page you were on?" I flung the book onto the bed next to him, and he pulled me in closer, looked intensely into my eyes, and said, "And it's no coincidence that you turned to *that* particular passage. No coincidence at all."

"This can't be real. These are your books! You know them!"

"Go and get another book, if you still don't believe me."

I don't know why I didn't just let it go, but the whole situation was intriguing and very exciting. I ran into Will's room. I had to find a book that had zero possibility of him knowing. I spotted a textbook on the bottom shelf that was simply called *The Vietnam War*. It didn't, in any way, seem like something that Gabriel would have been interested in or would have cared about. I took it and hurried back to his room. I stuck my head in, making sure that he couldn't see the book in my hands. "Okay, I've got one." He was still facing the other direction, but I held the book behind my back just in case. Then I turned my back to him and said, "Ready?"

"Yes. Just go slowly."

I opened the book to a random page and started reading. He jumped in right away and read aloud exactly what I heard in my head. "In 1965, the first major battle between American and North

Vietnamese soldiers took place in the Ia Drang Valley in South Vietnam. During the battle, a platoon of American soldiers was cut off and surrounded. Lieutenant Foster's platoon was among those sent to rescue the trapped Americans."

I turned to him, and my hands were shaking so badly that I could barely hold the book. "How the fuck are you doing that?"

"The mushrooms help me access a psychic part of my brain. We all have it. We just need help getting to it."

"But I don't understand. I've never-"

He moved towards me and took the book from my hand. "That was me, you know."

"Who?"

"Lieutenant Paul Foster. That was me. My men and I were sent there to rescue captured troops. When we came under heavy fire, I ran forward because that's what they teach you in the infantry, to lead by example. So I raced across open ground and hurled grenades at the enemy, but I was shot in the neck. I had your letters in my back pocket, and I took them out and held them to my chest as I slipped out of my body."

"*Come on.* That's not real. How could that be, that I just so happened to pick a book and a page that talked about *you*? That's a pretty big coincidence, isn't it?"

"*There are no coincidences.*" We were both silent for a moment, then he continued. "You were all I ever wanted. I watched you on campus for almost two years before I worked up the nerve to ask you out. We only went on one date before I went to Vietnam. I asked you to wait for me. I thought about you all day and all night. It was always you. But you didn't feel the same way about me. The day I was killed I got a letter from you saying that you married my brother."

"I married *your brother*?"

"Yes, my brother Joseph, who was actually Will."

"Wait, *what*? You're telling me that *your brother* in a past life was *Will*, and *I married him*?"

"Yes. You ripped my heart out."

"Gabriel, *seriously.* How do you *know* that?"

"I just know."

"This is very hard to wrap my mind around." I started pacing the room. I didn't know what to think. Normally I would have thought this was either a ploy to gain my trust, so he could get me into bed, or the ramblings of a person on drugs. But I couldn't explain how he knew what he knew.

"Can you see any other lives we've lived together?"

"I don't know. Should I try?" he replied, slowly closing his eyes.

"Maybe. But this is kind of bugging me out."

"Let me concentrate for a few minutes." I sat down next to him as he leaned his head back onto the pillows. Then he reached out for my hand with his eyes still shut and started deep breathing. Just having him hold my hand was almost too much. I wanted to straddle him and shove my tongue down his throat. His face started twitching a bit then he murmured, "Horses."

"Horses?" I repeated.

"Yes. Your father hired me to take care of the horses. We've been meeting secretly in the afternoons. Your horse is beautiful and white. Mine is black and much bigger."

"Why do we have to meet in secret?"

"I'm a peasant, and your father wouldn't approve. You always bring your maid with you to meet me."

"Why do I bring my maid?"

"I think I make you nervous. You always ask to ride my horse. I told you that if you meet me alone, I'd let you." He was silent for a few minutes and then blurted out, "Oh, your maid is Lizzie."

"What!"

"That wasn't her name then. Her name was Mary. She's very protective of you, so you had to sneak away to meet me alone at night."

"How old are we?"

"We're both 18. My parents died, and I live alone in a small cottage in the woods."

"What happened when we met alone?"

"We made love in a field far from your home. We kept meeting every night to make love, and I asked you to marry me."

"Did we get married?"

"Yes. You ran away with me one night, and we live several days' journey from your home."

"What year is it?"

He was silent again and then said, "1370" with certainty. He smiled and said, "We had a little girl."

"We did?"

He continued to smile. "Yes, she's beautiful. Like you." Then his expression changed to a look of terror. "Your father is looking for us. He wants me dead."

"Holy shit! Why?"

"Because I stole you from him. You were supposed to marry someone else."

"Well, that's ridiculous."

"He set our house on fire."

"Oh my god!"

Gabriel's face started to twitch, and he called out, "I had to kill him but only because he was going to kill *me*!"

"You had to kill *who*?"

"Your father. I stabbed him in self-defense. He lunged at me but I moved, and he accidentally slashed you across the hip. *He almost slit my throat!* "

"Then what happened?" I was totally captivated by this insane tale. *"Wait!* Which side of my body was I cut?" I asked.

He concentrated and almost seemed to be squinting with his eyes closed. "Your left-hand side. You never got over the fact that I killed your father. Even though I didn't have a choice."

"This is fucking crazy. Like, what are you even telling me right now?"

His eyes popped open, and he sat up and looked me dead in the eyes. "Jane. *Your father was Will.*"

I stood up and pulled my shirt up to reveal the birthmark I had on my left hip. It was a very thin, light brown splotch about two inches across. He reached out his hand to touch my hip, but I jerked away. "What is even *happening* right now? Is this *real*?"

He pulled me back onto the bed beside him and pressed his lips onto mine. "Now that I have you…" he said into my mouth, "I can't let you go."

"I'm not going anywhere," I whispered back. "But I'm really freaked!"

"He needs you. And he's going to take you away from me," he responded cryptically.

"Who?"

"Will."

"*Will*?"

"Yes."

Suddenly, my phone rang inside my bag, and I shook my head. "I'm not answering it."

He pulled away. "You have to. He *needs* you."

I took out my phone and looked at the number. "I don't know the number," I said as I flung the phone onto the bed and turned back to Gabriel.

"It's him. You have to answer."

I sighed and clicked on the phone, but I didn't say anything.

"Jane? It's Will."

"Holy shit."

"What is it? Are you alright?"

"Yes. I'm fine. I just… What time is it there?"

I looked at Gabriel, and he looked worried. "A little after 6 AM. Did I wake you? I hope not. I just can't stop thinking about you."

"It's okay. I was just having a really weird dream."

"Where are you?" he asked. I didn't know how to answer, so I went with the truth. "I'm at Red House." Right after I said it, I wandered into the hallway and into Will's room because I knew what he would ask next.

"It makes me happy knowing you're there. Are you staying in my room?"

"Yes. I'm here right now."

"I wish I were with you."

"How are you holding up?"

"It's been difficult. I was the only one who was really close with my grandfather. My mum and dad are more concerned with his money than his memory."

"Fuck. They don't deserve a son like you."

"It just brings up a lot of darkness, you know?"

"Yes. Death has a way of doing that. Does it help you to think of your grandparents being together again?"

"I don't know. I'd really like to believe that, but it seems silly."

"I believe it. 100 percent."

"I really wish you were here with me right now. I can still get you a ticket."

"I know, Will. I just can't."

"Jane, are you… Are we… I mean…"

"It's really late, Will. I'm exhausted. Can we talk tomorrow?"

"Yes, of course. I'm so sorry to bother you."

"Hang in there. I'm with you."

"Thank you. That means a lot."

"Goodnight."

"'Night."

CHAPTER 20

GABRIEL

"Napalm Love"—Air

RESTING ON MY BED, I WAITED FOR HER TO RETURN AS random images erupted behind my eyelids. There were neon fractal patterns, swirling tunnels plunging through the blackness, and bright blue and purple vines forming complicated grids, which all connected somehow. Vertigo quickly took over, so I sat in a chair beneath the open window, hoping the crisp November air would help me gain my bearings.

I focused on the sounds outside, and everything was humming with activity. The wind whipped through the branches, pulling the leaves into frenetic swirls, and the air felt charged with life. The autumn energy was alive and buzzing with excitement. I shut my eyes and inhaled deeply, taking in a mix of rich soil, wet bark, and Jane's sweet caramel scent.

I didn't open my eyes. I didn't need to. The energetic pattern of her body outlined in neon pinks and purples appeared behind my eyelids. I held my hand out for her and felt her reach out for me before we actually touched. I gasped when her skin made contact with mine.

"Are you okay?" she softly asked me.

"Shh. Come here."

I took her into my lap, and I could feel the sexual energy rising off her body. It was like warm, golden wisps of light surrounding me. Her face was inches from mine, and I kept deep breathing to fully inhale her presence.

"Gabriel," she whispered into my ear. "Can I ask you a question?"

"Yes," I answered without opening my eyes. I saw the energy around her face turn orange, and sparks started to travel up her spine from deep in her belly.

"Why don't you want to have sex with me? I mean, I don't get it. Weren't you trying to get me into your bed for months? Now that you have me, you won't fuck me. Aren't you into me anymore?"

I slowly opened my eyes and put my nose to hers. "Jane, are you fucking kidding me? I want to fuck you *so much* that it fucking *hurts.*"

"So… now seems like a good time." She grinned and put her hand on my chest. I wrapped my fingers around her hand.

"The thing is that I don't want to just fuck you, Jane. I want to make love to you."

"So make love to me."

She moved her leg over, so she was straddling me; then she stared at me with complete desire and what felt like a hint of sorrow. I instantly knew I could completely lift up her soul or break her down into pieces with my response. So I didn't respond. I took off my shirt and put her hand onto my bare chest, right over my heart. I pushed her palm down until I was sure she could feel my heart beating.

"Do you feel that?"

"Yes."

She lifted off her shirt and pressed my hand into her chest above her heart too. Then she put her other hand on top of mine. As soon as I registered her heartbeat, I exhaled deeply. We sat there for what felt like a very long time, feeling each other's heartbeats and breathing slowly and deeply. She released her hand and pressed her bare chest onto me. As her warm skin met mine, she put her face into my neck. One hand rested perfectly on my collarbone, and the other ran through my hair and stopped on my scalp. Her hips pushed into mine, and she softly moaned into my ear. Under normal circumstances, I would have thrown her onto the bed and fucked the living daylights out of her. But this wasn't normal, and I didn't want it to be. Thousands of years of karmic walls and boundaries started to fall down.

I reached behind her and grabbed my phone off the desk. I was able to put in the passcode; however, the screen was too bright, and the numbers and letters kept melting off the screen onto the ground. She giggled and took the phone from me.

"What are you trying to do? *Are you getting bored?*" she jokingly asked.

I leaned towards her ear and whispered, "Aqueous Transmission," the name of the song that played when we first met. A knowingness spread across her face, and she searched it up for me.

"I'm going to make us a little playlist," she stated.

"Okay. I need to lie down. I'm getting dizzy again."

She swung her leg over and got up as I crashed down onto the bed and slammed my eyes closed. The song started to play, and I felt her warmth move close to my body. I gazed over at her and admired her flawless naked form.

"You're glowing," I told her. "You're so warm."

"I'm not even touching you," she noted.

"You don't have to."

Her smoldering skin was so close that I started sweating, and I felt her unbutton my pants and take them off. Before she touched me again, I knew she was going to go for my boxers, and I reached out and grasped her hands and shook my head. She sighed with frustration, and I sat up and pulled her on top of me.

"Wrap your legs around me again."

Her hot naked body climbed onto me, and she encircled my waist with her legs. I rested my forehead on hers. "I can really feel you. *Fuck.* You're on fire." I started gasping for air as she leaned in and caught my mouth with hers. She seemed to be getting on my wavelength because she didn't act upon the frenetic sexual energy I felt pouring off her. She just held my lips against hers and took a deep breath.

"Everything we've been and everything we will ever be, that's us right now," I told her.

She grabbed the back of my neck and nodded.

"This is it, Jane. The universal, cosmic vibration. Do you feel it?"

She didn't say anything, but I saw a tiny blue orb fall down her face. I lifted my hand and wiped the tear away. We were becoming one.

Whatever intense feelings she was having, I wanted to redirect them away from the sadness. "Listen to the music. Can you feel every instrument? How the sound is echoing off the walls and bouncing back and surrounding us with the most beautiful energy? It's glowing blue, just like when we met that night. Can you feel it?"

"I... I don't..." she seemed distracted.

"Breathe with the music, Jane. Breathe with me."

Our breath matched the rhythm of the music, and I saw her energy field turn a brighter, twinkling gold. Then the song changed to that deeply sexual song she had played in the car earlier. We synced up with the new energy, which was dark crimson and orange—a purely base, sexual vibration. We started sweating, and she slid one hand behind my neck, and the other held onto my chest. Our breaths were more frenzied, and the sexual tension we'd been sending back and forth for months bubbled up to the surface. She moved forward until she found the perfect position on my throbbing hard-on, which was still under my boxers. When she settled into the right spot, we both sucked in a huge breath.

We kept breathing in unison, and she started rocking back and forth. I ran one hand down her back and gently guided her ass while my other hand slid into her sweaty hair. It wasn't an intense movement, just slow, constant, rhythmic circles.

"I can feel you melting into me."

I tried to hold her face, but she turned and sucked my fingers into her mouth. The sensation was so wet and warm that I cried out, and she slammed her hand onto my chest and moaned.

"Open your eyes," she commanded between gasps, and when I did, her eyes were piercing into mine. She held my chest tightly and moaned back and forth in perfect rhythm with the song, and I saw a soft, pink light start to spread from between her legs and up the middle of her body. As the glow moved upwards into her chest, she called out my name followed by "Oh god," and the pinkish light spread through her veins like ink spreading through water. I pressed my hand over her heart, and the light spread into my hand. She screamed "Yes!" and her face slammed down onto my chest as she bit down really hard, keeping the same movements going.

"Ahh fuck!" I called out as my orgasm started, and as I came, I saw golden light seeping from the bite mark she left on my chest. I stopped moving with her, and she bit my neck while slamming her hips into mine.

"Don't stop! Don't fucking stop!" she screamed and bit down again. The pain in my neck was so intense that I pulled her by the hair so we were nose to nose, and we both started coming again. "I fucking love you," I breathed into her mouth.

Her eyes shot open, and she stopped moving as the song changed to something dark that I didn't recognize. She jumped off of me and pulled my t-shirt on.

"Don't get dressed," I murmured. "I want to see your glow."

She started pacing the room and chewing her nails. A swirl of dark purple and red ink moved around her head and chest. "What is it?" I asked. "What's wrong?"

She stopped moving and stared at me for a moment and then bolted from the room, leaving traces of dark colors behind. My body felt like it weighed a thousand pounds, but I forced myself to run after her. I saw traces of colors leading into the bathroom and found her in the empty tub with her knees to her chest.

I kneeled down beside her and held out my hand, but she shook her head and refused to look at me. "Jane, please don't put your veil back up. We were so connected. Come back to me." I reached for her hand, and she let me hold it, though it hung limp in my grip.

"You said that you love me."

"I do."

"You barely know me."

"Haven't I proven to you that I *know* you? Don't you believe?" I climbed into the tub and faced her. "Can't you feel it?"

"I don't know! This is fucking crazy!" She hid her face in her knees. The red color of the stained glass tree above us shone down on her, and she looked like an absolute goddess. It took everything

I had not to furiously make love to her in that tub, but I could see and feel the intense fear pouring from her body.

"Jane. Look at me. *Please.*" She picked her head up, and a tear that looked like red watercolor fell down her cheek. I took her face into my hands. "You have been mine before, and you will always be mine."

She let out a huge sigh and closed her eyes. "I'm scared."

"I know."

I turned the water on and fixed the temperature. I took off my boxers and helped her pull off my t-shirt. I leaned back against the side of the tub and held out my hands. She turned around slowly and laid down on my chest, and we both exhaled deeply. I wrapped my arms around her, and we melted into each other and fell asleep.

I woke up alone in a cold bath. I dried myself off, tied a towel around my waist, and went back to my bedroom. There was a note on my pillow.

> *Ed drove me home. I need some time to myself. A close friend of mine is getting married this weekend. If you'd like to be my date, pick me up at 1 PM on Saturday. It's a few hours from here, so I'll be staying till Sunday.*
> *-J.*

I didn't want to give her space. I wanted to wrap my arms around her and keep her with me forever. Her sweet smell was all over my room. I wasn't sure if she was mine completely yet, but I knew that the coming weekend would be the turning point, one way or the other.

CHAPTER 21

Jane

"Once Upon A Dream"—Lana Del Rey

I SPENT THE REST OF THE WEEK EITHER WORKING OR STALKING Lizzie. The only information they would give me was that she was still in intensive care, and no visitors were allowed yet. I looked out my window at 12:55 on Saturday, and Gabriel was waiting for me in the hottest convertible car. I waited another 15 minutes before joining him outside. He smiled when he saw me and got out of the car.

"Where the fuck did you get this car from?" It was an Audi R8 in the most beautiful shade of dark blue.

"Borrowed it from a friend." He grabbed my bag and tossed it into the tiny space behind the passenger's seat next to his bag and guitar. "Ready?"

"You brought your guitar?"

"Of course."

He was wearing a fitted white t-shirt, tight black jeans, and those worn-in leather boots. His style and magnetism were always so effortless, and I had to keep reminding myself not to stare. But every time I looked at him, I saw flashes of his face between my legs or the look on his face as we came together. He still seemed so cool and nonchalant. Did he remember that he told me he loved me? I couldn't bring it up because then he would know how hard I was falling for him.

He started the engine, and when my favorite Jack White album started blaring from the speakers, I couldn't stop smiling. "So where are we headed?" he asked as he peeled out of the driveway.

"The middle of fucking nowhere," I informed him.

"Does that have an address or…?"

"Yes. Lemme look it up." I found the address and typed it into the GPS.

"Wow. That *is* in the middle of fucking nowhere!"

"It's not too late to turn back!" I announced.

He turned to me and flashed that flawless fucking smile and said, "Not a chance babe. You're stuck with me." Then he winked and turned the music up and accelerated so fast I felt like I was going to fly out of the car and into the fall colored trees that hung above us.

We drove for a while just enjoying the crisp air, the music, and the intense energy between us. Then "Love Interruption" started playing, and we both turned to each other and laughed. It was the song he failed to guess was my favorite at the museum. I didn't realize, as we sang the lyrics to each other, what a giant fucking metaphor it was. It was one of those moments when you feel so good, so high on life, that you wish you could capture those minutes in a little jar to return to again and again.

As the song ended, it started raining, and he put the top up. "So give me the details. Whose wedding is this?"

"My college roommate Ally. She's a sweetheart. She's not someone I'd normally be friends with. We're just really different. But living together made us really close. She started dating Dan on the first day of freshman year. He's a good guy, and they're really cute together. She rented a bunch of houses on a lake. We'll be staying in one of them with a few other couples."

"Sounds cool."

"The only thing is… my ex will be there."

"Oh *shit*. The one who tried to fuck you in that haunted castle?"

"Yup. His fiancée will be there too. The one he cheated on me with."

A huge grin spread across his face and he said, "This is going to be fun!"

"It *is*?"

"Making that fucker jealous? Fuck *yeah*, it'll be fun!"

"I'd prefer to avoid him if possible… and his whore too."

"Whatever you want. I'm yours, and I'll do your bidding."

"Thanks. Maybe you can avoid excessive drug use while we're there? Or just not do drugs at all?"

"You got it. I'm glad you're not going alone."

"Will was actually supposed to go with me."

"But you decided you wanted a better piece of arm candy to show off?"

"No. His grandfather died, and he left the country."

"Right. Well, whatever the reason, I'm happy to be here with you."

I grinned, and he took my hand. Then my thoughts jumped to Lizzie, and my expression fell.

"Jane, what is it?"

"I just haven't been able to get in touch with Lizzie. I'm worried."

He immediately took out his phone and called someone. "Hey, Mike? It's Sam Wilson. How are you, brother?" He laughed and said, "She's alright, just really worried about her best friend." He listened and then hung up.

"He'll call us back in 10 with an update."

"*Who?*"

"That nurse who checked out your foot."

"*You got his number?*"

"Figured it might come in handy."

I squeezed his hand and whispered, "Thank you. Who's Sam Wilson?"

"A character from Captain America," he said with a look of amusement. I lifted an eyebrow, and he added, "Don't worry about it."

Just a few minutes later, the phone rang, and Gabriel handed it to me.

"Hello?"

"Hey! It's Mike. I just talked to the doctor who's overseeing your friend's care, and it looks like she's doing a lot better. Still in ICU but off the machines and improving quite a bit."

"Oh, thank God!"

"Listen, if you call me during my shift tomorrow afternoon, I can probably get her on the phone. Say 1 PM?"

"That would be amazing! I really appreciate it!"

"You got it!"

I hung up and gave the phone back to Gabriel. "Good news?" he asked.

"Yes. She's doing much better. If I call him tomorrow, he'll put her on the phone."

"Excellent!"

He switched on the radio and a Guns N' Roses song was playing. "Hey Jane," he said. "Check out what station this is on." I looked down and saw the station was called, "Classic Rewind," and gave him the finger.

The sun emerged from the clouds, and he put the top back down and turned the music way up.

We arrived at the wedding venue a few hours later. There were four houses in a semi-circle around a lake. The huge one in the middle was where the wedding would be that night. The front door of the wedding house burst open, and Ally came running out and embraced me.

"Jane, I've missed you so much! It's been so long!" She pulled away and looked Gabriel up and down. "Well, *hello* there! And who is this handsome fellow?"

He smiled and held out his hand to shake. "Gabriel. Congratulations! I'm so happy to be here. Thanks for having me." She used his hand to yank him into a hug and he laughed.

"Let me show you where you'll be staying!" As we followed her, she turned to me and said quite audibly, "He's fucking gorgeous! Where'd you find him?"

I rolled my eyes, and Gabriel answered, "At an art museum."

"You picked up a guy at an art museum? That's so fancy!"

"I was only there waiting for Lizzie, and he started following me around like a lost puppy dog."

"She plays hard to get pretty well," Gabriel commented.

"Tell me about it," Ally responded as she opened the door to one of the lake houses. "Okay, so you guys will be in the snowy mountain room. Follow me!" We went up a small wooden staircase and down the hall. "This is the best room, in my opinion."

She opened the door to a very bright and airy room. There was a highly arched ceiling with several skylights and tons of windows overlooking the lake. The walls, curtains, linens, and rugs were all white. Gabriel whistled to show he was impressed. "There's more!" she said. She opened another door revealing a huge bathroom with a shower that could probably fit the entire wedding party. Then she crossed the room and opened a door that led to a balcony with a giant hot tub. "I saved the hot tub for you," she said to me and winked. "Good thing you brought *him*!" she said as she elbowed Gabriel in the arm. "I wouldn't want it to go to waste."

"That's so kind of you," he answered. "I promise not to let that hot tub go to waste."

I cleared my throat loudly. "So what's the plan?"

"You have about an hour to get dressed. Quick rehearsal at 5:30 outside and then the ceremony at 6:30. Sorry, Gabriel. I'm going to have to borrow your date for a bit. But you'll have her back after the ceremony. I promise."

"No worries. Do your thing. I'm sure I can find some ways to occupy myself," he said as he leaned over and looked at the hot tub.

"Great! Help yourself to whatever's in the fridge downstairs. There's lots of beer and wine. Okay, I better go. I have a million things to do!" We hugged, and she quickly left.

As I went to close the door after her, I saw the bedroom door next to ours fly open, and my ex Jake came out. He looked exactly the same, maybe even better than the last time I saw him, which was two years before when we had broken up.

"Jane?" he said with a bit of surprise, like he didn't realize I'd be there. I ran past him and caught Ally before she walked out the front door.

"Hey! Ally! Did you know that my room is right next to Jake's?"

"Shit. That was an oversight. Dan assigned the rooms. I meant to fix that, but I totally forgot!" I pushed out a huge puff of air. "Jane, I'm so sorry! I've been so overwhelmed!"

"Well, can't you move him? Or us?"

"Not really. There's nowhere to move to. Every room is taken. I guess we could ask someone to switch, but most people got here yesterday and are all unpacked and-"

"Okay, forget it. I'll just deal."

"Do you hate me?"

"Of course not! *Fuck* him! He doesn't fucking matter. This day is about you and Dan."

"You're the best. Besides, the new guy you got is waaaaay hotter! Damn girl. He's fucking beautiful. But so are you!"

"Okay, okay. Thanks for the confidence boost!"

"Your babies will be supermodels! Is it serious?"

"We're not exactly ready to talk about having babies."

"Have you said 'I love you' yet?"

"He did. But he was on shrooms."

"I bet he meant it. Just doesn't have the balls to say it sober."

"Who fucking knows? Love you. See you in an hour!" I scurried back to our room without running into Jake again.

"What's up? Is everything okay?" Gabriel asked.

He was stripped down to his boxers with a towel in one hand and a beer in the other. I wanted to wrap my legs around his waist and kiss him.

"Nothing. Just my piece of shit ex is staying in the room directly next to ours."

"Oh fuck, really?"

"Unfortunately."

He moved closer and softly said, "Wanna make him ridiculously jealous?" He leaned in and kissed me on the neck. I shivered, visibly, and he grinned. "Got time for the hot tub?"

"No, I have to get dressed."

"She said you have an hour. It doesn't take that long to put on a dress."

"I have to do makeup and hair too."

"Please? Twenty minutes?"

I rolled my eyes. "Okay. Twenty minutes! I'm setting an alarm."

"Need help getting undressed?" He didn't wait for an answer and started unbuttoning my shirt. I let him unhook my bra. Then he stood back and looked at me for a moment.

"Yes?"

"It's just... your tits are amazing."

"Kay, thanks."

"Thank *you*."

He held my breasts and felt them gently while leaning in to kiss me. I kissed him back as he pinched my nipples and swirled his tongue into my mouth. "Come *on*!" I yelled as I pulled away.

He grinned and moved closer. "I want you."

I pulled away further this time. "Yeah, I know, but I can't get into this right now!"

"Why not?"

"I think I'm just going to start getting dressed. You enjoy the hot tub." He took a swig of beer.

"Suit yourself." He went towards the balcony and then turned back. "Are you sure everything is okay?"

"Yeah. Just... nothing. I'm good."

"I'm here for you. Just tell me what you want me to do."

"You don't have to do anything right now. Just enjoy yourself."

"You sure?"

"Yup."

He walked away and then turned around again. "Jane?"

"Yeah?"

"I fucking love it when you're a bitch to me. Gets me really worked up."

"I'll keep that in mind."

I almost barfed when I saw myself in my bridesmaid dress. Ally was obsessed with Disney, and we all had to dress as Disney princesses. I had to be Sleeping Beauty, which didn't really make sense with my skin and hair coloring. I swallowed my pride and tied the pink satin bow into my hair. Then I went onto the balcony to say good-bye to Gabriel before I left for the rehearsal. When he saw me, he looked confused.

"Wait. Is this a costume party? I brought a regular suit!"

I sighed. "No, it's not a costume party. Ally is kind of a giant cheeseball who's obsessed with Disney. The wedding party has to dress as Disney princes and princesses."

He started laughing and said through giggles, "That is so fucking cheesy! I love it!"

"Go ahead and laugh at my pain."

"Even though it's kind of ridiculous, you make a magnificent princess. I'm kind of jealous of whoever gets to be your prince."

"Uh-huh. I have to go to the rehearsal. I'll see you at the ceremony out by the lake at 6:30."

"Come over here."

"No way! I'm not letting you get me wet!"

"I'm not going to get you wet. I just really need to kiss you."

"It'll have to wait till later. I have to go." I left the balcony and picked up my pink lace parasol and opened the door. I felt him clutch my wrist and place a folded piece of paper into my hand. Then he whipped me back around to face him. Standing there dripping wet in his soaked boxers, he took my face and kissed me deeply. I almost pushed him away, but he felt so good that I lost myself.

"What's this?" I asked as I held up the paper.

"I wrote you a poem about our last night together." He kissed my cheek and neck and trailed kisses across my collarbone.

"I wrote you a poem too," I told him.

"*You did?*"

I took the paper out of my bag and slipped it between his fingers. "You're definitely waking something up inside me."

He looked down at the paper. Then he kissed my neck and ran his tongue along my lips. I moaned, and he grabbed my ass as I opened my mouth for more. Then he pulled away and said, "Are you sure you have to go?"

I exhaled. "Yes…"

He ran his finger along my cheek and said, "Skin as white as snow."

I rolled my eyes. "Nice try, but that was Snow White. I'm Sleeping Beauty."

He looked behind me and grinned. I turned around and saw Jake standing in the hallway watching us. Gabriel nodded his head in Jake's direction and said, "Hey man. How's it going?" Jake looked annoyed and walked away.

"Gabriel, I have to go."

"Okay, but remember you're mine."

"I am?"

"Always have been. Always will be."

The coordinator lined up the bridesmaids and groomsmen to walk down the aisle. By another oversight, I was paired with Jake. He went to hook onto my arm, and I yanked my arm back and stalked after the coordinator. "Excuse me? There's some kind of mistake. I'm not supposed to be paired with him."

"Oh. Well, he's in the matching outfit."

"They're all dressed as princes. Does it really matter?" I wouldn't have cared so much if the bride wasn't forcing us to dance with our chosen partners as well.

Ally came over with a frantic look on her face. She was dressed as Cinderella. "Jane, what's wrong?"

"I'm paired with Jake, so I was just seeing if I could switch. No big deal."

"Oh, no. This is terrible! There's no time to switch outfits!"

"Do they have to switch outfits? Aren't they all Prince Charming?"

She looked offended. "No. *Dan* is Prince Charming. There is only *one* Prince Charming, and he marries *Cinderella*. Princess Aurora marries Prince Philip!"

"Who's Aurora?"

"You!" She started to look very worried, and her breathing got heavy.

"Ally, it's no big deal! I'm a big girl. I can walk next to him. Don't worry about it!"

"Are you sure?"

"Yes! Positive."

I begrudgingly joined my piece-of-shit prince in the procession. Angrily linking elbows with him, I looked away, and he asked, "They wouldn't make the switch, huh?"

"No," I answered, avoiding eye contact.

"You're still angry with me?"

I whipped my head around to face him. "Let's see. You cheated on me for months and lied to my face over and over and over again as you told me you loved me and wanted to spend the rest of your life with me. Then you ripped my fucking heart out and moved your homewrecking *slut whore* into *my* home that very same day, without giving me any notice. No, Jake. I'm not angry at all."

"I never meant to hurt you. I was hoping we could be friends."

"I'll have to think about that one. Yeah, no fucking way."

"Who's the guy you're with?"

"None of your fucking business."

"I hope he treats you well, Jane. You're very special."

"Fuck you!" I said way too loudly as the entire wedding party turned to stare at me. I faced the other direction and pulled Gabriel's poem out of my bra as time seemed to stand still.

As Souls Converge

So close she leaned and poured her heart through me,

My hand on her chest as I felt the eloquent throbs of her soul,
The smooth dark stream of hair spilled around her face,
Sweet fluttering sheet, surrounding the piece of my heart that
      she stole.

Let her silent song show me her burning soul,
which her eyes cannot help but reveal,
I watched her when at some warm thought,
Her heart's secrets she could no longer conceal.

From that sudden union I caught a brief glimpse,
As her veil completely fell and her soul sought mine,
That part of her she buries deep inside,
The part that makes her love the most divine.

I finished reading just as we started to walk down the aisle towards the lake. I felt a warm glow pour from my face as I thought of that night and our intense connection.

As we approached the altar and lined up alongside the groom, I noticed Gabriel was sitting next to Jake's fiancée, and a huge pang of jealousy coursed through my veins. But he was staring at me the entire time. He was in the same fitted suit he wore the night I tied him to his bed, and I couldn't control the smile that grew across my face. He was too gorgeous in that suit. It was unbearable.

I looked down at the ground. When I looked back up, he winked at me, and I had to look away again to compose myself as we started the readings. Each pair of bridesmaid and groomsman had to read a passage from the movie their costumes came from. It was so embarrassing; I wished I had taken a few shots before I walked down the aisle like I saw some of the groomsmen doing.

It started with Snow White and her prince. They read lines about having one love and some other cheesy crap I can't remember. The reading was really dry, and they were obviously pretty embarrassed. It felt like a comedy skit.

Next was Rapunzel's turn. You could tell that she was kind of goth by her dark makeup, black nail polish, and the combat boots that stuck out from under her purple gown. The contrast was hilarious. She reluctantly read the lyrics to "Now I See the Light" from *Tangled*, along with the groomsman, who had a ridiculously deep voice. He read his part completely monotone.

Then the groom's brother, who was dressed as the beast from *Beauty and the Beast*, stepped forward with Belle. He was very overweight, with a huge bushy beard, so he didn't need the headpiece. The poor guy had to read the lyrics to "Beauty and the Beast." I couldn't hold it in anymore when I glanced over at Gabriel. I busted out a huge laugh, but Rapunzel shoved me to shut me up.

Then it was my turn. I sucked in a huge breath and read my first part. "I know you. I walked with you once upon a dream. I know you. The gleam in your eyes is so familiar a gleam."

Jake answered with, "I know it's true that visions are seldom all they seem, but if I know you, I know what you'll do. You'll love me at once, the way you did, once upon a dream."

I almost couldn't do the last part, which was to be read simultaneously with Jake, but I found Gabriel's eyes and read directly to him. "I hope it's true this vision is more than what it seems, because if dreams come true, I know what we'll do, we'll dance once again, the way we did then, once upon a dream." I still wanted to laugh, but Gabriel had a serious look on his face which helped me compose myself.

Next the bride and groom read vows composed of lines from *Cinderella,* and finally, the fucking ceremony was over. I immediately found Gabriel, and he took my face into his hands and kissed me gently and slowly. The sun was setting on the lake, and I didn't want the moment to end. He didn't either. He wrapped his arms around me, and we watched the sun sink behind the horizon. Finally, I pulled away and admitted, "That was so painful."

"But cute."

"*Adorable*. Did that whore try to steal you from me?"

"Whore?"

"The girl sitting next to you in that red dress that makes her look like a fucking she-devil. That's Jake's fiancée."

His eyes grew wide with surprise. "Let me get this straight. He left *you* for *her*?"

"Apparently."

"She looks like a fucking horse."

"Oh my god, she totally does."

"Total horseface and not attractive in the least. He must be blind and completely brainless."

"I have to agree," I said as we walked over to the bar. I ordered an amaretto sour, and he got another beer. I needed a buzz, and fast.

"You know," he said between swigs of beer, "I know what went wrong there."

"Do you?" I drank the entire glass through the tiny straw. "Please enlighten me." We started to wander over to the lake.

"He can't handle a strong woman."

"What makes you say that?"

"I talked to her a bit. One of the easiest lays I've ever met. I could have had her sucking me off under my chair in less than five minutes."

"Umm, eww."

"What I mean is, there isn't much there. She's the type that will agree with whatever the guy says and let him take the lead in every aspect. Girls like her are a dime a dozen and boring as fuck."

"I'd have to agree with you again."

"*You* are the opposite. You're strong, confident, clever as fuck, and magnificent. A guy has to be pretty secure to handle you."

"Geez. I'm like heavy machinery, huh?"

"More like a rare jewel."

I rolled my eyes. "So what makes you so sure that *you* can handle me?"

"I'm not so sure. But I'm damn fucking sure I'd like to try."

"I think I'd like to see you try too."

"I'm just getting started baby."

He started to kiss me, but we heard the DJ inside the house summon the wedding party.

"I think that's you."

"Walk me there?"

"Of course."

"I'm gonna need more drinks. She's making us do a dance routine."

"Shit. Let's run by the bar real quick." We walked to the bar hand in hand, and Gabriel ordered two amaretto sours.

"You like these too?" I asked.

"Fuck, no. That girly shit would make me puke my guts out. They're for you! To get you through the next half hour."

"How thoughtful!" I said as I took both glasses from him and started to chug. As we approached the house where the party would be, he said, "There's something I'm curious about."

"Uh-huh."

"What did you see in that guy? He seems kind of... basic."

"I thought he was pretty basic too when I first met him. Total lax bro. But Ally was dating Dan, and he was Dan's best friend. So he was around a lot. We'd get left alone when they were making out or whatever. He just kind of grew on me."

"Like a fungus."

"Yup."

"Is that what I'm doing? Growing on you like a fungus?" he asked as we approached the back door of the house.

"No, I wanted you from the beginning. I just didn't trust you." The alcohol was loosening up my tongue a little more than I would have liked.

"And now? Do you trust me?"

"Not really. But I think it's too late."

"Too late?"

"In case you haven't noticed, I've kind of given in." I kissed him lightly on the cheek, and he looked shocked as I entered the house.

I joined the wedding party on the dance floor. Ally asked if we had received the videos she sent which explained, in great detail, the dance moves we were expected to perform. No one answered, and she seemed annoyed. Although it was hard for me to understand why she was putting us through this crap, she was a good friend, and we had a lot of fun together. So I swallowed my irritation and spoke up. "I got the video, Ally. And I watched it several times. I'm just afraid it'll be very challenging for us, never having practiced it." It was mostly a lie. I didn't watch the video in its entirety even once. It was too ridiculous. We were expected to do a rather complicated ballroom dance to a mix of various Disney songs. I looked around at the apathetic group of people who were staring at Ally with venom, and I knew the whole thing was about to fall apart.

"Well, let me just see you run through it once!" she insisted.

She ran over to the platform where a band was setting up their equipment, and she had them hook up her phone to the speakers. "Love is an Open Door" from *Frozen* started blasting, and everyone looked around in confusion. I started doing the dance moves from the only part I watched, stepping back and forth and then turning my back to Jake and crossing my arms over my chest. Again, everyone just stood there, not moving at all. Trying to be supportive, I grabbed Jake's hand and turned inward, and then spun back out. The best man grabbed the maid of honor's hand and tried to spin her as well, but she tripped over his gigantic feet and crashed to the ground. I kept doing the steps I could remember, and Ally yelled out, "Follow *her*! Just do what *she's* doing!"

A few more people tried to follow me while several others refused. "Come *on* you guys! This looks terrible!" The bridesmaid with the combat boots had had enough.

"Excuse me. I just have to get this off my chest. I'm very happy for my cousin Dan, and I'm sure you're a very nice person. But just because you are having a wedding does not mean we are your fucking puppets! You are the very *definition* of a *Bridezilla*!" Ally's face started to turn red and tears spilled down.

I quickly took her aside. "Listen, sweetie. They obviously didn't study the video, and they're embarrassed. I have a better idea. How about each couple enters the room in a different, creative way? The band can introduce us that way. It could be really cool!"

"But I saw this routine online, and it was so beautiful!" she said as she sucked back a nose full of snot from crying. I grabbed a napkin and gave it to her.

"Maybe they were professional dancers. This group is definitely not."

She growled a bit. "*Fine*. We'll do your idea. Can you explain it to them? I have to check on the favors. They're supposed to be on the tables when the guests enter!"

"Of course."

I went over to the bar and asked the bartender for eight of the strongest shots she could produce. She laughed and asked, "All for you?"

"I kinda need it, but nah, it's for the wedding party. We had to dress as Disney characters, and now the bride is making us learn a choreographed dance."

Her eyes bulged a bit. "Shit. I've worked a lot of weddings, but I've never seen *that*! I better make it two shots each!"

"You're our savior!" I said as I shoved a $20 into her tip cup. She poured a bunch of stuff into 16 shot glasses. The only thing I recognized was Wild Turkey, and I knew she was definitely hooking us up. I sauntered back over to the wedding party with the tray of shots and a big ol' smile on my face. "Good news guys! I got her to let go of the dance idea."

"Thank god!" Rapunzel announced as everyone else sighed with relief.

"We *do* have to do something creative though."

"Ah, fuck!" the Beast called out.

"Don't worry. It doesn't have to involve dancing! The band will introduce each couple, and we'll enter in a different way. And the bridesmaids will decide that part."

"What do you mean?" Snow White inquired.

"Maybe you can ride in on the prince's back like piggyback style," I suggested.

Snow White's prince added, "I can carry you on my shoulders." Snow White nodded with understanding.

"So each of you decide how you and your partner will enter. And to sweeten the deal, you get two shots each!" I chugged the first one and shook my head at the strength of the alcohol. I grabbed the other shot and one for Jake. Then I went back to him to explain my idea.

"Alright, fuckface. Here's what we're gonna do. I am going to enter by myself, with my hands on my hips, and my head held high, *like the fucking goddess I am*, while you crawl on all fours after me, like a *fucking dog.*"

"Very funny," he responded. "There's no way I'm doing that. What else you got?"

"Ally made it clear that this idea was to be decided by the ladies. Do you really want me to go find her and tell her you refuse to cooperate?"

"*Seriously*, Jane. Gimme a fucking break."

"No. You don't deserve one. Do this little task, and I will consider your karma with me wiped clean."

I held out a shot for him. He threw it back and said, "What do you mean?"

"I won't hate you as much. I'll always *kind of* hate you, but not as passionately. Deal?"

"Ugh, whatever. Can we get this nightmare over with? I'm gonna need more shots."

"Same," I said as I forced the second one down. We went back to the alcohol tray, and Jake had a second shot while I forced back a third. I felt lightheaded, and I realized I had barely eaten anything. I briefly considered grabbing a few rolls off a table when suddenly the guests came running in from outside to escape a massive downpour. Gabriel entered smoothly, completely unbothered by the rain that soaked his hair and jacket. He grabbed a beer from the bar, sat down at a nearby table, raked his hands through his wet hair, and winked at me. I couldn't control my smile. He was amazing, and he was mine.

The wedding coordinator came running over. "You all need to get in the hallway! The introductions will be starting soon!" We trudged into the hallway like good princes and princesses. She lined us up in a particular order behind the closed doors. Jake and I were set to enter right before the best man and maid of honor. Snow White entered first while sitting on her prince's shoulders, and everyone cheered. Rapunzel went in piggyback style with her man, but just before they made it to the dance floor, he totally dropped her on her ass. They scrambled to join the first couple in line.

Next was my turn, and I turned to Jake and said, "Well?"

"Well, *what*?"

"Get on your knees!"

I started swaying a bit from the intense buzz. "I can't believe I'm doing this," he murmured as he got down on all fours.

"I can believe it. It's your destiny, Jake!" The doors swung open. I sauntered into the room with my hands on my hips, and my head held high as the chorus of "Kiss the Girl" from *The Little Mermaid* played. I heard gasps and laughs, and then everyone clapped, cheered, and whistled like crazy. I glanced back and saw Jake crawling on all fours with a very resigned look on his face. It was exhilarating.

When we reached the rest of the wedding party, I slammed my foot down onto Jake's shoulder as he tried to rise, forcing him back into position. Then I rested my foot there and looked at my nails. The guests went crazy, and I locked eyes with Gabriel, who had the widest grin across his beautiful face. I winked at him and smiled.

The Beast entered holding Belle's hand, and they both looked bored. Then Cinderella and Prince Charming had their grand entrance, and the MC announced that the bride and groom wanted everyone to join them for their first dance. The band started playing "A Whole New World" from *Aladdin,* and I immediately went and yanked Gabriel out of his chair. We wrapped our arms around each other on the dance floor, and he put his nose to mine and said, "You're a fucking queen!"

"I know."

"That whole thing was orchestrated by you, wasn't it?"

"Of course!"

"I am so turned on right now." He took my hand and showed me how aroused he was. I ran my tongue over my top lip and then bit my bottom lip as I started to gently massage him. His eyes lit up, but he noticed an older couple watching us. He blushed and pulled my hand off.

"Since when are you so fucking shy?" I asked as I pressed my hips into his and sucked his earlobe into my mouth. He shuddered but pushed me away a little.

"Come on, you fucking prude!" I said playfully. Then I dropped my head back and let my hair sway back and forth across my back. I started to lose my balance, and Gabriel caught me and yanked me back up.

"How many drinks have you had in the last hour, Jane?"

I rolled my eyes. "Why? Are you concerned I might have a little too much fun?" I leaned in and bit his bottom lip.

"Yes!" he said as he pulled his lip from my teeth. "I *am* a bit concerned. I think you need to eat something." I scoffed as he led me over to a table and gently pushed me into a chair. He held a roll out for me, and I turned my head and crossed my arms across my chest. "Please?" he said with true concern in his eyes.

I grabbed the roll and angrily ripped off a bite.

"What are you mad about? I don't want you to get sick."

"I'm not going to get sick," I declared as I continued to ferociously eat my roll. "And I don't need a caretaker."

"I know that."

"Can we dance now?"

"Eat another roll, and it would be my honor." I growled at him and shoved another roll down my throat. Then he held out a hand for me and led me back to the dance floor as the band started to play Walk the Moon's "Shut Up and Dance."

He put my arms around his neck, and we danced and swayed and laughed. He kept picking me up and swinging me around, and it was pure, cheesy fun. At one point, Jake and his girlfriend danced near us, and Gabriel let out the most realistic horse neigh I've ever heard. They both looked at us with confusion, and he just coughed and said, "Excuse me!"

The band started another cheesy song, and I leaned into Gabriel's ear. "Is it just me, or does the band suck really bad?"

He laughed and yelled back into my ear, "It's not the band; it's the guitar player! He's all over the place!" We turned towards the platform, and the guitar player was swaying back and forth and seemed drunk.

The singer announced it was time for dinner, and we sat down at the table where I had eaten the rolls. An older woman came over and said, "Excuse me dear, but I think you might be at the wrong table. Did you get your seating card?" She held out a magic wand with a tag on it that said her name and the number of the table we were sitting at. "You're probably at *that* table," she said as she pointed to a table next to where the bride and groom were sitting. The entire wedding party was there, and there were two empty seats.

"Fuck," I spat. The woman looked shocked. "Listen," I looked at her tag and continued, "Katherine. Any chance you want to switch with us?"

"Oh, I don't think we should. It seems like the wedding party is meant to be there."

"I'll give you 20 dollars!" I grabbed my purse and fished around then added, "No, 35 dollars!"

The woman looked irritated, and Gabriel stood and pulled me up from my chair. "I'm sorry, ma'am. I think she's had a bit too much to drink."

"No, I haven't! If I have to sit with that cheating piece of shit and his horseface girlfriend, I'm gonna need *a lot more drinks*! Excuse me!" I snatched my purse and stomped over to the bar.

"Hey! Me again! I'm gonna need more of those shots!"

"Are you sure? You seem pretty lit!" I took out a wad of cash, and she said, "Coming right up, Sleeping Beauty!"

I let out an "ugh" and yanked the pink ribbon from my hair. Gabriel joined me as she presented me with two more shots of the same mixture from earlier. "Bottom's up!" I said to the bartender, and I gulped down the awful substance.

"Woah, there!" Gabriel grabbed the other shot from me, smelled it, and made a yuck face. I tried to get it from him, but he moved it away. "I think you've had enough, my dear." I tried to grab it again but he dumped it into the little sink behind the bar. "Come on! That cost me 35 bucks!"

"I'll pay you back. Let's go sit down." He took my hand, and I turned to him and got right in his face. "If I have to sit with *them*, I *need* to be drunk."

"No, you *don't*. Here's why. *They* are garbage people and are *not* worth your energy. You *cannot* let them get under your skin like this. You are above them. Show him that he no longer has any power over you. If you've truly moved on, you wouldn't even notice that he's there."

I blew out a long breath. "I guess I haven't moved on then. And maybe I never will. That's how bad he hurt me."

He got closer and took my hand. "Jane, listen to me. I understand that he hurt you. And don't think I don't want to beat the living daylights out of him. But that proves nothing and accomplishes nothing."

"It would make me smile!"

"I know. But what he needs is time for that shit relationship over there to blow up in his face and to see that you've moved on from him. You not giving a fuck that he exists is the best revenge, trust me."

"But-"

"And you're here with *me*. And I'm *way better* in every possible way than that toolbag. Focus on me, and I guarantee his jealousy will come pouring out. Now let's go sit down and completely ignore them like the nothings that they are. Okay?"

"How do you know so much about how to handle douchebags?"

"I *was* one for a long time."

He winked at me and then led me over to the table. We sat down at the two empty seats next to them as the first course was being served. A waitress placed bowls of thick orange muck in front of us. I leaned in, smelled it, and gagged. "Excuse me? What is this?"

"Brie and Cheddar Apple Beer Soup with Cinnamon Pecan Oat Crumble, ma'am."

My eyes widened at the description. "Sounds… interesting."

Gabriel leaned towards me. "You first."

"Uh-uh! No fucking way! It smells like vomit!" I said way too loud. Rapunzel cleared her throat to signal that I was being rude and took a big ol' spoonful into her mouth. Then she promptly opened her mouth to let the substance pour back out into her bowl. I cleared my throat in the same way that she did.

Gabriel signaled a waiter. "We're gonna need a lot more rolls over here."

"Yo," I said to him with a big smirk on my face. "I *dare* you to eat that soup."

His eyebrows twisted as he answered, "No fucking way! I don't want to get food poisoning!"

"Aww! Come on! Don't be a pussy! It's just soup!"

He rolled his eyes and the best man called out, "Don't do it, man! It ain't worth it!"

Gabriel laughed. "I don't know, dude. She called me a pussy."

The best man answered, "You may be a pussy, but you won't have your head stuck in a toilet all night!"

"You make a strong point." He held his hand out for a shake. "Gabriel."

The best man shook his hand and said, "John."

"I think before I make a decision on whether or not to accept the dare, I need to hear the terms."

Everyone looked at me with anticipation. I had a pretty intense buzz going on, and the next statement just kind of slid out. "Eat three spoonfuls, and I'll give you a BJ later." Gabriel's eyes almost fell out of his head. He turned to John and put his hands up as if to say he didn't have a choice.

John replied, "Just hold your nose when you swallow. I'll get you a ginger ale."

"Wait. Jane, do I have to swallow?"

I batted my eyes at him and said, "*Do I*?" His eyes bugged out again, and he grabbed the spoon.

Then he turned to me and said, "Can I get these terms in writing?"

"Oh, just do it already! Let's go!"

He held his nose and took three quick spoonfuls of soup. Then he let go of his nose, gagged a bit, and chugged the glass of champagne that was in front of him. He gagged again and drank my entire glass of champagne too. The whole table erupted in laughter, except Jake and horseface, who looked rather angry. I suddenly realized that I hadn't even noticed they were there, and I grabbed Gabriel's face and kissed him long and hard. Then I pulled away and stuck my tongue out to show my disgust from the leftover taste of soup in his mouth. Rapunzel held her champagne out for me, and I chugged it down and gave her a thumbs up.

"You two are hilarious!" John called out as the singer of the band announced it was time for the best man's speech. "Ah, shit!" John said as he stood up. "Alcohol! More alcohol!" he demanded. The remaining members of the table held their champagne glasses out, and John threw them all back. I grabbed Jake's glass as Gabriel took horseface's glass, and we held them out for him too. He gratefully chugged them and announced, "This is going to suck."

As he walked towards the platform, Gabriel whistled and cheered for him, and I joined in. Rapunzel cheered too. Horseface crossed her arms across her chest and declared, "You two are ridiculous!" Gabriel neighed, then cleared his throat and excused himself.

I laughed obnoxiously loud and turned to him and said, "You are so ridiculous, Gabriel!"

He replied, "And so are you, my love. So are you."

Then we kissed for an inappropriately long time. I didn't bother to look for a reaction from Jake as the best man's speech started. He was moving from side to side, clearly unable to keep his balance from all the alcohol. He cleared his throat into the mic five separate times and then stumbled backward into the drum set. Some of the band members tried to help him up, but he insisted he was fine. Then he stared into the crowd with a blank look for a while. The wedding coordinator came over and whispered into his ear, and he angrily responded, "I got it! I got it! Get out of here lady!" She put her hands up and backed away. Gabriel was squeezing my knee too tightly from the hilarious tension. I moved his hand and placed it on my inner thigh and winked. He started rubbing me over my underwear, and I closed my eyes.

"I don't know anything about love, alright," the speech started. "But I *do* know one thing! My brother Dan knows how to get pussy!" Everyone gasped, Gabriel spit water out of his mouth, and my eyes flew open. The wedding coordinator started to approach the platform again, but John stopped her. "I'm sorry! I know that was bad! I won't say pussy anymore, I promise!" I took Gabriel's hand away. I needed to concentrate on what this guy was saying because it was amazing. "Okay, so what I meant to say is that my bro has always been pretty good with the ladies, if you know what I mean. And I *know* you *know* what I mean!" Everyone laughed awkwardly, and he pointed at horseface and said, "*She* knows what I mean, *am I right, Olivia?*"

Gabriel and I both called out, "Ohhhhh!" and she galloped out of the room as Jake chased after her. The way the whole thing with them was playing out was beyond perfect.

"*Anyway*. My point is that Dan was so good with the ladies that I think without him I never would have gotten laid! So I just want to say thank you, bro. For helping your awkward big brother get some pussy! Us big boys need love too. I fucking love you!"

Just as the wedding coordinator tried to steal the mic from John, he dove off the platform directly onto his brother. It was probably meant to be a hug; however, he ended up knocking his brother's chair back, and they both fell backward. The bride was bright red and did *not* look pleased. It was eerily quiet until John stood up and pulled the groom up with him and yelled, "We're okay!" Everyone cheered as they hugged, and John returned to his seat. "How'd I do?"

"That was absolutely the most memorable best man speech I've ever heard!" Gabriel announced.

"Aww, really? I had a whole thing planned, but I couldn't remember it."

"Off the cuff is better," I added. "From the heart!"

"How bout I get us some shots?" he responded and stumbled towards the bar as they started serving dinner. They put a very odd-looking piece of meat in front of each of us as Belle started her speech. She was quite sober and very obviously nervous. As she started to babble about friendship and memories and stuff, Gabriel and I discussed what exactly the gray slab in front of us was supposed to be.

"I'm thinking this is fish." He leaned in to smell it, then verified, "Yup. Definitely fish."

I smelled it too and gave my theory. "Beef. Really old, weird, rubbery beef."

His face twisted with disbelief, and he said, "Wanna bet on it? I'll ask the waitress."

I grinned. "Sure. What are the terms?"

He thought for a moment and said, "If I win, we leave this shitshow early and get in the hot tub."

"Sure. And if I win, I don't have to give that BJ, *and* I get a striptease from you later."

"Sheesh. The stakes are high!" Gabriel said as he flagged down a waiter. "Excuse me, sir. I'm so sorry to bother you, but can you tell me what this is exactly?"

"Of course, sir. Petit filet of beef in a balsamic demi-glaze."

I mouthed, "*Yes!*" to him.

"Can I just ask you one more question?"

"Yes, of course, sir."

"Have you ever eaten any of this food?"

The waiter twisted his face in disgust and replied, "*Fuck no.* Excuse me. I meant that I have not tasted the food."

"Is there anything in the kitchen that isn't so fucking disgusting? I'll pay extra!"

The waiter handed him a card from his back pocket. Then he whispered, "That's your best bet!" and walked away. I leaned over and saw it was a business card for pizza delivery.

Gabriel stood up and said, "Would you all excuse me for a moment?" just as Jake and horseface returned to the table.

"I'll join you! I have to use the ladies' room." He held out his hand and escorted me into the hallway. It wasn't until I was up and walking that I realized how drunk I was. I needed to hold onto Gabriel's arm to keep my balance. He led me to the bathroom and asked if I needed help in there too. "Thanks, I think I can take it from here."

"I'll be right here if you need me."

I forgot that I was dressed as fucking Sleeping Beauty, and when I saw my reflection in the full-length mirror, I was startled. Then a laughing fit started. Gabriel knocked and asked if I was okay. "Yep! Just forgot I was a Disney princess for a moment!" I had some issues lifting the layers of the dress, so I just took it off completely and plopped down to pee. The room was spinning, and I had a profoundly joyous feeling. I got the dress back on, but I had to have Gabriel lace up the back in the hallway. I leaned against the wall while he navigated the ribbons and such. When he was finished, I spun around and whined, "Do we really have to go back in there?"

"I was hoping you'd wait outside with me."

"For what?"

"Pizza!"

I took his hand, and he wrapped his arm around me to help me stay upright as we made our way outside. It was drizzling but not too cold, and I spun around in circles in the middle of the street. He came over to me and took my hands. "Okay, princess. Time to get out of the road." I giggled and used his hands to spin me around a few times. Then we sat on the sidewalk as the pizza delivery car pulled up. A man took out 10 boxes of pizza.

"Where do you want these?"

Gabriel led him inside to an empty table in the hallway. Then he handed him a wad of bills and thanked him. "How'd you get him to come so fast?" I asked.

"Hundred dollar tip!" He opened the first box of pizza, and I swear I heard angels singing.

"Ladies first!"

I grabbed a slice and ate it ridiculously fast as Gabriel inhaled two slices at once.

"This is the best pizza I have ever had ever, *ever*," I exclaimed.

"I think you're just hungry and drunk."

We took more slices as John the best man stomped over in a frenzy, screaming, "Yeeeeesssssss! You got enough to share?"

"Of course!" Gabriel answered.

John grabbed all the boxes and headed for the ballroom. "Wait!" I called out. I turned to Gabriel with concern. "He can't bring that in there. That's so trashy!"

"I think it's too late."

We entered the ballroom, and John smashed the boxes onto the middle of our table. People started running over and fighting over slices. I made a sad face at Gabriel. "I wanted more."

"Me too."

The band started playing "Ain't No Mountain High Enough," and he turned to me and said, "Shall we dance?"

"Fine. But when the cake comes out, I'm knocking bitches out to get the first slice."

"If it's any good."

"How do you fuck up cake?"

"Good point."

We joined a few other couples on the dance floor, and as the old cliché goes, we danced like no one was watching. Gabriel spun me and dipped me and even attempted to lift me into the air a few times. We were laughing so hard that I could barely breathe. Then the guitar player stumbled over to the side of the platform and vomited. Everyone turned and gasped. A bunch of staff started to clean up after him as the wedding coordinator and the lead singer helped the guitar player hobble out of the room. The singer came back and said into the mic, "Any guitar players here?"

Gabriel and I looked at each other, and I shrugged my shoulders. "Totally up to you."

"Just a couple songs. Promise."

I nodded my head, and he handed me his jacket and loosened his tie. I stood in place as he jogged over to the platform and grabbed the electric guitar. There was nothing sexier than Gabriel playing guitar. He exchanged a few words with the other band members, and they started playing Talking Heads' "Burning Down the House." They sounded really good, and people started to fill the dance floor. Then they played The Beatles' "Twist and Shout," and Gabriel had his back against the singer's back as they shared a mic. I was so turned on I almost had to sit down, but Ally came over and started dancing with me. We twisted and shouted and giggled, and there was so much joy. Then she grabbed me and screamed into my ear, "I'll be right back! Don't move!" I stayed put and enjoyed watching Gabriel play the shit out of the guitar, and she returned with a tray full of shots. "Fireballs! For old time's sake!" Then she grabbed one and tossed it back. I started to back away, but she was pretty buzzed. "Come on! It's my wedding day!"

"I can't. Seriously. I'm really drunk already." She made a pouty face and yelled at me again.

"Okay, *one*!"

"Woo!" she yelled as I drank the shot and shook my head from the taste. Then she did another shot and yelled, "One more! For good luck!"

"Seriously, Ally! I *can't*!"

"Don't be a baby!" she said as she threw back another. I growled at her and drank another. She slammed the tray down on a nearby table, grabbed my hands, raised them up in the air, and screamed "Woo!" at the top of her lungs.

I screamed too as the singer announced, "Okay. We have a special request from the best man."

John stumbled onto the stage and took the mic. "This is for my little brother. We used to listen to this every night in the summer of '98! Love you bro!"

The band started to play Guns N' Roses' "November Rain," and John sang pretty well considering how drunk he was. I, meanwhile, was the most drunk I had ever been in my life, and I plopped down in a chair and leaned my head back. When the guitar solo started, I lifted my head and watched Gabriel absolutely kill it. I couldn't wait to get him back to the room, so I could fuck his brains out. As the song ended, I slammed my head onto the table for a little rest.

Then I heard his voice in my ear. "Jane? *Jane?* Are you alright? Lift your head up!" I tried to lift my head, but it was too heavy and just hung down in front of me. I heard him say, "Shit," as he lifted me up. "Can you walk?"

With my head still hanging down, I slurred, "Yes, I can fucking walk. What kind of fucking question is that?" Then I fell right onto him with all my weight. He swept me up into his arms. The next thing I knew, I was gently placed in a bed, and I tried to sit up.

"No, don't get up."

"Why not?" I slurred. It took me a few tries to get my head up, but eventually, I did. Gabriel came over to me and held out a glass of water. I pushed it aside and started to unbutton his shirt.

"What are you doing?" he asked.

"I still want my striptease. Get this fucking shirt off!"

He put the water down and took off his shirt. "Pants!" I commanded, and he slid them off too. "Okay, now do a sexy dance." He just stood there with a blank look. "Come on." He didn't move, and I hopped off the bed and into his arms. Then I smashed my mouth onto his and shoved my hand into his boxers.

"Jesus!" he called out.

"What?" I yelled.

"Nothing." He leaned in and started kissing me gently, and I grabbed the back of his head and kissed him way more intensely.

He seemed reluctant, so I pulled away. "What is it?"

"I just think we should slow down."

"What! *Why?*"

As he started to answer, vomit exploded out of my nose and mouth and landed all over him. I put my hand over my mouth, but the spew just kept coming out. I bent over, so it wouldn't spray on him again.

"Oh my god! I'm so sorry!" I yelled as he helped me into the bathroom.

"It's okay," he answered as he helped me kneel in front of the toilet. As I vomited a few more times, he sat behind me and held my hair, and rubbed my back. I was so sick that I didn't even know who was there or what was happening. I just felt taken care of. When the vomiting finally ended, I sprawled out on the little bath rug and closed my eyes. I woke up in bed the next day next to Gabriel, who was staring at me with that little smirk.

CHAPTER 22

GABRIEL

"I Wanna Be Your High"—Chad Tepper

THAT WEDDING WAS THE TACKIEST SHIT SHOW I'VE EVER witnessed. But it was the most fun I've had at a wedding by far. Jane's veil was falling more and more, and it wasn't just because she was so drunk. There was a comfortable feeling between us before the alcohol. She was starting to feel like home. I almost enjoyed fucking around with her more than I would enjoy actually fucking her. *Almost.*

I would have let it happen that night, for sure. But when we got back to the room, my instincts told me she was just about ready to blackout. I might be a piece of shit in a lot of ways, but I don't fuck unconscious or even partially unconscious girls. Also, I can't believe I'm saying this, but I wanted to save our first experience for a better time. Yes, a more special time. (*Fuck*, that's lame.)

After she blew chunks all over my bare chest, I helped her to the bathroom where she continued to throw up for another half hour. Considering she had only eaten one piece of pizza the entire day, I had no idea where all that vomit came from. When her stomach was completely empty, she passed out on the floor in front of the toilet. I cleaned off her face and hands, changed her clothes, and put her in bed. Then I showered her puke off my chest and arms and put on clean clothes. I watched her sleep for a while, and then I went onto the balcony for a cigarette. I briefly thought about smoking the joint I had in my bag, but something about it seemed wrong. I wanted to be fully present in case she needed me. I considered getting in the hot tub, but it felt pointless to do it alone.

I heard some banging noises, and I went to the end of the

balcony to see where it was coming from. From that angle, I could see directly into the bedroom that Jane's ex and his girlfriend were staying in. The curtains were wide open, and the lights were on. He was banging her doggy style in his dress shirt and black socks. I shook my head and laughed because the dude had no idea what the fuck he was doing. You would think it wouldn't be that complicated, especially in that position, but I can tell you with 100 percent certainty that she wasn't getting anything out of it. I don't even know if he was aware that she was in the room. Maybe he forgot there was a girl there, and he just thought he was humping his pillow. No wonder Jane never got off.

I went back in and searched my pants for my lighter and found Jane's poem. I sat outside and enjoyed my cigarette in the cool moonlight while I read her words.

Flowering Arms of Completion

My soul is lost inside this hollow body tree.
You attempt to find me with your godlike heavenly breath,
as the tips of your fingers and tongue
weave this magnificent cerebral death.

My roots creep across you,
Penetrate your flesh and link up with your veins,
As your hands upon my body
Help break these invisible chains.

My blood is the river I suck from your ground,
Cherry blossoms bursting on my branches,
You fill me—
My soul is found.

I went back into the room and got under the covers next to her. There was no tension in her face. It was one of the only times I'd seen her completely calm. No sign of that defensive bitch who turned me on more than anything. While I missed her just a bit, seeing her face and body completely at ease helped put me right to sleep. I woke up early and snuck into the kitchen before anyone else. I grabbed every breakfast food I could find and a huge bottle of aspirin.

Jane was still out cold, so I decided to go for a run. I changed and started running laps around the lake. The trees were covered with lush orange, red, and yellow leaves. Their reflection on the water made it look like the lake was on fire. The smell of the wet ground reminded me of the smell of the olive trees outside my family's villa in Montepulciano. There's a path out back where Christina and I used to ride our bikes. The path goes up several hills, and from that height, you can see the vineyards, old villas, and even a few old castles. I used to love the times when I was able to ditch her and ride alone. I always felt I could connect with all of it more by myself. As I thought of what was probably my favorite place in the world, I had a strong urge to take Jane there. Surely she would say she couldn't, but I had to convince her. The nagging feeling that my time with her was limited was becoming more intense. I had to have as many meaningful experiences with her as I could.

I showered and got back under the covers in my underwear just as she awoke. She looked peaceful and content. Then her face suddenly dropped, and she asked, "Did I throw up on you last night?" I nodded yes with a grin. She instantly flung herself out of the bed, ran into the bathroom, and slammed the door behind her. The shower turned on, and I heard her talking enthusiastically to someone. She came out smelling fantastic and slid back into bed next to me.

"Sorry about that," she began.

"You're not the first, and you probably won't be the last."

"To vomit on you?"

"Yup."

"Why do you get vomited on so often?"

"That's a very good question. I should ponder that more. Hungry?"

"Ugh, *no*. I'm still kind of nauseous, and my head is fucking killing me."

I brought her the bottle of aspirin and water. "How many of these do you think I can take?" she asked as she spilled a bunch into her hand.

"At least three."

"Four it is!" She drank the entire glass of water and slammed her head back down onto the pillow.

"Who were you talking to?" I asked.

"Lizzie called!"

"How is she?"

"A lot better! She's mostly just being monitored to make sure she doesn't relapse. No visitors for at least another week."

"I'm really glad she's doing so much better."

"Me too."

"You should eat. Can I bring you something?"

"I don't know. I guess."

I grabbed a muffin and a banana and brought them to her. She opened one eye and made a face at the banana and then grabbed the muffin and took a huge bite with her eyes closed. "I'm still a little drunk," she murmured.

"I know. I have a question for you, and I don't want you to answer until you've taken enough time to really think it through."

"Oh, no. Did I mention I'm not feeling well?"

"It's not like that. Just listen. I know that whenever I bring up traveling you're very hesitant because of your job and whatever else, but I have someplace very special that I would like to take you to."

"Okay. Let's go. Where is it?"

"Italy."

"Italy?"

"Yes. My family has a villa in a suburb of Siena. It's incredible there. We have 250 acres, and this time of year… it's impossible to describe it with words. I really want to share it with you. I've never taken a girlfriend there or even *wanted to*. I only go with family or alone. Please consider it before you say no. We could go for just a few days if you want."

A hint of a smile appeared on her face, though she kept her eyes closed. "I have a better idea."

"*A better idea than Italy*?"

"Yes. London."

"*London?* Jane, have you ever been to *Tuscany*?"

"No, I haven't. But there's a reason I want to go to London."

"And that reason is…?"

"Will."

"Oh."

She opened her eyes and looked at me very sincerely. "You said yourself that he's having a really hard time, and he needs me. I think he could use our friendship right now."

"Our friendship, *or your love*?"

"*Our* friendship *and* love. So what do you say?"

I grabbed my phone and started searching for flights. "What day should we go, and how long do you want to stay?"

"Lemme think. How about Thursday to Monday?"

I quickly found a flight. "Okay. Two first-class tickets to Heathrow Airport. Departs Thursday at 4 PM and arrives the next morning. You in?"

"I'm in! But don't tell Will. I want to surprise him."

"I won't tell. Promise."

I jumped on top of her and kissed the shit out of her. She leaned back and said, "Did you call me your girlfriend?"

"I don't know. Did I?"

"Sort of."

"Can I do it again some time?"

"Maybe. But *not* in front of Will."

I rolled my eyes.

"No, *seriously* Gabriel. I don't want to hurt his feelings. That's not why I want to go there."

I leaned in close to her face. "*Jane.* If we're going to be together, he's going to have to find out at some point."

"I realize that. But I don't think it needs to be during a visit we make for the main purpose of cheering him up. Then it's just like we're rubbing his nose in it."

I sighed dramatically. "Okay, I'll *try* to keep my hands to myself in front of him."

"Don't just *try*. Forget that you even know me like that. We're *just* friends."

I stared at her. An image of her calling out my name as I made her come flashed into my brain and my dick got rock hard. I growled at her and grabbed her bottom lip with my teeth. Then I pressed my dick into her thigh. "This is *not* how I react to my *friends*, Jane."

"Oh, come on. Ed never got that reaction from you?"

I growled again and kissed her aggressively. She gave in immediately and raked her nails through my hair as our tongues swirled in unison. I ripped the blankets off her, and she was only wearing a t-shirt. She grinned and opened her legs, revealing her perfectly shaved pussy. "I'm gonna make that headache go away," I told her. She responded by closing her eyes and spreading herself open more.

"You have the most perfect pussy in the entire fucking universe."

"You already told me that."

"It's worth restating. But I want you to turn over."

"Hmm?"

"Turn over. I want to see your ass." Her eyes flew open.

"*Why?*"

"Because I want to worship you."

"You want to worship my ass?"

"Yes." She giggled and looked at me like I was a complete idiot as she turned over and stuck her face in the pillow. But her legs were closed.

"Jane. Open your legs."

"No."

"No?"

"*No*. You have to make me *want* to."

"Challenge accepted."

I gently kissed across the crease where her ass cheek met her thigh, and then I moved to the other. I kissed around her hip and gently bit down on the flesh there. She jumped a bit, and I continued kissing up her hip and across the top of her ass until I hit the small of her back. I paused; then I gently ran my tongue from the top of her ass crack down to her pussy. I stayed there a while just kissing and making little circles with my tongue. She started to moan and open her legs just a bit.

"That's it, baby. Open for me."

"No." She closed her legs back up with a grin.

"I love it when you fucking fight me like that." She looked satisfied with herself until I ran my finger down her ass crack and slid it inside her. She gasped and inadvertently opened her legs a little as her ass went up a bit. I caught her there and dove my tongue in and ran light circles around her asshole while I slowly moved my finger in and out of her wet pussy. "Fuck you taste good." She moaned louder and grabbed the pillow with her fist. "You like that, baby? You like when I lick your asshole like that?" I asked as I continued licking and fingering.

"Fuck, yes!" she moaned. "Don't stop."

I slid my tongue down to her clit and made circles while I pressed on her asshole with my thumb. A trickle of wetness fell down her slit, and I licked that shit up. She tasted amazing, and I couldn't get enough. "I fucking love doing this to you."

She started to shake, and I could tell she was close. "Turn over. I wanna watch you come." She turned over and looked at me so intensely that I thought she might slap me, but she ripped her shirt off and jumped on top of me. We kissed so intensely it was almost combative. Then she ran her hands down my chest, pulled my dick out of my boxers, bent down beside me with her ass in the air, and took the entire thing into her mouth. I gasped and started rubbing her clit. She moaned onto my dick, and it made me tense up even more. I leaned over and shoved a finger inside her.

She pulled me out of her mouth and called out, "Oh god!"

"You like that baby?"

"Yes. *More.*"

"Louder!" I told her.

"More! I want more!" she called out. I yanked her off the bed and pushed her up against the bedroom door. Then I spread her open and started flicking her clit with my tongue as she stared down right into my eyes. Her breathing was getting more intense, and I slid a finger inside her as I continued the same pace with my tongue. She started to shudder, and I moaned into her pussy as she called out, "I'm coming! Don't stop! Please!"

"Say my name!" I demanded as I shoved another finger inside.

She screamed, "Gabriel, fuck! I'm coming! Fuck, Gabriel!"

She shoved me off her and then dove on top of me, and we fell back onto the floor. We kissed passionately. Then I told her to turn around, and I pulled her ass onto my face and started licking like crazy. She shoved my dick into her mouth, and we pleasured each other with the most amazing rhythm. We moaned together until we both exploded at the same time, and she screamed my name as loudly as I screamed hers. Then she rolled off of me, and we both laid next to each other catching our breath. She started giggling, and I sat up.

"What?"

Her laughter got more manic. "That was fucking crazy."

I leaned in and gently held her breasts. "Yeah, like *fucking amazing*, you mean!"

"Yeah, but like, *really loud*!"

I smiled at her and winked.

She looked confused. "Wait. Did you…? Did you want that to be loud on purpose?"

"Maybe."

"Why? It's embarrassing."

"I'm not embarrassed at all. I wanted that toolbag next door to know what he's missing. And by the way, I caught a glimpse of them going at it last night. I'm pretty sure *she* knows she's missing out too!"

She looked angry for a second, but then an insane laugh

burst out of her mouth. She leaned in and kissed me with sincere warmth. Then she looked at me all serious again. "Okay, but I'm not kidding. In front of Will, *we're just friends.* Got it?"

I took her hand and put it on my dick, which was still completely hard. "Yeah, whatever *friend.* Round two?"

She sighed and collapsed backward. Then she yelled, "Just kidding!" and jumped on top of me again.

CHAPTER 23

Jane

"I Will Possess Your Heart"—Death Cab for Cutie

Fuck, that boy knows what he's doing in bed. I'm sure he's had plenty of practice, but I don't care what the reason is. I came four times that morning, and everyone in the house heard it. After we finished, we took a shower together where he made my fourth orgasm happen, which surprised me completely while he had that little smirk of knowing satisfaction. We packed our shit and went downstairs where the entire wedding party stared us down, some with disgust (horseface), others with anger (Jake), and most with grins and giggles. John, the best man, immediately got up and gave Gabriel a high five and announced that he's the man. Ally responded with, "So we've heard!" Jake stared him down with hatred, and I realized that everything Gabriel had said the day before was true. The best revenge was truly not giving a shit about them, and it had unfolded beautifully.

Knowing that Lizzie was going to be okay completely lifted my mood. I was really excited to travel with Gabriel and to see Will, but I was aware of the complicated triangle I was in. I almost wanted to cancel, but in my mind, I heard Gabriel say, "Memento mori." So I stuck with the plan, vowing not to allow anything to happen that would hurt Will.

A few days later, on the way to the airport, I reiterated to Gabriel that all affection had to stop. Even though he had that sexy smirk that drove me mad, he seemed to understand how serious I was.

I had never flown first class before so that in itself was a fabulous experience. The food was really good, and the seats were comfortable and huge. We sat next to each other, though there was a large console between us. We shared earbuds and played different songs for each other. He showed me his sketchbook which was filled with sketches of Lizzie and me. He was so unbelievably talented. He had a way of taking our likeness and making it appear ethereal and timeless. Eventually, I fell asleep with my head on the console, and he gently woke me up to show me how to completely recline my seat into a bed. I wanted to kiss him passionately just over that revelation, but I controlled myself and went back to sleep.

We arrived at 10 AM and took a cab to a hotel he booked. When we pulled up to the Mandarin Oriental in Knightsbridge, I almost passed out. I'd walked by the Mandarin in NYC, but I barely registered it as it was beyond my lower-middle-class existence. The building itself looked like a castle, and the entrance was so shiny and vast that it was overwhelming. Everything was made of a different colored marble—brown, green, gray, white, and black. The lobby was decorated for autumn, and there were huge trees everywhere, dripping with orange leaves, red berries, and little twinkling lights.

We got a few looks from people indicating we seemed out of place. But after Gabriel gave the front desk the details of our reservation for the "Executive Suite" and handed his black AMEX over, the vibe changed immediately. It was over $10K for the four nights we were staying. I tried not to show my complete shock at the price tag. But as a man in a ridiculous outfit that included a furry top hat took us to the elevator, I couldn't help but comment.

"You're *that* rich?"

"Hmm?"

"10 G's?"

"You know I like to make the most of my experiences," he said with a wink. "If we're gonna do it, let's fucking do it! Am I right, my man?"

He addressed that last part to the uptight bellhop who rode with us in the elevator. His response was, "Certainly, sir."

We followed the bellhop down to the end of a lovely hallway where he unlocked the double doors to our suite and handed Gabriel the keycard. He put our luggage in the humongous walk-in closet and asked if we would like him to unpack our belongings for us. Gabriel declined and handed him a wad of folded pounds, and he bowed to us and left.

I started to tour the suite. "Good thing we have two walk-in closets! I wasn't sure if there'd be enough room for everything in my one bag!" I moved on to the bathroom, which was made of floor-to-ceiling gray marble that was so shiny it looked wet. Then I checked out the sitting room with its purple velvet couch and giant, flat-screen TV before I moved on to the bedroom.

Gabriel wrapped his arms around my waist. "Do you like it?"

"One bed, huh? A bit presumptuous of you."

"I suppose I could sleep on the couch," he said with his signature grin. I turned my head so he could kiss me.

"I don't think that will be necessary," I said with half-closed eyes.

"Come see the view!" He led me over to the French doors on the other side of the room and opened them up. We stepped out onto a white stone balcony and moved to the edge. It had a breathtaking view of Hyde Park.

"Holy shit!"

"Hungry? Why don't we get room service and eat out here?"

"Okay, but then we're calling Will."

"You got it."

We ordered "afternoon tea," and two bellhops set up the most beautiful lunch on the balcony. It was almost too pretty to eat. Every little sandwich and pastry was like a work of art. Gabriel didn't seem that blown away as he started tossing mini sandwiches in the air and catching them in his mouth. Each time he caught one, he smiled proudly.

"Lemme try!" I threw a pastry covered in whipped cream at him, and it hit him right on the nose and bounced onto the floor.

He put his hands up like "what gives" but smiled. "Why didn't you open your mouth? You just wasted like ten bucks right there!"

"I thought you were going to try it yourself!" he answered as he attempted to get the cream off his nose with his tongue.

"Here," I threw a napkin at his face, and he picked it up and wiped himself off.

He grabbed a cream puff and aimed it at my mouth. "Ready?"

"I guess…" I opened wide and tried to catch it, but it hit me at the top of my forehead and landed in my lap. "Come on! It's in my hair! I'm gonna need a shower!"

"That's my master plan," he said with a wink.

I shoved the cream puff in my mouth and growled at him. "I'm calling Will before you get any more food in my hair."

"But you haven't even tried any of the tea yet. What flavor do you want?"

I slid my teacup over to him. "Surprise me."

I ran inside, looked up Will's number on my phone, and called from the landline. I wanted to surprise him from a local number.

"Hello?"

"Will?"

"Who am I speaking with?"

"You don't recognize my voice?"

"Umm, not really…"

"It's Jane!"

"Jane? That was utterly confusing! My phone is showing a London number."

"That's because I'm in London!"

"Are you fucking with me?"

"I am totally *not* fucking with you!"

"Where are you exactly?"

"The Mandarin Oriental."

"In Hyde Park?"

"Yep!"

"I'm about two miles from you! When did you get there?"

"Just a few hours ago."

"Can I pick you up immediately? There's no reason to waste your money on a hotel room. My flat has five empty bedrooms."

"Well, it's Gabriel's money I'm wasting, but I would love to see you!"

"You're with Gabriel?"

"Yeah. We decided it would be cool to surprise you. Are you surprised?"

"*Extremely.* Wait for me outside. I'll be there in 15 minutes. Bring your things."

"I'll see you soon. Cheerio!"

"Did you just say 'cheerio'?"

"Sorry. I got a bit carried away. See you soon."

"Right."

I went back onto the terrace where Gabriel was busy texting. "Will is picking us up. He's insisting we stay with him. He's only a few minutes from here." He didn't look up or acknowledge me. "Hello? Gabriel? Did you hear me?"

He still didn't lift his head and just said, "Hold on a sec." I waited another few seconds and went inside to freshen up in the bathroom. I should have showered before I called Will. I looked as jet-lagged as I felt. I mashed deodorant into my underarms, sprayed a little perfume, brushed my teeth, and freshened my makeup. When I came back out, Gabriel was still on the terrace texting.

"Okay, I don't know what's going on with you, but I'll be waiting for Will outside."

He texted a bit more then followed me into the room. "Sorry about that. I was just catching up with some old friends. Did you say Will is picking you up?"

"Picking *us* up. He's insisting we stay with him."

"Are you sure he wasn't just talking about you?"

"Yes, I'm sure. Let's go!" He looked down at his feet and hesitated. "What is it?" I asked.

"Why don't you go spend some time with Will while I catch up with friends? We can all meet up for dinner later."

"What? What friends?"

"Just some old friends. I haven't been to London in two years, so it would be nice to catch up."

"But I thought we came here to be with Will."

"*You* came here to be with Will. *I* came here to be with *you*."

"And *I* will be *with Will*."

He sighed and moved closer to me.

"Jane, I care about Will too. But I truly think he would rather spend time with you than with both of us. I'm not saying I'm not going to hang out with him. But do I have to spend every minute with him?"

"Well, no. Okay, fine. Go see your friends." I grabbed my duffle bag, threw it on my shoulder, and walked towards the door.

"Are you mad?" he asked.

I turned around as I tried to figure out what exactly I was feeling. "I'm not mad, it's just…"

"What?"

"Isn't there any part of you that's jealous or at least… worried?"

"About you being with Will?"

"Yeah. Alone."

He smiled and swiftly walked forward, then he stopped in front of me and said, "Kiss me."

"Umm, what?"

"Kiss me!"

"No. I'm trying to have a discussion with you."

"I know. I'm actually trying to make a point. So fucking kiss me." My face contorted into a confused and somewhat pissed expression as he crashed his lips down onto mine. I protested at first by trying to shove his chest away with my fists, but he grabbed my wrists and used them to bring me in closer. I moved my head away, and he followed my face with his and kissed the side of my mouth and down my cheek to my neck. It felt so good that I forgot I was mad. I grabbed the back of his head and brought his mouth back up to mine so I could kiss him properly. Not only did I forget what we were talking about, I didn't give a shit. All I wanted was for him to pick me up and take me into the bedroom. Suddenly, he pulled away and stared at me with that fucking smirk.

"What! What the fuck was that?" I demanded. I felt toyed with.

"Did you feel that?"

I wanted to pretend I didn't know what he was talking about, but I knew exactly what he meant. I huffed and let out an irritated, "*Yes*."

"*That* is why I'm not worried about it."

"Point taken." My phone started buzzing in my pocket, and I pulled it out and saw it was Will. "So… dinner later?"

"Yes, please."

"I'll text you."

"I'll answer."

"You better."

"*I will*."

I spun around and left the room without looking back. In the elevator, I started to feel really confused. Just as I started to question if I could trust him or not, my phone buzzed, and I opened a text from him that read, "You have been mine before, and you will always be mine."

I immediately wrote back, "Don't be so sure of yourself. You've also lost me before, and you could lose me again."

He responded with the same lines again, "You have been mine before, and you will always be mine."

"Yeah, yeah, Nostradamus. See you at dinner."

Will was waiting for me in the lobby. He looked more disheveled than usual, but when he saw me, the light returned to his face. My natural reaction was to run towards him, and he opened his arms and scooped me off the ground. As he gently placed me back down, I saw he was about to kiss me. I turned my head to make sure it would land on my cheek. It was really awkward. He took my bag and asked if I was hungry.

"You're always trying to feed me! I'm not hungry, just jetlagged."

"I'm so glad you're here. It means so much to me. You have no idea."

"Of course. I can't wait to see where you live!"

"Where's Gabriel?"

"He's seeing old friends. He said he'd meet up with us for dinner."

"I see," he said as we exited the hotel.

I looked around at the luxury vehicles parked in front. "Which car's yours?"

"None of them. I took the underground. Is that alright?"

I smiled. "Of course! I just expected…"

"That a spoiled, rich boy like me would have a driver?"

"Well… yeah. Or a hot sports car!"

"It's literally one stop from here. But I can get a cab…"

"I'm just teasing, Will!"

We rode the tube in silence, just enjoying being together. The few blocks' walk to his place was lined with luxurious townhomes. They were all white, with grand stone columns and intricate iron balconies.

"*Shit*, Will. I don't think my net worth allows me to even *walk* on these streets."

He rolled his eyes playfully and held out his phone. "Shall I wire you some funds?"

"Sweet! I could use a new car!"

He started to ascend the steps of one of the immaculate townhomes. The black door had two huge potted trees on either side.

"*This is where you live?*" I asked in amazement.

"At the moment," he said with no emotion. He unlocked the door and led me into a lovely and immaculate townhouse. The floors and walls were made of shiny white marble and lined with black and gold candelabra. There was a strong scent of citrus and pine. I had to stop myself from commenting on how out of place I felt again.

I followed him down the hall past several doors, and I noticed one of them had a panel of buttons next to it. "What do those do?" I asked.

"Elevator," he responded.

"Shit. How many floors does this have?"

"Five and a terrace."

I bit my cheek to prevent my stupid comments from falling out as he led me into a large dining room where everything was black, gold, and white. The table was covered in a mess of papers, some of them crumbled up.

"What's all of this?"

"Paperwork."

"Yes, I can see that."

"Sorry. It's all having to do with my inheritance." He sighed as his face fell. "Can I take your coat?"

"Sure. So this is complicated stuff, huh?"

"Yes."

He gestured to the couch on the other side of the room. I sat down, and he sat next to me.

"Can I get you a drink?"

"No, no. I'm fine. But I'm worried about you."

"I'll be alright once this is all over."

"Do you want to tell me about it?"

He paused. I sensed that he was about to unload the details, so I waited patiently.

"My grandfather had the bulk of the family's wealth. Half a billion pounds. His will remained a secret until he died. I was called to his lawyer's office, and it was revealed that he left everything to *me*."

I wanted to say that was a great thing and that I was happy for him; but he looked distressed, so I just kept listening.

"My parents were angry as well as my aunts and uncles and their children. No one else was named. Not only did he leave me all the money, he also gave me his company and all of his properties."

"I have to admit, I don't know why this is a bad thing."

"It's not necessarily a bad thing. But it's an enormous responsibility. On the will was one statement…" He went over to the table and sifted through a bunch of papers until he found the right one and read from it. "'I give the entirety of my property, estate, personal belongings, and my corporation, Morris & Co., and any item that I shall be entitled to, at the time of my death or thereafter, to my grandson, William. He alone will know the proper manner in which to distribute my assets.'"

"Wow! That's quite a compliment!"

"And an enormous fucking burden!"

"So what's all the other paperwork?"

"It's all of his stuff. Cars, bank accounts, vaults filled with jewelry, real estate in several different countries. He even left me a few dozen horses, so I have to figure out what to do with *those* bloody things."

"Okay, I can see how this is a huge responsibility. And a burden. But it's not a *bad* thing. I mean, there are worse things in life, right?"

"I'm not trying to sound ungrateful, Jane. But the issue is my family. They all have requests and demands, and they all feel entitled to the same things. They're calling me non-stop, and I wish they would all just fuck off. I want to mourn my grandfather. They couldn't care less that he's gone. His body was still warm when they swooped in like a bunch of bloodthirsty vultures."

His face was turning red, and he was gripping the chair so tightly that his knuckles were white. I went over to him and took his hand.

"Will, I understand. I mean… *I don't understand at all.* But I hear you. And I wouldn't want that responsibility either. He must have thought very highly of you to want you to take over everything. But clearly, he didn't consider the burden he was putting on your shoulders."

"The hardest part is his company. There are thousands of employees that need to be managed. I don't give much of a shit about construction."

"What *do* you give a shit about? I mean, what kind of company would you want to run?"

"Is it possible to have a company that produces art? No, that doesn't make much sense. Art is an individual thing."

"Of course, it makes sense! There are plenty of companies that make beautiful things!"

"Yes, but the manufacturing of art and beauty is something the brotherhood is strictly against."

"Well, what if you could combine these things somehow? Bring art and beauty to people on a more personal level?"

"That's something to consider." He looked down at his feet and then into my eyes. "Thank you. For being here. I've really missed you." He leaned down to kiss me, and I backed away.

"So… Can I get a tour of this place?"

"Of course. Can I ask you a question first?"

"Shoot."

"It's more of a favor really."

"No problem!"

"My grandfather's memorial service is tomorrow. Would you…?"

"Yes, of course I'll go."

He exhaled deeply. "Thank you. You have a way of keeping me calm, Jane."

"Shit. I don't have anything to wear. I mean, I should wear black, right?"

"Yes, I suppose."

"Shit."

I kneeled down next to my duffle bag and started digging through it. "Yeah, I've only got jeans. *Shit.*"

"Then we'll have to go shopping."

"Yeah? Alright. But *I'm* paying!"

"We'll see. Any place in particular you'd like to go?"

"The only store I know of in London is Harrods."

"Then you'd better let *me* pay."

He held out my coat, and I grabbed it and threw it on.

"No, I'll pay. They must have a clearance rack!"

"Surely."

Will and I had so much fun wandering around Harrods. I dragged him through every department, including the jewelry counter, before we hit the women's clothing section. The cheapest thing I could find was a very plain black dress for 170 pounds. It annoyed me to spend that much on a dress I knew I'd never wear again, but there was no way I was going to let Will pay. I wasn't his girlfriend, and I was trying to keep the mixed messages to a minimum. I needed shoes too, so I grabbed a pair of ugly black sandals from the clearance rack.

I've never been that into fashion, but there was a pair of Jimmy Choo heels that were breathtaking. They were black satin and had tiny crystals shaped like leaves creeping all along the sides and onto the slim little heel. I've always loved anything with ivy on it, and there was just something about those shoes that I couldn't resist.

Will insisted that I try them on in my size, despite the 765 pound price tag. I agreed, just for fun. I rolled up my jeans and slipped them on and walked in front of the mirror. I expected them to be uncomfortable, but they fit perfectly and felt amazing. It was like they were made just for me. Will was staring at my feet and shaking his head slightly.

"What?" I asked. "Ridiculous, right?"

"They're *perfect* on you. And I hope you don't mind me admiring your legs. Because they're *spectacular*. Your feet are lovely too."

I could feel the blood rushing to my cheeks. "Stop that!" I immediately flung off the shoes and placed them back in the box.

"Well, that was fun!" I turned to speak to the salesman. "I'll just take this dress and these sandals please."

The salesman wrapped the dress and shoes in an elaborate package of tissue paper and ribbons and then placed them in a shopping bag and handed it to me. "Have a wonderful day, madam!" he exclaimed and began to walk away.

"Wait. What do I owe you?"

"It's been taken care of, madam. Is there anything else I can do for you?" I whipped my head towards Will, and he winked at me. I slapped him on the arm and reminded him that I wanted to pay.

"You can buy me a scoop of gelato," he responded.

"Deal."

We both got scoops of Nutella gelato and wandered into the home section. I plopped down on a huge, overstuffed couch and closed my eyes.

"You alright?"

"Just tired. Jetlag."

"Why don't we go back to my flat, and you can have a nap?"

"That sounds wonderful."

He helped me off the couch, and we made our way back to the front of the store. As we exited, the salesman from the shoe department handed Will two huge shopping bags, and Will thanked him. I asked him what was in the bags and he said, "Just a few odds and ends."

When we returned to his flat, he said he would show me all of the bedrooms, and I could choose which one I wanted to stay in. "You're also welcome to stay with me," he added. "I'd really like that."

"Oh! Umm, you know what? I'm just so exhausted; I'd love it if you could take me to the nearest bed or couch. I don't need a choice."

"As you wish."

He ushered me down the hall to a bedroom with a delicate crystal chandelier hanging over a massive bed with a fluffy white comforter and a ton of white pillows. Everything in the room was white except for the floor, which was a dark mahogany.

"Will this do?"

"This is *amazing*! Thank you!"

"There should be plenty of fresh towels in the bathroom. Can I get you anything else?"

"Maybe just my bag?"

"Of course."

He returned with my duffle bag and placed it inside the closet along with the Harrods bag with my dress and sandals. Then he placed the other huge shopping bags onto the bed.

"What are these?"

"Just a few odds and ends… for you." I wrinkled my eyebrows with confusion. He smiled and added, "Have a good nap," and closed the door behind him. I started pulling things out of the bags, and my mouth fell open. Every single thing I had admired in the department store was there, including a silk designer dress worth almost 1,800 pounds, a designer coat with a price tag of almost 7,000 pounds, ridiculously overpriced satin and lace pajamas, fancy French perfume, a 24K gold cigarette lighter I thought Gabriel would like, Hermes lipstick I had tried on, a gold and sapphire bracelet, a box of insanely priced truffles, and of course, the Jimmy Choo shoes. I sat down on the bed in shock. It was the sweetest thing anyone had ever done for me, but there was no way I could accept any of it.

I ran into the hallway and called for Will. I found him at the dining room table filling out paperwork.

"Will!"

"That was a quick nap!"

"*Will!* I can't accept any of those things!"

"Why not?"

"Because… it's ridiculous!"

"What's ridiculous? Buying things for someone I care about?"

"It's too much! Too much money!"

"Well, now that you basically know my net worth, you're aware that it isn't a lot of money to me. And in a way, it was a selfish purchase."

"Huh?"

"It makes me happy to make *you* happy."

I plopped down into the seat next to him. "Jesus Christ, Will. That is really fucking sweet. But I just can't."

"Well, I could find some use for the lighter, and I might be able to pull off the lipstick and perfume, but the heels and dress will definitely *not* fit!"

"Just return them! I don't need that stuff."

"Not returning them. So either you take them, or they will sit in the closet completely unused. And that would be a shame."

I huffed in frustration while he changed the subject.

"Do you like Thai food?"

"Sure. But-"

"How about I pick up dinner from my favorite Thai place?"

"Okay. Don't forget, Gabriel said he'd join us."

"Right. Six okay?"

"Yeah."

He picked up his pen and continued with his paperwork. "Enjoy your rest," he said without looking up.

I left the table and then turned back and whispered in his ear, "You forgot the crystal vase." The pen stopped moving, but he didn't lift his head. I added, "Just kidding!"

His pen started moving again as he commented, "It's on back-order and will arrive here tomorrow."

"Are you fucking kidding me, Will?"

"Not kidding at all, Jane."

"That vase was 3,000 pounds!"

"Was it?"

I huffed again and stomped back to the bedroom. Will was so generous and sweet, but my thoughts instantly returned to Gabriel. I grabbed my phone and sent him a text.

"Hey. Dinner at Will's at six. His address is 20 Chester Terrace, Knightsbridge. It's one tube stop from the hotel. Hope you're enjoying your time with your friends."

I napped for about two hours then checked my phone. It was almost 6 PM and there was no response from Gabriel. I took a shower and joined Will in the kitchen.

He was setting up a huge spread of the most yummy-looking Thai food.

"Hope you're hungry! How did you sleep?"

"Really, really well! That was the most comfortable bed I've ever slept in in my entire life."

"I'm glad. I forgot to ask if you like spicy food or not, so I got a lot of options."

I sat down on a stool next to him and grabbed a fork. "Okay, I'm going to need some descriptions because I don't really like spicy food, but I do want to try everything."

He kept taking out more and more dishes from a bunch of big shopping bags and spreading them out on the island. "Are you expecting company? Of like half the city?"

"Won't Gabriel be joining us?"

"He's supposed to. But he's not answering my texts."

He lifted his eyebrows as if to say, "Are you surprised?"

"What's that face supposed to mean?"

"Nothing," he said with no emotion. "That's prawn and chicken satay. You *must* try it with the peanut sauce."

I dunked it into the sauce. "Holy shit, this is fucking delicious!" He smiled and grabbed one for himself.

"So what's the deal with you and Gabriel?" I asked with a mouthful of food. He slid a tray over to me with beautiful purple dumplings that looked like flowers. I took one and popped it into my mouth.

"What's the deal with *you* and Gabriel?" he responded as he ate a dumpling too.

"We're friends. Good friends." I shoved another dumpling in my mouth so I wouldn't have to talk.

"Us too," he said.

"Okay, but it kinda seems like you hate him," I said. "These are phenomenal by the way."

"Chor muang. Caramelized chicken and peanut dumplings." He went over to a cabinet and took out two wine glasses. He brought them over with two bottles of wine. "Red or white?"

"Whatever you recommend." He grinned and plunged the corkscrew into the bottle of white wine and filled our glasses. I took a sip. "You didn't really answer my question." He put another dish in front of me. I rolled my eyes and grabbed what looked like a spring roll. He pointed to the orange sauce on the plate. I dipped the roll into it and took a bite. "That's the best fucking spring roll I've ever had."

"Duck roll," he corrected as he shoved one in his mouth followed by another. He washed them down with a few huge gulps of wine and sighed. "I suppose my friendship with Gabriel is... complicated. We formed a strong bond at school. We both felt extremely passionate about art and the need to return to the basics. I appreciate how much he's helped me push my own boundaries and limitations. But after sharing my home with him for a few years, our differences are getting in the way of the original reason we all chose to live together. I don't agree with much of his philosophies on life... and women. I'm starting to feel the need to separate."

I dug my fork into a pile of what looked like onion straws. "Careful! Those are spicy!" he warned.

I ate one anyway. "Not *that* spicy. And really good!" I ate a few more. "I completely get where you're coming from. Lizzie and I were so close; we were like family. But we've both grown and changed so much, and we're definitely moving in opposite directions. The love is still there. But it often feels like more of an obligation."

"Just like family!" he added. "Try the soup." He slid a bowl of thick white soup over and handed me a spoon.

"I'm getting full," I said as I tried a spoonful.

"*I'm* not!" he said as he grabbed a huge forkful of food.

"Seriously, Will. Where does it all go? You don't have an ounce of fat... anywhere!" I looked him up and down and laughed.

"It's a gift really," he said as he ripped a chunk of beef off of a stick with his teeth. "You must leave room for dessert."

"In that case, I call uncle!" I dramatically dropped my fork onto the table.

"What will you call your uncle for?" he asked.

I giggled. "It's a saying. I guess it's American. It means I'm calling it quits."

"Right. That's fucking weird."

"So is calling everyone a wanker. It's like you're constantly accusing people of masturbating."

"Well, there's some truth to that, isn't there?"

"You mean that everyone masturbates?"

"Right."

"So why is it used as an insult?"

"I suppose there's shame in it, particularly in a repressed culture like mine. It's also quite a funny image."

"Yeah, for guys it is."

"Oh, you don't find the image of a woman wanking off to be funny?"

"When you put it like *that*, it sounds pretty funny." We both gulped down more wine.

"So do you think you'll ask Gabriel to move out?" I asked.

"I dunno. I was hoping that would all progress naturally. I never expected to spend the rest of my life with four blokes."

"You have a better idea?" I asked. "Cuz it looks like a lot of fun to me!"

"Well… that depends. What are *your* plans for the rest of your life?" My eyes grew wide when I realized what he was asking.

"I'm living day to day. Who can think about next week even? Right now I'm in London, in an incredible flat, with a wonderful friend, eating amazing food. My next goals are to see Lizzie make it out of the hospital and then figure out a possible career path."

"Lizzie's in the hospital?"

"Fuck, I haven't told you. She caught pneumonia and has been in the hospital since you left."

"How awful. Will she be alright?"

"Yes. I think so. She's moving in the right direction, but because she had cancer and only has one lung, they have to be really careful that she doesn't get another infection."

"She had cancer? What kind?"

"Lung cancer. Pretty rare for someone her age. But she beat it."

"I am so sorry I wasn't there to help."

"I know. I found her unconscious in the tub. Gabriel helped me get her to the hospital."

"Must have been terrifying for you."

"Yes. Very."

"Is there anything I can do?"

"How about dessert?"

"Of course."

It was almost 8 PM. While Will cleared our plates, I checked my phone, but there was still no answer from Gabriel. I didn't know whether I should be mad or worried. I considered sending another text, but I didn't want to seem desperate. I put the phone back in my pocket and helped Will with the dishes.

"How about a movie with dessert?" he asked.

"Sure!"

"Why don't you find us something to watch in the living room while I get dessert together?"

"What genre are you in the mood for?"

"I think we could both use a comedy."

"Agreed."

I sat down on the pristine white sectional couch that looked like it had never been sat on even once. The throw pillows were lined up so perfectly that I checked to see if they were attached. Everything in the flat was a shade of cream, gray, taupe, or stark white, and it didn't look lived-in at all. There were eight remote controls, and after playing with them for a while, I gave up. I went over to the bookcases and shelves surrounding the flat-screen T.V. and examined them. There was one large, vintage photo of a couple at their wedding, a graduation photo of Will with his grandparents, and a photo of a huge wedding party in front of Red House that included Will and his little sister. There was a large framed picture of his sister as a flower girl, and a laminated card was lying next to it. On the front was an image of an angel kneeling down to pick up a little girl. On the back it said, "In Loving Memory of Emma Rose Morris" in beautiful script, and underneath was a very sad but beautiful poem about God having called her soul home.

The pain that his family had gone through in losing that beautiful little girl hit me like a punch to the gut, and tears started pouring down my face. I couldn't stop thinking about Lizzie. I was terrified of losing her, and part of me saw her as an innocent little girl.

Will entered the room with several plates and placed them down onto the coffee table. "Find any good films?"

I tried to suck in the snot that was leaking from my nose, and I used my sleeve to wipe the tears away. "I couldn't figure out how to turn the T.V. on," I said, trying desperately to hide the sorrow in my voice.

He knew right away that I was upset and rushed over and took my hand. "Jane! What is it? What happened?"

"Oh nothing, just allergies. No big deal."

"Allergies, my arsehole. What are you upset about? Is it Gabriel?"

"What? No. I don't think we should talk about it."

"Why not?"

"Because I'll just make you sad too."

"Well, seeing you sad has already done that, so we might as well talk it out. Let's sit."

We sat down on the couch, and I checked out the desserts. "Fuck these look good. What are they?"

"Changing the subject, are you? Caramelized banana sundae, mango cheesecake, coconut rice dumplings, and starfruit in mango orange sauce." He handed me a spoon. "Now tell me what's making you sad, so I can try to fix it."

"We're just going to eat right here? Like this?"

"What do you mean? Why not?"

"Look at this place! It doesn't look like anyone has ever *sat* here, let alone *eaten*, on this immaculate white couch!"

"This was one of my grandparents' properties that they rarely used. Not a lot of love went into it. It was more of an investment. I didn't want to stay with my parents while I'm here sorting this shit out, and this is an excellent location. But I really don't give much of a fuck about any of it."

"Really?"

He took a spoonful of the banana sundae and flung it onto the couch between us. "See?"

"Well, there's no need to ruin a perfectly good couch! This couch probably cost a year's worth of rent for me!"

"It's worth it to me if you can relax and not worry about getting these wonderful desserts on this stupid couch."

He picked up the cheesecake and handed it to me. "Now can we talk?"

I took a big spoonful of the cheesecake and slowly ate it. "Wow, that's delicious. And I don't even like mango but… wow!" He stared at me blankly. "Alright! I saw a memorial card over there, and it made me think of Lizzie. I also felt really sad for your family and that little girl."

He looked down at his hands and drew a deep breath. "'Broken Chain?'"

"Hmm?"

"The poem on the card. Was it about a broken chain?"

"Yes."

"It's for my sister Emma."

"Lizzie told me that you lost your little sister, but I don't know any of the details. We don't need to talk about this, Will. You have enough to be sad about."

"No, it's alright. I don't get to talk about it much. My family gets very uncomfortable about it."

"I'm sure it's very painful for them. For all of you."

"Yes. But they *blame* me. My parents do, anyway."

"Blame *you*? Why?"

"They hold me partially responsible." He looked at me with the saddest eyes. I wanted to wrap my arms around him, but I was still trying to keep the lines clearly drawn. I didn't think we would be alone in these intimate settings together. Otherwise, I wouldn't have visited. I considered myself in a relationship with Gabriel or at least moving in that direction with him. But I didn't want to outright reject Will either because I cared about him. It was a fucking mess.

"Will. I don't know what happened, but I'm sure that you did everything in your power to keep that little girl safe. I highly doubt you were at fault."

"It has a lot to do with Red House. My grandfather loved it there, and he was planning to sell his company and move there permanently. My parents and my uncle talked him out of it because they were hoping when he became old and feeble, they could take the company away from him and run it themselves. My grandfather continued working like a bloody dog well into his eighties because he didn't trust anyone else to run his company, and he was right not to. They didn't actually care about what he had built from nothing and just wanted to squeeze as much money out of it as they could and sell it off in pieces. Since Red House was sitting vacant, I asked if I could move in with the brotherhood. No one cared except my grandfather, who was thrilled that I would be taking care of the place. I think my parents were happy that I was leaving the country because I wouldn't be in the way when they manipulated my grandfather into giving up his business. Soon after we moved in, my cousin announced that she was getting married to an American, and they wanted to have the wedding near New York City. I convinced them to get married at Red House, and my sister was the flower girl. After the ceremony, everyone was scattered outside having cocktails when we realized we didn't know where Emma was. It happened so quickly. One moment she was there, and the next moment she had disappeared."

My hand instinctively went to my mouth. I didn't know exactly where this was going, but I knew it would be terrible. As he spoke, he made eye contact, but it seemed like he was trying not to connect too deeply with me or with the story he was telling. I think if he did, he would have fallen apart.

"An hour later the groom found her floating face down in the lake."

I gasped and grabbed his hand. "She couldn't swim?"

"Not really."

"Will. That is so, so terrible. I'm so sorry." He glanced downward and ran his thumb across my hand. "Wait a second. I don't understand how that's *your* fault!"

"My parents said that it's my fault they were even *at* Red House in the first place. If I hadn't moved in and insisted my cousin get married there…"

"That's ridiculous! That makes absolutely no sense. I'm sorry to say this, but they sound like major assholes."

"Don't be sorry. They *are* major assholes. I'll never understand how my dad came from my grandparents. They were wonderful."

"They must be where *you* come from then!"

He held my hand up and kissed it. "I haven't spoken about that in a long time. I feel better."

I tried to nonchalantly remove my hand from his, and I picked up a dessert plate instead. "Will, I just realized something. Did you know that another little girl drowned in the same lake?"

"What do you mean?"

"A few weeks ago, Gabriel, John and I were hanging out at Effie's house and she told us this crazy story about a little girl who drowned in that same lake."

"Who's Effie?"

"The wife of that religious old nut who lives on the other side of the lake."

"Oh, the young, naked wife?"

"Well, she wasn't naked at the time. But I kept thinking I saw a little girl in her house and she said it was the ghost of a girl who drowned in the lake like fifty years ago."

"Really? That's freaky. I've never heard that."

"Do you think there's some kind of connection?"

"If it was fifty years ago, I don't see how. But I'll admit, even though I've always loved Red House, I've always thought there was an eerie feeling at the lake. Even before Emma died."

I sucked in a huge gulp of air. "I think I'm ready for a comedy now; how about you?"

He nodded and pressed a bunch of buttons until a screen with movie selections came up. He pulled up the comedy menu and started to scroll. *Step Brothers* was first on the list. "Even though I've seen it about a million times, I could definitely go for *Step Brothers* right now."

"Looks daft but whatever you'd like."

"Wait. You've never seen *Step Brothers*?"

"No. Am I missing out?"

"Boats and hoes?"

He looked confused.

"The Catalina wine mixer?"

He tilted his head a bit.

"I want to roll you into a little ball and shove you up into my vagina?"

His eyes looked like they were going to fall out of his head. "Run that last one by me again," he said.

"They're quotes from the movie! It's *life-changing* good. Play it immediately!"

"As you wish!"

I considered our viewing of that movie a true test of Will's sense of humor and personality, and he passed with flying colors. He loved it so much that he kept pausing to repeat lines and rewinding to hear them again. At one point, we were laughing so hard that I snorted, which made him turn bright red. It was just the kind of therapy we needed. After it was over, there was an uncomfortable tension. I could sense he was going to try to kiss me, so I insisted we watch another movie. I pretended to fall asleep; then I did actually fall asleep, and he did too. At around 2 AM the doorbell rang, and we both sat up. He told me to wait on the couch and went downstairs to answer the door. Minutes later he reentered with Gabriel, who threw his black leather duffle bag onto the ground and stared at me.

My mind started to race. I was mad at him for not being in touch; however, I couldn't act too emotional in front of Will, or it would seem suspicious. Plus, he looked fucking gorgeous in a tight thermal shirt and his peacoat, and I kind of wanted to mount him. He tried to break the tension with a simple, "Hey."

"Hi…"

"You're mad?"

"I'm not mad. It's just a bit rude of you, considering we had plans."

"I know. I'm so sorry, Jane."

"Whatever. I'm glad you're okay."

"Listen," he said as he sat down next to me and went to take my hand. "I haven't seen my friends in years."

I felt Will watching us so I yanked my hand back. He smelled strongly of alcohol, and I could see he was a little tipsy. I noticed a smear of red on his neck and the collar of his shirt. "Is that blood?" I asked, pointing to it.

He looked confused as he swiped at the area and looked at it closely. "No, it's paint."

"Paint? You were painting?"

"Yes. I sort of got pulled into working on a mural."

"Okay… I'm going to bed."

I walked over to Will. "Thank you so much for dinner. It was really great. What time should I be ready tomorrow?"

"We'll leave here about 9:30. The service is at noon, but it's a bit of a drive."

"What service?" Gabriel asked.

"My grandfather's memorial."

"I'm sorry, man. Where is it?"

"Canterbury Cathedral."

"No shit? Wow. I thought they only bury clergymen and nobles there."

"He's not being buried. His ashes are being interred. But he was a special person, yeah."

"Wait," I interrupted. "Canterbury Cathedral… as in *The Canterbury Tales*?"

"That's the one."

"That is so cool!"

Will didn't answer. He just looked at Gabriel and said, "There are open bedrooms on the second and third floor." Then he turned to me. "Is there anything you need?"

"Just sleep. Thank you."

"Goodnight," he said softly, and he left the room without looking back at Gabriel.

After a minute Gabriel said, "Come here."

"I'm tired. I'm going to bed." I started to leave the room, but he came after me and blocked the doorway.

"You're mad."

"Sort of."

He took my face into his hands. "I will make it up to you."

"Okay, great. Goodnight."

I tried to walk away again, but he held me tightly and whispered, "I want to make it up to you *now*."

He pressed his mouth onto mine and tried to slide his tongue in, but I kept my lips shut. He wasn't deterred and kissed down my neck instead. I closed my eyes and enjoyed it for a moment before moving away. None of this could happen in Will's house. It was straight-up rude.

"Let's just go to bed." I kissed him on the cheek and walked away, but he followed me down the hall. "Which room are you gonna stay in?" I asked.

"Yours."

"Umm, no. You're not."

"We should have stayed at the hotel," he commented as he followed me into my room.

"You still can," I told him.

"I want to be with you."

"I know. But it's fucking rude to do that in Will's house."

"Well, when we go back home and resume... *this*, it will be in his house. Maybe we should just rip the Band-Aid off right now."

He grabbed my ass and pulled me into his hips as his tongue dove into my mouth. I kissed him a bit and then shoved him hard. "*Please* respect my wishes on this. He's hurting. And he has feelings for me. His grandpa's memorial is tomorrow. Have a fucking heart, Gabriel."

He sighed very dramatically and put his hands up in submission. "Alright. You made your point. I'll fuck off now."

"Goodnight."

"How about a shower? You can help me wash the paint off."

"*Gabriel. Goodnight.*"

He shoved his bottom lip out like a whiny toddler and left the room. I washed up, popped a sleeping pill to assure I would actually sleep, and got into bed. Not long after I drifted off, I awoke to the delicious sensation of someone kissing my ankles and up my legs. I was groggy from the pill and just let it happen until it reached my inner thigh, and I felt a tongue lapping over my underwear. I moaned but then came to my senses and ripped the blanket off.

There was Gabriel, in his underwear, smiling at me from between my legs. I sat up and drew my knees to my chest. "What the fuck are you doing?"

He gave me that playful grin but no words.

"Seriously, Gabriel. Get the fuck out."

"Come on. I can be really quiet."

I growled at him. "First of all, I have my period."

Without missing a beat he said, "I don't care," and grabbed my knees and shoved my legs open.

I didn't actually have my period, I just thought it would keep him away. I used my foot to shove him off. "Well, *I* care!"

"Why?"

"Cuz it's gross!"

"It's not gross. It's amazing. It's your power source."

"It's my uterine lining."

"I think it's amazing. And it just makes everything wetter, which is hot. And I know how sensitive it is when-"

"*Not happening*! Moving on!"

He threw his hands up. "*Okay.* How about a massage? Do you have cramps?"

"Gabriel. Seriously. Fuck *off.*"

He stood up next to the bed and stared down at me. He looked so fucking gorgeous that it was hard to refuse him. But I was *not* going to let it happen in Will's home.

"Look. I want you too. But I'm not doing it in Will's house. End of story. I'll see you in the morning."

He leaned over and kissed me very gently on my mouth and then my nose and forehead. "Goodnight."

CHAPTER 24

Jane

"Dream"—Bishop Briggs

AFTER PERFECTING MY HAIR AND MAKEUP, I STOOD IN the closet looking over the clothes Will bought me the day before. The boring, dumpy dress I had picked out hung sadly next to the designer dress worth 18 times as much. It was also black and would look a thousand times better on me. But some part of me felt uncomfortable wearing it, like I was pretending to be someone I'm not.

I tried on the cheap dress and stood in front of the mirror. It was okay, but not exactly flattering. It looked like a black sack with a belt tied in the middle. Then I slipped into the expensive dress. It gave the illusion of a tuxedo jacket and skirt and was made of the most luscious silk. It appeared expertly tailored and hugged my curves perfectly. Underneath the satin lapels of the jacket was a thin panel of delicate black lace. It was just the right mix of sexy and classy. I'd be a fool not to wear it, I thought, and I wanted to look good for Will. Not as his love interest but as a close friend who took the occasion seriously.

I eyed the two shoeboxes and tried the clunky sandals first. They looked awful with the designer dress, so I had to wear the Jimmy Choos. As I glanced in the mirror one last time, I barely recognized myself. A sophisticated, wealthy-looking woman was reflected back at me, and I had to fight the nagging feeling that I was a ridiculous imposter.

I went to grab my coat when I saw the coat that Will had bought for me hanging next to it. I felt completely unworthy of wearing a coat worth almost six grand, let alone *owning* one, but it was black. My coat was red, and I wanted to be dressed appropriately. I snatched it off the hanger and told the judgmental voice in my head to shut the fuck up.

I went into the hallway and heard Will and Gabriel talking in the kitchen. As I entered the room, Gabriel was sitting at the island in a t-shirt and boxers, and Will stood by the sink drinking coffee. He was wearing a dark blue suit, and his hair was combed down with gel, which I had never seen before. He looked really handsome. When they saw me, they both stopped talking and froze.

"Gabriel, why aren't you dressed? Don't we have to leave soon?"

"Jane, you look *stunning*," he stated. I rolled my eyes as he came over to me and got close to my face. "Seriously. You're exquisite," he whispered.

I grinned and then backed away. I saw over his shoulder that Will was staring at me with an open mouth. I stepped away from Gabriel and moved closer to him. "I clean up nice, huh? Will provided me with a few items that are worth more than a year's rent!"

"Worth every bloody penny," he said as he stared at me with bulging eyes.

Gabriel sat back down and ate his cereal, very obviously avoiding eye contact with me as he spoke. "I was just telling Will that I was offered a commission from the parents of an old friend. He doesn't mind if I miss the memorial today. So I'll meet up with you two tonight."

I stood in place, staring him down. "What kind of commission? Is it really worth not being there for your friend?" There was a tense silence between the three of us while Gabriel searched for a response. "Okay, whatever," I said with irritation.

"Jane, I told him to do it. Don't be angry with him. There's no need for him to come with us today and miss a huge opportunity."

Again, I had to control my emotions because I didn't want Will to know there was more going on between us. "Okay, whatever you guys think is right. Can I get some coffee?"

"Of course."

Will poured me a cup of coffee and held out a basket of scones and muffins. I grabbed one.

"Shouldn't we get going?"

"Yes."

"See you later, Gabriel. I guess."

"You will. I'll be finished around 6 PM, I hope."

"Don't rush for us!" I said as I put on my gorgeous new coat. I held my arm out for Will, and he hooked his arm around it. I turned back to Gabriel and smirked as we left the room. He looked just a bit angry, which is what I was hoping for. The main purpose of our trip to London was to support Will, and I didn't think that Gabriel would be somewhere else the entire time.

The sights along the drive to the cathedral were breathtaking. It was a foggy, overcast day, which fit the somber mood of the occasion. Once we left London, we sped past mile after mile of lush pastures and farmland. The countryside was dotted with little stone cottages and lots of sheep. Will seemed preoccupied, so I didn't press him to talk. But it wasn't awkward at all; it was peaceful.

He looked over at me a few times and smiled, and a warm feeling passed between us. "It's so beautiful here," I told him, and he nodded slightly. "Do you want to talk?"

"I suppose I should get it off my chest."

"I'm ready."

"I just feel like I'm the only one who actually cares about my grandfather as a person. Most of the people who show up today will only be there because they have to be, because of some title or business relationship, or because of family obligation. No one actually spent any time with my grandfather, especially when he was sick. My parents treated him like rubbish until they realized they needed to stay in his good graces to ensure their inheritance. Then they feigned care and love, but it was quite obvious how full of shit they are."

"You have every right to be angry and to dread this memorial.

I can't even imagine having parents like that. Actually, now that I think about it, my father ruined our family for the sake of money, so maybe I *can* imagine what it's like. It *hurts*."

"It's also the place of the burial. My family arranged for his ashes to be buried at the cathedral, but my grandmother is buried at the family's estate. It's not right, and it's not what they wanted. They should be together."

"Why aren't they burying him with her?"

He sighed loudly. "Because it's considered a great honor to be buried at the Cathedral. Only kings and archbishops are buried there."

"Who cares? If that's not what your grandparents wanted, it doesn't mean shit!"

"Exactly. I cannot wait for this day to be over and for all the business to be settled so I can leave the country and return to my life."

"Can I just ask you why your parents are pushing so hard for his money? I mean, I know everyone always wants more, but aren't they already rich?"

"It's complicated. My parents don't have much anymore. I mean, my father is a barrister, so they're comfortable. But they don't have wealth like they want to *appear* to have, like my family used to have. They're obsessed with making people think they have the kind of wealth my grandfather had."

"I don't understand. Why didn't he share any of it with them when he was alive?"

"My family's wealth goes back several hundred years. For generations, they just spent the money that was left to them and didn't work or bring in additional income. So by the time my grandfather got his inheritance, there were only about 100,000 pounds left."

"*Only* 100,000 pounds? That would change my life quite a bit!"

"I know. But my family was living in a bloody castle with dozens of staff and caretakers. They needed a lot more than that to pay for the lifestyle they were accustomed to."

"Oh, I see. They were already living like millionaires."

"Yes. Most of them were completely unaware of how little they had left, including my grandfather. He thought he was about to inherit a fortune. And he almost gave up my grandmother for it."

"What do you mean?"

"She was from an American middle-class family. They fell in love and wanted to get married, but his family refused to support the marriage because she wasn't up to their standards. They said they'd take away his inheritance if he married her."

"Those fuckers!"

"He decided he wasn't willing to give her up for money, and he married her anyway. No one came to the wedding. No one."

"That sucks. But it's also kind of romantic."

"It is. And they always said they wouldn't have it any other way. It was just them, and it was special."

"So how did he become so rich?"

"He was never actually taken out of his father's will, and he inherited the £100,000. Then, against everyone's wishes, he invested it into a number of different things. With the money he made from those investments, he started housing developments in London and later in New York City. He loved New York, and once he moved into Red House, he didn't want to leave."

"So he took £100,000 and turned it into half a billion?"

"Yes."

"*Amazing.*"

"He tried to bring my dad into his businesses many times, but my dad wanted to do his own thing, which my grandpa supported. He went to law school, but then he refused to get a job. It was obvious he cared about money for the wrong reasons, especially when he married my mum, who's always been obsessed with nobility and fitting in with high society. My grandfather gave them the family's castle and lands, and neither of them worked for almost 20 years. They kept taking money from him and wasting it on meaningless things like jewelry and cars, instead of taking care of the property. Finally, he cut them off, and my dad had to get a job, which he's still all broken up about."

"Well, boo-fucking-hoo."

"Right? Then they started selling off all kinds of family heirlooms and bits of land to get more money."

"It all makes sense now. I totally get why your grandfather left everything to you. You seem to be the only one who has any honor."

He looked at me with a little smile. "You think?"

"You are probably the most honorable man I've ever met. Your grandfather would be very proud."

"Thank you. That means a great deal to me."

I saw a playground in the distance, and an idea popped into my head. "Will! Pull into that parking lot!"

"Where?"

"The playground."

"What? Why? I know you're trying to cheer me up but-"

"Just turn!" I called out, and he veered into the parking lot and screeched to a halt.

"What's going on?" he asked.

"Do you have a plastic bag or a bottle? Some kind of container?"

"Let me look."

He got out of the car and looked through the trunk. He got back in and held out an empty gas can and an enormous first aid kit. I grabbed the kit. "This is perfect. Come on!" He had left the trunk open, so I dumped the contents of the first aid kit into it and slammed it shut. Then I walked towards the playground, and Will followed close behind.

"Do you mind telling me what's going on?"

When I got to the sand, I knelt down and pointed to it. "I have an idea. Think about it for a minute before you react."

"Alright…"

"This sand looks a heck of a lot like ashes, doesn't it?"

"I don't know. I've never seen human ashes before."

"That's probably because once it's in the urn, no one looks at it. Right?"

"Right…"

"What if we took this sand and switched out your grandfather's ashes with it? Then we could bury him where he belongs. With his wife."

He went from a kneeling position to sitting and stared down at the ground. Then he cocked his head in my direction. "Do you really think we could get away with this?"

"I think we could give it a good try. And if we get caught, you have enough money to buy us out of the situation!"

He grinned with a devious look in his eye. "This is a fabulous idea and kind of fucked up as well."

"*They're* the ones who are fucked up. They should respect a dead man's wishes. And they won't even know about it. So they can brag all they want about his burial place while he rests in peace somewhere else!"

"Right. Let's do it."

I scooped up a bunch of sand and picked out the little pieces of dead grass and a cigarette butt. "There. Now all we have to do is get to his ashes when no one's around and quickly switch them out!"

"I hope it proves to be as easy as you make it sound."

"Worth a try, no?"

"Absolutely."

As we walked back to the car, he turned to me and started laughing.

"What?" I asked.

"Always an adventure with you."

"In a good way?"

"*Always.*"

As we drove through the lovely village of Canterbury, he took my hand into his, and I didn't mind at all.

We drove up to an elaborately carved gateway, with shields, angels, and flowers. The doors were open, and he drove through and parked the car off to the side. I got out and looked up at the cathedral looming above me. "Jesus Christ!" inadvertently slipped out of my mouth.

"Yup!" Will responded.

It was massive and absolutely majestic. It had a Gothic style, with tons of columns, towers, and steeples sticking up into the clouds. The entire facade was covered in intricate carvings, and the stained glass windows had a decorative pattern on them that looked like lace.

"Will, this is breathtaking!"

It started to rain, and he opened an umbrella and held it over me. "My grandfather loved it here."

I smiled as a black Mercedes pulled up next to us. "Here we go," he whispered to me with dread in his voice.

"What?" I asked.

"Mum and dad are here."

"Oh."

I took his hand as a show of support and gave it a squeeze. He squeezed back but didn't let go as they got out of the car. A pretty blonde woman with a fancy black hat that looked like an upside-down basket hurried over.

"Your father forgot the bloody umbrella! Let's go!"

We followed her through the massive arched doors as his dad jogged behind us. When we entered, Will closed the umbrella and shook it out as his mother stood on the tips of her toes to touch his hair. "William, I rather like your hair like this. You look very put together!" He rolled his eyes as she finally noticed me. "Oh goodness! How rude of me. You must be Jane. I'm Carol, Will's mum."

She held out her hand, and I smiled and shook it. I wasn't sure if I was expected to kiss it or something, but at that point, I didn't care. "It's so nice to meet you. I'm so sorry for your loss."

She smiled brightly and then turned to Will. "William, you didn't mention how lovely she is on the phone!"

Will looked embarrassed but didn't say anything. His father stepped forward and held out his hand. "Lord George Morris, Earl of Suffolk. How do you do?" I couldn't help but giggle at how silly he sounded.

"For fuck's sake, dad," Will started. "She doesn't need your whole bloody title."

"William! We're in a church!"

"It's nice to meet you, sir," I said as I awkwardly shook his hand.

"Yes, well, she is American, isn't she? I suppose titles don't mean much to them, eh?"

Will looked away with disdain as his mother noticed the first aid kit I was holding. "Are you alright?"

I had forgotten what was in my hands. "Yes!"

She seemed to be waiting for more of an explanation, so I glanced down to my feet. "My foot! I need a bandage. New shoes, ya know?"

"Why don't we go patch up your foot, Jane. Excuse us." He took my hand and led me away.

"I'm sorry they're so insufferable," he said with a pained look on his face.

"Ah, your mom's not that bad. Dad's kind of a dick. Could use a breath mint too."

He busted out laughing, and it echoed throughout the humongous church. "Shall we have a look around?" he asked.

"We shall!"

We strolled around the cathedral admiring the stained glass, and he pointed out the various aristocrats and archbishops who were buried there. There were a lot of creepy effigies of dead kings laid out on top of their coffins. As we approached the pulpit, we tried to act like we were tourists and continued having a casual conversation about the art.

"I don't see an urn," I whispered.

He pointed to a wooden box on top of a pedestal. "You think that's it?" I asked. He nodded, and we quickly moved towards it.

"Okay, grab it!" I told him.

He held his hand out and then hesitated.

"What? What is it?" I asked.

"I... I can't."

"You don't want to?"

"I want to... but I can't. That's his body in there."

"Do you want me to do it?"

"Yes."

"I got it. If you're sure."

"I'm sure. I just can't… do anything with the ashes… myself…"

I nodded and lifted up the box, surprised at how easily the lid opened. Inside was a big plastic bag of ash that was barely sealed. The texture and weight were similar to the sand, but the color was definitely off. I told myself it was unlikely that anyone would open the box as I looked from the first aid kit to the bag and realized we needed a third container to make the exchange. Will kept watch near the doorway. I searched around for a container and spotted three golden goblets on the altar. I ran over and took them; then I went back to the bag of ashes and carefully dumped them into the cups as Will looked on in horror. He started waving his arm to signal that someone was coming. I poured the sand into the plastic bag and shoved it into the box, but I had to leave the ashes back in the cups as a man dressed in a very fancy robe entered.

He eyed me suspiciously and said, "Is everything alright?"

Will jumped in. "Your grace! My apologies. I hope we aren't intruding. My grandfather's memorial service begins soon, and we just wanted to have a few moments alone with… him."

The man turned to me, and I smiled awkwardly and looked back to Will.

"Of course. Please let us know if there is anything else we can do. Your grandfather was a highly respected member of our church and will be greatly missed." Will nodded, and the man gently added, "Peace be with you," and left.

"That was the archbishop!" he whisper-yelled.

"Do you think he knows something's up?"

"I have no idea!"

I immediately ran over to the cups and poured the ashes from them into the first aid kit. There was still some residue in the cups, but Will signaled me to hurry up. I blew into the cups to scatter the rest of the ashes and joined him as he went down the corridor towards a staircase. As we descended the stairs to the crypt, he put his finger to his lips to quiet me until we reached a far, empty corner.

The crypt was as beautiful as it was creepy. It was mostly dark and lit only by candles. When we reached the furthest corner, Will stood in front of me and whispered, "Holy shit! We did it!"

"I know!" I whispered back as I instinctively threw my arms around his neck. He wrapped his arm around my waist with a grin, and I awkwardly put my arms back down and tried to deflect.

"Just pray no one examines the box… or those goblets… too closely."

He went to a row of lit candles and held out a stick for me. "Would you like to light a candle?"

"Sure. What for?"

"Whatever you like. It's like a prayer or a wish. Or you can light it in remembrance of someone."

I took the stick and lit it. "In loving memory of your grandfather," I declared.

He nodded, and we lit two candles, side by side, and returned the sticks. "Thank you," he said.

"Of course. Should I just hold onto… him? Or would you like to?"

I held out the first aid kit, and he bent down close to my face and merely said, "You."

I gave him a friendly smile, hoping he would pull back, but he kept his face close to mine until I turned to face him directly. He looked very serious, so I giggled and asked, "What're you thinking?"

"Nothing. Everything. I don't know. We better go back up. The ceremony will start soon."

He gestured towards the stairs, and I went up. On the third step, I wobbled a few times on the thin heels I wasn't used to wearing, and I fell backward. He caught me as I let out a ridiculous shriek, and we both laughed way too loud. I looked up at his face. "I'm still getting used to these rich-people shoes!"

An enormous smile spread across his face as he leaned in and kissed me. And I let him. It was a beautiful moment, but I was thankful that we were sort of in a public place and had somewhere we needed to be because I didn't want it to go any further than that.

As we climbed the rest of the stairs and entered the chapel,

I couldn't stop thinking about Gabriel. Should I tell him that we kissed? Would he be jealous? I realized that I *wanted* him to be jealous as Will led me to two empty seats in the front row next to his parents. The chapel was packed with people, and I felt like they were all staring at me.

"Are you sure I should be in the front row?" I whispered.

"Of course. You're with me."

We sat down as the organ started to play a sad, creepy song, and a procession of men dressed in fancy gowns came down the aisle holding giant candlesticks. One of them had the box of ashes on a satin pillow. He placed the box on the altar, and the priest began to speak. "Glory be to the Father, and to the Son, and to the Holy Ghost."

The crowd answered, "Amen."

"As it was in the beginning, is now, and ever shall be: world without end."

Again everyone answered, "Amen."

"We have gathered here today to honor the life and legacy of Lord Edward Morris, 18th Earl of Suffolk, and to commend his immortal soul to almighty God." He continued with the "Our Father" prayer, and everyone spoke along with him, except for me. I wasn't raised with any religion, and I didn't know any of the words after the first line.

After that, the priest talked about delivering us from the burden of flesh, so we may experience everlasting bliss. Everyone eagerly shouted, "Amen!" I started to wonder if anyone was going to speak specifically about Will's grandpa. It seemed like a regular church service to me.

"And now Lord Morris, the 19th Earl of Suffolk, shall read a passage from Ecclesiastes in honor of his beloved father." As Will's dad approached the podium, Will took my hand and squeezed it pretty hard. I looked down at our hands and then up at Will's face, which was staring at his father with anger and pain.

"To everything there is a season and a time to every purpose under heaven. A time to be born, and a time to die; a time to plant, and a time to pluck up that which is planted. A time to kill, and a time to heal. A time to break down, and a time to build up. A time to weep, and a time to laugh. A time to mourn, and a time to dance. A time to cast away stones, and a time to gather stones together. A time to embrace, and a time to refrain from embracing. A time to get, and a time to lose. A time to keep, and a time to cast away. A time to rend, and a time to sew. A time to keep silence, and a time to speak. A time to love, and a time to hate. A time of war, and a time of peace." As he left the podium and returned to his seat, Will loosened his grip a bit. I stroked the top of his hand in support.

"And now the Earl's grandson, Sir William, would like to read a eulogy for his beloved grandfather." Will stood up and looked at me with warmth before his eyes went down to the floor, and he approached the podium. He took a folded paper out of his jacket, and it took him a bit to collect himself before he started reading.

"In Proverbs 13:22, King Solomon writes, a good man leaves an inheritance to his children's children." He paused and stared directly at his parents as he repeated the line with emphasis. "*A good man leaves an inheritance to his children's children.*" They shifted uncomfortably in their seats. "Today I want to speak about the inheritance my grandfather left to me, for which I am enormously thankful. And I am not speaking here of money or possessions, though I am also grateful for the very comfortable life he has afforded my family and me. I am speaking of the passing on of something much more valuable. The inheritance of his soul.

"How can I explain to you what my grandfather's spirit was made of? It is an impossible task, but let me try. My grandfather's spirit was made entirely of tireless, relentless love for his family, his community, and for life itself.

"From my grandfather, I have inherited honor and faithfulness, as exemplified by his marriage to my grandmother. Married for 70 years, he did not go a day without telling her how much he loved and appreciated her. But that was not enough. It was his personal mission each and every day to *show her* how much he loved her by his level of concern and care. Even after several decades of marriage, he continued to seek new ways to keep romance in their relationship. He brought my grandmother breakfast in bed, every day, for 70 years. Even when he had to use a walker, and it took him close to an hour to make it to her bedroom from the kitchen, he still brought her breakfast. I can only hope to be blessed with the opportunity to be the same kind of husband for my own wife one day.

"There's another part of my grandfather's soul that I am thankful to inherit. Persistence. There are many key moments in his life when he showed an enormous amount of determination. When he first met my grandmother, she didn't really like him. And he knew it because she told him directly."

The crowd laughed a bit which broke the tension really well. Then he added, "I've been in a similar situation myself," and he looked directly at me and grinned. I could feel myself blushing as he continued, only this time he wasn't reading from the paper. It was like he was speaking off the cuff. "But I know not to give up so easily on something that means so much to me. Something I can see my future in." I looked down into my lap as he continued.

"My grandfather persisted in showing my grandmother his heart and eventually she gave in and had no choice but to love him back. She knew she would never find another man who would love her and care for her as completely as he would. And they both persevered when his family disapproved of their relationship. They were determined to be together, and eventually, the family embraced them as a couple. And when my grandfather was given the last bit of the family's inherited wealth, he did what he thought was best, again, against the advice of everyone he knew. He wrote his own story, trod his own path, hand in hand with his love, and proved everyone wrong, time after time.

"I am honored to inherit from my grandfather his humility and integrity. He never showed off his wealth or saw himself as better than anyone else on earth. He never spoke of his accomplishments, though they were many. He always told me that everyone has a story worth listening to, and he had enormous compassion for his fellow man.

"Which is another huge legacy I seek to emulate: service to others. My grandfather poured a significant amount of money into helping people. He gave more than half of his net worth to create a grant-giving organization that supports education, medicine, science, and the arts. But he also gave so much of his time. He spent every Sunday at the local nursing home, talking with the lonely residents, and lifting their spirits. When he became a resident there himself, he still went out of his way to spread kindness and cheer to everyone around him.

"I could talk about my grandfather's wonderful qualities and contributions to society for hours. But I will end with the most important lesson I have inherited: money does not bring happiness, only love can do that. I hope that everyone here understands the privilege it was to know this man. Thank you."

He returned to his seat, and I whispered, "That was so beautiful, Will. And it was kind of badass too."

"You think?" he mouthed to me.

I winked and whispered, "We'll talk in the car."

The priest signaled the family to follow him to the front of the altar, and Will's parents got up, along with a few others who were in the front row. Will stood up and followed them. I felt uncomfortable sitting in the front row by myself because it looked like I was part of the family and choosing not to join them. He looked back and winked at me, and I felt a bit better. They followed the priest off to the side of the altar where one of the slabs of stone from the floor had been removed. Another man in a black robe with a red sash walked the ashes over and got down on his knees in front of the hole in the ground. The family bowed their heads as the priest spoke.

"We have entrusted our brother Edward to the Lord's mercy, and we now commit his mortal remains to the ground. Earth to earth, ashes to ashes, dust to dust, in sure and certain hope of the resurrection to eternal life." The man put the ashes in the hole, and Will's mom and another woman placed flowers on top. I couldn't help but feel exhilaration knowing what Will and I had done and that we were the only people in the world who knew.

There wasn't much more to the ceremony except a few more standard Christian prayers. The organ played to signal the end of the service, and everyone got up and started mingling and chatting. His mother turned to us. "Will you be joining us at Powderton?"

Will sighed. "Only for a bit."

"Lovely. Your father and I would like to speak with you... in private." He didn't respond, so she turned to speak to me. "Wonderful to meet you. See you soon!" She kissed both of my cheeks, hooked her arm around her husband's, and sauntered away.

"What's Powderton?"

"Their home."

"Oh shit! We're going to a castle?"

"Only for a bit. There will be some awful people there, so brace yourself."

"I'm starting to think this is why you bought me all these fancy clothes. So I'd fit in."

"Jane, of course not! I don't *want* you to fit in. That's what I like about you!"

"That I'm some kind of misfit?"

"No, that you're never afraid to be who you are and say what you feel. It's... Well, after being around these tight-arse people my entire life... it's downright refreshing."

"So I shouldn't be concerned that I'm the only female here who isn't wearing a ridiculous hat?"

"I'd be concerned if you were!"

An older woman in a gray suit with an enormous gray top hat that had ridiculous bursts of black and white feathers embraced Will. A man with messy gray hair and fucked up teeth stood beside her, staring at the ground. "Oh, William!" she proclaimed as he tried to pull away from her. "I know how hard this must be for you! You were thick as thieves, your grandfather and you!"

"Yes, Aunt Catherine. We were very close."

The man stepped forward and simply said, "William," and shook Will's hand very dramatically. "We will see you at Powderton then?"

"Yes, sir."

"Good then. Come, Catherine."

She hesitated like there was something she wanted to say but couldn't find the words. "Ah, William. I was wondering…"

"*Catherine*," her husband insisted. "Not now."

"No, Aunt Catherine. I haven't made any decisions yet," Will said with no emotion. "But I will take your requests into consideration."

"Oh, I wasn't… I didn't…"

"*Catherine*."

"We'll see you at Powderton," she said with an awkward smile, and they hurried away.

"*Fuck,* that was awkward," I said to Will.

"My dad's sister," Will answered. "As subtle as a sledgehammer."

"Just plain rude! We're still at the man's memorial for god's sake."

A dainty, manicured hand tapped Will on the shoulder. When he turned around, a girl in her mid-twenties was standing there with a little grin. She was wearing a massive fur coat and an equally massive purple hat with a gigantic flower on top. She didn't take any time to reveal her agenda. "William, we've missed you!" She tried to kiss both of his cheeks; however, his height prevented it, and he didn't bend down for her. Instead, she just pretended to kiss each side, then said, "Oh, Will! Before I forget! I wanted to ask about the flat at Queen's Square. You see, it's very close to Imperial College, which I'll be attending in the fall. I'm sure my mum told you…"

"Anne, please. This is neither the time-"

"Oh, forgive me! Where are my manners?" She held her hand out to me and said, "Lady Anne Bottomley, Will's cousin."

I shook her hand and said, "Jane."

"We'll see you at Powderton, Anne." Will took my hand and led me away.

"These people are really rude, especially considering their fancy titles and all. Shouldn't they know better?"

"Money trumps everything."

A very pretty bleach-blonde girl looked directly at us and started walking over. Will whispered, "Oh fuck," and turned to look the other way.

She was wearing a tiny little black dress that was way too short for the occasion and a black hat that looked like a saucer attached to the side of her head. It had a black veil pulled down over her face. Her shoes were silver and covered in little pearls. No doubt they cost as much as mine or more. She held her hand out in front of him. He begrudgingly took it and kissed it and she curtsied and said, "My lord."

His eyes closed halfway as though he was bored, and he answered, "Hello Laura," with no emotion. I wondered what this one was going to ask for.

"I've missed you. Why haven't you answered my calls?"

"I've been busy," he said as he looked everywhere but at her. The more I stared at her, the more I realized she was fake as fuck. She definitely had too many nose jobs, or one really bad one, and tons of filler in her lips and cheeks.

"How long have you been back in London?"

"A few weeks," he said with irritation.

"Aren't you going to introduce me to your friend?" she asked as she batted her eyelashes like a little doll.

I didn't wait for him as I stuck my hand out towards her. "Hi. I'm Jane. It's nice to meet you."

She looked at my hand like it had cooties and lightly touched it with hers. "Oh, you're American. I'm Lady Laura Hollister of Sandwich."

"Umm, okay. So how do you two know each other?"

She looked at Will and giggled. "How do we know each other, Will?"

"We grew up together."

"Our fathers serve in the House of Lords together. We spent almost every summer of our childhood at my family's estate. Remember, Will?"

"Yes, Laura. I remember."

"We went to Oxford together as well."

"Will, you went to Oxford? You never told me that."

"Well, he only went for one term, before he left me to pursue… whatever it is you're doing across the pond."

"Oxford isn't exactly known for its arts programs."

"Nonsense! Oxford is Oxford. Whatever you study, you will be taught by the best. But what exactly you will *do* with that degree is the more important question. Seems a bit impractical, doesn't it?"

"Well, Laura, I suppose that's why I left. An impractical man like me doesn't belong in a practical place like Oxford. Please excuse us." He grabbed my hand and pulled me away from her towards the front doors.

"I'll see you at Powderton!" she called out.

"Was she your girlfriend?"

"Why? Are you jealous?"

"Not really. It's just that… she's terrible."

"Fuck *no,* she wasn't my girlfriend. Our families have been shoving us together since birth, but she makes me want to fucking kill myself."

"Oh, I see. She has the fancy title and breeding."

"Yes. Her father is the Earl of Sandwich."

"The Earl of Sandwich? That's like, a real thing? Not a joke?"

"It's quite real. And she'll inherit 750,000 pounds from him on her 25th birthday."

"Holy fucking shit! Wait, isn't that a restaurant? The Earl of Sandwich?"

"Yes. That's part of where their fortune comes from. He licensed their name to a chain of sandwich shops in the U.S."

"I could go for a sandwich right now."

"Right. Let's get out of here, so we can beat these people to the good liquor and food."

"Race you?" I said.

"In those shoes?"

I took my shoes off, held them in my hand, and then did a stance like I was about to start running. "You sure?" he asked, looking down at my bare feet.

"Go!" I yelled as I burst through the crowd in front of us, which got me some whispers and stares. Will followed right after, and we busted through the cathedral doors and into the sunshine.

I held the first aid kit full of ashes tightly as we drove through the countryside. We went up a steep hill, and when we came back down, I could see a huge, gray castle in the distance. The enormous manor house had several towers jutting up into the sky.

"Will! That's legitimately a castle!"

"Not exactly. It doesn't have a moat."

"When you said it was a castle, I didn't really think it was a *castle*. But-"

"It's ridiculous, huh?"

"No! It's beautiful!"

The closer we got, the older it appeared. Large areas were covered in well-trimmed ivy, and the stone exterior looked quite weathered.

"How old is it?"

"About 600 years old."

"You know it must be haunted as shit!"

"I used to think so. Especially as a kid. My sister wasn't born until I was 13, so I had an entire wing of this place to myself. Got rather spooky at night."

"You grew up here?"

"For the most part. I spent my time here and at my grandparents' estate. Not a lot of happy memories here."

He took a deep breath as we inched closer to the front entrance. Then he suddenly jammed on the break and put the car in park.

"What is it?"

"I just... really don't want to go in there. Everyone will be having a great time, drinking and eating and bullshitting, and there will be no mention of my grandfather."

"We don't have to."

He sat in silence, staring out at the castle for a while.

"Why don't we go have our own ceremony?" I offered as I held out the box of ashes, and he nodded. "Is there an urn or container that you'd like to put... him in?"

He thought about it for a bit before answering. "I think I'd like to just return him to the earth."

I smiled and nodded. He put the car in reverse and peeled out of the driveway so fast that I almost dropped the box. "Where are we going?"

"There's a much quicker way to get to the garden. From here, it would be quite a walk."

"I wouldn't mind the walk, especially around here. But in these shoes..."

He drove for another five minutes around some winding roads and then turned onto a makeshift road in a densely wooded area. It was really bumpy, so I held on tightly to the box until we arrived at an iron gate. He put the car in park just as my phone dinged with a message.

He got out of the car and approached the gate as I took out my phone. Gabriel had sent a picture of him standing in front of a huge mural of a naked woman. It covered an entire wall, and the woman had flowing watercolor hair that stretched out all over her body and out into the air. Behind her were wildflowers and weeds. He was shirtless with smears of paint all over his perfect chest, neck, and face, and his hands were stained blue and purple. Under the picture he texted, "You were my inspiration." She did look a bit like me, especially the shape of her body. I was about to answer when I noticed a huge mirror at the very edge of the photo. Reflected in it was a tall, blonde girl taking a picture with a fancy camera. The painting looked a hell of a lot more like her than me. I switched off my phone and threw it on the floor of the car and ran to catch up with Will inside the little cemetery.

There were only about a dozen headstones and a few large stone slabs that were about the size of a coffin. Will was standing in front of one of the stone slabs. It stood out because most of the stones were very weathered and sinking into the ground, but this one was bright white and looked new. As I turned to address Will, a pattern on one of the old headstones caught my eye. I moved closer and tried to figure out what was so familiar about the strange design that was etched across the top of a weathered headstone from the year 1794. It was a series of squares and dots. I couldn't place where I knew it from, so I turned back.

"Do you need more time to yourself?"

He kept staring at the stone. "No. I'm alright."

The slab read, "Annette Morris, beloved daughter, wife, mother, grandmother." As we stared down, Will started to shake his head.

"What is it?" I asked.

"They didn't put her title."

"You think it was on purpose?"

"I know it was on purpose."

"I'm so sorry, Will."

"What does it even matter to them? I'm the only one who ever comes here."

"They have a lot to learn. I don't know if you believe in reincarnation, but if it's real, they're going to have to come back again and again."

"Maybe they'll come back as a bunch of flies on a pile of horseshit."

"Most likely. Did you realize that we didn't bring a shovel?" I asked. He made an "oops" face, and I pointed to a shovel leaning against a tree in a far corner.

"That was easy," he replied.

I held out the box for him, and I started to walk over to get the shovel. After a few steps, one of my heels sunk into the mud, and I stumbled forward. I stood back up and took my foot out of the shoe; then I yanked it hard to get it out of the ground and slid it back on. A few steps later, the other heel sunk into the mud, and I screeched in frustration and stepped out of the shoe. I took the other one off and walked barefoot in the mud. I grabbed the shovel and pulled the shoes out of the mud on the way back. Will was laughing at me as I held out the shovel.

"Fuck these shoes."

He continued to laugh as he broke ground. I looked around for something to help him dig with, but I didn't see anything. Then I held out one of the shoes. "I can help you dig with these!"

"Thank you, but I think I'd like to do it myself."

"Right. Of course."

I stood and watched as he dug a shallow hole.

"Probably doesn't need to be very deep, right?"

"That looks perfect."

He kneeled down with the box, and I knelt next to him. He closed his eyes for a while, and I watched him in awe. He was such a sweet, wonderful man, and it was charming how much he loved his grandparents. He opened his eyes, lifted the lid to the box, and whispered, "Here we go." He slowly dumped the ashes into the hole and paused with a deep breath before using his hands to fill the hole back in with dirt. He patted it and then stood up and held his hand out for mine. I placed my hand in his, and as we walked out of the cemetery, I pointed back to the headstone with the mysterious pattern.

"Does that mean anything to you?"

"The headstone?"

"The symbols at the top."

"Not really, but I do feel like I've seen those symbols somewhere."

"It's familiar to me too, but I can't place it."

"Hmm. I can ask my dad about it."

"No, it's not important."

When we got back in the car, he turned to me with a serious look. "Jane, you have no idea how much it means to me that you were here for me today."

"It means a lot to me too. I'm glad we did what we did."

"What can I do for you?"

"You don't have to do anything, Will. We're friends. That's what friends do."

He looked down at the console. "Friends. Right."

He backed his way out, and I took a folded piece of paper out of my bag. "Actually, there *is* something you can do for me."

"Name it."

I unfolded the paper and held it out for him. He glanced at it, and his forehead wrinkled in confusion.

"I found it in the tube station yesterday. Can we go?" I asked.

"What's a foam party?"

"It's a dance party where they pour tons of bubbly soap on everyone."

"I see. I'd be happy to drop you off and pick you up."

I shoved his arm playfully. "No way! You'll go with me and participate fully!"

He looked like he was in pain as he answered, "If I must."

"You must."

"They have hard liquor, I'm assuming?"

"Of course."

"Isn't that a gay club?"

"I don't know. Is it?"

"I believe so."

"I'm sure they let others participate as well."

"I'm going to need to get sloshed. Really sloshed."

"I'm guessing you mean drunk. And I assure you, we will get you quite sloshed."

"Right."

I grabbed my phone and wrote back to Gabriel. "Meet me in Heaven at 10 PM."

He immediately sent a question mark back, so I sent the address of the club. He wrote back, "Can't wait."

CHAPTER 25

GABRIEL

Listen to the Heaven Playlist
bit.ly/PlaylistinHeaven

I GOT TO THE CLUB EARLY, SO I COULD WATCH HER FOR A BIT. I wanted to see how she was with Will to make sure there wasn't anything I needed to worry about when they were alone. I was pretty sure she was mine, but it was obvious that I didn't have all of her trust yet. It was entirely possible for him to suck her in at a weak point, if she was feeling vulnerable or jealous.

I got a drink and stood against the wall in the corner. I had to refuse the advances of at least five guys by the time they showed up. Some were bolder than others. A few asked me to dance, one dove right in and tried to kiss me, and another one invited me to the bathroom for some head. I'd never been there before, but I was pretty sure it was a gay bar.

They entered wearing the same clothes from earlier in the day. She looked fucking perfect in that tight dress, and the heels really showed off her legs. I never noticed how hot her legs were because she was always wearing jeans. As they walked in, that Lady Gaga song "Stupid Love" started playing, and she jumped up and down with excitement and tried to pull Will onto the dance floor. He kept shaking his head and refusing, and she even tried dancing on him a little to persuade him. He looked really uncomfortable and pointed to the bar. She threw her hands up and started dancing by herself on the dance floor as Will ordered drinks.

I leaned back and enjoyed watching her dance in that black dress with blue and purple lights swirling around her. Two guys who were pretty much humping each other noticed her and danced into her space. She was receptive, and they sandwiched her in and started dancing a little too close. Since they had just been making out, I assumed they were gay and not interested in her like that, but they started feeling her body and rubbing their fucking crotches on her. I was about to run over and pull them off her, but she shoved one pretty hard and yelled something at him. The other one laughed and grabbed her by her hips. She kneed him in the dick, and he fell to the floor in agony. Will walked over and handed her a drink. She took a sip and danced away from the two horny guys towards the middle of the floor. Will stood in place chugging his drink. She signaled for him to come to her with a sexy wave of her finger, and he reluctantly joined her. She tried to put her arms around his neck, but her hands went to his hips instead. She kept trying to get him to move with her, but he just stood there with a big, dumb smile. She let go and spun around a few times and then turned and looked directly at me.

I smiled at her, and she smiled back but then turned back to Will like I wasn't even there. She put her arms around his waist and hung her head back, shaking her hair around. "Such a Whore" by JVLA started, and it was just too fucking sexual for me to be watching from the sidelines. It was on.

I put my drink down and went directly to her and pulled her into me. She yelped with surprise and then gave me a hungry look like she was going to devour me. It was time to show Will how to handle a woman like this.

I put my knee between her legs and pulled her closer. I wrapped one arm around her waist and grabbed the back of her neck with the other, and we danced on each other with our lips an inch apart. I noticed Will was back at the bar ordering more drinks and grinned. I felt like I had already won.

I started sucking on her earlobe as we were grinding on each other, and I felt her legs loosen. I pulled her mouth to mine, but she flung her head back and shook her head no. I tried to kiss her again, but she kept refusing.

"Why are you playing games with me?" I said into her ear, so she could hear me over the music. Then I ran my tongue down her neck.

She closed her eyes for a second. Then she leaned into my ear and yelled, "Why are you playing games with *me*?"

"I'm not!" I yelled out.

"Who was that mural for?" she yelled back. I instantly knew I was dealing with jealousy.

"An old friend!"

"A very *hot, female* old friend!"

She started to turn away, and I grabbed her by the back of her neck again. "It's not like that!"

"Did she pose nude for that mural?" she demanded. "You must think I'm an idiot!"

"No, she did *not* pose nude. Her fiancé was there. It was her face but *your* body! Didn't you notice?"

"I just noticed that you ditched me to paint a naked female friend."

"Listen to me!" I called out as she started to walk away. "Fuck!" Arguing with her over the blaring music was infuriating. "Jane! Please! Come with me!" She shook her head no and quickened her pace towards the bar. Before Will saw us, I lifted her up and threw her over my shoulder, and stomped towards the bathroom. She was kicking and punching my back, but I couldn't let her go until I had fixed the situation.

I kicked open the men's bathroom door and marched past a few guys peeing and one who was getting head from another guy. I shoved open the door to the handicapped stall and dropped her to her feet. She shoved me and went to leave, but I caught her and held her against the wall.

"Listen to me! Nothing happened! What do I have to do to prove that to you?"

"You could start by letting me off this disgusting wall."

"If I let go, you can't leave."

"Fine."

I let her go. She went for the door again, but I slid in front of her with my back against the lock.

"Come on! It's gross in here!"

"Do you want me to call Claire, so you can ask her about today?"

"Claire?"

"The girl in the painting."

"No, I don't want you to call Claire."

"How can I get you to trust me?"

"I don't know! Isn't that something you have to earn, by like, not doing anything shady for a long period of time?"

"I thought I was doing that." She rolled her eyes. "What if I asked you to be my girlfriend?"

"Huh?"

"If we were officially a couple and I said I was committed to you, would you trust me?"

"I don't know if that's what I want." Her words stung at first, but I saw a hint of a smile in her expression. It was time to seal the deal. "I have something for you." I told her to close her eyes and give me her hand. She hesitated until I said, "Please!" She held out her hand, and I gently slid the ring onto her ring finger. She looked down at it happily, but then her smile dropped.

"What is this?"

"I've had this ring for a long time. I've been waiting for the right person to give it to. I was waiting for *you*."

"What does it mean?"

"It's a double Ouroboros, an ancient Egyptian symbol. The two snakes are eating each other's tails, forming a knot, with no beginning or end."

"You have this tattooed on your back."

"Yes. It's the first tattoo I ever got."

"Seems like it means something sinister. Like they're destroying each other."

"Not at all. It symbolizes infinity, eternity. Infinite return."

"The cycle of rebirth."

"Yes."

"It's beautiful. But what does it mean… in terms of… us?"

"You're mine. And I'm yours. And this should serve as a reminder for you. A reminder of what I've been telling you. You've always been mine and-"

"I'll always be yours."

"Exactly."

"In this life and the next? And the next? And the next? It's a bit much."

"Don't worry. We're going to get it right this time."

We leaned in and kissed each other as the guy getting head came really loudly.

"Uh, let's get the fuck out of here please."

"Yes."

"I still want to hide this from Will a bit longer. He's had a really rough day."

"Of course."

The dance floor was packed, and they had already started pouring foam onto everyone. There were huge metal tubes dumping soapy liquid directly into the crowd.

I knew Will was drunk because he was on the edge of the dance floor with his shirt halfway unbuttoned as a girl in a bikini top rubbed foam onto his chest and arms. She took his hand and led him further onto the dance floor, and he threw his arms up as the foam fell directly on top of them. Then the girl tried to reach up and kiss him, and he leaned down and let her. I turned to Jane and pointed at him, and her mouth dropped. "No way!" she called out. "How many drinks do you think he had?"

"Too many! I've known him a long time, and I've never seen him let go like that. Not even close."

"I love it! Let's go!"

She led me to Will, and he didn't even notice us as we started sliding around in the slippery soap. Jane stumbled a bit and then took off her heels and threw them across the room in frustration. They hit a guy in the back of the head, and he looked pissed. Then he picked them up and smiled as he tried to squeeze his feet into them. I leaned into Jane's ear and yelled, "You just made that guy very happy! But I don't think they're his size!" She winked at me and pulled me into her body by my shirt. When we were nose to nose, she spread her hands out on my chest and looked at the ring with joy. I tried to kiss her, but she shook her head no and nodded in Will's direction. "Yeah, I don't think he even knows where he is right now!" I called out as I tried to kiss her again. She wagged her finger in my face and spun around. Her perfect ass was just barely touching my dick, and it was a major tease.

The DJ called out, "Are you ready for more?" and the crowd went wild, screaming and jumping up and down. "I don't think you're wet enough! How wet do you wanna get? I can't hear you!" The screams were so loud that it created a painful buzz in the air as the tubes poured a massive amount of foam onto us. We were up to our waists in soap and completely soaked. People were flinging off their clothes and stripping down to their underwear. A couple of girls had their tits out. It was pure hedonism and memento mori in action. They were living like it was their last day on earth, rubbing soap all over each other. It started to feel like an orgy, and I wanted Jane close to me to protect her and to touch her all I wanted.

I used my shirt to wipe off my face and combed my fingers through my hair as she drew me in by my collar and unbuttoned my shirt. As she tossed my shirt behind her, I tried to pull off her jacket, but it was stuck. I grabbed the collar and yanked as hard as I could and apparently the whole thing was one piece. Suddenly she was standing there in her black pushup bra and part of a ripped skirt. She looked shocked and then giggled and called out, "That dress was like four grand!"

"I'll buy you another one. Get over here!"

We danced and slid our slippery hands all over each other, and she finally got caught up in the moment and let me thrust my tongue into her mouth. She met my kiss with an equal amount of desire. I started to undo her bra, but she grabbed my hands and flung them off. We kept kissing, and I couldn't stop myself from sliding my hand down her skirt. She was so wet, and my hands were already slippery from the soap. She moaned into my mouth and started rubbing me. I contemplated taking her back into the bathroom stall when I noticed two huge hands rubbing her shoulders and moving down to her chest. My jealousy raged, and I went to throw him off when I realized the hands belonged to Will. His eyes were closed, and he looked totally out of it. He was barely holding himself up as he leaned down to the side of her face and said something into her ear.

I didn't know what the fuck to do. She didn't want him to know we were a couple even though we had just made it official. I wasn't all that threatened by him, but still, this was my girlfriend he was groping. I tried to ignore it as Jane turned her head in response to something he said, and she opened her mouth to receive his tongue. I started to take my hand out of her skirt when, without removing her mouth from Will, she shoved my hand back in and guided me up and down. I obeyed, honestly turned on while watching her make out with another guy, as he ran his hands under her bra. She had one hand on the back of his head as she continued rubbing me over my pants while she kissed Will passionately.

I decided that if this was what she wanted, I could deal with it for one night as long as it didn't go much further than that. She pulled her head away from Will, and her eyes seared into mine. She took my hand out of her skirt and sucked on my fingers while staring at me. I slammed her into me by her ass and dove my tongue back into her mouth. Will watched us for a moment and then started to walk away. She grabbed him by the arm and shoved his hand down her skirt as another two feet of foam was dumped onto us. He was rubbing her and looking into her eyes as she leaned in to kiss him. I backed up a step or two to find something to wipe my eyes with. The soap was starting to burn. She saw me backing away and hooked her hand around the top of my pants and flung me back against her ass. I licked her neck as he rubbed her. Then I slid my hand down the back of her skirt and down her ass. I found her pussy and shoved two fingers in. She jumped with surprise and then leaned her head back to look at me. I winked at her, and she closed her eyes and let us work her into an intense orgasm. I had to shut Will out of my mind. It was too weird.

She came so loudly that I could hear her cry over the blaring bass of the music, and she shuddered harder than I'd ever seen. Will took his hand out of her skirt, and she kissed him gently before he stumbled towards the bar. I kept my hand inside her from behind and shoved my other hand down the front of her skirt. She started shaking her head like she couldn't take it, and I kept pumping my fingers from behind and rubbing her clit until she came so hard that she screamed my name. I released her, and she leaned into me with exhaustion. Then she said into my ear, "Bathroom?"

"Please."

"Women's bathroom this time."

We hurried into the women's bathroom, but all the stalls were taken. She shoved me up against a full-length mirror at the end of the row of sinks and yanked my pants down and began giving me the hottest blow job of my life. Two girls came in, and she didn't stop at all. "Oh shit!" one called out. "He's fucking gorgeous, honey! I don't blame you!" she added.

Her friend said, "See! A guy like that could turn me straight!" and they started doing their makeup in the mirror, like it was nothing out of the ordinary.

Once I focused on what she was doing to me, I came pretty quickly. She washed her mouth out in the sink and grinned at me. I could barely stand up anymore. We walked out together all blissed out, and Will was standing there waiting for us. The three of us stayed quiet for the rest of the night. We just kept drinking until we woke up at Will's place the next morning, having no idea how we got there.

CHAPTER 26

Jane

"Swollen"—Bent

WE ALL ACTED LIKE IT HAD NEVER EVEN HAPPENED. I woke up the next morning and found Will shuffling through paperwork again, his hands buried in his hair with frustration. I sat down next to him.

"How long have you been up?" I asked.

"A while."

"I'm pretty hungover," I admitted.

"Same."

We sat there in silence as he shuffled through his paperwork.

"You know, I've been thinking," I began. "The only problem with this money situation is your perception of it."

"Oh?"

"You see it as an enormous burden because your family is expecting you to give them all what they want, when they want it, right?"

"Right."

"Well, what if this was actually *your power*?"

"Power *over* them?"

"In a way."

"I think that's the reason it was left to me in the first place and not them. I don't see money as power."

"I know. And I'm not saying you should change who you are. But maybe you should change how you view their expectations of you. *You* are in the driver's seat. *You* will make these decisions when you are good and ready. *If* and *when* you see fit!"

"Uh-huh."

"I also think you should come back home. It will be much easier to get them off your back if you're in another country."

"I like that idea."

"Come home with us."

"I might need a bit more time, but I think I'll be home shortly after you."

"Good."

Right after Will dropped us off at the airport, Gabriel turned to me with a strange look on his face.

"So about last night…?" he began.

"Yeah."

"I was sober. I think you were too."

"Yes. During… *that*."

"I'm not judging any of us. But I'd like that to be a one-time thing."

"Agreed."

He tapped the ring on my finger and smiled. "My one and only?"

"Apparently so."

When we got back to Red House, we were inseparable for four days straight, only parting when I had to work. We slipped into a comfortable yet romantic routine. We ate every meal together, showered together, and slept together.

Both Lizzie and Will were coming home soon, and I was ready to tell them about our relationship. Things seemed like they were falling into place.

On our fifth night together, as we ate dinner and drank vintage wine, Gabriel said he had a very special place he wanted to share with me.

"Where is it?"

"In the house."

"There's part of the house I haven't seen?"

"A very special part. A sacred place. So sacred, in fact, it's part of our oath not to share it with anyone outside the brotherhood."

"Then why are you sharing it with me?"

"I think it's time. Your presence here has become integral to the creation of our art. You're our greatest muse, and I think the guys would agree."

He took our wine glasses and the bottle and told me to follow him.

"Maybe you should ask them first?"

"I've always thought it better to apologize for something afterwards than to seek permission and be denied."

I rolled my eyes as he led me towards the library. "I've been to the library!" I called out. He shushed me as we entered the library doors, and I followed him to a back corner where he stood in front of a tall bookshelf.

"You must promise to keep your knowledge of this place a secret."

"What place? The library?"

He wrapped his fingers around the side of the bookshelf and pulled it forward. A doorway opened, and he walked inside and switched on a light. I followed him, and he told me to close the door behind me.

It was a massive art studio. I wondered why I had never considered it before. Most artists have a dedicated studio, and they had a massive house. Of course they would have one.

There were canvases and sketches on easels, hanging on the walls and from clothing lines, on the floor, and spread across massive tables. The floor was white marble, but there were splatters of paint all over the place, including the white walls. It was an industrial looking space, with high ceilings, fluorescent lighting, and only one window towards the back. The tables had countless cups full of brushes in all states of use, tons of tubes of paint, pencils, watercolor palettes, and charcoal.

Gabriel went around turning on all the swing-arm lamps on the worktables as I looked closer at the paintings and sketches. I realized the majority of them were of Lizzie and me. He switched off the overhead lights and held out my wine glass for me. "I hate those fluorescent lights," he commented as he filled my glass. "So unnatural."

"Umm, Gabriel?"

"Yes?"

"Is it me, or are a majority of these paintings of Lizzie and me?"

He looked amused. "Are you pleased or freaked?"

"A bit of both."

"I told you, Jane. You're our muse."

"Apparently Lizzie is as well."

"Yes. In a different kind of way. But yes."

I stepped away from him and began to take a closer look at the art. There were sketches of me asleep in bed and in a chair, dressed as Marie Antoinette, and angrily eating a sprig of berries. There was a drawing of Gabriel kissing my forehead, and one of me swimming nude. "What's with this one?" I asked. "I don't recall swimming naked around any of you."

"Wish fulfillment?" he said with a smirk. There were tons of sketches of Lizzie doing all kinds of mundane things like sitting, sleeping, eating a lock of her own hair, and kneeling at a church altar. Then I noticed on one table that there were about a dozen sketches of a woman who looked like me as far as the body and hair, but she had no face. "Why don't these have faces?"

"Those are Will's. He said he can't get your face right. It's been frustrating him a lot." He pointed to a painting that I remember posing for in the library. I was standing with my hands folded in front of me. In the painting, I wore a long white dress and a crown of leaves in my hair, but there was no face.

"I remember posing for this."

"La Belle Iseult. It's been plaguing him."

"Because of the face?"

"Yeah."

"This is Will's table?"

"Yup."

It was fascinating to see the difference in each artist's workspace. Except for the sketches which were strewn about, Will's workspace was perfectly neat, with his immaculately clean brushes lined up by size. The table itself had no traces of spilled paint or charcoal bits. Above the table was a shelving system, with every supply carefully placed. Next to Will's workspace was obviously John's. The table was filthy, covered in dribbles of every color paint, and bits of charcoal and eraser shavings were scattered about. There were sketches of Effie pinned haphazardly to the wall above the table, and there were tons of little watercolor paintings of her on the table, with a few sketches of Lizzie in a bathtub. I noticed on the side of the table that there was a canvas sticking out. I picked it up and immediately recognized it as the one Lizzie posed for in the bathtub. It was extraordinary. "Ophelia! I'm glad it came out so beautiful since it almost killed her."

"I know."

"Why isn't it hanging up?"

"I think he feels weird about it because of what happened."

"All the more reason to put it on display!" I placed it on the back of the table and leaned it up against the wall. I glanced over to the table next to John's, and I couldn't figure out who it belonged to. There were tons of sketches of Lizzie, and a lot of tragic literary and biblical scenes. "Who did all these sketches of Lizzie?"

"They're self-portraits."

"*Lizzie did these?*"

"Yes. She's very talented. A natural."

"No kidding! I can't believe it! So she has her own workspace in here?"

"Mhhm."

All her self-portraits were sad and weak looking. I wondered if that was how she felt inside. Hanging above her table was a huge painting of me dressed in a green dress and carrying a strange object.

"*Lizzie painted me like this?*"

"No, that's mine. She was studying my use of color."

"What am I holding here?"

"A chalice of the soul."

"Which means?"

"This is you as Mnemosyne, the mother of the nine Muses."

"That's awfully flattering. Not only am I your muse, I'm *the mother of the Muses?*"

"Absolutely. I told you that the day after we met. You are not *a* muse, you are *the* muse."

"So what's with the cup?"

"In Greek mythology, Mnemosyne oversaw a pool of memories in the underworld. Some dead souls would drink from her cup before being reincarnated so they'd remember their past lives when they went back to earth. She'd dip her cup into the pool and allow you to drink."

"So your weird ability to see past lives has something to do with drinking from my cup?"

"In a way. Being with you awakens that part of me. Actually, in the last few weeks, I've had a lot more visions, completely sober."

"Really? Shit. I don't know if I can handle more of that at the moment. I'm a little overwhelmed."

"By?"

I gestured around the room at all the pictures of me. "Right," he answered. "I never considered what this must be like for you. Is it creepy?"

"Yes. But also really, really cool." I saw a curtain in the corner of the studio and walked over. "What's behind here?"

"Open it."

I moved the curtain aside, and there was a platform with a wooden box in the middle and a white sheet next to it. On the floor was an easel and a stool.

"Is this where you seduce your prey?"

"If you're asking if this is where models sit for us, yes, that was the idea. But it's only been used a few times."

"Uh-huh. You've never seduced anyone in here?"

"No. This is a sacred space, as I told you. That's why this area has barely been used. It goes against the idea of this being a private space if we bring in models."

"I see. So why are you all so adamant about your studio being private?"

"There's a few reasons. When you're in the middle of an artistic process, it feels really vulnerable. You don't want outsiders and their judgment fucking up your energy."

"I can understand that. I don't know that it needs to be hidden behind a bookcase, but I get the vulnerability part."

"I think Will just wanted an excuse to make a secret passage."

"It *is* pretty cool."

"Plus, it's part of our philosophy that art should be made in its natural state. If you're painting a woman in front of a tree, you should be outside in the woods with her."

"That makes sense."

"So will you?"

"Will I…?"

"Pose for me?"

"Do I have to go outside? It's pretty cold out."

"No, this painting is set in my bedroom. But I'm finished with the background. I just need you."

"What would I be wearing for this?"

His finger pointed to the white sheet behind me, and I raised my eyebrows suspiciously. Then he took a canvas from the side of his table and brought it over to show me. "I was hoping to work on this."

Sketched onto the canvas was an image of me asleep on my side with a sheet draped across the bottom half of my body. I was naked from the waist up. "When did you…?"

"I started it after the first night you slept in my bed. I've been adding to it, but I need to see the real thing to get it right."

"What makes you think I want there to be a painting of me topless? Did you consider that maybe it's a little bit of a violation?"

His face dropped, and he stood directly in front of me. "*Fuck,* you're right. I just, I never considered that. I'm so enamored with your body; it seems so natural to me. I can easily cover you with the sheet or just throw the whole canvas in the fireplace if you want. It would be a shame not to share this with the world though." He put his hand onto my neck. "It's your call."

I bent down and picked up the sheet. "So just wrap my bottom half in this then?"

He exhaled audibly. "Yes. I'll give you some privacy while I get the space heater. It gets a little drafty in here near that window."

"Maybe some pillows too. The floor doesn't look very comfortable."

"You got it."

"And more wine!" For that, I got a sexy wink.

He unrolled a thin mattress and placed a few pillows on it. He took a while setting up his paints and brushes next to the easel. I was in my underwear, but I kept my shirt on until he was ready. He put his glasses on and kneeled down next to me.

"Ready?"

"I guess."

He paused and glanced down at my t-shirt. "Right," I said apprehensively before lifting it over my head and handing it to him. He looked at my chest and smirked.

"*What?*"

"Cold in here?"

I looked down at my chest and frowned. "*Yes*, it is a bit cold in here!" I pinched his nipple through his shirt. "Too cold in here for *you*?" I teased.

He pulled the space heater over and turned it on. Then he started positioning my body. He went back over to the easel and turned it around to face us, so he could get the positioning right.

He draped one of my arms over the other in front of my belly. His hands gently moved my legs forward, and he kept repositioning my feet inch by inch. A tilt of my chin, a tug on the sheet that covered my bottom half, gently moving a lock of hair behind my shoulder, with that serious look of concentration… It all drove me wild.

He put small bits of paint onto his palette and examined a few different brushes before settling on one and lightly dabbing it in the paint.

"Can I talk? Cuz if I have to just lie here like this for hours, I might die."

"You can talk. Just don't move."

"Okay. So which do you love more? Music or art?"

"That's like asking a parent to choose a favorite child."

"I think most parents have a favorite kid, and it's actually an easy question for them. They're just not allowed to answer it."

"Yeah, you're probably right. I guess I'd have to choose visual art. It was my first love and my driving force most of the time."

"What made you start painting?"

"My mom. We never really got along growing up. Our personalities just didn't gel. But when I was being creative, I guess she could relate to me because she was an artist too. It was the only time I felt warmth and acceptance from her. I wanted more, so I kept creating things."

"So when did you get into music?"

"My dad was the musician in the family, which is why I refused to learn how to play an instrument growing up."

"Because you hated him?"

"Yeah. He's not a bad guy, but we also don't see eye to eye on many things. So I equated music with him and just completely rejected it."

"So when did the switch happen?"

I moved my hand to scratch my face, and his eyes widened when I placed my hand back in the wrong position. He came over, repositioned me with a grin, and then went back to work.

"I was 15, and this girl I was really into mentioned that she loved musicians. So I lied and told her that I was the lead singer of a rock band. She asked if we would play at her birthday party in a few weeks and stupidly I said yes."

"Figures. So did you pull it off?"

"I gathered up my closest friends and told them we had two

weeks to form a rock band. When I promised them that lots of hot girls would be into it, they agreed. I picked up a guitar for the first time that night, and it sort of came naturally."

"Of course it did. Doesn't everything happen like that for you?"

"No, I wouldn't say that. There are some things I have to work pretty hard for." I lifted an eyebrow in disbelief, and he tilted his head towards me as if to say, "Case in point."

"Did you write any original songs for the party?"

"No, just covers. We practiced every night for five or six hours, and we weren't terrible."

"So did you get the girl?"

"I sure did. And a bunch of her friends too."

"Jesus, Gabriel."

"You asked."

"I guess I did. So how long did the band stay together?"

"A few years until we went to different colleges. They wanted to pursue music, but I didn't. So I just kept playing for fun and studied art."

"Why did you drop out?"

He made a sound of disgust before answering. "It was just a bunch of bullshit. There was no nurturing of the creative process. It was like they were trying to take our natural abilities and inspirations and stamp them out. We had to fit into a formula, which is suicide for an artist. The whole thing made me feel suffocated, and it was the least creative period of my life. As soon as we formed our brotherhood… it was like the floodgates opened. Ideas and inspiration poured out of me."

"So let me ask you this. Why are most of your paintings of scantily clad women? Aren't you inspired by anything else?"

"Of course I am. I'm just *the most* inspired by women!"

"Because you're horny?"

He paused and looked at me. "*Because* they're the greatest mystery to me! Even more mysterious than the universe and *life itself*. I mean… you *create* life. You have the entire universe of possibilities in your womb."

"Come on. You equate the female species with the mystery of the universe and life itself?"

"Stephen Hawking was a genius, right?"

"From what I've heard."

"And he dedicated his life to unlocking the secrets of the universe."

"Okay…"

"He had an obsession with Marilyn Monroe. He had a huge poster of her over his desk. When asked why he had an image of her over his workspace, he said, 'She's cosmological. A celestial object.' He also said that she had the same curves as the universe."

"Did he happen to say anything about what was going on inside her head by any chance? Because she had a higher IQ than both him *and* Einstein."

"I'm not surprised. And I'll bet Hawking *did* know that because he said that women were a complete mystery and the most puzzling thing about the universe. Their curves are only a *small part* of that equation."

"Okay, so women are super mysterious and celestial. I agree. But have you ever tried to paint any of your other feelings? Like the past life visions or the connection you feel when you're on shrooms? Because the images you described to me that night seem like they would make a pretty amazing work of art."

He paused and put the end of the paintbrush in his mouth. "You make a strong point. I just don't think there's a canvas big enough to hold those ideas."

I sat up and pointed to the wall. "This huge, blank, white wall seems like it's begging for that sort of thing."

One of his eyes squinted as he meditated over my suggestion. "Shouldn't I run that past the guys before I decide to paint a huge part of our work space?"

"Wasn't it *you* who just said you'd prefer to ask for forgiveness later rather than seek permission first?" He smirked and rolled his eyes. I stood up and wrapped the sheet around my chest like a towel and put my face right next to his. "*Memento mori*, Gabriel."

"You up for this *right now*?"

"Now is all we have."

"We're going to need a lot more paint."

He led me to a closet filled with gallons and gallons of every paint color imaginable. I grabbed all different shades of blue and purple with some pink and gold hues as well. I turned around, and he was holding cans of black, red, and orange colors. He looked at my choices and laughed. "We're the yin yang, huh?"

"Or just polar opposites."

"The earth needs balance. And so do we."

"Somehow when I think of balance, you're the last person I picture."

"That's why I need *you*."

We laid out our paint in front of the wall and picked out brushes. He went to a corner and started typing furiously into a laptop. Ambient music poured into the room from tiny speakers in each corner of the ceiling. He started pouring paint into trays as I unraveled the sheet and started to put my shirt back on.

"Uh-uh!" he called out, yanking the shirt away from me.

"*What*?"

"I need my inspiration!" He outlined the curves of my shoulders and breasts with his hands.

"Well then take off *your* shirt too!"

He tore his shirt off and chucked it into a corner, and I instantly swooned. I wanted to feel the curves and dips of his muscular chest, trace the lines in his upper arms, and run my fingers down that sexy V that dipped below his jeans. He saw me staring, and I felt myself blush so I turned to stare at the wall. "Where do we begin?"

He looked at the wall and started chewing on his nails. "I've got it! Be right back." He brought in several huge jugs of black paint, two rollers, and a ladder. He poured the paint into a tray and handed me a roller. I stood there waiting for him to explain his thinking. He rolled his roller into the paint, climbed to the top of the ladder, and said, "Begin at the beginning, right?" I shrugged my shoulders as he continued. "In the beginning was the void." Then he started covering the wall in black paint and motioned for me to join him. I dipped the roller into the paint and started smearing it across the bottom of the wall. Moving the roller back and forth to the rhythm of the music was a soothing experience. Before long, the entire wall was black. He came down from the ladder and stood next to me as we stared at the wall.

"Okay, here's the void. But then what?" I asked.

He looked me up and down and smirked.

"*What*?"

"You give me inspiration."

"And?"

"And then God created the heavens and the earth." I looked off to the side with confusion, and he came closer and embraced me. "God created the *heavens*!" he repeated as he ran his hands all over my body.

"*Please* don't quote the bible while touching me like that!" I pushed him away playfully. "It's fucking weird."

"Noted," he commented, running his gaze over my chest and legs.

"So shall we paint the heavens or the earth?" I asked.

"The heavens of course. Earth comes later."

"Got it. So paradise colors. I'm thinking pink, gold, and light blue."

"Let me think back to my last trip." He closed his eyes, and his head swayed a bit. Then his eyelids popped open, and he ran back into the supply closet and came out with an armful of spray paint and two huge masks. He dropped the cans down and held out a mask for me. I looked at him like he was nuts, and he shook it at me. "Trust me, you'll want it."

I reluctantly took the mask and waited for him to put it on first. Somehow it didn't look ridiculous on him, but the idea of standing there topless with a very post-apocalyptic looking mask on my face was just too much. He gestured for me to put mine on too, but I stepped back a few feet and sat on a stool. "I'll watch first."

He bent down and took a can of yellow and stared up at the

wall for a bit. Then he started spraying a huge line in the middle of the blackness. He climbed up the ladder to extend the line to the top. Then he made smaller lines creeping out of it. It almost looked like a bug. Next he sprayed neon orange all around the yellow, like a border, and added some bright red. It looked like a beautiful flower until he sprayed more black through it like veins.

He took off the mask and stood next to me, gazing at the wall. Then he grabbed a sponge off one of the desks, dunked it into the black paint, and started dabbing the colors very methodically. After adding a lot of black, he sponged on some metallic gold. It really started to look like images I had seen of nebula and cosmic haze. But he was using my least favorite colors.

He slid the mask onto the top of his head and turned to me. "If you're just gonna sit there all night, I might as well be painting you!"

I sighed and grabbed my mask. "I was waiting for a spark of inspiration!"

"And?"

"And I guess I have to *inspire myself*!"

"Is that so? Well, stick around. I'm just getting started, babe!"

I put the mask on and went to the supply closet and took out all different shades of blue. I marched to the opposite side of the wall and copied his technique but with the blue. I had never spray painted before, and it was exhilarating. I worked faster than him, refusing to think. I just let my hand go where it wanted with the paint. Then I dabbed with a sponge, but I didn't like the pattern it made. I poured some aqua paint into a tray and dipped my fingers in and started flicking them at the wall. It made tiny little spots, like stars.

"I like your technique!" he called out as he tried it with his colors. We went crazy flinging paint at the walls on our respective sides. It really looked beautiful, like the cosmos, both light and dark. He started to add little details with a small brush. I got carried away and flung paint in his direction, and it landed on his chest and face. We both stood still until he reacted with a smile.

"Sorry about that," I said casually. He just nodded and kept painting. About a minute later, he dipped his brush into my blue paint and flung it directly at my face. I gasped and turned to face him.

"Sorry about that," he said through a huge grin. I swiped the paint off my face and bent down to grab a brush.

"You know, I'm not too sure about your color choices," I told him.

"Is that so?"

"So... bland. All black. You need some color."

He turned to face his side of the wall. "All black? What do you mean? I've got-" Before he could finish I dunked my brush into the turquoise paint and ran it down the middle of his back.

"Ah! That shit's cold!" he called out.

"I was talking about your tattoos!" I told him. "Now they're more colorful."

His eyes narrowed. "What about the ones on my arms?" I plunged my brush into the dark purple and slowly filled in the images on his arms while he watched with amusement.

"*Better?*" I asked.

"And my chest?" he said softly. I took his paint palette that had metallic gold on it and used it to color in the skull on his chest. He wrapped his hand around mine while his eyes burned into me, and he slid the brush from my fingers. "My turn."

"Umm..." I started to back away, and he slowly followed me until the back of my legs hit the platform.

"Are you afraid?" he asked.

"Of paint?"

"Of *me*."

"No."

"Good."

He lifted the brush and slowly ran it across my collarbone, and I closed my eyes. "This color won't do," he said, and he grabbed a nearby jug of bright red, poured it into a cup, and covered his brush. Then he took the brush and lightly placed it on my chest. "*This* is your color."

"Is it?"

"*Yes.*"

He painted a flower over my heart. The gentle strokes of the cool paint made me shiver. He dunked the brush back into the paint and ran it down my belly. Then he gently ran the tip of the brush across my nipple and looked directly into me. I couldn't take it anymore. I shoved my entire hand into the cup of paint and ran it down his chest. He placed my paint-covered hand on his cheek and slowly brought me in. When our mouths met, I saw flashes of the nebula he painted behind my eyes. Our tongues danced together as we ran our hands all over each other's bodies. I pulled back and looked at him. He tried to kiss me, but I kept pushing him away. I just wanted to tease him, but he wasn't in the mood for games.

He took my hand and held up the ring he had given me for both of us to see. Then he put my hand over his heart and pushed it in so hard that I thought he wanted me to hurt him. He had a serious, determined, almost angry look on his face. "You feel me?" he demanded. I nodded, and he held my hand up and kissed each finger and then my palm. I drew him in, and we devoured each other as he took me down to the floor. As he kissed my neck and chest, I took the cup of red paint and poured it down his back. He lifted his head and exhaled as the paint spilled down his body. His eyes bore into mine as he started grinding into me. I dug my fingers into his slippery back and moaned.

He sat back and took the tray of blue paint I had been using and submerged his hands in it. Then he held them above me and let the paint drizzle onto my chest. He ran his fingers through the paint on my body, making little swirls on my stomach and chest, and I unbuttoned his pants. He took them off but kept his boxers on and told me to turn over. I shook my head no because I still wanted to play. He growled and tore off my underwear with one hard yank, and I smacked him across the face. It wasn't hard enough to leave a mark, but it was harder than I had intended. He paused and looked at me suspiciously, unsure if I was angry, so I smiled and rolled onto my front. As he went to touch my ass, I rolled over again, just out of his reach. He sat there on all fours, panting, like a wild animal staring down their prey. I bit my lip and grinned as he launched himself at me, knocking over a stool with a tray full of dark blue paint that spilled directly on top of us. We both knew it was fully *on*.

I raked my hands through his messy, paint-splattered hair as he ran his tongue all over me, not caring about the paint getting in his mouth. He put his hand behind my head, so he could get even deeper into my mouth, and his other hand slid between my legs. I cried out as he rubbed me gently. Then he brought his fingers up and sucked on them, looking at me with total lust and admiration. I took hold of his hips and started grinding into him over his boxers. He dropped his head down to mine and whispered, "Fuck."

"Come on, baby," I begged. "I want it."

He shook his head. "Not yet."

"Please!"

I gasped as he slammed my knees apart and ran his tongue up and down my slit over and over. He moaned as he shoved his tongue as far in as he could. I arched my back, and he shoved my hips back down to the floor and spread me open with both hands.

"I could do this for hours," he said as he started to suck on my clit.

"Oh god!" I called out. "Please!"

"Please?" he repeated as he ran his tongue up and down, over and over.

"Please!" I yelled.

"Please, what?" he asked as he slowly entered me with a finger.

"Fuck! *Please!*"

"Please *what?*"

He started to get a rhythm going with his finger as he made light circles with his tongue.

"Gabriel!" I screamed as I started to shake. "*Please* fuck me!"

He grinned and asked, "Are you about to come?" as he kept the same rhythm and added another finger.

"Yes! I'm gonna come!"

"*When?*" he demanded.

"Now!" I screamed, and he suddenly pulled his fingers out and said, "Good." He moved backward looking very satisfied with himself, having just denied me a major orgasm, as he awaited my response.

I sat up, chest heaving, body on fire, and called out, "You motherfucker!" before I jumped on top of him. His back slammed down to the ground, and we kissed with all the passion, confusion, longing, and angst of all the lives we had lived together. I slid his boxers down forcefully and rubbed him on me as we kissed.

"Are you sure?" he asked through kisses, looking up at me with what felt like love.

"Condom!" I demanded. He pointed across the room and rested his hands behind his head.

"So go get it?" I said with irritation. He leaned his head down and bit my nipple. "Come on!" I pleaded.

"In the front pocket of my backpack." He pointed to the bag on his work table.

I huffed at him. "You must not want it that badly."

"I just wanna see your ass as you walk over there." I quickly got off him and strode over to the table, loving the feeling of his eyes on my body. I grabbed a condom, got back on top, put it on him, and slid him inside. We both gasped as I sat back to get him in deeper.

"*Fuck*," he whispered as I held onto his chest. I cried out to the ceiling as he grabbed my ass to move me back and forth. "*Fuck*, Jane," he breathed out and pulled me in for a kiss.

I moaned his name into his mouth and said, "Right there."

"Right there?" he repeated as he rocked me into him harder and faster.

"Yes!" I called out. "Oh god! Gabriel! Fuck!" I came hard, shuddering and slowing down as he rolled us over to take control. I was still riding out my orgasm when he pressed my knees to my shoulders and slowly fucked me as we stared deeply into each other. He shoved his thumb into his mouth and then gently rubbed me with it.

"That's it, baby. Come for me."

I immediately started having another orgasm as he said, "*Yes. I* love making you come." I started to shudder as he pressed his fore-head into mine and said, "Fuck, I love you, Jane."

"I love you too," I said through moans. He started fucking me faster and harder, and I called out, "Oh god! Gabriel!" as he came and grinned before collapsing next to me. He yanked off the condom and chucked it behind him. We laid there naked, sweaty, and covered in paint, and I started laughing and couldn't stop.

"What?" he demanded.

"We're filthy!"

His eyes shot to the ceiling as we heard rain pounding hard upon the roof. "Follow me!" He seized my hand and lifted me off the floor.

"Wait! Where are we going?"

"To get clean!" he said as he dragged me towards the back window.

"I'm naked!" I yelled.

"So am I! No one's home!" He flung the window open, and a gust of cold air blew in.

"It's freezing!" I protested.

"It's not that cold out tonight."

"Memento mori," I told myself as I hopped out of the window and into a muddy flower bed. We ran into the middle of the garden and let the cold rain clean off our naked bodies. I spun around in circles while laughing and screaming, "I'm fucking freezing!"

"I know! Isn't it great to be alive?"

"Yes!" I yelled as he lifted me up, and I wrapped my legs around his waist. We kissed and kissed as the rain beat down on us until I started shivering, and he led me inside through the backdoor. Then we scurried upstairs to his bedroom and wrapped ourselves in towels and blankets and collapsed onto his bed.

"Can I ask you about one of your tattoos?"

"Of course. Ask me anything."

"The one across your shoulder blades. I think I saw it on an old headstone in the cemetery behind Will's parents' house. Is that possible?"

"Entirely possible. It's an old, secret language that was used on headstones all the time."

"What does it mean? What language is it?"

"It's pigpen cipher."

"Huh?"

"An ancient secret code. It goes back as far as the Knights Templar."

"So what does it mean?"

He turned on the bedside lamp and grabbed a notebook and pen. "Look." He drew three large hashtags and put a series of dots in the boxes and showed it to me.

"What's this?"

"This is the code. See how each box makes a shape similar to the letters on my back?"

"No…"

He traced the first box on the first hashtag, which only had two lines like a backwards L. "See? If I isolate that, it looks like this." He drew a backwards L.

"Okay, so what does this mean?"

He drew a letter of the alphabet in each box. "Each box makes a different shape. Now you know which letters correspond to them." He stood with his back to me, so I could see his tattoo.

"Okay, let's see."

I started to decode the shapes on his back the way he showed me, and it spelled out, "Fate cannot be taken," which I repeated to him.

He turned around and looked down at the notebook. "You learn quickly!"

"Fate cannot be taken?" I asked.

"Right."

"What does that mean?"

"It means that what is meant to be will be, no matter what."

"You sound pretty sure about that."

"I am."

"Why would that be on a headstone?"

"That probably wasn't what you saw. But it was very popular in the 1700s to write 'remember death' in pigpen cipher or to have an hourglass with wings to remind people to live life to the fullest while they can."

"That seems a bit redundant. You're already in a cemetery looking at a gravestone. Chances are, you're already thinking about death."

"It means more than that. It's not just about death. It's about-"

"Seizing the day and all that! I know. It's a good reminder I guess." He laid down next to me and turned off the light.

"You guess?"

"You guys have any dessert in this bitch? Cuz I can't stop thinking about all the ice cream I won't be able to eat when I'm dead."

He rolled over and looked at me with a blank expression and said, "I got you," and left the room. I rolled onto his pillow and deeply inhaled his scent. I wanted to stay in his bed for eternity and tried to push away the intense feeling of longing, sadness, guilt, and fear that suddenly swept over me. Somehow I knew in my bones that it couldn't last. And he knew it too.

He came back with a bowl of chocolate, vanilla, and strawberry ice cream and two spoons. "How's this?"

"It'll do, but don't you want any?"

"Haha," he said as he grabbed a spoonful and shoved it in his mouth. "So you ready to hear the vision I had about us the other night?" he said through a mouthful of ice cream.

"I guess. Is it terrible?"

"No, it's actually really cool. I was listening to this audio book about recalling past lives, and it walks you through the techniques and meditation practices to get into that hypnotic state. I sat on my bed with a pen and notebook and wrote everything I saw. And it was a *fucking flood* of information." He took a bunch of notebook pages off the desk and handed it to me. Scribbled across the pages were the words, "Justin, Thea, 527, Byzantine, Turkey, Flavius, blue demes, hippodrome, purple shroud, rioters."

"What's all of this mean?"

"First, let me just tell you that I never studied this stuff in school. Not that I can remember, anyway. I've never heard of these people. When I looked it up and it all fit together, it blew my mind but also confirmed what we already know."

"Which is?"

"We've always been together."

"Oh."

"I saw myself as a young soldier during the Byzantine Empire, helping my uncle Justin as he'd just taken the throne and needed a lot of help getting local support. You and I met at the Hippodrome. We were both fierce blue fans, and when I saw you and heard you speak, there was that magnetic pull, just like now. You were stunning and so confident and so intelligent. I had to have you. But you were an actress and a whore, so I was forbidden to marry you."

"Woah, woah, woah! Stop right there! What the fuck do you mean *I was a whore*?"

"Like, *literally*, you were a prostitute. It was common for actresses at the time."

"Yeah, I'm not feeling any connection to this story at all. Sorry." I ripped the bowl from his hands and turned away.

"But Jane, that's just the beginning. We fell in love. I begged my uncle to let me marry you, but his bitch wife convinced him not to allow it. My uncle, by the way, was Will. I think he had feelings for you."

"Jesus! That's fucking nuts!"

"I'm pretty sure Lizzie was his wife, and she was really jealous of you." I didn't know how to respond to all of this, so I just listened and continued eating ice cream.

"His wife died, and he let us get married. Then he died right after that, and we became Emperor and Empress. That was the year 527."

"What was my name?"

"Theodora. And my name was Flavius, but I changed it to Justinian to honor my uncle."

"Flavius, eh? *Sexy*."

"Yeah. But Jane, seriously, we did amazing things together. You were my equal in power and influence. You fought fiercely for the rights of women, and gave them the right to divorce and own property, and you made laws that protected prostitutes and poor people."

"Yup. Sounds like me. What's the thing about the purple shroud?"

"At one point, the people rebelled against me. It was chaos, and I was afraid for our lives. I made a plan for us to flee, but you refused to go with me. You gave a speech to me and my advisors that convinced us to stay and fight."

"Did it say something about you being a giant pussy?"

"In much fancier terms, yeah. You basically said that we're all going to die anyway. And if we were to flee, when we got to safety, we'd want to die anyway from shame. You said that you would rather wear your royal robes as a death shroud than run away like a pussy."

"So what you're telling me is that I used the old *memento mori* line on you? *Don't you think that's interesting?*"

"I didn't even realize!"

"So did my speech work?"

"Yup. My men and I slaughtered tens of thousands of rioters and secured our throne."

"Mhhm. It's starting to feel familiar now." I handed him the empty bowl. "Do you need another pep talk, or can we sleep now?"

"Don't you want to hear the rest?"

"I've heard the best parts, I think. But lemme guess. It all ended tragically?"

"Mostly, yeah."

I kissed him on the cheek and declared, "I'm good. Goodnight!"

"Goodnight, empress."

He drew me in close and wrapped his arms around me. I exhaled deeply and closed my eyes.

"Oh, Gabriel?"

"Mmm?"

"I wasn't a whore. Those were vicious rumors started by your enemies."

"Got it."

We were both quiet for a moment, and then I started thinking aloud. "I wish we could actually visit that time period again. It sounds a lot more interesting than this one."

He sat up a bit and turned his head towards me. "You mean like time travel?"

"I don't know. I'm just thinking, what if somehow we could go back to one of those times and then we could change things? Like if we know what went wrong in the past, maybe we could fix it."

"You mean go back and make different decisions so it doesn't end tragically?"

"Yeah. I guess. Just a thought."

"Even if time travel were possible, there's a lot of problems with what you're talking about, like the butterfly effect."

"That's the idea that if you change even the tiniest thing in the past it would fuck up the future really badly?"

"Pretty much."

"I don't see it that way. The future would just be different, a different outcome as though it was meant to be that way in the first place. And it could be much better, because going back with the knowledge of how things will turn out could be pretty useful. You could prevent major disasters."

"Sounds like you're thinking about parallel universes."

"Parallel, like next to each other?"

"Yeah. The idea is that there's an infinite number of universes, including the one we're in, that are made up of everything that exists or has ever existed. So there's an infinite number of us living similar realities, side by side, each making slightly different choices and living out the consequences."

"That's interesting but I'm talking more about one timeline. Like if you could go back and change things, in this life let's say, would you?"

"You know there are several schools of thought that claim that's actually possible."

"Really? How?"

"I've only heard about two ways of moving backwards in time: LSD or near death experience."

"Shit. Why those?"

"Apparently we all have the ability to move forwards and backwards in time, but it's too hard to actually *believe* it's possible, which then makes it *impossible*. But when you're on acid or close to death, it cuts through those mental blocks and makes it possible."

"You lost me."

"Quantum physics says that thoughts are things. So if you can remove the mental blocks and believe 100 percent that you can visit a different time period, it will happen."

"Okay, so once those blocks are gone, what do you do?"

"Have you ever had a lucid dream?"

"You mean a dream where you realize you're dreaming?"

"Yeah."

"Only a few times," I answered, "but yeah."

"What did you do when you realized you were dreaming?"

"I immediately started to try to change things and go to places I wanted to be."

"So you just pictured where you wanted to be and the dream changed?"

"Pretty much."

"From what I understand, it's the same idea when you try to go back in time. Picture it, believe it, and you're there."

"Wow. It's a damn shame I'm not willing to do LSD or bring myself to the brink of death."

"I might be willing to do one of those."

"Well, of course you would."

"But the difference is, I wouldn't change a damn thing."

"Really? Nothing at all?"

"Nope. Nothing at all."

"But what if your life could be even better than it is now?"

"I wouldn't risk it. Because I might not be here right now, with you."

"But I thought that what is meant to be, will be, no matter what!"

"Excellent point. But that also means there's no point in trying to change it either."

"So I don't have to worry about you doing acid?"

"Nah. I think this reality is enough for me." He slid back down to the pillow and pulled me into his body again.

"I hope that's true."

CHAPTER 27

GABRIEL

"Black Swan"—Thom Yorke

THE FIRST TIME WE HAD SEX WAS EVEN BETTER THAN I could have imagined. Jane, true to form, drew me in with her ideas, criticism, and fickle moods. I never really knew where I stood with her, which made it more exciting. It wasn't until she straddled me and actually put me inside her that I felt sure of how she felt about me. And the games she played with the fucking paint… I couldn't get enough.

After I told her about my vision, I wasn't sure if she really believed me or not. She fell asleep in my arms right away, but I couldn't relax. I wanted more. More of her body, her mind, her fucking soul. I needed to hear her tell me she loved me again. That she needed me inside her.

I woke her up with my tongue between her legs, and just when I thought she would kick me off, she arched her back and moaned. Then she pulled me on top of her, and we made love for what felt like hours. It was slower this time, more thoughtful. The heat was up too high in the house, and I felt the sweat dripping off my body onto hers. The whole night was just mind-blowing. The best sex I'd ever had by a long shot.

Eventually we fell asleep, and early the next morning we awoke to the sound of a girl's voice downstairs.

"Hello? Is anyone home? *Hello?*"

Jane rolled over and whined, "Who the fuck is that? What fucking time is it?" with her eyes still closed.

"I got it. You sleep." I pulled on sweatpants and kissed her cheek as she drifted back to sleep with a grin.

I went downstairs and found Lizzie in the kitchen looking through the fridge. "Lizzie, you're back! It's so good to see you!" I went to hug her, and she turned around with half-closed eyes and a weird little smile.

"My love!" she called out, her voice a bit slurred. She put her arms out to embrace me, and all of her body weight fell into me. I wasn't expecting it, and I stumbled backwards with her in my arms.

"Woah! Alright. Shit. Are you feeling okay?" I helped her into a chair. She plopped down listlessly, but she looked so happy. "Are you feeling alright? Can I get you something?"

She smiled brighter. "Just some cold water." I grabbed a bottle of water from the fridge and opened it for her, and then I leaned back on the counter.

"What time is it?" I looked around and saw it was just after 8 AM. "Is everything okay? Are you better?"

She looked down at her lap and then up at me with drowsy eyes. She pointed to the chair next to her. "Sit. Please."

I sat down as she asked.

"I'm great. I'm doing really great, Gabriel."

"I'm so glad! Totally recovered? Nothing to worry about?"

She leaned in and put her hands on the table as I leaned back in the chair. She smiled and gestured for my hands. I reluctantly reached out, and she dropped her hands into mine and looked straight at me. "I have some news."

"Okay. Should I be worried?"

"I hope not." I paused and waited, and the next thing she said changed the course of all of our lives forever. She exhaled deeply and grinned. "I'm pregnant."

My blood ran cold. "What? What do you mean?"

She giggled and looked at me with such love that it scared the shit out of me. "I mean, I'm pregnant. With a baby. *Your* baby. *Our* baby." This is going to sound absolutely horrible, but I was hoping the next thing she was going to tell me was that she couldn't keep it because of her health condition. Then I prayed she was pulling some kind of prank, and I waited for Jane to burst into the room laughing. She just kept staring at me, and then I begged the gods to wake me up from the fucking nightmare I had just woken up to.

The only words I could manage to speak were, "Are you sure?"

She laughed again and squeezed my hands. "Am I sure that I'm pregnant, or am I sure that it's yours?"

"Both?"

Her smile faded. "They took my blood about three times a day for a month, so I'm sure I'm pregnant. And you're the only one I've ever had sex with, so aside from some kind of miracle from god..."

I dropped her hands and raked my fingers through my hair. "I'm sorry. I just... need a minute to process this." I stood up and walked over to the sink and bent over a bit. I started to feel nauseous. I jumped when I felt small, cold hands on my bare back.

"I know it's a lot to take in. I was pretty shocked myself. But don't you see? This happened for a reason. It's meant to be. *We're* meant to be." She took my wrist as I turned to face her, and she put my hand onto her belly. "We're going to be a family." I felt like the walls were closing in. I yanked my hand away as Jane entered the room and ran to Lizzie.

Lizzie's eyes stayed on mine, but she let go of my hand. All I could think was that I had to be the one to talk to Jane first. I didn't know what I was going to say or how I could fix it, but I had to be in control of the situation.

Lizzie turned to face Jane as they embraced. "Hey, ladybug!" Lizzie said with that odd, slurred speech.

Jane pulled away and stared into her face. "I was so fucking worried about you! They wouldn't let me visit you, and I couldn't get you on the phone, and your fucking parents suck and-"

"I know. It's okay. I'm fine, my dear. Just fine."

"Are you sure? We have so much to talk about! You look kind of pale. Are you sure you're okay? Come sit down!"

As Jane led Lizzie to a chair, I jumped between them. "Jane! Can I talk to you for a quick second?"

She sat down next to Lizzie. "Yeah, what's up?"

They were both staring at me, and I hesitated. "I just... I just really need to talk to you alone for a second." She scoffed, and Lizzie stared at me with a weird look I couldn't decipher.

"Gabriel, I haven't seen her in a month! Can't it wait?"

I felt dizzy, and I couldn't think straight. "Yeah, okay. Nevermind."

"Put a shirt on, for fuck's sake. It's December," she added with a wink.

"Yeah, right. Let me go do that."

It was inevitable. It was like watching a train coming at me head on, and I was paralyzed on the tracks. I just had to get the fuck out of there. I quickly left the room and ran upstairs to the bathroom. I splashed cold water on my face and stared at myself in the mirror. I had never felt such self-hatred before. I wanted to break my own nose. I threw a shirt on and waited at the bottom of the stairs for the fallout. I couldn't hear anything, but it wasn't long before Jane burst out of the kitchen and came marching towards me. I stood up and tried to speak to her, but she walked right past me to the front door, without acknowledging me at all. She grabbed her keys off the table and went for the door handle, but I stood in front of her. "Jane, *please*! Please listen to me!"

"Get the fuck out of my way. *Now*."

She looked at me with such venom, such hatred. Like I was all the proof she needed not to trust men, or anyone, ever again. "Jane, listen to me! It was one time! *One time!* And you and I weren't together yet! It was the night of the party, and you had just rejected me for Will-"

"So you fucked my best friend? Without a condom?"

"I was drunk and angry!"

She rolled her eyes and tried to shove me out of the way. "I know that's not a good enough excuse! But I swear to you, on my life, I didn't even enjoy it. I was thinking about *you* the entire time. Ask Lizzie! I even called out *your* name!"

"Oh *shit*! I feel *so* much better now! You called out my name while you were fucking my best friend! That is *so* reassuring! Let me just go ask her about it! That won't hurt her feelings at all!" She used both hands to try to shove me over with all her strength, but I didn't move.

"Please, Jane. Please listen to me. *I love you.* I made one mistake. One huge, gigantic, colossal mistake. And if I could do anything to take it back I would. But this doesn't have to mean the end of us! I'm in love with you. You're the one I want to be with!"

She looked at me with seething hatred and said through gritted teeth, "If you don't move out of the way, I will fucking kill you." I laughed at her ridiculous threat, and she grabbed a letter opener from the table near the door and put it to my jugular.

"Do you wanna find out if I'm kidding or not?"

I could have easily taken it from her, but the look of pain in her eyes was so intense that I knew I had to let her go. I put my hands up and moved away. She flung the door open and started running to her car, and I ran after her.

"Jane! Please tell me what I can do! What do I need to do to prove to you how much you mean to me?"

She stopped for a moment and spun around to face me. The anger was gone and tears started to fall. As she spoke, she battled to control her trembling bottom lip. "If you ever truly loved me, you'll do what I ask. You'll take this ring and give it to *her*. You'll let me go, and you'll go back inside and tell Lizzie that you love her, and you're happy. Then you will support her and take care of her… like a man." She took off the ring I gave her and held it out to me as more tears streamed down.

I stepped forward and took her hand. "This ring is for you and cannot possibly be for anyone else. I cannot tell those lies. You're the one I love."

She sucked back her tears and took a deep breath. The anger was back. "Then you don't know the true meaning of love. Love is about sacrifice, Gabriel. Sacrifice and honor. For once in your life, stop being so goddamned selfish and think about something other than what *you* want." She wiped her face with her hand and threw the ring on the ground at my feet. As she got into her car, another car pulled up and Will got out with his luggage. He looked at me with confusion and then peered into Jane's car and saw the distraught look on her face. He immediately ran to her and started demanding to know what was wrong. She rolled down her window and said through tears, "Ask Gabriel." Then she sped away. Will didn't ask me anything. He didn't even look at me. He collected his bags and went inside and closed the door behind him.

CHAPTER 28

Jane

"Slow Dancing in a Burning Room"—John Mayer

THE PAIN WAS MORE INTENSE THAN ANYTHING I HAD EVER felt. My heart had been ripped out by several men before, including my own father, but those times were entirely different. I had given my love and trust so easily to them, without question. The fallout seemed almost inevitable, a lesson that had to be learned. But with Gabriel, it was a unique kind of pain. My instincts told me not to trust him from the very first moment, and I fought against the intense longing for him so fiercely. Finally, I gave in to what I wanted most, an intense connection and chemistry like I never thought was possible. I gave myself to him one tiny piece at a time, trying desperately to protect myself from the destruction I somehow knew was inevitable. He had me fully, heart and soul, and we both knew it. And I truly believed that I possessed him completely as well.

And I still believe that. I believed it then, and I still believe every word he said to me that day. It was a stupid mistake he made, prompted by alcohol and jealousy. And there's no doubt in my mind that Lizzie wanted it to happen, despite the obvious feelings he and I had for each other. But none of that mattered anymore. In that moment, the past meant nothing. All that mattered was the future. And in my view, the future was about the blameless soul who was being pulled into this complex web of feelings and desires. No matter how much I believed that Gabriel truly loved me, the only thing that was true for me anymore was the fact that the man I loved was having a baby with my best friend. All I could do was focus on supporting her and making sure she and the baby had every chance of thriving.

My phone rang over and over with relentless calls from Will, Lizzie, and, of course, Gabriel. I could hide in my apartment as long as I needed, though they all knew they could find me at work. So I left my boss a message that I was having a crisis and needed time off. Then I shut off my phone, took two sleeping pills, and slept for three days straight.

When I eventually got out of bed, it was late in the afternoon. I showered and went for a long drive to the beach. Though it was December, and the air was frigid, I sat on the sand and stared out at the gray waves crashing on the shore. I considered every possible path moving forward. Finally, I reached a peaceful agreement with my heart, which consisted of two words I repeated over and over like a mantra: support Lizzie, support Lizzie, support Lizzie.

I would have complete tunnel vision until the heartache subsided, I told myself. To be there for Lizzie and her baby, I would have no choice but to be near Gabriel. So I had to steel myself and refuse to feel. I would not leave my dearest friend in the dark. She needed me, and I would not let *anyone* stand between us. I was going to be the best aunt I could possibly be. Nothing else mattered.

I drove home feeling a painful but strong resolve. When I entered my apartment, I was shocked by what I saw. Every surface was covered in flowers and lit candles. And these were not ordinary flower shop flowers. They were delicate, lush, obscure blossoms that definitely did *not* grow in the winter, and they were dripping down from every surface of my tiny apartment. Huge branches covered in bursts of cherry blossoms sprayed out of giant crystal vases. Bunches of wisteria cascaded down the doorways and window frames. But the most breathtaking part was the arrangement in my bedroom. The bed was covered in lacy white orchids and vines of ivy, and it all looked like it had grown naturally over my blankets and pillows. In the center of the bed was a massive painting of me with angel wings, flying above a wild garden. In the middle of the garden, there was a poem painted into the vines in a lovely script.

You Were Born to Fill Me

Your spirit was born to fill my blood with fire,
to burn through me;
To breathe upon my gazing eyes,
To laugh and murmur in my ear,
To touch my soul and show me colors
That flutter down from the farthest parts of heaven.

Within your voice, within your heart,
Within your mind is a spirit who was born
To lift apart my trembling wings and reveal me;
When on my mouth your finger lays,
And Eden's gates open to paradise,
I see your soul clearly and worship only you.

I cannot erase your hair, hands, and lips,
Heart, mind, and voice,
Your words that come from deep within.

Do not let my greatest hope be slaughtered,
Let me find in you my heart's deepest goal.
Truth in love cannot fall victim to thoughts
Of what is right or wrong.

I will never stop needing you,
Your body and your soul.

D.G.R.

Unsure of what to do, I dropped onto the bed next to the painting and closed my eyes. "It's over, it's over, it's over," I chanted in my head. "I'm made of steel. I'm made of concrete. I'm made of stone." I felt the sting of tears behind my eyes, so I bit down on my cheek as hard as I could and resumed my chanting. "It's over. It never even started. It never happened. I'm made of steel. I'm made of concrete. I'm made of stone. Support Lizzie, support the baby, this is for Lizzie, Lizzie, Lizzie, Lizzie." I sat up and turned on my phone, ignoring the barrage of texts and voicemails that kept coming through. I saw that my boss had left a message.

"Hey Jane. I am so sorry to do this to you, but we're going to have to let you go. You're a great employee, and a wonderful friend, but you've missed so many shifts in the past few months with little to no notice. We just have to find someone else. I hope that whatever you're going through turns out okay." I felt nothing in response to that news. Compared to everything else, it didn't seem to matter.

Next, I dialed Lizzie and left her a voicemail. "Hey! I'm so sorry I haven't been in touch! I've been really sick. I think I had food poisoning or something. I've just been doing nothing but throwing up and sleeping. Anyway, *please* can we see each other? I'm sorry for how I reacted. I just… I was shocked. And worried. I always worry about you. You're my family, Lizzie. And I'm here for you. Whatever you need. You have my support and my love always. Please call me."

A few minutes later, she texted, "Hey lady! So glad you called. Not feeling so good. Everything's okay, just a little nauseous. How about you come over for brunch tomorrow? So much more to talk about! Love you!"

I was unsure if she was inviting me to Red House since that was where she was living before she got sick. I wrote back, "Sure! Talk in the morning!" though I had no intention of ever going there again. I looked up the nearest locksmith and made an appointment to get my locks changed. Then there was a knock at the door. "I am steel. I am concrete. I am stone," I told myself as I tiptoed to the door and looked through the peephole, mentally preparing myself in case it was Gabriel. I exhaled when I saw Will and opened the door.

"I'm so sorry to intrude, but I've been really worried about you. You haven't been answering your phone."

"I know. Come in."

As soon as he stepped in, he stopped and reacted to the massive amount of flowers. "*Jesus!* It looks like a garden vomited in here!"

I giggled. "Yes, it does. Maybe we should talk outside?"

"If you like. It's quite cold outside though."

"Okay, forget it. Please sit." I gestured to the couch, and he brushed a bunch of flower petals off before he sat. "Can I get you anything? Water or something?" I asked.

"No, no. I don't need anything. Just tell me that you're alright."

I sat down next to him and sighed. "I'm okay. I just wasn't feeling well."

"I suspect your illness might have something to do with the news you received the other day?" He was jumping right in, refusing to pretend that what I was going through was anything other than the obvious.

I inhaled deeply and dropped my head. "It definitely sent a shock through my system."

"Mine as well."

"I just… I'm worried. I don't know if Lizzie is healthy enough to have a baby."

He gave me a look that said, "We all know that's not what you're upset about," but he had the decency not to say it.

I still didn't want him to know that Gabriel and I had anything going on, and for some reason, I thought I could hide it.

"I'm sure that her doctors will be monitoring her closely. But I can understand your fears. You're a wonderful friend." There was an uncomfortable pause before he continued. "Alright, so, I have to ask about the floral display here. I'm sure you have many admirers, but this seems a bit over the top."

I couldn't believe he was asking me about something that he obviously knew all about. He was nudging me to admit everything, and I just wasn't ready to do it. I didn't want to lose his respect. "Yes, one in particular is quite enamored with me it seems."

"Seems like an apology of sorts. He must have hurt you quite badly." I stared back at him and shrugged my shoulders. I almost started to cry, but thankfully he changed the subject. "Jane, I have something to ask you." I lifted my eyebrows to show that I was listening. "Would you consider moving into Red House?"

The question immediately struck me as ridiculous. The place where Lizzie and Gabriel were living was the last place on earth I wanted to be. "Hear me out," he continued. "Hunt moved in with Annie, Ed moved back home to California, and John and Effie moved in together…"

"They did? Did she leave her husband?" I asked.

"Yes."

"That's great! He seemed terrible."

"Yes. He is. So… as you know, Lizzie is pregnant with Gabriel's child. I've been wanting to ask them to leave, as I told you, but now doesn't seem like the right time. I can't just throw them out in the middle of all this. They have a lot to work out. But being there alone with them… It's a daunting task. I'm worried for Lizzie's health, as you are. She's been acting strange, and I know she's pregnant. I'm the last person who knows anything about that, but something doesn't seem right to me. And I don't trust Gabriel to properly look after her. She needs you." I blew air through my lips audibly and looked away before he moved in closer and added, "*I* need you." I turned my head back to him, and he was looking at me with such love and warmth that I started to cry. "Oh shit! Jane! I didn't mean to upset you!"

He scooted closer and took me into his arms. I unloaded all of my pent up emotions onto him and his sweater. The tears were streaming and snot was pouring from my nose, and I was sobbing like a maniac. He rubbed my back and kept saying he was so sorry. When I leaned back, I left a trail of liquid from my nose to his shoulder. He glanced down and made a funny face, and we both laughed. "I better get *us* some tissues."

He went to the kitchen and came back with a roll of paper towels. He handed it to me, and I took a wad and gave it to him. "I'm sorry! That looks like a nice sweater."

He sat down next to me again. "Fuck the sweater. *Are you okay*?"

"Yes. I didn't mean to unload on you like that. I guess I had a lot of stuff I was holding in." I paused and blew my nose a few times.

"Lizzie *did* seem weird, now that I think about it. Her speech was weird. Slower. She seemed out of it."

"Yes."

"I don't know if moving in is the best thing." He waited for me to continue. "But I *did* just lose my job." He grinned as I sunk down into the couch and flung my head back. "I don't know what the right thing to do is anymore. I don't know anything."

"There's a difference between the *right* thing and the thing you *want*."

"Exactly. And I don't know what either of those things are anymore!"

"How do you feel when you're at Red House?"

"Depends who I'm with. With you, I feel peaceful. Happy. Light."

"I feel the same way."

"About Red House?"

"About *you*."

I hesitated and then tried to steer the conversation away from deep feelings. "You have an extra bedroom? Far away from your current housemates?"

"I do. Several."

"I suppose a few months of looking after my friend in a beautiful old mansion couldn't hurt."

"I'll have a moving company here tomorrow. What else do you need?"

"No need for movers. This shit furniture was here when I moved in. I'll pack my clothes and be there in a few days."

He smiled warmly and nodded. "I'll leave you to your enchanted garden now."

I rolled my eyes and walked him to the door. "Will?" He turned around, and I kissed him on the cheek. "You're the best human being I think I've ever met."

He looked down and shook his head. Then he put his hand to my cheek. "I feel the same about you."

"No. I'm not. I'm… a fuck up."

"Hey. Don't say that. We're all fucked up. We're all broken. You're just so much more in touch with how you feel than the rest of us. It's… You're…"

I wrapped my fingers around his hand and whispered, "I know." He nodded and backed away as I slowly shut the door.

I went around my apartment gathering up all the flowers and stuffing them into trash bags. There were 15 bags in total, and I sat on the couch and stared at them for a while before I grabbed the painting from my bed and stuffed it in too. After several trips to the dumpster, I collapsed onto my bed and drifted off.

I woke up to the sound of guitar music, and people yelling outside my window. I kept trying to ignore it, but it seemed to be getting louder. Then something hit my window. I ran over and pulled the curtains aside. Under my window was Gabriel, looking up at me while singing and playing guitar. His face looked drawn, and he was wearing a sleeveless shirt despite the freezing December climate. People were yelling at him to shut up from their apartment windows. I closed the curtains and sat on my bed as the shouting continued. I heard someone say they were going to call the cops. I flung the window open and heard him singing "Sweet Jane." It was a beautiful, soft version, and it pinched my heart for a moment. I repeated my mantra about being made of concrete and called out to him like he was an unwanted nuisance.

"Gabriel! What the fuck are you doing? Just go!" He kept singing and ignored my request. "Gabriel! I'm serious! Just fucking leave!" He shook his head and kept playing. "This isn't a fucking eighties movie! You can't just play a song under my fucking window and fix everything! Just fucking go!"

He shook his head. "Not until you talk to me." He kept singing as someone threw a shoe at him. He ducked and continued.

I grabbed my coat and ran outside barefoot. Then I shoved him as hard as I could. "What the fuck is wrong with you?"

He looked at me with intense pain in his eyes. "You know what's wrong with me. I need you."

I shoved him again. "I don't fucking care what you need! How about what *I* need?"

He reached out to take my hand, but I pulled away. "Tell me what you need, Jane."

I gritted my teeth and tried to ignore his lips, his eyes, his words, the true longing in his voice, and the beauty in the song he had played. "I need you to go home and be there for Lizzie."

He came closer and spoke softly. "I *am* there. I *will be* there, and I *am* there. But she's not the one I'm in love with." I growled in frustration because I was deeply in love with him too, and we were in an impossible situation. He read it on my face. "I know you feel the same way."

I stepped back and steeled myself. "I'm not going to say whether that is true or not-"

"You don't need to say it, Jane. I can feel it. Can't you?"

"It's irrelevant! It's pointless, meaningless, and irrelevant now! Don't you see? You and I… whatever this is… it's been over since before it started. We were always doomed!" I saw his hands curl into fists at his sides.

"Help me understand this!" he shouted. "You and I are in love with each other. Lizzie is pregnant. Can't we both be there for her *and* be together as well?"

"What fucking reality are you living in Gabriel? Do you think that's what I want? Don't you think I deserve better? Or how about what Lizzie deserves? She deserves better than that! And the baby! That innocent soul should be the focus of this entire thing! This is not about what *you want* anymore. It never will be again." He started to shiver, and I wasn't sure if it was from the cold or frustration or both.

"So what are you saying? *I have to be with her?*"

"Yes."

"*Why?*"

"Because it's the right thing."

"The right thing is going against how I feel? Denying myself love and forcing myself into a relationship that I don't want to be in? *How is that the right thing?* It's not the 1950s, Jane! Just because I got a girl pregnant doesn't mean I have to marry her!"

"But it does."

"*Fuck!* Why? *Tell me why?*"

"Because Lizzie is fragile. Her emotions are extremely delicate, and her health is hanging by a thread. If she feels in *any way* that this baby is unwanted, or that *she* is unwanted, or unloved, it could kill her. It could kill *them*."

"Do you honestly believe that?"

"I do. In my heart of hearts, Gabriel. I know it. I don't want to let go, but we have to."

"I don't have to. I don't live my life like that. I never have, and I never will."

"I know. But things change. People change. Priorities change because they have to. You've lived every day using death as an excuse to do whatever the fuck you wanted, rarely considering the effect you have on others. But it's time to stop thinking about death and start thinking about *life*. *Remember life,* Gabriel. The one that's growing inside Lizzie right now is more important than what *we* want."

Suddenly something changed in him. I saw a light inside his eyes go dim. And it was one of the saddest things I've ever seen. He closed his eyes, and when he opened them, they were filled with tears. He nodded over and over, like he finally got it, before inhaling deeply and straightening his back. "Goodbye, Jane," he whispered.

I wanted more than anything to run to him, cradle him in my arms, and tell him that none of it mattered. But the opposite was true. This was *the only thing* that mattered now.

CHAPTER 29

Jane

"I Know"—Fiona Apple

I MOVED INTO ED'S OLD BEDROOM, BETWEEN LIZZIE AND WILL. Several weeks passed, and I only saw Gabriel once. He was rarely at the house during the day, only coming home a few nights a week to sleep before leaving again. One morning, I got up earlier than usual, and he brushed by me in the hallway on the way to his bedroom. He was drunk and disheveled looking. His shoulder slammed into mine, and he looked away and laughed before stumbling into his room and kicking the door closed.

He didn't go to any of Lizzie's weekly doctor appointments. He barely acknowledged her at all. She slept most of the time, which was good because the doctor said that rest was the most important thing for her. She was really weak and breathing for two with only one lung. She had to be extremely careful not to overexert herself. When she was awake, she seemed to be really lightheaded and almost fell down the stairs at one point. Will and I made her promise not to go down the stairs without asking for help. We also had to wake her at various points during the day and beg her to eat, but she couldn't hold down any food. She would usually nibble on a bit of bread and go back to sleep, only to wake up later and throw up.

Will and I took her to her appointments, and we'd sit in the waiting room together laughing at all the newborn babies. He told Lizzie she could stay as long as she wanted, and he would make a nursery for the baby. He felt as bad for her as I did, and the way he treated her as though she was part of his own family was just beautiful. I wondered if she was filling a bit of the hole that his sister left behind.

Christmas was approaching, and Lizzie hadn't told her parents about her pregnancy. She was going to spend a few days with them and finally let them know. I was really nervous about how they would react. They were very traditional people who were generally more concerned with appearing like the perfect family than actually holding their family together.

We dropped her off and reminded her to eat and rest as much as possible. She was very skinny and pale, with dark purple rings under her eyes. She looked sicklier than when she had chemo, and I was terrified. I asked if she wanted me to stay at her parents', but she insisted that she was fine.

When I got back in the car, I started to cry. Will put his hand on mine and looked at me warmly. "I know. I'm scared for her too." He wiped a tear from my cheek. "Jane, please stay with me tonight."

"It's Christmas Eve. I usually spend it with my mom." He looked down with disappointment. "Will, would you like to come?"

"Oh, no. You don't need me following after you. Spend the time with your mum."

"Well, what will you do?"

"I'll be alright. Perhaps I'll finish a painting or two. I haven't finished anything in months."

"You know what? Fuck it. My mom will be with her new boyfriend, who's a dick, by the way. She has the worst taste in men. I'll tell her I'm sick, and we'll spend it together. Maybe I'll help you with those paintings! I mean, I can't really paint, but I'd be happy to keep you company while you work!"

"Jane, you don't have to do that. I'll be fine."

"I know I don't *have to*! I *want* to!"

His face lit up with joy. "Shall we go out for dinner or stay in?"

"I'd love to stay in. Maybe we can cook something ourselves. But first, you need a tree!"

"Do I?"

"It's not Christmas without a tree!"

"I don't have anything to decorate it with."

"My mom's got a storage unit with boxes and boxes of ornaments that haven't been used in years."

"I love that idea. Will you let me finish the painting of you I started months ago?"

"Sure. Can't get the face right, I heard."

"I think I need the real thing to fully capture it."

"It's a plan."

We grabbed the boxes of ornaments and went to buy a tree. We picked out the biggest, most lush tree at the tree farm and set it up in the library near the fireplace. Then we cooked pasta and had a picnic in the library in front of the fire before he asked me to sit for the painting.

"Okay, but I should let you know that I get bored easily, and I will probably fall asleep or annoy you with my chatter."

He grinned and looked at his hands. "You *never* annoy me."

"Don't you want to use the studio? It's not a secret anymore."

"Yes, I know."

"I'm sorry if you didn't want me to know."

"The only thing I'm sorry about is that *I* wasn't the one to show you."

I looked up at the mural over the fireplace. "Think maybe it's time to remove this?" I asked. "I mean, don't get me wrong. It's beautiful. But it's... *her.*"

"Will you help me paint over it?"

"*Me?*"

"Yes, *you.* I saw your mural in the studio. You have some natural talent."

"I hope you don't mind that we did that. It just kind of... happened."

"I don't mind."

The awkward energy was thick, so I jumped into the chair where he had originally painted me. "So which way should I face?"

He pulled the easel closer and gently turned my head, bit by bit, until it was at the perfect angle. "There. Please don't move." I nodded and smiled. "Don't smile," he added. "She's supposed to be in distress." I nodded slightly and dropped my expression.

I sat quietly for about an hour, and just when I was going to lose my mind from boredom, Will threw his paintbrush across the room in frustration.

"What's wrong?" I asked.

"I'm just shit at painting you."

"Oh, come on. Can't be that bad. Can I see?"

He huffed and spun the easel around for me to see.

"Oh."

His mouth formed into a half smile. "See, you can't even pretend it's any good!"

"The other parts of the painting are great! The whole background and my dress and hair. The face is just a bit…"

"Terrible?" I didn't answer, and he exhaled intensely. "It makes no sense. You'd think of all the people in the world, I would be able to paint the one I'm in love with!"

I froze and felt my eyes widen. "*What*?"

He kneeled in front of me and looked up into my eyes. "It's true. I cannot paint you, but I love you."

"You… love me?"

"More than I've ever loved anyone in my life."

My breath caught in my throat, and I took his hand. "How… do you know?"

He laughed. "I just know." I kept staring at him, and he continued. "If you need more explanation than that…" He put his forehead to my knees and took a deep breath before looking up at me again. "The last time I saw my grandfather, he said that I seemed different and asked what had changed. I insisted that nothing had changed, and he smiled and said, 'You have a glow. *The glow.* I'd recognize it anywhere. What's her name, William?' I laughed and said I had met a girl named Jane, but we were just friends. 'For now,' he said. 'So tell me about her.' The first thing I said was that you make me laugh. He smiled and said, 'She's the one, isn't she?' I asked what made him say that, and he said whenever I had talked about girls in the past, I would always say how pretty or smart or talented they were. But I'd never said that they made me laugh."

I scrunched my face to show my displeasure at hearing the other girls were pretty, smart, and talented, and I was just funny. He knew what I was thinking right away.

"I told him you were *also* the most beautiful and clever girl I'd ever met as well. But he insisted that the laughter was a sign. Laughter, he said, is the true test of everlasting love. If you can laugh together, at yourselves, at each other, at everything… you can make it through *anything* in life together. And that's when I re-alized that whenever I'm with you, I'm laughing or smiling or just excited about life, and I haven't been for a long time. And when we aren't together, all I can do is think of you and all the things I want to do with you. You make me feel like life isn't a prison, like escape is possible, risks are worth taking, and getting lost is just part of the plan. I…"

He took a piece of paper out of his back pocket and started to read. "I want to follow random dirt roads with you to see where they lead, walk through patches of snow deeper than our knees, get lost in a thick mountain fog, leap from cliffs into faraway seas, and sip wine near a bonfire on the beach at dusk." I gently started to play with his hair, twisting it in little circles, as the warmth between us grew. "You have set my world on fire in the best way possible. I'll do *anything* to prove to you how happy I will make you. I will ded-icate my life to you. Please, give me the chance to show you." The wonderful heaviness of his words pressed down on my chest, and tears flowed down my face. He dropped the paper to the floor. "Oh god, Jane! Why are you crying? Did I say too much?"

"No, no. It's nothing you said. It's just… Why would you want to be with me? I don't deserve you, Will. I don't." My cries became sobs as he took my face into his hands.

"Hey! Look at me! Don't ever say that. *I* decide who deserves me. And if you let me, I would like to *prove to you* that *I* deserve *you* every day of our lives."

I barely registered what he was saying and started shaking my head.

"What?" he asked. "What is it? You don't feel the same way?"

"I was with Gabriel! We were *together* and-"

He put his fingers to my lips to quiet me. "Jane, do you honestly think I don't know that? I'm not an idiot. And I don't care." He removed his fingers from my lips and wrapped them around my hands.

"You don't care?"

"Don't get me wrong. I *care*. It was torture for me knowing you were with him when you should have been with me. I just had to be patient and trust that the universe would somehow bring us together."

I was so overwhelmed; all I could do was hang my head and continue to cry until he spoke.

"Jane? Do you have feelings for me?"

I stopped crying and pointed to a tissue box. He brought it to me, and I wiped my face and nose to buy time because I couldn't figure out what to say.

"Jane." I looked up at him as he stood above me. "Can I make love to you?"

A wave of energy shot through my body, and a smile spread across my face.

"Is that a yes?"

I nodded and giggled.

"*What?*"

"I've just never had anyone ask me like that."

"Just trying to be honorable."

"I know. And I love that."

He held out his hand, and I gently took it. We slowly walked up the stairs, smiling at each other, the anticipation hanging heavily in the air. This was it, the true test of whether or not we belonged together, and we both knew it. We entered his bedroom, and I stood with the back of my legs pressed against the bed, unsure of what to do. If I were with Gabriel, I would have ripped my shirt off, crawled onto the bed, and turned around with a look of playful anticipation. But with Will, I felt nervous and a bit shy, which was weird but… good.

He lit a few candles on the night table and the two that hung in old sconces over the bed. Then he slowly approached me with a very serious look on his face. He took a piece of my hair and slowly ran it through his hand and then he pressed his forehead into mine and smiled. I thought he was going to say something, but he took my face into his hands and gently kissed me. I kissed him back, and we opened our mouths at the same time, mutually deepening the kiss. Our tongues danced together in harmony. We had the same rhythm and pace, and I slid my fingers into his messy hair. He slowly ran his lips from my mouth across my cheek and to my ear. "I have thought about this every night since the first day we met," he whispered into my ear.

I felt him inhale as he kissed down my neck, and I clutched his shirt in my hands. He pulled it over his head and threw it aside as he continued to kiss my neck and collarbone. It was the first time I had seen him without a shirt. "You have so many tattoos!"

He responded into my neck between kisses. "You sound surprised."

"I just didn't peg you as a tattoo kind of guy."

He stopped kissing my neck and looked directly at me. "What kind of guy did you peg me as?"

"I don't know. I was wrong… about so many things." He smiled and pulled me back into him. "Is that a skull on your arm?" I asked as he slowly took off my shirt. He turned to show me his upper arm where there was a tattoo of a skull with roses in its eye sockets and a snake coiled around it.

"This was a stupid mistake. My roommate at art school had just started doing tattoos, and I let him practice on me. I was so drunk that I didn't even ask what he was giving me." I traced the snake with my fingers.

"The snake is making an infinity symbol," I told him. "That's so meaningful. You have no idea."

"Is it?" he asked as he slid his hands from my collarbone to my chest and swiftly unhooked my bra.

"You never noticed?"

"I don't look at that one really. It's shit. I meant to have it redone or covered over." He turned around to show me his back where a line of Latin was written across his shoulder blades, surrounded by leaves. It was the same line that was etched into his fireplace.

Virtute et valare luceo non uro

"This one is the most meaningful to me," he explained. "It's the inscription from my family's coat of arms."

I traced the lines with my fingers. "Of course it's something about virtue, which makes a lot of sense," I said.

He turned back to me. "By virtue and valor I shine but do not burn."

I slowly closed my eyes. "That is *so* you."

He took my breasts into his hands and admired them. Then he looked up with a grin. "Do you know how beautiful you are?"

I shrugged and put my hands on top of his, making him squeeze me harder. "You don't have to be so gentle with me, Will."

He caressed my face with one hand. "Would you rather I was more rough?"

I giggled nervously. "I don't know. I just don't want you to hold back. I'm yours now. Do what you will."

His eyes widened, and he pulled me into his body. His mouth crashed down onto mine, and we resumed our rhythm but with more intensity. "You don't know how good it feels to hear you say that," he breathed into my chest, and he ran his tongue over my nipples.

"Yeah?" I grabbed the back of his neck and scratched my fingers through his scalp.

He got on his knees and kissed down my belly and then looked up at me as he pulled down my pants and underwear. "Say it again."

"I'm yours."

His eyes burned, and he stood up and kissed me with such intense feeling that my whole body hummed. As he kissed me, he slid his hand between my legs and whispered, "Say it again," as he ran his fingers up and down.

I could feel myself getting wetter as I grabbed his face and looked directly at him. "I. Am. Yours."

He responded by sliding a finger inside me, and I gasped with pleasure. I could feel how much he wanted me, but it wasn't just desire; there was so much love and admiration. He moved his finger deeper as he pressed his open palm into my clit, and I moaned into his ear. He laid me down on the bed and kissed my feet. Then he ran his tongue up my leg, stopping to kiss the side of my knee, my outer thigh, and my hip. He kissed all over me before sliding his tongue between my legs with a smile. Then he used both hands to spread me open and looked up at me and said, "Mine."

I nodded, and he very gently started flicking me with his tongue. "Oh fuck!" I called out, and he grinned as he spread me even wider and picked up the pace. "Will! Holy shit!" He gently traced the outside of my entrance with his finger as his tongue moved faster than I even knew was possible. I wanted to come, but I wanted him inside me even more.

"Come here!" I called out. His eyebrows went up, and he slowed his tongue. "Please!" I called out. He sat up as I scooted back to the headboard.

"Everything alright?"

"Make love to me. *Please.*"

"As you wish."

He pulled open the drawer in the night table and took out a condom.

"I'm on the pill."

"Are you sure?"

"Have you been with anyone since we've met?" I asked him.

"Of course not."

"I used a condom with Gabriel because I guess I didn't trust him completely. But I trust you. More than anyone in the world."

He returned the condom to the drawer and pulled his pants and boxers off. Then he climbed on top of me and put his nose to mine. "I love you, Jane."

I smiled as warmth coursed through my body. "I know." We kissed with that perfect rhythm, and as he entered me, I answered, "I love you too."

The pace was slow but intense, and we kissed and kissed. At some point I sat up and leaned into him as we brought each other to orgasm. We were sweaty, exhausted, and equally as relieved as I collapsed onto his chest. As we caught our breath I started laughing.

"What is it?" he asked.

"Thank god!"

"Right. I know what you mean."

"No, seriously. Thank God you don't have a tiny dick. I've heard horror stories from friends who dated really tall guys with freakishly small dicks. Their height makes it look that much smaller. I didn't know what to expect."

"I'm glad my dick isn't small as well. That sounds terrible."

"Sorry, that wasn't very romantic, was it?"

"Jane, comments like that are why I love you. I never know what to expect." I kissed his sweaty cheek before he leaned over to grab something from the night table.

"Can I ask you a question?"

"Shoot."

"Will you be my wife?"

"*What*?"

"Will you marry me?"

He held out a huge ruby ring surrounded by tiny diamonds that glittered in the candlelight, and I sat up.

"Are you serious, Will?"

"I tried to ask you earlier today, but it didn't go quite as planned. Did you want me to get on one knee?"

"Yes!"

"*Right.*"

He stood up and started to kneel beside the bed. I grabbed his arm and yanked him back into bed. "No! I meant yes! I'll marry you!"

"Are you sure? I don't want to pressure you."

I held out my hand. "Will. Shut up and put the fucking ring on me."

"Right." It fit perfectly.

"This is so beautiful. It looks like a flower."

"It was my grandmother's. I know it's not the conventional ring you might have wanted, so we can-"

"Are you kidding me? *I love it*."

He smiled and moved me onto his chest. As I started to fall asleep, he said, "Will you still be sleeping in Ed's room?"

"Maybe. Do you snore?"

"Not that I'm aware of."

"I'll let you know in the morning."

We snuggled back in before I woke him with a question. "So, does this mean I'm a duchess or something?"

"You would be a lady. When my father dies and I become the Earl of Suffolk, you'll be a countess."

"*Shit!* I better get my act together. I have a lot to learn about what forks go with what courses and how to bow to fancy people."

"God, *please*, don't learn any of that. I want you just like this."

"Just like this?"

"Just. Like. This."

CHAPTER 30

Jane

"Bad Blood"—Godz

THE MONTHS BEFORE OUR WEDDING SEEMED TO SLIP AWAY in an instant. We decided to have a small ceremony on the patio. The only people we invited were the brotherhood, Will's parents, my mom, and Lizzie, who was seven months pregnant.

The baby was healthy, but Lizzie was clearly struggling. She still couldn't hold down food and didn't gain much weight. She was pale and sickly and became the focus of my daily life with Will. We hadn't seen Gabriel in months. We had no idea where he was or what he was doing. After Lizzie told her parents about her pregnancy, they refused to help her in any way. Will and I had to have a serious conversation about Lizzie, and we agreed to let her live with us and help her raise the baby.

It was the morning of our wedding, and Lizzie helped me pick flowers from the garden to carry down the aisle. I was in Will's bedroom doing my hair and makeup when he knocked on the door. Lizzie opened it and yelled at him to leave because it was bad luck to see the bride before the ceremony.

"I just wanted to give her this!" He handed Lizzie a pair of earrings and told her they had been in his family for 400 years. She brought them to me, and we both swooned as she lovingly hung the diamond teardrops from my ears.

"Let's get you dressed."

I refused to make a big fuss. Of course I could have had any dress I wanted and the biggest, fanciest wedding I could come up with, but none of it felt right. I just wanted to marry Will at Red

House and start our lives together. I chose a very simple, airy, white linen gown that reminded me of the little sun dress I wore as a kid at the beach.

I stepped into my dress and stood in front of the mirror as Lizzie slid a blush colored peony behind my ear and whispered, "You look perfect."

I pulled her in for a long, tight hug. "I love you so much, Lizzie. You're part of our family. Always will be."

"I know. I love you too. I'm not feeling well. I think I'm going to lie down for a bit before the ceremony."

"What's wrong? What can I do?"

"Nothing. Just a little lightheaded. A little rest will help."

"Can I walk you to your room?"

"It's just next door! I'll see you soon."

We hugged again, and I sat down in front of the mirror to touch up my makeup. I heard the door open and close again, and I assumed it was Lizzie. "Everything okay?" I asked without looking up.

"Fucking fabulous."

I stood up and spun around to face Gabriel. He was dressed in his fitted black suit, and he looked gorgeous but definitely thinner. His eyes showed his exhaustion.

"You shouldn't be in here! You have to go!"

"Jane." He scrubbed his face like he was in agony. "You look… *magnificent.*"

"Thanks. But you really shouldn't be in here."

"I have to admit… I didn't think this day would come. I didn't think you would actually marry him."

"Oh, okay. So we're having a conversation? Then let me ask you this…" I stood up and stomped over to where he stood. "*Where the fuck have you been*?"

"Just trying to move on with my life as you've done so easily. Do you mind?"

"Yeah, I *do* mind. Because my best friend is pregnant with *your* child! Or did that slip your mind?"

"No, it has *not* slipped my mind. But what did you expect?

For me to continue living here while you rubbed my fucking face in your new life with Will? Was I supposed to watch you be with someone else after you ripped my fucking heart out?"

"I expected you to be a man! If you don't want to live here with me, then get your own place, and take Lizzie and your baby with you *and fucking take care of them*!"

"That's what you want, huh? You want me to lift the burden from you, so you can be free to travel the world and spend Will's money?"

"*Fuck you*, Gabriel. It's not like that, and you know it! Take some fucking responsibility!"

He stood there seething while looking me up and down. Then he moved closer and slammed his mouth onto mine. I'd be lying if I said that I didn't have sparks all over my body. I gave in for a moment and kissed him back before I came to my senses and shoved him away. "*What the fuck are you doing?*"

"What the fuck are *you* doing? You didn't love him before! *What changed?*"

"*I* did! *I* changed, Gabriel!"

We stared at each other, our chests rising and falling with exasperation. "Maybe you love him, but are you really *in love* with him?" he finally asked.

"Yes. *I am.* Just go." I sat back down and wiped off my smeared lipstick.

He slowly moved closer and spoke softly into my ear. "Fine. But just answer one question for me. *Can he make you come like I can?*" I stared at him in the mirror. He had a satisfied look on his face as though he was sure of the answer.

"Fuck off, Gabriel," I said with no emotion as I continued to reapply my lipstick.

He stomped towards the door and turned and said, "Just remember. You have been mine before, and you'll always be mine."

"Not in *this* lifetime. Not anymore."

He grabbed the doorknob, but before he left, I called out to him.

"Oh, Gabriel? In case you were wondering, she's having a girl." His eyes narrowed with anger, and he slammed the door behind him.

As I stared at my reflection in the mirror, feeling a torrent of conflicting emotions, I noticed a piece of paper on the bed. As I read its contents the room twisted in breathless circles around me.

Severed Selves
D.G.R.

Two separate divided souls which
brought together, find a loving voice,
Two glances which together, in love,
would forever rejoice.
That joy is now lost like stars beyond dark trees,
Our two hands apart but that touch alone gives such ease.

My chest on yours, both filled with a mutual flame,
And meeting in one clasp, our souls are made the same.
Two souls, two shores assailed by violent breaking seas: such
are we now,
My deepest hopes long for one loving word from you, some
fragment of a forgotten vow.

You came to me at love's hour most ecstatically,
Your light upon this darkened stream surrounded me.
Into my heart you showed me that you have always been present,
When clothed with fire your heart gave to me it's testament.
I have been near and felt your soul to be,
the innermost chamber of my heart's sanctuary.
Before we were born your life with mine was already done,
As from the heavens I shouted, "I am yours, and you and I
are forever one!"

When trapped in the darkest part of eternity, one glance from
you is all it will take,
To draw up my imprisoned spirit, from
the murkiest waters of this unceasing heartache.

Please, my soul, be one with me again. Only you can set me free.

I collapsed onto the bed, holding the paper to my heart. All my feelings of love for him crashed over me in a raging storm as tears leaked out. My phone buzzed and jarred me out of the emotional haze.

"Ready?" a text from Will read.

"Almost," I answered.

"Jane, you have made me the happiest man on earth. Thank you." I let the poem fall to the floor.

"I love you. See you in five."

"I love you too. *Always in all ways.*"

I plucked the poem from the ground, swiped a lighter off the mantle, and set the paper on fire. I tossed it into the fireplace, dried my face, and took one last glance at myself in the mirror before I married the man I was meant to be with.

CHAPTER 31

Will

"Golden Slumbers"—Ben Folds

I'M NOT STUPID, AND I'M NOT BLIND. I KNOW SHE'S STILL IN love with Gabriel and probably always will be. But it's a fact I have to accept if I want to be with her. And she's not just something I want. She's someone I *need*.

I watched him enter her room that day. I knew she was alone. I waited at the top of the stairs and felt incredible relief when he came out only a few minutes later, slamming the door behind him in anger. He stopped in front of me and declared, "You won, Will! *Congratulations*. The better man won."

"It's not a game, Gabriel. It's life," I told him.

"Same fucking thing," he replied before shoving me over to stomp down the stairs. I waited a few minutes before texting her. I could sense that her feelings were all over the place. But when she came out and saw me waiting at the top of the stairs, she had the most serene expression as she gave me her hand. And I knew we were okay.

We walked together to the solarium. Before we went out onto the patio where our guests were waiting, I turned to her. "I can't believe I forgot to mention how absolutely perfect you look. Forgive me."

She leaned in and whispered, "Only if you forgive *me*."

"For what?"

"Not really seeing you."

"Do you see me now?" I asked.

"That's why I'm marrying you!"

She bent forward to kiss me as the wedding coordinator she didn't know I hired opened the doors. I withdrew from her kiss and whispered, "Not yet!" as I motioned towards the patio.

Her gaze widened as she gasped. "*Will!* I said I didn't want to make a fuss!"

"So sorry, dear." She shoved me playfully as I added, "Not sorry at all actually."

The orchestra started to perform The Beatles' "Golden Slumbers," and Ben Folds played piano and sang. She was so overwhelmed by the massive amount of wildflowers and candles that covered the patio that she barely noticed the music. We went arm in arm to the ivy-covered archway where the Archbishop of Canterbury stood. When we turned to each other, she looked back at the orchestra and realized who was playing. "Will! Is that *Ben Folds*?" she called out. He lifted his arm from the piano and waved to her as he finished the song. She grasped my face and pulled me down and into a long kiss.

"Goodness!" the Archbishop said through a laugh. "We better get the show on the road, so we can get to that part!" She came away beaming, and her eyes didn't leave mine for the rest of the ceremony.

The Archbishop mentioned that the ceremony was held in honor of loved ones who could not join us but were surely with us in spirit. He said that my grandparents were smiling down from heaven, and Jane took my hand and gave it a squeeze. I put her hand to my mouth and kissed it.

The ceremony was short, as we both wanted. The only reason we had any religion involved at all was to honor my grandparents. The parts the Archbishop said that resonated with me were when he quoted a passage from Proverbs that said, "A wife is far more precious than jewels." He commented, "Jane, all of us here who truly know William know that he will dedicate his life to you, and he will treat you as though you are more precious than the finest jewels."

I didn't register much else that was said. I was completely focused on Jane. The way she smiled at me with such love and devotion, it was as though we were there alone, with no one else in the world around.

Lizzie read a passage from Kahlil Gibran's *The Prophet* that Jane and I chose. She was so weak she could barely stand, so we pulled a chair over for her to sit in as she read. The lines truly embodied how I felt about love and about my life with Jane. In that moment I wanted to be with her for all eternity.

Lizzie read, "'When love beckons to you, follow him, though his ways are hard and steep. And when his wings enfold you, yield to him, though the sword hidden among his pinions may wound you. And when he speaks to you, believe in him, though his voice may shatter your dreams as the north wind lays waste the garden. For even as love crowns you, so shall he crucify you. Even as he is for your growth so is he for your pruning. Even as he ascends to your height and caresses your tenderest branches that quiver in the sun, so shall he descend to your roots and shake them in their clinging to the earth. And think not you can direct the course of love, for love, if it finds you worthy, directs your course. Love has no other desire but to fulfill itself. But if you love, let these be your desires: To melt and be like a running brook that sings its melody to the night. To know the pain of too much tenderness. To be wounded by your own understanding of love; and to bleed willingly and joyfully. To wake at dawn with a winged heart and give thanks for another day of loving; to return home at eventide with gratitude; and then to sleep with a prayer for the beloved in your heart and a song of praise upon your lips.'"

We both kissed her and helped her back to her seat, and finally, the moment came when we exchanged rings and were pronounced husband and wife. I kissed my bride as though it was my last kiss to give on earth. Everyone stood and cheered as we walked back down the aisle to the sounds of the orchestra playing "Golden Slumbers" once again. As we passed the aisle where Gabriel stood, I thought I saw them make eye contact, but I couldn't be sure. It didn't matter anyway, for she was finally mine.

I guess he was right. I had won. That's what it felt like anyway.

CHAPTER 32

Jane

"Shiver"—Coldplay

I REALLY DIDN'T WANT MUCH OF ANYTHING FOR OUR WEDDING but should have expected Will to make it special, and it was. It was the greatest few hours of my life. I felt like I had finally grasped the meaning of things and what my path should be moving forward. Will was my life, and nothing else mattered. Even though we were married, I had a lot to prove to him. I vowed to show him that he made the right decision every day of our lives.

There were more people than the few we agreed on, but it was still a small wedding. We sat at our table underneath the archway where we were just married and watched our guests eat, drink, and dance in the candlelit twilight. I had him tell me who each person was who I didn't recognize, and it was mostly family, with a few friends from his childhood and art school. Lizzie helped him choose a few of my old friends to invite as well, including Ally and Dan. Gabriel sat with Lizzie and had his back to me most of the time. I tried not to even look in his direction, but I did notice that he seemed to be treating Lizzie with care, which made me happy.

After dinner, Will excused himself for a moment and stood with the orchestra behind him. He spoke into the mic, "Good evening, friends and family. Thank you all so much for being here. I know a lot of you traveled a long way to spend this special day with us, and we are very grateful to you. As many of you know, I am complete shit at dancing, so instead of a first dance, I'd like to play a song for my new wife."

He grabbed an acoustic guitar and started to play. I was shocked by how good he was. He sang "Shiver" by Coldplay, which was so meaningful. He played directly to me, looking into my eyes from across the patio the entire time. By the third stanza, Ben Folds joined in on piano and sang backup, and the orchestra of about 30 or 40 musicians started at the chorus. By the end of the song, I was a complete mess, with tears streaming mascara down my face. I ran to him and wrapped my arms around his neck, and he spun me around. When my feet hit the floor, I grabbed his face and kissed him for a full minute. When I opened my eyes, I said, "I didn't know you could play guitar!"

"We both have a lot to learn about each other."

Out of the corner of my eye, I saw Gabriel angrily stride towards the door to the solarium and slam it shut behind him. Lizzie followed after him, and I worried that she was under stress. I started to go after her, but Will held me back. "Let her go. They need to work out their shit." I nodded and pulled him into another embrace.

Not long after, Lizzie approached me with excitement in her eyes as I came out of the bathroom. Gabriel was standing behind her staring at me with daggers. "Jane! I have amazing news!"

"What is it? Tell me!"

She held her hand out, and she was wearing the Ouroboros ring that Gabriel had given me. "I'm engaged!"

I tried to hide the look of shock and worry that appeared on my face. "Oh wow. I mean, that's great! When did *that* happen?"

She turned to smile at Gabriel who had a pissed off expression. "Just a few minutes ago! We worked everything out!" She rubbed her belly and took Gabriel's hand. "We're going to be a family!"

I forced a smile and kissed her cheek. "I'm so happy for you. Congratulations, Gabriel."

"Congratulations to you too, *Mrs. Morris*," he said with venom. We stood there in an awkward triangle, with a volatile mix of emotions brewing.

Suddenly, Lizzie leaned against the wall to steady herself. "Lizzie! Are you okay? What just happened?"

"Oh, nothing. Just got a little dizzy. I'm fine." I got closer to her and looked into her face. She looked pale and sick.

"Have you eaten today?"

She waved me off with her hand. "I had a little something. I'm fine. Don't fuss."

"I think you should sit down." I gestured to a nearby armchair.

"I said *I'm fine*! Stop babying me! I'm a grown woman!" She walked back outside with irritation, and Gabriel and I were left alone, staring at each other.

"What's the plan here, Gabriel? What's your motive?"

"*Motive?* For what?"

"For marrying her! You haven't given a shit about her this entire time, and all of a sudden you want to *marry* her? I'm not buying it!"

He moved in closer to my face and looked down at my lips before he whispered, "I don't really give a shit *what* you're buying, *Mrs. Morris.* My life is none of your business."

"Once again, that would be 100 percent true… if my best friend, who happens to be very sick, wasn't having your child!"

At that moment, Will stood between us. "Is everything alright?"

I stepped back and ripped my eyes from Gabriel, who looked like he was going to strangle one of us. "I've just heard some interesting news, Will. Gabriel and Lizzie are engaged."

Will turned to Gabriel and gave him a gentle smack on his back. "Is that right? Well, look at you! Got the marriage bug, huh? That's wonderful!"

Gabriel didn't respond or even look in Will's direction. He kept gazing at me with such intensity, it scared me.

"When's the big day for you two?" Will asked, pretending not to see the exchange of overwhelming emotions between the two of us.

"Tonight," Gabriel murmured, not looking away from me.

"Tonight? Well, *shit*! Are you hopping on a plane to Vegas?"

Gabriel finally turned to face Will. "Your priest agreed to marry us tonight."

A small gasp escaped from me as Will responded. "Lovely. Will you need witnesses?"

Gabriel turned back to me. "We were hoping you two would help us with that."

Will saw the look on my face and gently took my hand and gave it a squeeze. "We'd love to. Isn't that right, Jane?"

"If that's what Lizzie wants. I... I just..." I broke away from them and went outside to Lizzie and knelt in front of her. Is it true that you and Gabriel want to get married *tonight*?"

She looked at me with hesitation because she knew I'd protest. "Yes, it's true. And before you say anything, I'd like to remind you that he's the father of my child, so how you feel about him isn't really relevant anymore."

I held her hand. "I know. You're right. I just want to make sure this is what you really want."

"Why wouldn't I want this? I'm having his baby, *and* I'm in love with him!" I could see that she wasn't going to listen to anything I had to say. I had to tell myself that this was the best thing for her and the baby and pray that he would do right by them moving forward.

After the guests started to leave, the four of us met the Archbishop in the ballroom underneath the stained glass dome. Lizzie held my bouquet, which was tied with a blue ribbon. She wore the diamond earrings Will had given me that morning as something old and borrowed. When I asked her what she wanted as something new, she pointed to her belly and smiled. For rings, she would use the Ouroboros, and Will gave Gabriel an old wedding band that he inherited. He didn't really know whose it was or where it came from.

Will and I stood next to them, and I held his hand so tightly that I must have been cutting off his circulation. The Archbishop opened a book and looked down at Lizzie's belly as he spoke. "I am always happy to bring a family together. And while I take the sacrament of marriage quite seriously, as I hope you both will as well, I must make this a quick one, for I have a plane to catch." Lizzie nodded and smiled while Gabriel remained expressionless the entire time.

The Archbishop started the vows, and Gabriel repeated each line after him with zero emotion or emphasis. It was like he was on autopilot. Lizzie's vows were so heartfelt that she actually teared up at the end. I wanted to hit Gabriel over the head to get him to care.

They exchanged rings, received a short blessing, and were pronounced husband and wife. The kiss was heartbreaking for me to watch because Lizzie's face showed complete joy and love while Gabriel kissed her like he was doing a menial task that meant nothing to him.

The Archbishop congratulated all of us and excused himself. Just as he exited the room, Lizzie said that she didn't feel well and needed to lie down. I was relieved that we wouldn't have to spend anymore time with them that night. She took Gabriel's hand and led him out of the ballroom and up to her room.

"So *that* happened," Will said to me as we stood there in shock.

"I really hope that was the right thing, Will."

"I hope so too. And it is. They're having a child together, whether he likes it or not. This *is* the right thing."

"The right thing *in theory*… But it could very well lead to a lot more heartache for her."

"Let's just hope that if he is going to hurt her, he waits until the baby is born safely."

I let out a long sigh. "Well, aside from that odd situation, this was the best day of my life."

"I really hope so. And I feel the same."

"Shall we retire to our bedchambers?" I said jokingly.

"We shall!" He swept me off my feet and carried me the long way to the staircase and up to our room. He gently placed me on the bed and knelt in front of me. "Thank you for making me the happiest man in the universe."

"Eh, it was nothing."

CHAPTER 33

GABRIEL

"Playa"—Dennis Lloyd

I FELT CURSED. THE GODS WERE ANGRY WITH ME; THAT WAS clear. Maybe I *had* lived selfishly for most of my life, but I never did anything to hurt anyone *intentionally*. And I didn't deserve the sharp fall off a cliff that my life had suddenly taken.

I made one mistake in the midst of love, passion, and jealousy. I didn't deserve to pay for it for the rest of my life. At first, I vowed to be there for Lizzie unconditionally, to prove to Jane that I *was* capable of doing the right thing. But after Jane moved in, it just seemed like she was trying to torture me. How could I live in a house with the woman I loved desperately, who told me there was no chance in hell she would ever love me again? I refused to watch her and Will fall in love while I sat back and accepted my fate. I alone was in charge of my destiny, and I needed to get back in control of my life.

I stayed with Hunt and Annie for a while. I was drinking way too much, and it didn't take long for Annie to seize the opportunity to take from me what she had been trying to get for years. One night I passed out on their couch in a drunken haze, and I woke up with my dick in her mouth. I was so smashed that I could barely lift my head up, let alone fight her off. I murmured Hunt's name, and she shushed me and pointed to their closed bedroom door. So there I was, getting sucked off by my best friend's fiancée while he slept on the other side of the door. I threw my head back and let her fuck me without a condom. That's when I knew I was really in a fucked up place.

I woke up the next morning, vowing to myself that I wouldn't let anything like that happen again. I wasn't that person, and I couldn't let heartbreak turn me into a fucking trainwreck. I started running, and I didn't stop until I collapsed in a park, several hours later. As I stumbled home, so weak from thirst, a convertible full of college girls pulled up next to me and asked if I wanted to join them. My only reaction was to say, "Water," before I put my hands on my knees and dropped my head. The girl in the passenger seat held up a huge bottle of water and shook it at me. As I approached them, she opened the door and slid over. I sat down next to her, grabbed the water, and drank the entire thing as she leaned across me to shut the door. "More," I cried as they turned up their shitty pop music and sped away laughing.

The next three days were spent at their sorority house in a cloud of alcohol, drugs, and sex. Every time I tried to get sober and leave, another cute girl would jump on top of me and drag me back into the haze. It was probably a fantasy scenario for most guys, but as I walked from their house trying to get my bearings and figure out where I was, I felt almost suicidal. *What the fuck was I doing?* I needed to stop drinking and get my shit together.

I hitchhiked back to Hunt's apartment, and I started to write. I wrote 60 pages of poetry, mostly about Jane. I refused Annie's advances for several nights in a row and painted instead. Hunt rented a garage space at their apartment complex that he used as a studio. I dragged in a sleeping bag and painted and slept there. A few days later, Hunt came in to tell me that Will and Jane were getting married, and we were invited. I felt the floor slip out from under me, and I punched a hole through the garage door before Hunt pointed to his punching bag which hung from the ceiling behind me. I apologized and beat the shit out of it for a few hours while I decided what to do next.

Sweaty and exhausted, I collapsed onto the floor as Annie entered the garage in a robe. She said she understood how I felt and was there to take the pain away as she dropped her robe, revealing dominatrix-looking lingerie. I was weak and needed something to numb the pain. So I fucked her brains out with gritted teeth, unleashing all of my pain and anger, and she seemed to really get off on it. At one point, she even asked me to hit her, and I did. She tasted the blood on her lip with her tongue, smiled, and told me to do it again. I refused but spanked her ass as hard as I could, over and over, leaving handprints behind. I wondered if Hunt would see them, but I didn't even care that much if he did because he deserves someone better than her anyway.

It was the morning of Jane's wedding, and I had no plan other than to confront her before the ceremony, pull her into a kiss, and show her who she truly loved and was meant to be with. I was certain that when our lips met, all of the intensity of our connection would come flooding back to her, and she would call off the wedding. And when I kissed her, for a moment, it did feel that way. She kissed me back with an equal amount of passion and longing, and I felt relief wash over me. But she shoved me away, chewing my heart up with her words and spitting it back out at me. The look of disgust in her eyes told me it really was over.

I was broken. I felt like an abandoned mansion in winter— bleak, hollow, forgotten. No emotion, no passion, no desire. I was just a body with barely a soul left inside. So I decided to do what everyone said was the "right thing" and marry Lizzie. I did care for her. She was very smart and lovely, like a delicate porcelain doll on a shelf. After seeing my soulmate marry another man, I accepted the fate I was given and gave Lizzie my hand. She didn't have my heart, my soul, or even my body, but she had my hand.

We barely spoke that night as I watched her take a pill bottle from a shoebox in her closet and slip a pill into her mouth. She fell asleep soon after, and I snuck into her closet to check the shoebox. It was filled with empty bottles of prescription painkillers, all in her name. I opened more shoeboxes, and there were dozens of empty bottles. I woke her up and questioned her. She was pretty out of it but said they were given to her after her last visit to the hospital. I asked if it was safe for the baby. She nodded yes before her eyelids fell, and her head dropped down to the pillow. I checked her vital signs to make sure she was just passed out and not in serious trouble before I fled. I'd be damned if I was to be blamed for her drug problem.

That night, I stayed with my sister. After collapsing on the couch in the dark, I tried to make sense of what my life had become as the phone rang. It was Will. Lizzie woke up covered in blood, and they took her to the hospital. I woke up Christina, and we sped there together. I didn't want to be married to Lizzie nor did I want to be a father, but I didn't want her or the baby to die.

When we got there, Jane and Will were still dressed up from their wedding. Will sat in a chair with his head in his hands while Jane paced the waiting room barefoot. When she saw us arrive, she yelled at my sister, "What the fuck is *she* doing here?"

Will took her arm and pulled her back as I got in her face. "She's my *sister*, Jane!" She growled at me as I asked Will what was going on.

"We don't really know. She started screaming from her room, and when we went in, she was covered in blood from the waist down. They took her back, and we haven't heard anything since."

"Where the fuck *were* you?" Jane yelled at me. I ignored her and went past them to the front desk. I explained that I was Lizzie's husband, and they let me through right away. Jane followed me. "Where are you going? They said we aren't allowed in!"

"I'm her *husband*, Jane. Family is allowed in."

Her hands turned into fists. "Like *fucking hell* you're family! *I'm* her family! You aren't *shit*!"

I looked at her with sincere compassion. "Jane. I promise I'll let you know what's going on as soon as I can."

She dropped her anger for a moment. "Please, Gabriel. *Please*."

"I promise."

They took me back to her room, but there was no one there. I went into the hallway and grabbed a nurse. She brought me back to the same room and told me to sit down. She said that Lizzie was going to be okay, but she lost the baby. She was in surgery. They would let me know when she was in recovery, so I could see her. All I could think was that Jane should be the one going in to see her, not me. I was probably the last person on earth she wanted with her. I told the nurse that Lizzie's sister was in the waiting room and should be allowed into the recovery room. She went to get her.

Jane walked in and looked around in confusion. "Where is she? What's going on?"

"I think maybe you should sit."

"What? Why? What the fuck is going on? Where is she?"

"She's okay. She's in surgery."

She sat down and let out a sigh of relief. "Oh, thank God. C-section?"

"She... she lost the baby."

"Oh my god. Oh shit. No. No. Are you... are they sure?"

"Yes."

"Fuck. But she's going to be okay?" I nodded my head, and we sat in silence staring at the floor. "Gabriel. I'm... I'm sorry." I nodded again and looked away. We didn't look at each other or say anything again until a nurse came in to get us. I insisted that Jane go first, without me.

"Are you sure?" she asked. I nodded again, and she leaned in and took my hand. "Thank you."

I texted Christina to let her know what happened and to tell Will. I waited for many hours until they wheeled Lizzie in with Jane at her side. Her face was very pale and sickly. I went to take her hand, but she moved it away. When I tried to talk to her, she turned her head in the other direction. I didn't know what to do. As her husband, I needed to be there, but the truth was that I had no right to be in that room. And we all knew it.

I started to speak to her, and she closed her eyes and pretended not to hear me. "Lizzie, I'm so sorry about the baby. I just want you to know that I'm here for you. Whatever you need. I'm here. I'll be waiting in the hallway." Jane looked at me with sad eyes and then glanced down to the floor. I sat on the floor in the hallway for a while until I fell asleep. Eventually, Jane woke me up and told me to go home. They would be taking Lizzie back to Red House soon. I said I would follow them there.

"You don't have to," she said softly.

"I know. I *want* to."

CHAPTER 34

Jane

"Haunted"—Poe

WHEN WE GOT HOME WITH LIZZIE THE NEXT MORNING, she retreated to her room, and Gabriel went with her. Will's parents were still there, and they called him into the kitchen for a talk before they went to the airport. He tried to explain what we had just been through, but they showed no interest. About 15 minutes later, they walked past me without saying anything and brought their luggage outside to their cab. Will came out of the kitchen looking completely disheveled.

"What is it? What happened?"

"It's not worth discussing. Not now anyway. Please, can we sleep?"

"Yes, of course."

We got undressed and took a shower together, at my insistence. We had barely been alone since we got married, and I was dying for a bit of intimacy. But we were physically and emotionally exhausted.

We made love in the shower, and while it was incredible, I could tell his mind was elsewhere. When we got into bed, I turned to him and put my head on his shoulder. "Will. I know you're exhausted, but you can't hide from me. Please tell me what's going on with your parents."

"They want Red House."

I sat up and faced him. "What do you mean?"

"They decided they want this place for themselves."

"I don't understand. I thought they don't even like it here. Do they even want to leave England?"

"No. They want it, so they can sell it. While we were at the hospital this morning, they had someone come to appraise the property.

Apparently the dome in the ballroom is an original Tiffany's mosaic. Just the dome is worth 35 million dollars."

"Are you fucking kidding me, Will? They want Red House, so they can sell it? When you love it here so much? You're the only one who ever cared about it! Do they know how much it means to you?"

"They don't care."

"What about the fact that your sister died here? Does that mean anything to them?"

"All the more reason to let it go, they said."

"Well, do they have any claim to it? Isn't everything in your name?"

"Red House is in my grandfather's name. Even though he left everything to me, it gets complicated with assets outside of the U.K. There are different laws, and they could fight this one more easily."

"What do you want to do?"

"Stay here where I'm happy and live my life."

"So let them fight. They won't win."

"They said that if I don't hand it over willingly, they'll contest the entire will, on the grounds that he wasn't in his right mind when he wrote it. I could lose everything."

"That is unbelievably shitty. They care more about money than their own son!"

"Always have."

I took his hand. "Will. Whatever feels right to you, I'm on your side. The money is awesome, but we don't need it. If you want to fight this, I'm willing to take that chance."

"It's just… that's not what my grandfather wanted. I don't know. I have to think about it. Talk to some experts. But I'm not giving up our home without a proper fight."

"Then we will fight to the *death*!"

"Hopefully it won't come to that. Please, let me hold you now, wife?"

"Of course, husband. Should I check on Lizzie?"

"She's not alone. She's with her husband."

"Oh, right." I rolled my eyes and fell into his arms.

The next few months were filled with meetings with lawyers and experts and government officials. We were completely occupied with the legal fight we had taken on and weren't paying as much attention to Lizzie as we should have. But Gabriel stayed. He was there all day, every day with her, though after she fell asleep he would stay out for most of the night. I was just happy that he was looking after her.

We didn't speak or interact with each other much. He stayed locked in her room where he drew and painted her obsessively. I passed by when he left the door open one afternoon, and I was shocked by the amount of paintings there were of her. He stopped in the doorway and turned to me but didn't say anything.

"Gabriel, did you paint all of those? They're stunning! And there's so many!"

"It turns out I was wrong about you. Lizzie is my Beatrice. Not you," he said coldly before he shut the door in my face. It didn't bother me much, as long as he stayed with her and took proper care of her.

She wasn't speaking to me either. She rarely left her room, and when we saw each other, she would give me one word answers or ignore me completely. One night I heard her moaning from her bedroom, and when I entered her room, she was standing in the dark, rocking a bundle of blankets in her arms.

"Hey, Lizzie, is everything okay?"

She turned around and looked completely spooked. "Shh! You'll wake the baby!"

I moved closer. "Umm, what baby?" She didn't look up from the blankets she cradled and started singing a lullaby. "Lizzie, I'm worried about you."

Still looking lovingly at her bundle she said, "There's nothing to worry about, mother. Everything is wonderful. Isn't that right, baby?"

Her response shook me to my core. I went to get Will, and I

explained what was going on. He went with me to her room, and she was asleep in her bed. Still worried, I tapped her on the shoulder, and she slowly turned to me and mumbled something without opening her eyes.

"I just wanted to make sure you're okay. I'm worried about you." She opened her eyes and took my hand.

"I'm alright. Just tired. Really tired." She seemed like herself again, so I pulled the blankets up and shut the door.

I woke up early the next morning still scared about her mental health. I went to check on her, but the door was locked. Will and I both tried to open it. I started screaming for her to open the door, but there was no answer. I called Gabriel's phone over and over until he picked up. I asked where he was, but he wouldn't say. I explained that Lizzie was having an emergency and asked where the key to the room was. He said he had it on him and would be home later. I started screaming at him that he needed to get home immediately, but he hung up on me. Will said he would take the door handle off and went to get his tools. I spoke through the door, praying she could hear me.

"Lizzie, it's Jane. I'm so sorry for everything that's happened to you. You have not deserved any of the suffering you've had. I wish I could take it all away, just erase it from existence. But there's so much to look forward to, and you are so, so loved! Please open the door. You're my best friend. My family. I love you so much, ladybug. Please."

There was no answer, and I started to sob and pound on the door as Will tried to remove the handle without success.

"This isn't your average lock. It's over a hundred years old. They put the lock in a pocket inside the door. There's no way to break it."

"*So what do we do?*"

"I'm going to call a locksmith and get my hacksaw. I might be able to hack through the latch. In the meantime, keep calling Gabriel."

An hour later, halfway through Will's effort to saw through the latch, Gabriel appeared behind us. His shirt was ripped and dirty, and his face was covered in cuts and bruises. I tried to control my anger and ignore his pissy attitude.

"What happened to you?"

"Don't worry about it," he said as he held out the key. We opened the door and found Lizzie sprawled out across the bed, not breathing. Her skin was ice cold and gray. Next to her on the bed were several empty bottles of painkillers, and she held a note in her hand with a poem scribbled on it.

> *Never weep for love that's dead*
> *Since love is seldom true*
> *But changes his fashion from blue to red,*
> *From brightest red to blue,*
> *And love was born to an early death*
> *And is so seldom true.*
>
> *Never weep for what cannot be,*
> *For this God has not given.*
> *If the merest dream of love were true*
> *Then we should be in heaven,*
> *And this is only earth, my dear,*
> *Where true love is not given.*

I let the poem flutter to the ground as I scooped her up into my arms and rocked her like a child. Will took her from me and tried CPR a few times after calling for an ambulance. Gabriel stood in the corner of the room, motionless, watching the scene unfold in horror.

"She's gone," Will said softly as he put her back in my arms. I screamed *no* over and over and kissed her face and tried to shake her awake.

"She's not gone! She's asleep!" I called out as Will tried to calm me. I kept trying to wake her up as the paramedics rushed into the room and took over.

"*Where were you?*" I screamed at Gabriel. "Where the fuck *were* you?"

He stared at me, frozen.

"This is *your* fault! Do you hear me? This is your fucking fault! All of it! If we never met you, she'd still be alive!" I lashed out at him and hit him in the chest with my fists, but he still didn't move.

Will pulled me out of the room and held me in the hallway as I collapsed onto him and sobbed.

CHAPTER 35

Jane

"Cruel World"—Phantogram

WE SAT IN THE PARKING LOT BEHIND THE CHAPEL watching everyone go in, but I couldn't move. My hand gripped the door handle, but I couldn't find the strength to open it. "It'll be starting soon," Will said.

"I know."

I kept staring at the chapel doors and squeezing the handle. "I think I need you to help me out of the car."

"Of course."

He came around and opened my door and held his hand out. His eyes were filled with such compassion, and I felt waves of his love surround me. I let him pull me up, and then I dropped my weight onto him. "I don't deserve you, Will."

He pushed my hair out of my eye. "Stop that."

We slowly walked a few steps, and I grabbed onto him tighter. "I don't feel good."

"What's wrong?"

"I feel weird… lightheaded."

"We don't have to go in, Jane. There's no rulebook for these things. You can grieve for her in your own way. She would understand."

I paused for a moment and shook my head. "No, it's not right. It's my best friend's funeral. I have to be there."

He looked down at his watch as we heard an organ start to play. "We better hurry."

We moved quickly to the front doors, but before we opened them, I peered into the window and saw Gabriel approach the pulpit. He glanced down for a moment, then his head shot up, and his eyes found mine in the back window. A surge of nausea exploded inside, and I bent down and threw up a bit. Will handed me a bottle of water and suggested we go back to the car. I took a big swig before responding.

"No. I feel better now. Let's go in."

We entered the chapel as quietly as we could and slid onto the last bench. The chapel was packed with people, and dripping with pink and white lilies. I sneered as I recalled how much Lizzie hated lilies.

"They smell like a funeral," she used to say. Her favorite flower was baby's breath. If she got a bouquet of flowers, she'd remove everything but the baby's breath. We used to argue about whether that was even a flower or a weed. "It's a flowering plant," she insisted. "In the carnation family. Like teeny, tiny carnations." I laughed and said, "And carnations have to be the shittiest flower ever! It's the cheap-ass flower you give to your grandma."

"No, lilies are the worst! They're the most common flower used at funerals because it's supposed to symbolize innocence, like the person's soul has returned to innocence, just because they're dead. And they smell so bad. They're just like smelly, virginal death flowers."

"I love your knowledge of random, useless facts. But baby's breath isn't a flower."

"Shut up."

I almost laughed aloud at that memory as Gabriel started to speak. I put both of my hands into Will's and took a deep breath.

"In the words of the poet Homer, 'She did not seem to be the daughter of a mortal man, but of a god.' That is how I think of Elizabeth."

Will and I both looked at each other and mouthed, "Elizabeth?" at the same time. No one called her that, not even her parents, who were huddled together in the front row near the open casket. It was just the beginning of a very contrived load of bullshit from Gabriel. I dug my fingernails into Will's palms as he continued.

"She was never meant for this world. She was too good, too pure, too lovely. When you remember her, do not look down and think of her as she is today. You must gaze upwards to heaven, where her gentle soul has flown. Do not cry with endless sorrow for the loss of this gentle dove, but hear the angels singing as the Lord called her back to where she belongs. In the words of poet Dante Alighieri, 'The heavens have no other defect but lack of *her*. The Lord says, suffer it in peace that at my pleasure *she*, your hope, remains there. My lady is desired by highest heaven: now I would have you know of her virtue.'"

He looked up from his paper for the first time and saw my confused face in the back row. I thought I saw a glimmer of shame as he cast his eyes back down and hesitated several times before he continued reading.

"None of us were worthy of her, especially me. A mortal thing she was, and yet her beauty, wisdom, talent, and purity were not meant for this world, and they were certainly not meant for me. The Lord created in her something so rare, the greatest good that nature can possibly create. I think that Lizzie slipped from heaven down to earth to show us a miracle. But a miracle cannot last forever, as beauty, youth, and innocence are not made to be everlasting. And in that sense, it is better that she returns to the angels from where she came, before sickness and age, and the corrupt poisons of this world, took from her all that made her beauty so rare."

I was wondering when he was going to say something specific about her, like how kind and generous she was, especially to animals and children, or something about her unbelievable talent in music and art, or how fucking smart she was, as opposed to all the Dante crap. But I realized the reason he wasn't saying anything personal about her was because he really didn't know her at all.

He stepped down and approached her open casket. I was grateful that I couldn't really see inside from where I was sitting. I wanted to remember her the way she was in my memories, not a vision of her lifeless shell.

He tucked a notebook underneath her masses of golden hair

and peered out at the crowd. "I was often writing these poems when Lizzie was ill. I should have been attending to her. I should have taken better care of her. So with her, I leave my only copy of my poems. They shall stay with her for all eternity."

I turned to Will and he gave me a look that showed he was just as uneasy about Gabriel's eulogy as I was. It felt so inauthentic. Small pangs of nausea fluttered inside me as Gabriel went back to the podium and stood next to a veiled canvas.

"No photograph will ever do her beauty justice. So I have tried to immortalize her in this painting." He dramatically pulled the cloth off of the canvas and said, "This is Lizzie as Beata Beatrix, which shows the moment that Dante's Beatrice is carried up to heaven. Here she is seated at the balcony, when she is suddenly swept away from earth to heaven, where she belongs. I can only hope that when my time comes, Lizzie will forgive me for my sins, and bless me as my guide through paradise, as Beatrice did for Dante."

On the canvas, Lizzie sat with her eyes closed, palms turned upward, looking rather sickly and gray. In fact, it didn't look like Lizzie at all. Not when she was healthy or sick, or even when her soul was finally gone from her body. I didn't know who that girl was in that ridiculous painting. It seemed to be the version of her he had created in his mind, removing any trace of real life from her, probably to ease his nagging guilt. I guess if she was never meant for earth, then there is no reason to mourn her passing, or feel any remorse for the role he played in her demise.

A surge of vomit went up my throat and I ran for the back door. I made it outside just in time and violently threw up. When the vomiting turned into dry heaves, Will helped me back into the car. We had to stop several times on the way home, so I could throw up on the side of the road.

When we got back to Red House, Will helped me into bed and sat down next to me. "What did you think of Gabriel's eulogy?" I asked, as he wiped a bit of sweat from my hairline.

"Truthfully? Quite a load of bollocks."

"I know, right? I was waiting for him to say *anything* that actually felt like it was about *her*."

"No, that was entirely about *him*. His poetry, his art, his usual bullshit."

"He wasn't like that. I mean, when I first met him he was fake and pretentious like that. But then it went away and he was… better than that. More real."

"I think you brought out the best in him," Will said while looking at me with such warmth and love. "You have a way of doing that."

"I just wish he would have said something that wasn't so… contrived. Something that captured who she really was. But I guess he really didn't know her. So I don't know what he should have said. But not *that*."

"He didn't have to speak at all," Will pointed out.

"He *is* her husband," I said as I rolled my eyes deeply. "I briefly thought about going up there to speak, but I felt too sick."

"It doesn't matter. She knows what's in your heart."

He gathered my hands and gently kissed them. I paused for a moment, then looked deeply into Will's eyes.

"I can't believe I'm asking this, but do you think he'll be okay?"

"Gabriel?" He sighed before continuing. "He'll be fine. He said he plans to move to Italy with his sister for a while. I think it will be good for him."

"Maybe I shouldn't be, but I'm worried about him."

"I'm not. And it's not that I don't care about him, because I do. But I know him, and I know he'll be okay."

"How do you know?"

"Have you ever heard the quote 'A burnt child loves the fire'?"

"No, but I think I know what you mean."

"People like Gabriel thrive on drama, both good and bad. He'll use this to fuel his creativity. He'll make it about himself, as he did today. He'll be fine."

He curled up next to me and held me before I had to run to the bathroom to vomit again. The next day, we went to the doctor and found out I was pregnant.

CHAPTER 36

Jane

"Private Road"—Bent

I WAS TOLD I HAD "HYPEREMESIS GRAVIDARUM," WHICH PRETTY much means I had the most extreme version of morning sickness for the entire pregnancy. I couldn't eat or drink much, and after my third hospitalization for dehydration, Will insisted we get our own nurse at Red House. Though she was a nice lady, I found her presence annoying. I wanted more than anything to feel normal and experience a typical pregnancy with Will. I longed to go shopping with him at all the baby boutiques and pig out on huge tubs of ice cream instead of being confined to my bed and attached to the toilet.

Miraculously, in the middle of my 7th month, I suddenly wasn't sick anymore. To celebrate, Will took me on a road trip to a secret location. We drove south for several hours and at some point I fell asleep. I awoke at sunset and gazed out of the windshield in awe. We were in the driveway of the old beach house my family used to own when I was a kid. My hand flew to my mouth and I was speechless for a while. "*Will*. How did you…? How did…? *How?*" He laughed and just said, "Your mum." A warm tear streaked down my face. "These were my happiest memories." He put his hand on top of mine, which was resting on my belly. "I know. And it will be hers as well." I moved his hand lower to where I felt the baby's foot move. "Or his," I commented. "Or his," he repeated.

"Does that mean this place is…" The baby gave a good jab right where his palm was and Will's eyes grew wide. "Needs a lot of work but yes, it's yours." I pushed his hand in and said, "Ours."

"Right. *Ours*."

He bought the property sight unseen, so I gave him a tour and shared all of my memories. The electricity and water hasn't been turned on yet but it was fun using candles and roughing it a little. Later that night we sat on some old lounge chairs on the back porch that faced the ocean. He rubbed my feet while we stared at the stars and listened to the waves crash on the shore.

"I've never seen so many stars in my life," he said.

"I know. I love it here. This is what I want the baby's room to be like. Starry skies and calm waves."

"That's easy. I can paint this."

"I would love that."

We were quiet for a while before I spoke again. "Will, I don't think I'm going to make it through the birth."

"Don't be silly. Of course you will."

"I've dreamt almost every night for the past six months that I die in childbirth."

"That's why you've been waking up so much?"

"Well, that and all the barfing."

"I think your fears are getting the better of you. That's what dreams are. It's our mind working out all of our anxieties and unresolved issues. You've been through a lot in the past year. Not just the pregnancy, but everything else. Of course you would have nightmares like that."

"But what if dreams are also full of other things like memories and premonitions? Every night I have the same dream that I die in the hospital and it feels *really* real."

"I'm sure it does. But I am not worried one bit."

"Okay. But I just want you to know, in case something does happen to me, I want to name the baby after Lizzie."

"Of course. And if it's a boy?"

"Do you think he would mind being called Lizzie?"

He chuckled. "Perhaps. Or maybe we can use the same initial? We don't want him to hate us so early in his life. We'll give him better reasons for that later on."

"True. A little bullying builds character but I don't want it to be excessive. Did you have a better idea?"

He drew in a deep breath before he spoke. "I was thinking maybe Edward, after my grandfather."

"Edward? I guess Eddie is cute."

"Same initial as Elizabeth, too."

"So either way it works out."

"Exactly."

"Little Eddie Morris, the 21st Earl of Sandwiches or whatever."

"Something like that."

"You're going to be the most amazing dad, Will."

"And you will be the most wonderful mum."

"If I make it."

In the candlelight, I could see a hint of genuine fear in his eyes before he took my face into his hands. "Listen to me. You. Will. Be. Fine." My eyes got watery because I truly didn't believe I had much time left. "How do you know?"

"I just know."

I nodded my head and looked down at my belly. Though I didn't know what I believed anymore, I sent a little prayer up to the starry sky above us that he was right.

I can only remember shards and bits of the morning I went into labor. I woke up feeling a sharp burning pain that was almost unbearable. I could barely walk to the car. On the ride to the hospital, I floated in and out of consciousness.

As a paramedic helped me into a wheelchair, I grasped Will's hand and screamed, "I'm not going to make it, Will! I don't want to die!"

He held my hand with both of his as we rushed down the hall. "You're not going to die, my love. You're going to have a baby."

As they hoisted me onto a bed and started hooking up an IV, I looked into his eyes. "I'm not going to make it, Will. I know it. I'm not going to make it."

He tried to hide his terror as he pushed the hair off my forehead and kissed me. "You *are* going to make it. You and the baby are going to be just fine."

Sweat poured from my scalp, and I started to shiver. "I love you so much," I told him before a rush of doctors surrounded me.

I felt a strong pulling sensation in my belly before I faded out. I heard someone yell, "We're losing her!" and then only heard the searing whine of machines.

I looked down and saw a nurse performing CPR on my body. Then I was suddenly in the hallway watching Will pace back and forth. There was a flash of light, and I was in a white room with a young guy I didn't recognize. He took my hands into his as his face rapidly aged to that of an elderly man. "Tell him I'm so proud," he whispered, and I instantly recognized him from pictures I had seen. It was Will's grandfather. I went to embrace him, but the room dissolved.

There was another flash of light, and I was standing on a sidewalk looking down at a scrap of paper with the address for Red House scrawled on it in Gabriel's handwriting. I looked up and saw Gabriel's back before he turned the corner and was out of sight. I was standing in front of the art museum the day we first met him.

"Déjà vu again?" someone said, and I turned and saw Lizzie standing there with a big warm smile. She looked so much healthier and full of life. I grabbed her and pulled her into a hug and refused to let go. "Woah!" she said through laughs as I sobbed into her hair. "Are you alright? Why are you crying?"

I pulled away and wiped my nose with my sleeve. "I just love you so much."

"I love you too, ladybug. Let's go home." She started to walk away, and I took a lighter out of my pocket and set the paper with the address on fire. As it fell to the ground, she spun around and dove after it, but it was too late. "Why'd you do that?" she demanded.

I smiled before I felt an intense pulling sensation like I was being sucked down a drain.

I felt exhausted and so heavy, like a thousand bricks were piled on top of my chest. I opened my eyes, and Will was standing in front of me rocking our baby. He smiled warmly at me before looking down at the bundle in his arms. "Your mum is finally awake! Would you like to meet her, little girl?"

He bent down to show her to me. She was the most precious little thing, with closed eyes and a content little smile on her face. I tried to speak, but nothing came out.

"Would you like to hold her?" he asked. I nodded yes, and he placed her into my arms. Her rosy cheeks lifted as her smile deepened. Her eyelids opened, and she looked directly at me. "Look at that! She's looking right at you!" We stared at each other lovingly until her eyelids slowly shut.

"Are you okay with her for a moment? I'm going to get your mum from the waiting room. She's been quite worried." I nodded yes, and he left the room.

Soon after, I looked up, and Gabriel was standing in the doorway. I hadn't seen him since Lizzie's funeral. He had an unsure look on his face. "Can I…?" I nodded yes. He stood over me and looked down at us in awe.

"Are you feeling alright?"

I nodded and said, "Would you like to hold her?" with a very hoarse voice.

"I'd be honored."

He gently took her into his arms and looked at her with amazement. Then he walked around a bit and held her in front of the window for a while.

I knew I had just been through something profound, but I needed to know if it was real and if I had changed anything.

"Gabriel, how did we meet?" He turned around with a look of surprise.

"You don't remember?"

"Tell me again."

"We met at a concert in Amsterdam. Our connection was instant."

I interrupted him. "What about the second time?"

"I recognized you at the Museum of Modern Art. I invited you and Lizzie to Red House for dinner, but you never showed up."

"Oh."

"A few weeks later, I was searching different book stores looking for a certain translation of *Vita Nuova*, and I went to the store where you worked. I came every day for weeks until you agreed to get coffee with me. You brought Lizzie as a chaperone, remember? I guess you didn't trust me."

So I had changed things, and yet nothing had changed at all.

I wanted to explain what I had just been through to him, but I couldn't find the words. But the way he was looking at me, it was like he already knew.

He kissed the baby on her forehead before putting her back in my arms. "She's magnificent. Like you."

I smiled warmly at him.

"Does she have a name yet?"

"Elizabeth. Lizzie for short."

"That's perfect," he said before he leaned down and whispered into my ear, "Because it's *her*." My eyes darted to his, and he nodded before turning to leave. I called out to him, and he turned around.

"Gabriel. I'm… sorry. For everything." He looked down at his feet before lifting his head to me.

"Me too, Jane. Me too."

We drove up the long winding driveway to Red House, our little girl sound asleep in her car seat. Will put the car in park when we reached the house.

"Are you sure?" I asked.

"Yes. Very sure."

We exited the car and stood next to each other staring up at the house, half of it covered with fog. "Should we take Lizzie?" I asked.

He peered through the back window at her. "She's sound asleep. Better leave her be." I nodded and took his hand, and we entered the house together.

We stood in the foyer, looking around at the massive staircase and ornate mosaic floor. He exhaled audibly. "Ready?" I nodded yes, and he picked up two taper candles and handed one to me. He lit his and then mine, and we stepped in front of the staircase. We both bent down at the same time and placed the lit candles on their sides on the first step. He pulled me back into the doorway, and we watched as the flames started to creep across the first step and then up to the next. In less than a minute the entire staircase was aflame.

We quickly got back in the car and drove halfway down the driveway. Then we stopped and looked through the back window as smoke started to billow from the roof, and one huge flame shot up to the sky. He held my hand as we drove away, and we never looked back.

EPILOGUE

J ANE AND WILLIAM MORRIS MOVED TO LONDON, WHERE THEY turned Morris & Co. into a hugely successful design firm. Two years after Elizabeth was born, they welcomed a second daughter. Eventually, they moved to Kelmscott, a 16th-century manor house in the English countryside, to raise their children. Jane and Gabriel remained close friends, and many speculated about the true nature of their relationship, though Jane maintained they were nothing more than good friends.

Seven years after Lizzie's death, Gabriel had Lizzie's body exhumed to retrieve his poetry manuscript for publication. Those present that night in the graveyard reported that Lizzie's body was in perfect condition, and "her golden hair had continued to grow until it filled the coffin."

ACKNOWLEDGMENTS

First and foremost, thank YOU reader, for giving my story a chance. Out of millions of books, television series, movies, and other recreational activities, you chose to read my book. That means the world to me. If you liked or loved it, please consider rating it on Amazon and/or Goodreads. Every positive review makes a big difference. If you didn't like it, or hated it, why are you even reading the acknowledgments section? I mean, hey. Different strokes for different folks, so no hard feelings.

I dreamed of being a bestselling writer as a teenager, but I never really thought it would happen. So I became an English teacher because, obviously, I love books, but I also kind of love teenage angst. There's just something so relatable about it to me. It's like these little souls are just waking up to the reality of life on earth and it's a major shock to the system. I get it. But teaching is really fucking stressful and absurd (you can read more about that in my teacher misery books.) So I started writing as an escape. I held onto my sanity with this little sliver of hope that maybe one day people would read my writing and connect with it. Here we are today and my books have sold way more copies than I ever could have imagined! People relate to my stories. I'm letting go, knowing that wherever I take my readers, they'll support it! So again, thank you, my readers and followers, for supporting me and giving me a voice.

Thank you Emma and Rocky, my teacher-professor editors. Not only did you do an awesome job editing, you also dealt with my insecurities and gave me the confidence to put my story out into the world.

Thanks to the Pre-Raphaelite Brotherhood and their muses, Jane Morris and Lizzie Siddal. Without your interesting existences, I wouldn't have had a story to tell. See you in the next life.

Thanks to my kids. You are the most wonderful, interesting little creatures and you inspire me to just be myself and let it all hang out.

Thank you to my husband, for always supporting my ideas and pushing me to keep going. I know this genre was hard for you to get used to at first, so thanks for loosening up and taking this weird journey with me. And thanks for always letting me sleep way more than you. That's true love.

ABOUT THE AUTHOR

Jane Morris is the pen name of a bestselling author of four comedic books about teaching. She has taught high school English for the last 15 years. Morris received her B.A. in English and Secondary Education from a well-known university. She earned her M.A. in Writing from an even fancier (more expensive) university. She loves naps, dogs, trees and other things that can't talk. She has a big, obnoxious mouth, but is also overly sensitive, which is a ridiculous combination. You can visit her on social media where she has over half a million followers, or you can just keep living your life.

Made in the USA
Middletown, DE
26 June 2021